Book Three of the Life & Death Cycle

The
TOWERS
of
KNOLL

E.S. Barrison

DEDICATED TO GRANDMA RHODA & GRANDPA DAVID

THE STORY ISN'T OVER YET. AND I'LL KEEP ON WRITING IT FOR YOU.

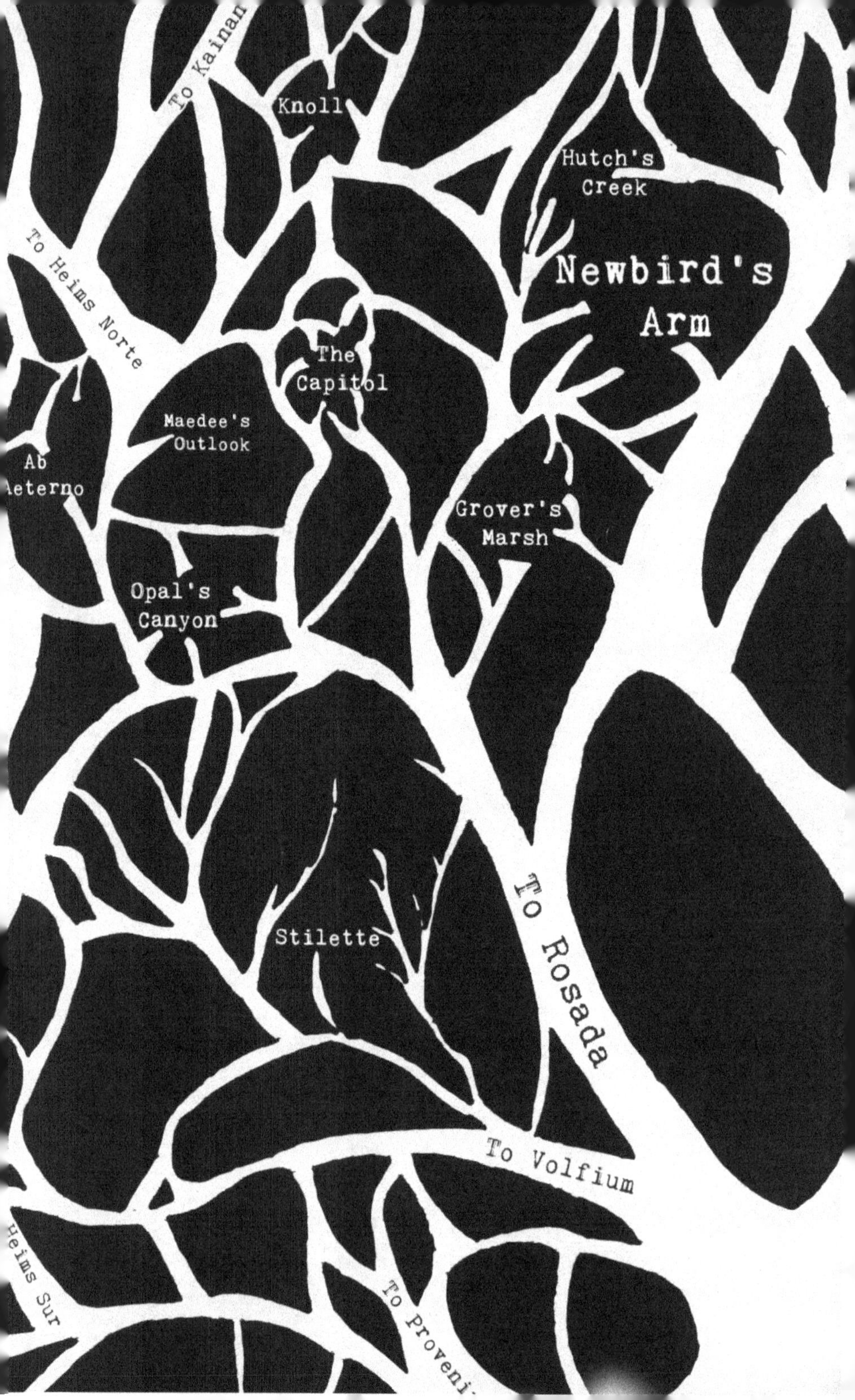

To Kainan
Knoll
Hutch's Creek
To Heims Norte
Newbird's Arm
The Capitol
Maedee's Outlook
Ab Aeterno
Grover's Marsh
Opal's Canyon
Stilette
To Rosada
To Volfium
Heims Sur
To Proveni...

rt
Graycott
To
Evylain
To Spinoza
To Delilah
Errat
To Yilk

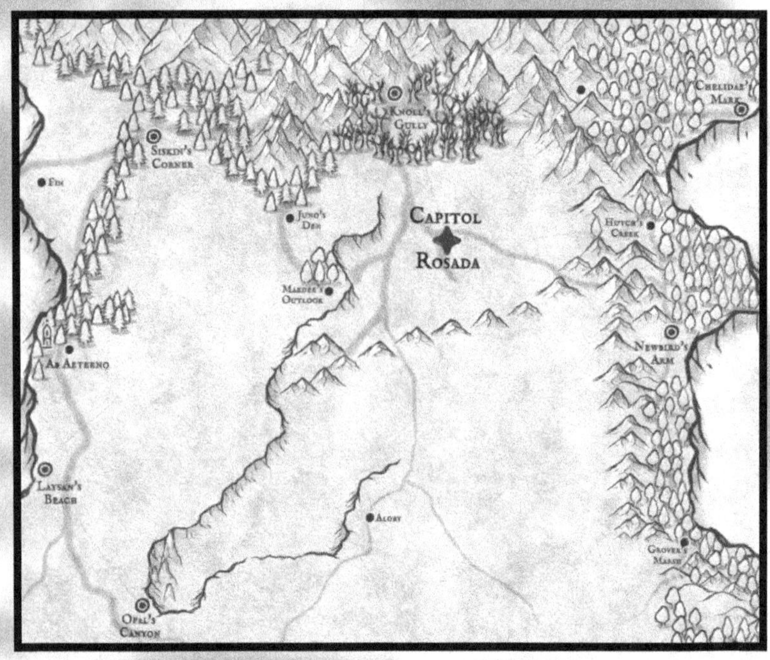

Chelidae's Mere
Knoll's Gully
Siskin's Corner
Fin
Juno's Den
Capitol
Rosada
Huver's Creek
Marder's Outlook
Ab Aeterno
Newbird's Arm
Laysan's Beach
Alory
Grover's Marsh
Opal's Canyon

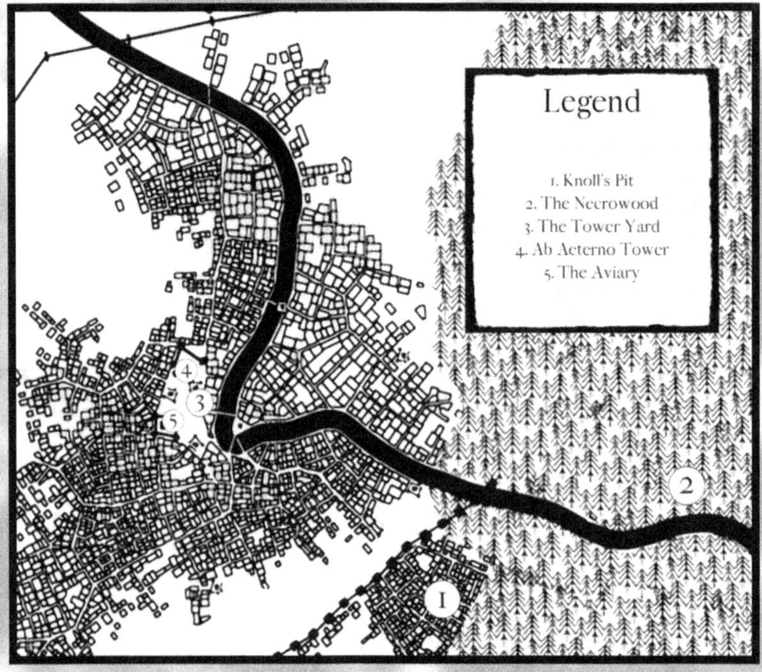

Legend

1. Knoll's Pit
2. The Necrowood
3. The Tower Yard
4. Ab Aeterno Tower
5. The Aviary

The Council of Mist Keepers

Ningursu
The God of Death

Aelia
The Healer

Tomas
The Peacemaker

Julietta
The Painter

Jiang
Null

Malaika
The Cartographer

Alojzy
The Architect

Caroline
The Illusionist

Brent
The Story Collector

CHAPTER ONE

THE GHOST ON THE HILL

Yaz hummed as she stood on her tiptoes to clean the tchotchkes wobbling on the shelf. With every buzzing movement of the tower beneath her, the knickknacks threatened to dive from the shelf. As they neared the edge, Yaz caught them, shifting them to the back of the shelves again before moving on to her next task.

Unlike the collection of goods in the moving tower, Yaz had long since learned to navigate the tower with ease. She ignored each lurch and twist of the engine below, focused instead on her chores. The sooner she finished, the sooner she'd be able to race to the platform on top of the tower to see where they had traveled this time.

As she dusted the last silver orb on the shelf, the tower skidded to a halt. Yaz caught the orb as it slipped off the shelf, stumbling herself into the nearby desk. The tower creaked once, and she regained her footing, a smile navigating across her lips.

"We're here!" Yaz exclaimed to herself. She replaced the orb, dropped her duster on the ground, and raced up the winding stairwell towards the platform on the roof.

For weeks, she'd been daydreaming about their arrival in Aeterno Village. She had found pictures of the glorious Tower of Ab Aeterno on the cliff overlooking the village in the books on Mr. Nasr's shelf. The sea glowed beneath it, casting a vibrant glow from the Effluvium. Per the books, the Effluvium served as the guiding mist of Life and Death. Yaz wasn't sure what that meant, but she could picture the mist rising from the sea, reaching to the tower. Some people even said that the tower was the tallest point in the nation of Rosada.

She pushed open the hatched door and climbed onto the platform. This was the first place in all Rosada she yearned to see. So far, the nation had been boring. It didn't have the seaside glass cities of Proveniro or the tropical jungles of Perennes, or the haunting swamps of

Volfium. Instead, Rosada sat dead, brown, and crumbling.

Certainly, seeing Ab Aeterno would change that.

She raced to the edge of the platform. Smoke wavered in the air, suffocating the landscape. Yaz's heart fell to her stomach. No tower waited for her. No glamor. Nothing.

"Where is it?" she whispered, removing her glasses to clean them. With the smudges gone, she examined the landscape again. Still nothing. For a few moments longer, she stared into the mist, willing for the tower to appear. Only shadows moved about the air—ghosts, monsters, and beasts. *Not real.*

Yaz shook her head, then raced to the floor beneath the platform, shouting, "Mr. Nasr!?! Ms. Kai!?!"

Below, Yaz threw open the door to the navigation deck. Mr. Nasr sat in the cockpit, staring through the navigation window and stroking the stubble on his chin. Beside him, Ms. Kai stood with her back to Yaz, her hand on a lever to direct the tower to its formal rest.

Yaz took a quick glimpse at the map on the wall; an electric bulb blinked just over Aeterno Village. Yaz loved that map. Ever since Mr. Nasr and Ms. Kai took her from Jrin Ayl, a small island at the tip of the continent, she'd loved counting each location on their map. They'd raised her as an apprentice to their little shop, promising her protection, glitz, and glamor.

Sure, they'd protected her for the last five years, but glitz and glamor? No. Most of the time, it had been work.

"Mr. Nasr! Ms. Kai!" Yaz caught her breath in the entrance. "Where's the tower? You said there would be a tower!"

Mr. Nasr glared over his shoulder. He was a stout fellow with a round face, uneven stubble, red eyes, and a bald head. Meanwhile, Ms. Kai bore a much kinder gaze, her one blue eye and one green eye watching Yaz with sadness. When Yaz first met Ms. Kai, she thought she was a goddess.

"We know Yasmin," Ms. Kai said. "We shall not be staying long."

"What? Why? Where is it?"

"It's gone. That means it is dangerous here," Mr. Nasr explained.

"But we've been traveling for such a long time!" Yaz bemoaned. "You promised we would stay here for a couple of days!"

Ms. Kai and Mr. Nasr exchanged a look. Yaz always thought it was the look a king and queen might share in a story. When she first told Ms. Kai and Mr. Nasr that, they laughed, but their interest in such stories wavered as they grew closer to Rosada.

"We do need supplies," Mr. Nasr grunted.

"Yes," Ms. Kai agreed. "It might be best we stop here for a day or so."

Yaz clapped her hands in excitement. "Thank you!"

Mr. Nasr turned and snapped with ferocity in his voice, "But you will stay here, Yasmin."

Her heart dropped even further. "But I wanna explore!"

"Not here."

"Yasmin, dear child." Ms. Kai knelt beside her. "You know we just want to protect you, right? Aeterno is not a safe place for children to play. When we reach Siskin's Corner in the north, then you can go play. Okay?"

"A'ight," Yaz mumbled.

"What was that?"

"Yes, Ms. Kai!"

"Very good. Now go finish stocking the shelves. We may have a couple customers come by." Ms. Kai tussled Yaz's hair, then returned to her gears and levers. Mr. Nasr stared at Yaz for a moment longer, his crimson eyes evaluating her every movement, then turned his chair around to face the window.

Yaz continued pouting as she left the cockpit. Why didn't they ever let her have any fun? She'd been in this tower for weeks now!

She dragged her feet as she returned to the ground floor. Usually, she took time looking at each of the pictures and artifacts on the wall. Despite living here for years, she still hadn't learned all the little stories each piece told. They bled of magic, of disease, but all of history. She hoped one day her own collection, hidden beneath her bed, would be as remarkable.

She continued to the ground floor, back into the curiosities. When alone, Yaz often dillydallied between the shelves to admire the oddities. People from far and wide ventured to see *Gisela's Curio Shoppe of Oddities Galore*. Items abound occupied the shelves, ranging from motorized toys and mechanized Year Glasses to strange artifacts rumored to hold magic.

Sometimes, Yaz disappeared into the farthest corner of the shop, where Ms. Kai kept old animal skeletons, geodes, and stones. Each of those skeletons told a story, and sometimes she wondered if their ghosts lived in the shop with their skulls. When Ms. Kai and Mr. Nasr weren't looking, Yaz would sit on the floor with the skulls and play with them, just like her dollies upstairs. She named each of them; Miss Pecker the bird skull, Arnold the deer jawbone, and Elizabeth the dehydrated lizard corpse had been her longtime favorites.

As she reached the bottom step, Yaz considered hiding in the shelves to play. It would be more interesting than cleaning the shop. But her attention drifted towards the doorway. She doubted that Mr. Nasr or Ms. Kai would notice her slip out of the shoppe, and she'd already done her chores this morning, too excited to sleep.

She refused to keep hiding.

"I'll be right back," Yaz whispered as she pulled on her boots. Checking once more over her shoulder, she creaked open the front door and hopped out of the doorway onto the riverbank.

A paved pathway waited beside the river, leading down to the town. Yaz didn't care about the shabby looking village; her attention fell solely across the river to the hillside.

Now that she was out of the tower, the image before her told a different story. Burnt trees and plumes of smoke garnished the hillside that once held the Tower of Ab Aeterno. Did it move just like Ms. Kai and Mr. Nasr's lopsided tower, with its mismatched pieces and crooked windows? Did it have as many smokestacks, filling the air with gray? Yaz closed her eyes, trying to picture the sight, but only saw Ms. Kai and Mr. Nasr's little tower.

With her imagination failing her, Yaz abandoned her thoughts and hurried over the rickety bridge across the river. She held her breath at each step, her stomach churning as the bridge rocked from one way to another. Even though the river slept beneath the bridge, the last thing Yaz wanted was to fall. *Mr. Nasr keeps promising to teach me to swim, but he hasn't yet. I should remind him.*

She breathed a sigh of relief once she arrived on the other side of the river. *I made it!* She raced over the trampled path and began her ascent up the hill, glancing back to look at her tower.

Unlike the Guard towers that frequented the landscape of Rosada, Ms. Kai and Mr. Nasr's tower comprised a hodgepodge of building blocks. It started with a base, followed by a house, only to be topped with a piece of an airship. Each part had its own charm. When they first took Yaz from her home, she stared at it with wide eyes. Even now, she admired it.

But she really wanted to see the Tower of Ab Aeterno.

As Yaz ascended the hill, she pulled at the charred branches and pocketed a few rocks. Leaves and ash skirted through the air, catching a few of Yaz's curls and hitting her glasses as she walked. Sometimes, when she walked in these forests, Yaz swore she heard ghosts. When she mentioned it to Ms. Kai, the woman laughed it off as a childish ploy. But why did they call her name so often?

Why did they pull at her now?

Yasmin...

Yasmin...

Help me, Yasmin...

She shook her head and broke a branch, using it as a sword to fight off the constant voices in her head. If Ms. Kai told her they didn't exist, then Yaz believed her. It was time to stop being a ridiculous child.

Yaz bushwhacked through the brambles, arriving at the top of the hill before the sun hit its apex. She collected a few odd rocks but nothing of interest; it wasn't like the forest held any *real* relics—at least not like what Ms. Kai and Mr. Nasr sold.

As she parted the last bushes, she entered a clearing obscured by smoke and soot. A skeletal building stood against the backdrop of smoke. Yaz wandered inside, checking the pews for anything of interest. Every footstep rang against the charred marble floor, but other than the stone pews and broken glass, nothing remained of the old Temple.

Yaz scuffed her shoe on the pavement in frustration. How could there be nothing here? This was where the Tower of Ab Aeterno once stood! Something had to remain. They couldn't have taken *everything*.

She passed through the doorway at the far end of the atrium. Rather than entering another part of the Temple, though, the door took her back onto the hillside.

Yaz exited the atrium. Just outside sat a giant sinkhole filled with an odd silver liquid. She gazed into it; the surface was as reflective as a mirror, and her reflection stared back at her with the same intrigue as an actual person.

Can I bottle this up and bring it to Ms. Kai? Then she won't be mad at me because it's so pretty! Yaz glanced around the area. She had brought no vials, and no cups or containers sat anywhere near the pool. *Maybe I can run back to the tower and—*

Bubbling pulled Yaz away from her thoughts. The liquid rippled, and out emerged a round white object.

What's that?

The water thrashed, bringing the white object to shore. With trembling fingers, Yaz lifted the object from the ground.

But this was no object.

In her hands sat none other than a human head. Rotting skin composed half the head, while the other half was nothing but a skeleton. Yaz's mouth dropped, and she caught a scream from exiting her throat.

Is this a ghost? Her fingers tightened around the skull as she scanned the water for the rest.

But there was no skin, no blood, and no body.

Only the head.

Yaz poked at the head's one closed eyelid. Another yelp lodged itself in her throat.

The eyelid flickered open to reveal an empty white eye. For a moment, the head even opened its mouth, and a deep fog exited from its lips.

"Ghost..." Yaz whispered.

The head blinked.

"Are you a ghost?"

No response.

She held the head up to eye level. "Are you alone?"

The eyelid fell again.

She pondered for a moment. How did the head get here? Was it alone, like Ms. Kai's other skeletons? She couldn't leave it here to rot.

"I'm gonna take you home and clean you up, a'ight? You can spend time with my dolly, then we can find your body or something so you can walk. A'ight?" If it disagreed with her ideas, it gave no sign. Yaz removed her coat and swaddled the head like a babe. "I'm going to call you Sir Jama, a'ight?"

No reaction.

Yaz didn't know if she expected one. It didn't matter. She would bring the head to Ms. Kai and Mr. Nasr, and her caretakers would be happy beyond measure!

Or maybe I'll keep you as my secret.

Yaz placed the skull in her bag, but before she had the chance to turn away, the water rippled again. This time, the ripples thrashed against the edge of the lake and kept moving back and forth like a pendulum.

Yaz ducked behind a bush near the pool. Just as she made refuge, a creature burst from the opposite side of the water. It landed on four legs, shook its body, then rolled over at the water's edge. It whined once.

Then barked.

Yaz perked up in her spot. *A dog?*

The water swelled again. This time, two humanoid figures ascended from the water, dripping like phantoms. The taller figure reached the basin, rolled onto the ground beside the dog, then turned back to the water. It helped the second smaller figure from the water. They embraced tight. Yaz swore they kissed.

The dog beside them whined.

But Yaz couldn't move. Part of her wanted to dash away, while the other part wanted to scream.

She watched as the figures stood there for what felt like forever. They spoke in quiet, hushed voices, their gazes fixated on the silver pool. She circled over to them, watching from the brambles. The taller figure, a man, stood hunched over as he spoke with the shorter figure, a woman. They looked odd and out of place. The woman wore a nightgown, her frizzy dark brown hair hanging in an uneven braid, a thick cowl hanging around her neck. Meanwhile, the man's curls stuck out in every direction, and his suspenders hung loose on his side as if he never finished putting on his clothes.

After a bit of time, the man finally turned to leave. The woman stopped him and whispered under her breath.

They kissed again.

Then she let go of him, her fingers lingering on his arm, and approached the edge of the pool. She placed her fingers into the liquid.

And at her touch, a geyser exploded from the center of the pool, releasing hundreds of red flowers across the hilltop.

PETALS

Silver. So much silver.
And red.
Peonies floated.
Spinning.
Twirling.
A dog barked.
Then light.

Bria clamored to the surface, sputtering. She struggled to stay afloat, bobbing up and down, the odd silver liquid clawing its way into her mouth. Where was she? What happened? Where was Brent? The last thing she remembered was that they jumped into the Pool in the heart of the Library. Were they still together?

Her head continued to spin as she tried treading water. Another wallop of liquid passed over her head.

She pushed up for air again. Two hands greeted her above the surface and yanked her to shore.

"It's a'ight. We're a'ight. Breathe."

"Brent? Is that you?" She blinked away the silver liquid.

"Yeah, it's me. We're a'ight. It's a'ight. Breathe." Brent enveloped her in a hug. They were still together.

Finally, her vision stabilized. Brent sat with her and Nix at the edge of a silver pool in a sinkhole. The sky glistened with the colors of dusk, and ash floated about in the air. She gasped and clutched Brent's shirt, trying her best to keep from passing out. The earth pulsated beneath her; she heard every breath, every gust of wind.

Just an hour ago, maybe less, the malevolent Ningursu, leader of the Council of Mist Keepers, had used his own abilities to set her magic into overdrive once again. This was the third time he'd attempted to control her now. She always fought back...

But it was getting harder.

Now the earth reached for her, its heartbeat as loud as a drum beneath her feet.

For now, they were safe. Relief washed over Bria, and she pulled Brent down into a kiss. The worry that somehow the Pool would separate them after they escaped the Library vanished with his eyes.

Nix, their gray box-headed dog, whined beside them.

"We're a'ight," Brent whispered again. "Let's get away from this goddamn pool."

Bria glanced at the pool once more. She couldn't shake the feeling that someone was watching them. It had to be the anxiety over the pool. These mysterious silver pools dotted the world with magical properties created by the immortal Magii and Alchemist Tehuti Thema Tarek Kamilah Kafele Kek. A universal lifeblood of the earth, composed of peony flowers and mist, they acted as transportation between locations, windows of communication, and cures for the wildest ailments.

Brent was right. The farther they got away from the Pool, the better. A constant fear that Kek or the Council would send someone after them remained.

After all, wouldn't the Council want to find Ningursu after his brother tossed him into the Pool?

But Bria didn't move. Her attention fell to Brent as he turned his back to the Pool. Exhaustion painted his face, sweat and grime matting down his curls, while he kept opening his mouth as if talking to himself. She couldn't fathom what was going through his head now. The Battle in the Library was fresh. Blood poured, people ceased...but most notably, Ningursu's brother perished at Brent's hands.

The old ghost, Nedo, begged Brent to take his story, thus ceasing his existence. After thousands of years of slavery, it was only the right thing to do. But Bria knew one thing: Brent was a good man, and even assisting someone begging to become one with the mist again would weigh heavily on his soul.

Or Brent's ability to retain stories using the mist would cause Nedo's death to haunt him.

As he breathed out, mist gathered around his face. Did it understand he was a Mist Keeper, the protector of souls and gatekeeper to death?

The Mist Keepers said they cursed Brent, but he still hadn't died. Sure, he had been to Hell and back, defeating a monster known as a Diabolo, absorbing its stories, and losing his mind in the process, but he returned. He was still alive and still a Mist Keeper. Brent continued to release souls and read the mist all while existing.

The curse might not break, but Bria promised it wouldn't take him from her. Never.

But they would have to keep hiding. With the endless tunnels beneath the earth as well as the pools, it would not be impossible to be uncovered by the Mist Keepers or Kek's Palaver of Immortals.

Plus, a third party was in the game now: The Order of the Effluvium. She and Brent discovered a connection between the Order and the Council after seeing Elder Don Van, the old leader of their home's Temple, in a smaller pool. With their detrimental hand playing games, even with Kek and the Palaver of Immortals now in control of the Library, nowhere was safe.

What could she and Brent do? They spoke of destroying the Pools and cutting off communication, but was that even possible? How many Pools occupied the world?

Bria placed her hand on Brent's back as he began to walk away. "Wait."

"Huh?"

"We need to destroy the Pool."

"What? How?"

"I know how to do it. I...I don't think it'll be hard...just draining."

"Bria...you can't right now. Not after what Ningursu did to you. I mean...what if...what if you..." His head fell, his curls falling over his face. "What if you don't wake up?"

"Brent..." She cupped his cheeks. "Trust me. Please."

"I do...I always do."

She kissed him again, letting her lips linger for a few seconds longer. Once they parted, she released Brent and approached the Pool. Her fingers trembled as she stared over the silver liquid. The Pool beckoned her. The peonies embedded in its liquid sang a song of blood and tears, like Madame Owiti's orb back in the city of Mert. That had been softer, less harrowing. Had blood spilled over this very Pool on this hilltop, like when Kek killed hundreds of seers to keep the Pool alive and well? Did Kek slaughter a seer right here?

Or was the song merely that of the peonies, begging for freedom?

Either way, Bria knew what she had to do. The calls enchanted her, and as Bria approached the Pool, she could no longer resist their tugging.

She knelt beside the Pool, tracing her fingers over the liquid. Her skin buzzed. It wasn't just the peonies; she felt every blade of grass, every dead beetle, every leaf that occupied the Pool. While the song was sad, life continued. Life demanded. Life yearned.

It pulsed from the Pool in a whisper, filling Bria's core. It was as if a sudden warmth overwhelmed her, wrapping around her veins and arteries. Her heart raced. Her ears buzzed. It touched every corner of her skin.

She gasped, and the energy filling her escaped. It bounced across the surface of the lake.

And the silver liquid exploded with a splash.

In a tsunami, it burst out of the basin and hit the trees. The geyser captured Bria in a fit of red and sent her flying backwards into the dirt. Pain ripped through the back of her head as she landed against the root.

The wind guffawed. Hundreds of peonies rode on the gusts, capturing the air, and raining with petals across the hilltop.

Like blood.

Bria couldn't move. Her head hurt. The dirt gripped her.

Roots wrapped around her arms and legs, crossing over her body. Vines clung to her hair and face. The earth beckoned. It needed life. It needed help.

And she could feel her soul reaching out across the charred hilltop.

She was everywhere. She was nowhere.

Her magic was out of her hands now.

And around her, the charred trees burst with life.

CHAPTER THREE

WANTED FOR CORNSTALKS

"B RIA!" Brent cried with the wind. Peonies blew through the air, masking the Pool from sight. She had been right there! What had happened? Did the Pool retake her? Did she get eaten by the Peonies?

Don't be ridiculous; peonies can't eat people.

She's not a person. She's a plant, the Diabolo in his head goaded.

No, she's not!

She has a branch growing from her ear. Plant!

Be quiet, Frankie!

Brent had grown used to the constant presence of the Diabolo, a demon composed of nightmares and mist that he had the unfortunate fate of harboring in his soul. It wasn't even the true Diabolo, only the creature's story riding close to his heart. For months, in the Independent City of Mert, he roamed the streets with his mind flittering between himself, the monster, and the stories of day-to-day life. Even now, despite the medications and therapies he'd endured, he had yet to shake the demon entirely. If the Diabolo didn't claw its way into his head, then it was the constant bombardment of stories hanging in the air. No matter where he looked, they followed.

But he had to stay focused.

Finally, the peonies cleared, the wind dying down to a quiet whisper. Bria lay on the ground, laden with vines, roots, and flowers.

"Bri!" Brent raced over to her and pushed a pile of peonies off her body. Each time he pulled at one, though, another flower or vine attacked from another angle.

Once he uprooted her and pulled her close, the roots attached to her skin snapped. She screamed out and dug her face into Brent's chest. Dirt crusted her skin, and the vines embedded themselves into her, just like the little branch behind her ear. Upon destroying the Pool, she'd become a part of the surrounding forest.

And to save it, she paid the price.

"I had to destroy it," she sobbed out. "We can't…Kek…or the Council…they would all…it would…I…"

"I know. Breathe. It's a'ight."

Her head fell against his chest. Tears continued falling from her cheeks, and the clouds above hung heavy with her sadness.

"You're a'ight, you're a'ight…" He pushed back the loose strands of hair from her face. "We're safe."

"Are we, though?" she whispered. "We don't even know where we are…"

Brent glanced around the hilltop. Now that he looked around, he caught the wisps of stories as they passed over him. He had been trying to ignore them since arriving, his head spinning still from harboring Nedo's ancient tale and the onslaught of horrors from the Library. The weight of Nedo's death haunted him, but he pushed it down to focus on the mist.

He saw it all: a fire eating away at a Temple where a pernicious Year Glass gazed from above everything. Then a tower, composed of gems and pearls, height defying imagination, shifted. It moved like the towers guarding the landscape of Rosada, but this time, bearing the fruits of the Order in its clutches.

Brent had heard of that tower; it was the pinnacle of glory rumored throughout Rosada.

"Ab Aeterno," Brent whispered.

"What?" Bria gripped his arm.

"We're in Ab Aeterno. That's where the Pool took us."

"Do you think Ningursu wanted to come here? That's why we're here?"

"Possibly..." Brent's heart still quavered from their experience in the Library. They broke into Ningursu's office only to discover a silver basin in the center of the room. There, inside it, they saw Elder Don Van, the leader of the Order of the Effluvium in Newbird's Arm.

The man responsible for putting the blank stamp on Brent's wrist when he was a child.

That confirmed the absolute truth for them: the Order and the Council communicated with each other. Their evils wove together like the threads of a sweater.

"Do you think Elder Don Van found Ningursu?" Bria glanced around, wincing in pain.

"I dunno. He's not here, though." Brent stared into the sinkhole that had been the Pool. *But we're back in Rosada.*

That wasn't necessarily a good thing. While there were pockets of safety throughout the nation for those like him—individuals with silver eyes, a penchant for stories, and magic—most of the time and in most places, if someone saw the black stamp on his wrist, they would throw him into the Pit. If they were indeed in Aeterno Village, persecution would not come lightly. He'd be a moving target. That much he knew.

Nix's whines pulled him from his thoughts.

Beside him, Bria's body began to weave its way back into the earth. Taproots clung to her, lacing into her skin, and a blanket of moss-covered her.

"Shite! Bri!" Brent stooped to her level and gathered Bria into his arms. Her eyes fell closed, her breaths uneven with each exhale. "Stay awake, a'ight? You're a'ight."

"I'm fine," she mumbled. Her head lolled to the side.

"No. C'mon, we can get into the tunnels or something and get out of here or—"

"No...Kek...the Mist Keepers..."

"A'ight...a'ight, um...I'll find us a place. C'mon."

Brent slung their bag off his shoulder, then lifted Bria off the ground. He grunted as he tried to stabilize her, then with his shoulders high, he followed along the path away from the sinkhole.

Stories followed in his wake. As he moved, he watched the past. The Tower of Ab Aeterno lurched away from its position, abandoning its place beside the sea. The Effluvium followed, an obedient soldier on the edge of the sea. Where was it going? And was Ningursu already with Elder Don Van? Or was his head floating in another pool far away?

Brent hoped it was the latter.

He adjusted Bria in his arms as he walked down the path. His black stamp lay hidden beneath his sleeve, and with his bangs over his face, he could only pray no one noticed his eyes. They'd be right to throw him in the Pit, especially with the way the Diabolo continued to nag at his thoughts.

Nix trotted ahead of them down the hill, shaking off the remaining bits of silver. The village of Aeterno sat embraced in the snow at the foot of the hill, gas lamps flickering in and out of life on the rows of the streets. Automobiles sat parked along the river with a couple of towers bordering the landscape. Brent couldn't help but feel like he was being watched.

Yet, despite the clear presence of the guard, the village itself was unremarkable. Simple. Outside of recent events, the stories held no intrigue: a farmer growing crops, a few children running in the streets, and an elderly couple walking their dog. And despite their insipid nature, Brent reveled in these silent tales. After the gnawing of the Diabolo or the detrimental heartbeat of Nedo's tale, these casual stories gave him a moment of serenity.

Brent repositioned Bria on his back as he crossed the river. Warehouses bordered the water. The walls told stories about guards, drunkards, and harlots hiding in the broken windows committing acts that, in daylight, most said belonged to demons.

He hunched his shoulders, adjusting the cuff of his sleeve to hide his hideous black stamp. Only back in Rosada for an hour, and his stamp once again turned him into a target. No longer did he have the freedom from the City of Mert; no longer did he rule over an empty library. Here, if they discovered him, his freedom might cease.

"Shite." He lowered Bria to the ground in front of the warehouse and brushed back her hair. In her sleep, she almost looked peaceful. Yet with foliage leaving a scar on her skin, Brent wondered how deep Ningursu kneaded his presence into her magic.

Brent took a moment to glance around the area. A few flyers decorated the wall. One advertised a tavern on the outside of the town, whispering of delights and freedom. Another showed a circus garnished in sunlight, just south of town.

The last one made Brent's stomach drop.

WANTED

BRIANNABELLA SMIDT

FOR TERRORISM, VANDALISM, AND ACTS OF

MAGIC

10,000 GOLD

A blurry picture of Bria occupied the space beneath the advertisement. While her face wasn't clear, the photograph showed enough: a girl controlling plants, a cowl around her neck, standing amid the ruins of Newbird's Arm from months ago.

"Bria…" He nudged her. "C'mon. We gotta…we can't stay in Rosada…"

"Hm?" Her eyes flickered open.

Brent tore the flyer from the wall and handed it to her.

She stared at it for a moment. "I know I'm wanted. This isn't new."

"Yeah, I know, but—"

"We can't go back into the tunnels."

"Not even to get out of Rosada?"

Bria shook her head. She didn't elaborate further before her eyes shut again.

"Shite. A'ight…shite." He placed a hand on Bria's head. Her skin burned.

She needs someplace to rest.

Just leave her here, his Diabolo chided.

You know I won't do that.

Lovesick fool.

He ignored the Diabolo's remarks, pulling Bria again into his arms. With a single glance around the warehouse district, he caught sight of a story about a drunkard and a harlot disappearing down an alleyway to find someplace safe.

Someplace safe for anyone.

Perhaps that same place would offer sanctuary for him and Bria.

Brent followed the stories of drunkards, harlots, and vagrants to a small inn on the outskirts of Aeterno Village. It hid in the wall beside Aeterno's Pit, a rundown shack, a communal bathroom, and no electricity. It provided sanctuary, though.

No one questioned his eyes or Bria's unconscious state as they entered. Black stamps shone on most of the patron's skin. Each person spoke with their head down, nursing drinks and speaking gossip and history. No guards. No Order.

Safety.

Brent received a key from a middle-aged barmaid. She nodded at him once, eyeing Bria carefully, then returned to work. No one said a word.

Brent lay Bria on the bed as soon as they entered their room. She didn't move, her skin burning beneath his fingertips. *Shite.*

He glanced at Nix and frowned. "What're we gonna do?"

Nix hopped on the bed and lay beside Bria.

Brent found a dirty washcloth in the bathroom, rinsed it, then lay it on her head. Once sure she wouldn't wake, he stepped out of the room and headed downstairs. The latest gazette and a hot meal welcomed him. The liquor whispered in his direction, but he did not move towards it.

You're afraid, his Diabolo teased.

Shut it.

Balancing a tray of food in one hand and the gazette in the other, he rejoined Bria upstairs. As the door closed, she jolted upright, arm outstretched, eyes bloodshot.

"I have food." Brent placed the tray on the table. "Bread and some sort of chowder."

Bria lowered her arm, but she didn't climb out of bed to join him.

Brent brought a bowl over to her, but she shook her head.

"You need to eat."

"It's too loud," she mumbled.

"Huh?"

"I can hear the vegetables in the soup…"

"You hear the vegetables?"

She nodded.

"You sound like me."

Bria snorted and wiped her eyes. "It's my magic. I think each time Ningursu tries to puppeteer me, he is unlocking more of my abilities. But I'm not a Mist Keeper or under his control. He wishes I was, though."

Brent placed the bowl down and sat beside Bria. He took both her hands, ignoring the stories gathering on her skin. Three times now, Ningursu had used his magic to control Bria. Somehow, after acquiring one of the camellia flowers from Bria's little branch, Ningursu maintained a connection with her.

She was too strong for him, though.

"You're able to fight it. I've seen you fight it," Brent said, refusing to take his eyes off her. "I think...Ningursu...he is scared of you. You are so strong and...I think...I mean...Ningursu doesn't know what to do."

"No, Brent, he knows exactly what he's doing!" Bria protested. "He knows that he is turning me into a weapon. Because everyone wants to use me as a damn weapon!" She closed her eyes. "Ningursu, Kek—shit, even the people of Rosada are saying I'm a terrorist."

Brent squeezed her fingers. "You're not a weapon."

"Who is to say that I'm not? You've seen what I do—"

Brent cut her off. "You are not a weapon. You're a fighter. You fight for your own cause. And I'll stand by you wherever you go."

Bria wiped her eyes. "That might not be the best idea."

"But I will. You should know that by now."

A slight smile formed on Bria's lips before she asked, "Even to eat pineapple?"

"Well...almost everywhere."

"I'll turn you into a pineapple lover someday."

"Never. Rather eat a fistful of alpaca hair."

"Have you ever eaten alpaca hair?"

Brent shrugged. "If I did, I was probably one of my stories."

Bria smiled and rested her head against Brent's shoulders, keeping the blankets close to her body. "I'm glad you're not a story anymore."

"Couldn't have done it without you."

"Kek cured you."

"And you kept me safe."

Bria fidgeted with the blanket. Her stomach gurgled.

Brent shoved the bowl back into her hands. "Eat."

She stared at the bowl. Nix hopped onto the bed beside her, panting.

"Or Nix might eat it first," Brent warned.

Bria finally lifted the spoon. Her hands trembled as she lifted the chowder to her mouth.

Silence settled in the room as Brent watched stories gather before him. They came to him nonstop, and in the small tavern, they were as vivid as ever, carrying the weight of struggles and heartbreak.

How many more stories could his mind handle before he slipped again into the Diabolo's grasp?

He reached into their bag and pulled out his jar of silver pills. His fingers trembled as he took one. The mere thought of being tied to these pills made his stomach churn, but they were enough to keep the demons at bay. He couldn't end up like he was all those months ago; he couldn't stay as the Diabolo's puppet.

I'm not my stories.

"What're we going to do?" Bria asked as she placed the bowl of half-eaten chowder on the table. Pieces of corn floated to the top.

"Right now, you gotta rest, a'ight?" Brent.

Bria opened her mouth to speak but then let out a profuse gag...

And out shot a corn stalk from her mouth.

CHAPTER FOUR

VANISHING HEADS

Yaz watched as the man and woman from the lake disappeared into the dilapidated tavern. It hid in the slums of Aeterno, blending in with the glaring metallic fence that marked the Pit. Prisoners, or vagrants, as Ms. Kai called them, stared out from cracks in the wall, their eyes empty with no color. Gray eyes, silver eyes, white eyes…they all bore little to no life in them.

What did they do to get put in the Pit?

Yaz didn't want to find out.

As curious as she was about the two people who emerged from the lake, the empurpling sky beckoned Yaz back to the Curio Shoppe tower. There was something that compelled her to those two; not only did they emerge from the lake, but the girl created a rainfall of red petals!

It was like something in a story. But Ms. Kai and Mr. Nasr always said magic was illegal in Rosada. Would they be safe?

The man was less interesting; he mumbled to himself as he walked, and a few times, Yaz swore he saw her.

She held her bag close as she strolled towards the tower. Every few moments, she placed her hand in the bag, reassuring herself that her new prize remained. *Sir Jama.* The skull was far more interesting than the bird skulls Ms. Kai kept in the back of her shop. They'd be able to fetch a pretty coin for it...or perhaps Yaz might keep it for herself, to play with her dollies in her room.

She followed Mr. Nasr's instructions as she headed back towards the tower. Yaz had learned quickly not to talk to strangers. "They're out to get all of us," Mr. Nasr had told her. Even when visitors arrived in the shop, they instructed Yaz not to speak.

It was for the best, they promised her.

But now she could show them how she took care of herself!

Yaz hopped over the stones by the river, keeping her eye on the misshapen tower in the distance. Its silver flag waved in the breeze, catching the flurries of snow falling from the sky.

Positioned like statues outside the tower stood both Ms. Kai and Mr. Nasr. Ms. Kai looked as though her one green and one blue eye might pop out of her skull. Mr. Nasr huffed in frustration as Yaz slowed her pace on approach.

"What did we tell you about leaving, Yasmin?" Ms. Kai spat.

"I just went out for a little, I promise!" Yaz hugged her bag tight. "I've been in the tower for such a long time!"

"Yasmin, we gave you specific instructions to not leave the tower," Mr. Nasr said.

"But you promised to let me explore—"

"Until we discovered the Tower of Ab Aeterno left."

"What does that have to do with it?" Yaz argued. "You don't let me go out anywhere!"

"Yasmin, you are a child and wouldn't understand."

"But I found something! You can display it in the shop!"

"We do not need any of your little trinkets." Ms. Kai added.

"But look!" Yaz reached into her bag.

Her heart sank. In the place where Sir Jama once sat, nothing more than air graced her fingertips. Tears welled in her eyes as she searched her bag. He was right there! She remembered pulling him out of the lake! Had this all been a figment of her imagination?

Or ghosts?

"Stop playing games, Yasmin. Go up to your room. Now," Ms. Kai insisted.

"But—"

"Go, or you won't get dinner."

Yaz's head fell. She didn't have the energy to argue with her guardians. Instead, with her body slumped, her bag against her chest, and her lips quivering, she wandered back into the tower. Mr. Nasr's red eyes felt like daggers on her back, and Ms. Kai's disappointment hung in the brisk air.

The tower didn't feel quite so welcoming. Some days, like today, it reminded her more of a prison. Why didn't Mr. Nasr and Ms. Kai ever let her out of their tower? All the other children played in the streets, but she had to work, she had to stay put, and she had to be obedient and gentle. Ms. Kai once told Yaz about the adventures she and Mr. Nasr had long ago; they used to travel the continent, meeting interesting people from Heims to the islands off the coast of Perennes and Proveniro. What happened to the people in those stories? Why did they hide away in the tower?

Or were they just lies?

Yaz climbed the stairs to her room. She'd created her own private suite in an old storage closet, big enough to harbor a bed, a dresser, and her chest of goodies. After shutting the door, she collapsed on the floor beside the chest and let out a loud wail.

I should have talked to the ghost people by the silver pool. Then I could have brought them back here and explained the situation to Mr. Nasr and Ms. Kai. They might know about Sir Jama!

She toyed with the lock on her chest. At least she still had her toys; they'd listen to her.

Even if they didn't speak.

Sir Jama would have been a great new toy, a fun new toy; it'd been so long since she added a new object to her collection.

But Sir Jama was gone now.

Yaz checked her bag one more time. Only dust coated her fingers. Perhaps he was never more than her imagination; besides, why would she find a human skull—half skin, half skeletal—lying at the foot of a silver pool? And in what world would someone cause the sky to rain red petals?

Ghosts.

Or magic, maybe?

Yaz opened her chest and rummaged through her toys. She pulled out three dollies: one made of string, one of sticks, and one of porcelain. Each one found a spot next to her bed, followed by a few rocks upon which she'd drawn eyes.

"I thought I had a new friend for all of y'all," Yaz said to her dollies. "Guess it's just us."

She brushed back the hair on her porcelain dolly's head. The doll bore a locket with a picture of a woman in it around her neck. A beautiful woman with long, dark hair, dark eyes, and a wide smile. Sometimes, Yaz imagined that woman holding her, rocking her to sleep. Together, they stayed in a house by the sea, telling stories and laughing.

But that was just another imaginary story.

Yaz wanted to believe that woman was her mother.

But she could have been anyone.

Now, she had Mr. Nasr and Ms. Kai. They'd given her a good life...even if strict.

Yaz sighed. She had no desire to play with dolls. Part of her wanted to cry, the other part wanted to sleep, but what good would that do anymore? Crying wouldn't make Mr. Nasr and Ms. Kai believe her.

"Stupid ghosts messing with me!" Yaz shouted. Of course, ghosts weren't real; they couldn't be. But at times, Yaz swore they existed, taunting her.

She knocked her bag off her bed. Real or not, why wouldn't they just go away?!

And as the bag hit the ground, Sir Jama's head rolled across the floor, staring up at Yaz with his empty eyes.

CHAPTER FIVE

THE BOXCAR

Lex jolted awake to the screeching of the train. Her body ached from sleeping against the wall. She's sacrificed the hay bale for her dear old friend, Madame Owiti; the old woman needed the bed more than her. Meanwhile, Lex's son, Garrett, slept on her lap. The boy hadn't said a word since the Guard pricked his finger a day earlier. When the needle touched his skin, he wailed as his blood dribbled into an odd silver substance in a petri dish. Once it hit the surface, his blood turned gold, as it had with Madame Owiti.

When they tested Lex's blood, though, it turned black.

Without a word, the Guard shoved Lex, Madame Owiti, and Garrett into one boxcar at the edge of the loading dock with other women and children. The door slammed shut, so the only slither of light came from a thin crack-like window on the ceiling. Lex's head buzzed as she waited for answers.

But none came.

And the train began to move.

She could only hope her husband was okay. When she last saw Toddle, the only words on his lips were simple: lie about everything. About what? She didn't know. The Guard didn't even ask questions; they merely pricked her finger and shoved her onto a train like cattle.

In the boxcar, a handful of other prisoners waited in shackles, moaning with hunger and distress. It had to be magic—Lex was sure of it. Why else would the Order gather all these individuals?

But she wasn't magic.

She could hardly be around magic.

Back in the City of Mert, Dr. Kafele of the Sanitorium diagnosed her with Phantom Rot. They called it a magical degenerative disorder. In simple terms, Lex was allergic to magic.

If that was the case, why did that strange liquid change for her? Why did they shove her in this boxcar?

Not that she cared; she would have fought tooth and nail to stay beside Madame Owiti and Garrett.

She shook her head in disbelief. They left Mert after the Order sanctioned the city. The plan had been to venture out to the country of Evylain, where no one would gawk at the black stamps on their wrists or at anyone's magical aptitude. Lex never wanted to leave Mert; she loved that city. She adored their little shop. But they had no choice. That chapter had ended.

And the Order now controlled the next page.

The train jolted again. *For the love of Diosa Ciénaga, surely they could drive this thing a little smoother. Some of us have children!* Lex cursed to herself, choosing her deity for the day in one breath.

Garrett fidgeted in her arms and whined. She squeezed his shoulder. What was the poor boy thinking? He rarely spoke, often only in single phrases, committing his attention to the made-up language he created with his dead brother. According to Madame Owiti, the ghost of Garrett's twin, Preston, always stayed near them. It was easier for Lex to pretend that Preston was alive, too...for Garrett's sake and her own.

While sight-of-the-dead was common in the City of Mert, feeding off the magic bleeding throughout the city, because of her *condition,* she could never see Preston. Or any other ghosts.

But Garrett saw. So did Madame Owiti.

She trusted them.

Garrett shifted on her lap again. Was he even aware of what happened? He was a precocious child, talented with his crayons and observant of his surroundings. He kept to himself mostly, only letting her, Toddle, or Madame Owiti touch him. Whenever someone fought, he hid. Loud noises frightened him. He often would chew on his fingers, despite his age. These were all small things, unnoticeable by most, but they were the things that made him undeniably 'Garrett.' Lex loved him for all of that.

Toddle always worried, though. His words still echoed in her head, *He ain't gonna have friends if he acts this way. He gotta stop having that imaginary friend and bullshite.*

Garrett would be fine. Lex was certain of it.

But what would the Order do to an atypical child once they arrived at…wherever they were going?

Madame Owiti stirred next to her, grunting as if to answer Lex's unspoken question. "We can't be at Knoll yet."

"Do you really think they're taking us to Knoll?" Lex asked.

"Where else, my dear?"

Lex drew in her lips and exhaled. Knoll's Gully made the most sense; it was the central base of the Guard and the place where the Order had the strongest power.

Their moving towers still haunted her memory, perfect shadows of her childhood when the Guard had experimented on her. She blocked most of it from her memory. As far as it concerned her, her life began in Knoll's Pit, where she tended to the wounded and listened to the vagrants rallying in distaste against the government. It was there that she and Toddle kindled a romance.

Everything else before then was a forgotten dream, locked away in a vault.

No matter how hard she pressed her memory, it was white.

Like her skin.

Like her hair.

Like a cloud-riddled sky.

Even her life as a child before the Order, back in Opal's Canyon, was nothing more than a song of blank faces. No mother. No siblings. Nothing.

She was the albino girl from the Pit.

She was Toddle's wife.

She was a fake seer.

That was all.

Madame Owiti kept rambling beside Lex. "They gotta be making a pit stop. Probably ain't bringing everyone to Knoll. They might even have real passengers or what-not, yes, yes. We're just a bit of cargo."

Lex stroked Garrett's hair. The boy hugged her thigh, then rolled onto his side. *He'll wake soon.*

Hungry.

Desperate.

She already expected his tears. What would she tell him? An adventure wouldn't quell him; neither would a prayer to a god. No, he needed comfort. It was dark. He was hungry.

Would he even be able to see Preston?

Her mind kept spinning. Even Madame Owiti's speech sounded distant.

Where is the Diosa Ciénaga? Are you the one whom I should pray to on this day? Or should I turn to the Effluvium?

No. She couldn't pray to the Effluvium now. Not when its Order saw her family as a plague.

Madame Owiti nudged her, removing a piece of candy from her bag. "You need to eat, dear. I snuck this in."

"Save it for Garr-bear," Lex replied.

"I have more."

Begrudgingly, Lex took the piece of candy and popped it into her mouth. *Chocolate.* It melted on her tongue, sending her into a momentary calmness. Its smooth, milky, sweet goodness transported her back to happiness.

Had life been happy only a couple of months ago? Ever since the Story Collector, Brent, broke into their little shop, things had gotten out of hand. She didn't blame Brent, though. Magic caused people to do strange things.

And Brent was a strange young man.

She smiled, thinking about the Story Collector and his lovely Magii girlfriend, Bria. They were nice kids. Lex had thought little about them as they fled Mert. What happened to them? Were they safe?

She prayed to the Swamp Goddess that they were somewhere far from the Order, far from the Guard, and far from Knoll.

Her train of thought snapped as Garrett woke. He rubbed his red eyes and peered around the dark train car.

"Pres…" He grinned and reached out for a space on the floor. "Wakey wake."

"Is he tired?" Lex asked Garrett.

"Yeah." Garrett stared at the ground.

"You must be tired too."

"Yeah."

"Are you hungry?" Madame Owiti interjected, offering Garrett two pieces of chocolate. "Why don't you share some of this with Preston, yes, yes?"

"Okay, Witi." Garrett took the chocolate without meeting Madame Owiti's gaze, then plopped on the floor cross-legged, his attention entirely on his ghostly brother.

At least he seemed unphased by the turn of events.

The train skidded again, finally coming to an abrupt halt. People huddled together as far from the doorway as possible. Lex gripped Madame Owiti's hand and pulled

Garrett back onto her lap. Madame Owiti made a motion with her hand to welcome Preston on her lap. *Thank Diosa for you, Madame. I wouldn't be able to handle Garrett and Preston alone.*

The door to the boxcar slid open, giving them no time to hold their breath. A tall captain with a curled mustache entered. His dark, beady eyes scanned over the prisoners. "I'm looking for Elexis Dray."

Lex's heart plopped in her stomach.

"I know you're in here. Fucking albino bitch. It ain't gonna be hard to find you…so let's make this easy, a'ight!?!" the captain shouted.

Madame Owiti squeezed her hand. "Stay strong. You have done nothing wrong."

"I know." Lex lifted Garrett onto Madame Owiti's lap, then rose to greet the captain. "I'm Elexis Dray."

The captain pulled her forward by the loose hem of her sleeve. "Come with me."

Lex didn't argue. It wasn't worth her energy. Fighting would lead to Madame Owiti and Garrett getting hurt. She couldn't risk that. Not now. Not ever.

She followed the captain out of the boxcar. The name *Carver* glowered at her from the badge on his uniform. Lex pulled away, taking in the drab scenery. Steam chugged from the train, mingling with the dead forest on the northern side of the train tracks. On the southern side, shacks and old warehouses coated the snow-covered landscape. *Madame Owiti was right. We're not in Knoll yet. This is too small.*

She didn't ask the captain where they were; she cared little. Answers would come, as they always did, yet her fear remained tight in her belly, somersaulting into her throat.

The captain led her into a different car. A long hallway of living quarters greeted her. Every part of her clenched with terror. She'd been in this scenario before, long ago, at the hands of a captain. They led her down a hallway filled with living quarters, then locked her in a room...

Alone...

Until a guard entered...

And stole her innocence with a laugh and a grunt.

A scream stalled in her throat, but she pushed it back into her stomach.

Breathe. Diosa Ciénaga will protect you.

The captain shoved her into a room in the back of the car. "You have five minutes." Then he slammed the door shut.

Trembling, Lex looked up from her spot on the ground. Two sets of boots connected to a gray uniform, marked by the black stamp.

The uniform rested on a tanned body with green eyes and dark hair. The face gruff and rugged but one she knew.

One she loved.

"Toddle?" she gasped, restraining her tears.

"Lex!" He pulled her close. "I was so worried about you and Garrett. Are you a'ight? Shite! Did they do anything to you? Are you okay?"

"They didn't harm us." Lex squirmed out of his arms. She eyed him; a new bruise blackened on his face, but he otherwise appeared unharmed. "Did you anger someone?"

"What do you think?" Toddle shrugged.

Lex sighed.

"I had to give the captain a piece of my mind. Got me to see you, though, so I think it's all a'ight, yeah?"

"Is it?" Lex narrowed her eyes at him. "You're wearing a Guard's uniform."

"I...yes. I am."

"Why?"

Toddle frowned. "It was the only way."

"Only way for what?!"

"To protect you!"

"So you joined the Guard?! Toddle! You spent your whole life running from them—"

"I spent my whole life protecting you! This was the only way to protect *you*! And Garrett! You're the most important things to me—"

"At what cost?!"

"I just had to give them some information. Nothing big. Just about Mert—"

"About Mert? No, you mean you told them about *people*! Toddle, how could you? We had friends there!" Lex clenched her fists.

"I had to protect you!"

"From what? We're still in the prisoner car!"

"But once we get to Knoll, you'll be a'ight! No one will take you away from me."

"Then why don't they let me out for good right now? Toddle, use your noggin!"

"They don't want to cause an issue with the other prisoners right now, that's all." Toddle didn't meet her eyes, though.

"Bull!"

"Elexis..."

"No. This...we shouldn't have come here. We would have been better off staying in Mert. Or hopping on a caravan across the Chessboard Plains or something like that! This..."

Lex closed her eyes. They had fled to Mert to escape all of this. Her husband abandoned the Guard and risked his own life for her safety. Now he'd returned…for the same reason? She couldn't wrap her head around it. All of it was wrong.

"You betrayed me, Toddle."

"Wha—What?" Toddle's voice quavered.

Lex still didn't open her eyes to meet him; she couldn't. She didn't want to see his heartbreak over the next sentences.

"I forgave so much. I accepted so much. But I can't forgive this. You so easily turned your back on your morals and gave into the Guard. Maybe you never left them."

"Lex, don't be rash!"

"I'm not being rash! I'm being honest!" She finally opened her eyes. Heartbreak had etched its way across Toddle's face. It broke her into pieces, but she continued, "I thought I loved a man of morals, of conviction, and of artistry. The past couple of weeks have shown I married a selfish man who has some heroic ideas that he has to protect his *weak* wife. I'm not weak, Toddle! And I would have rather you hold to your convictions than rejoin the Guard without a fight! You're putting lives at risk."

"I'm saving you!"

"You don't know that! By now, you should know that the Order and the Guard lie!"

"Lex, c'mon. I'm doing this for you!" Toddle groaned.

"No. You're doing it for *you*." Lex turned from him. "It's this damn hero complex you have...but it's not heroic! You've always hated magic. Even in Mert, you had a distaste for it. So now, you see a way to help end it under the guise of protecting *me*. I guess this lets your true colors shine."

Toddle called out for her again, but his voice fell on deaf ears.

As if on cue, the door slid open behind them, and the captain waited for Lex on the other side. "Come now, Ms. Dray. It's time to leave."

"Happily." Without another word, Lex followed the captain from the room, not bothering to look back at Toddle despite his pleas.

CHAPTER SIX

AETERNO VILLAGE

ria's whole body ached. As the morning light seeped into the room, her eyes fluttered open, but every movement creaked with the yearning to break. Moss decorated corners of her skin, and strands of corn stalk stuck to her teeth. When she closed her eyes, she could hear the trees outside and feel their death within the wooden floorboard.

The earth cried to her in Rosada.

But she couldn't save it.

Bria groaned as she rolled over on her side. Brent still slept, with Nix lying between them. He mumbled in his sleep. "Merta," "Brother," "Help me"—each phrase a mere remnant of Nedo's life. He'd freed the ghost from the story, letting his soul be one with the earth at last.

But at what cost?

Bria closed her eyes again. Where could they go now? When they jumped into the Pool, the last thing Bria expected was to end up in Rosada. The goal had seemed so simple: to find the Pools and destroy them, thus preventing Ningursu and Kek from continuing their watch over the world.

But she thought they'd end up somewhere safe.

Perhaps this was where they needed to be, though. If the Order had connections to the Council, she and Brent might be the only ones able to stop them.

Bria climbed out of bed. As her bare feet hit the floor, the wood cracked, sending her leg through the surface.

She cursed under her breath as she dislodged her foot. With her hand trembling, she ordered the wood to reform, leaving a trace of weaving branches in their place.

"Bri?" Brent sat up slightly in bed.

'I'm okay," she lied. Splinters stuck out of her foot. Blood congealed along them.

"You don't look okay." Brent joined her on the floor. "What happened?"

"I...I think there's something wrong with my magic. It's reacting to everything."

"Is that even possible?"

"I don't know." Bria stared at her hands. She ran her fingers over the floorboard. The mere hints of the trees beckoned to her. Could she turn this room into a forest with a single movement?

She didn't want to consider it.

"When Kek trained you...did they ever mention something like this?" Brent asked.

"They mentioned untapped potential. But I thought they meant in the forests or with storms, not...this." She still recalled the day Kek took her to the island. She met with one of the other Magii in the Palaver, a stout man named Yusef, who had a less powerful control over nature. Kek helped Bria unleash her abilities, helped her reach into the earth and bring life back to an otherwise dead landscape. From there, she birthed storms, controlled rain, and brought lightning down in the library.

What is my limit?

"Well, maybe we need to find a way for you to practice your magic. Someplace safe...so you can...I dunno...figure out your limits."

"I can't do that here." Bria turned to the window. The gray morning sky peered in at her, thick with the mist that ravaged Rosada.

There was something dead in the air in Rosada. But Bria couldn't quite figure out what. She felt it suffocating her in every breath. Her magic reached for life.

Just as it had back in Newbird's Arm.

Was it her magic that kept the gardens alive? What had become of them with her gone?

Brent mulled through the options. "Then we should leave Rosada. Hop on a caravan or a train or something."

"And go where?"

"Kainan can't be far, right? A couple days?"

"But does Kainan like magic?"

"Then we get to Heims or south to Volfium or…something. Back to Mert. If we take the tunnels—"

"No. Brent." Bria shook her head. "Kek might have said we're free to go…but I don't want to fall on their radar. And I'm sure the Mist Keepers are looking for us too. It's not worth the risk."

"A'ight, yeah, you're right. But then what do we do?"

Bria didn't dare look at Brent, instead peering out the window. Rosada. She hadn't planned on returning here, but the Pool led her here. It wasn't fate–Bria didn't believe in such foolish things—but everything always came together in Rosada.

Everything always beckoned her home.

"We're the only ones who know about the Council's connection with the Order. They're obviously planning something…" Bria picked at the floorboard. "Both of them have always hated magic. And the Council is getting more aggressive."

Brent crossed his arms. "Yeah, cause I fucked things up."

"Are you still blaming yourself for this?"

"I mean...I can sedate the Diabolo. I think that scares them."

Bria smirked at Brent. She liked when his confidence showed through his fear. Ever since she met Brent, he'd carried an aura of sadness on his chest. A pitiful boy who made mistakes because he was too afraid to act. Clumsy Brent Harley, goofy Brent Harley.

Kind Brent Harley.

But it was a rarity to see him confident.

"We're the ones who can stop this alliance," Bria said, trying her best to keep her voice steady.

"You really think we can?"

"I'm not sure. But we have to try, don't we?" Bria rose from the floor and walked to the window. A few guards marched beneath her window. Could she stop them all with a flick of her wrist? She wasn't sure she had the strength. "We can't be the only ones in Rosada who want to stop this."

Brent joined her by the window. "And we can always reach out to neutral parties. Like Malaika or Tilda."

Bria nodded, recalling the women she'd met in Mert only a few weeks ago. Malaika, though a Mist Keeper, didn't quite adhere to any standards set by Ningursu.

There were plenty of Magii who wanted nothing to do with Kek as well.

But really, Bria knew her talents were key to severing the connection between the Council of Mist Keepers and the Order of the Effluvium.

"We have to find out where the Tower of Ab Aeterno went," she said. "I don't think it's a coincidence we ended up here. I wonder if Ningursu was trying to connect with Elder Don Van or whoever he is communicating with."

"You think he could control the pools?"

"He's an ancient god-like skull. I doubt there's much he can't do."

"Good point." Brent's gaze fell to the window again, up towards the clifftop where the tower once stood. What stories did he see? Bria sometimes envied his magic; it was this magic that gave him truth, the magic that gave him knowledge. He wasn't just a gardener; he was a Mist Keeper, protector of life and death.

At least he knew how he'd gained his magic.

Meanwhile, Bria floundered in uncertainty with her powers.

"I might be able to figure it out...just gotta go see some more stories," Brent said.

Bria nodded. If Brent needed to see stories, then that meant one thing: they had to leave their hideaway in the tavern. But with Bria's faces plastered throughout Rosada, that wouldn't be easy in their current state.

She placed a hand on his back and followed his gaze out the window. "I guess we need a disguise then."

Bria put together a disguise using a few random items in her bag. She pulled on Brent's oversized clothes, then stuffed her hair into a yellow trilby hat they'd purchased a year ago in Mert. After scouring through the Gazette, they learned the only mention of Brent Harley was a single "wanted" line. For safety, though, Bria spent a good ten minutes combining his hair, then handed him her cowl to hide his own face. It wasn't a great disguise, but it was enough to hide their faces.

Brent groaned, running his hand through his newly combed hair. His attention remained on the newspaper.

"Anything interesting?" Bria asked.

Brent glanced at her. "Did you see that...I mean, did you hear about the Rosadian election results a few months ago?"

"Honestly? It was the last thing on my mind," Bria admitted. "I didn't really keep track of time during those months."

"Then I guess you didn't know about Elder Don Van..."

"What about him?"

"He's not an elder anymore." Brent pointed to an image in the paper. "He's the Senator for Knoll's Gully."

Bria's stomach turned. *Senator.* It was bad enough the man had pulled in Newbird's Arm and the Order. But now, he sat at the foot of the government, wringing his hands around weaker politicians. *No wonder he was here.*

She shook down her tears, and with Nix on their heels, they exited the room.

Bria clung to Brent's arm as they left the tavern. She didn't dare make eye contact with the old barmaid at the counter, her attention downcast. What if someone had already recognized her? The photograph from Newbird's Arm might have been blurry, but if someone looked hard enough or read the details, they might just report her to the Guard.

Bria didn't say a word as they walked, watching as Brent paused by each corner to take in the story. His expression never changed much, save for the way he creased his brows, then shook his head in disappointment.

Aeterno reminded Bria of Hutch's Creek, the town she lived in for the first eight years of her life. Smaller than Newbird's Arm but larger than the small villages scattered throughout Rosada, it bled with dust and smoke. The few automobiles in the town sat parked on the edge of the parched farmland, just past the train station. A gentle snow whisked through the air like smoke.

Bria caught one snowflake on her fingertips, watching as it melted into her skin. Brent shivered beside her.

"You have snow in your hair," Bria giggled.

"You sure I'm not just going gray?"

"That'd be quick." Bria hopped onto the side of a frozen fountain so she could reach Brent's hair. She stroked her fingers through his curls, brushing away the snow. "Any stories of interest yet?"

"No. A lot of guards…commotion over the fire. But the…the town is so old. It gives me a headache. I'll keep trying, though…"

Bria stopped him. "Don't push yourself."

Brent glanced past her. "I know the tower headed upstream…north."

"Knoll is north. And if Elder Don Van…erm…Senator Cordova, I mean, is the representative for that region, then maybe that's where they are taking it.'

"That would make sense. Or the Capitol…"

"Is there a river that leads to the Capitol?"

"Do I honestly look like I memorized geography? You're the earth goddess!"

Bria squirmed and looked away. "Goddess is a big word."

Brent took her hands. "You fought a Death God and lived. That puts you on par, if not better."

"Brent…"

"Don't downplay what you're able to do."

"Nix was the one who caught Ningursu, though." Bria glanced at their dog rolling in the snow. "She's the true goddess."

"Dog, God, same thing," Brent laughed. "But I won't change what I said about you."

Bria smiled. Brent Harley: hopeless romantic. He always had been, ever since they first kissed. He wore his emotions on his sleeve. But she needed someone like him, someone who kept her head up, someone who was goofy for no real reason.

Someone honest.

Someone forgiving.

Even when he shouldn't forgive.

Bria laced her fingers around his hands. "Perhaps we can see if there's a train station or something that has a map. See the river patterns. There might be a ferry or train heading towards Knoll. We can pass ourselves as seekers of the Effluvium or something like that, desperate to find Ab Aeterno after it vanished."

"Oh yeah, we're definitely some religious individuals." Brent lifted her up and spun her around. "Yes, I believe in the magical mist that blesses us! It is gorgeous and wonderful and perfect and will give us peace!”

“Brent! Stop it! You’re making me dizzy!”

He spun her once more, then placed her on the ground, laughing. “Let us give our souls to the Effluvium, that bastard!”

“You’re such a goof,” Bria laughed.

“Yeah, but you love me.”

“I do.” Bria stood on her tiptoes to kiss his cheek. “I’m so glad I didn’t lose you again. It would have been so easy in that battle, but...you’re here.”

“Eh, I’ll get lost again, I’m sure. It’s not like I have a good sense of direction.” Brent hopped back. “See! I dunno where I am going right now!”

“Brent!”

Before she could stop him, he dashed down one of the narrow roads, guffawing.

“Brent! Now’s not the time for games!” Bria chased after him with Nix on her heels. She restrained a laugh. Only Brent Harley could be ridiculous while attempting to hide. Now he was off, rushing through buildings and alleys, avoiding guards. Was it a story taking hold of him?

No. This was Brent at the core.

She continued chasing after him, rounding a bend into a dead green park. A steam engine sat at the far edge of the park, pummeling with smoke. Brent ran across the field, his legs loose and bouncing like a mare, unable to run in a straight line.

He glanced back over his shoulder at her, grinning like a child.

Bria didn't have time to stop him as he ran straight into a hulking figure in a colorful outfit.

"Oi!" the figure boomed as he turned, revealing a curly mustache and thick bushy eyebrows. "What you doing here?"

Brent stepped back as Bria reached him. She caught his arm.

"Sorry...sorry. I mean...I was...we were...I was being dumb. Sorry." Brent flushed.

"You're not a kid. What kind of idjit behaves like that? Grow up."

"I...um..."

"Let's go." Bria took his hand and tugged. "We were going to the train station."

"Hold on!" someone shouted from behind the big fellow. "I know exactly what type of idiot acts like that!"

Bria swore she recognized that voice.

A man approached them, hair pulled into a messy bun, grease and stubble layering his face.

"Micca!" Bria exclaimed.

Micca Fein, her and Brent's longtime friend, grinned widely. "Bria Smidt and Brent Harley! You're the last two

I expected to see out in Aeterno!" He nudged the hulking, mustached man. "Timothée! These are my friends I done told you about!"

The hulking man's face relaxed, and he bowed his head in greeting.

"Don't mind him. He's not one for words. But you two! I ain't think I ever seen you again! Come here!" Micca threw his arms around both Bria and Brent, tugging them close into a hug. His smile contaminated Bria, and she returned it with equal enthusiasm.

"What are you doing here?" Bria asked, stealing a glance at Brent. She was sure he already saw glimpses of the story.

"That's kinda a long story. But eh, we've got time. C'mon, let's get some grub, and I'll catch you all up."

SWALLOWED

Knoll emerged in the distance from beneath a smog-made blanket. Jemma watched as the multiple towers that dotted the city came into view from her perch in the Year Glass Atrium of Ab Aeterno. The tower pushed through the river up towards the city, navigating through the barren landscape dusted in a blanket of late winter snow. She imagined how people envisioned the tower as it approached; it probably appeared as a beacon, peaking out over the horizon. Awestruck, they probably collapsed their knees, praying for the kindness in the Effluvium's prowess.

When she first saw the tower, it compelled her to kneel.

Only for fire, rumored to be cast by a rogue Magii, to take away the dazzling sight.

Even now, worn by scorch marks yet shimmering like the moon, the tower did little to illuminate the landscape. From beneath the smog, Knoll appeared broken. Jemma had always pictured Knoll like this: dusty smog-ridden and with dark towers as shadows to be told. She looked down from above it all, a Sister of the Order, loyal to the Effluvium and nothing else.

"Welcome home, Sister Jey Ma," Senator Cordova stood beside her, his hands on his waist, his blue eyes focused with guile. "It is time to bring order back to Rosada. We'll make the Effluvium pure once more."

Jemma nodded. She'd maintained a silent composure over the last few days since the senator offered her passage on the Tower of Ab Aeterno. She'd ventured all the way from Newbird's Arm, abandoning her family and duties, in search of Newbird's Arms's late spiritual leader, Brother Roy Al. With the help of vagrant Micca Fein, she crossed the country; she only discovered destruction and dismay in the spiritual grace of Ab Aeterno, though. Brother Roy Al was dead, shot and burned by detrimental hands. Jemma truly believed the senator and his men were to blame...but part of her wondered if something more was afoot.

It didn't matter, though. Jemma had agreed to travel with him to Knoll. She'd feared that refusing would mean he would cut her future short, send her to live as a vagrant in one of the Pits throughout Rosada. She would be no better than Micca, running for an undetermined future. All that she stood for would vanish.

Between her failed betrothal to Brenton Harley, her foiled attempt to bring peace back to her hometown of Newbird's Arm, and her desolate venture across Rosada, she'd sacrificed so much to the Order already. When pressed with the choice, Jemma knew she had to follow Senator Cordova—the former Elder Don Van of the Newbird's Arm Temple—to Knoll. Only then could she learn the Effluvium's true history; only then might she be able to cleanse the world of demons.

"Senator." An elder with beady black eyes and a receding hairline entered the room. "We shall arrive within the hour."

"Thank you, Elder An Drew." Senator Cordova beamed.

"There are a few matters of concern, though, I am afraid. There have been reports of Yellow Storms in the North."

"Then I suppose we need to get started as soon as possible. Has there been any news otherwise?"

"Captain Carver has arrived back from Chelidae's Mark with a new batch from Mert."

"And the city is still under our control?"

"Yes, sir."

"Very good. Please prepare for arrival."

Elder An Drew bowed his head, then scurried out of the Year Glass Atrium without another word, like a squirrel with secrets buried outback.

Jemma said nothing; it wasn't her place. She instead directed her gaze up to the Year Glass. Unlike the fixtures back at home, she could literally stand beneath this Year Glass. She watched as the silver liquid dripped from above, filling the hallowed walls around her and into the basin below her feet. She spent all day up here, only venturing out of the atrium for bed or the lavatory. Cadet Christof Carver sometimes joined her, bringing her meals and sitting opposite her. Neither of them said a word. Sitting beneath the Year Glass of Ab Aeterno was hardly the place to talk.

Senator Cordova broke that tradition, though. "I am sure you have questions, Sister Jey Ma."

"Yes, but it is not my place to ask," Jemma replied.

"I implore you to ask, Sister." Senator Cordova smiled. It sliced his face, causing his blue eyes to shine like his silver-streaked hair. "I am but an old man. I know that to cleanse the Effluvium and bring prosperity to

Newbird's Arm, I must listen to the next generation. You represent that to me, Sister Jey Ma. I saw it in you as a young lass in Newbird's Arm. If Brother Roy Al didn't have the ridiculous notion that he could fix a vagrant through marriage, it is quite possible you would already run your own Temple in the Newbird Region."

Jemma saw it for a second in her mind's eye: a small temple somewhere in the mountains, her draped in a blue robe. It was everything she'd ever dreamt...but that was for a different lifetime.

"Never mind that, of course. You are here now." Senator Cordova led Jemma towards the window as he continued to speak. The tower passed alongside a farm, its fields turned brown and lifeless by the chill in the air. "So, please, humor me, Sister Jey Ma. Tell me what you want to know."

Jemma kept her gaze on the nearing city. Her mind ran in circles. For the past few days, she'd been trying not to think. She wanted to cleanse herself of doubt and worry. But questions remained, and even as she meditated, they did not vanish.

"What are you hoping to accomplish in Knoll?"

"Knoll elected me as its representative, so I intend to represent it," the senator stated.

"But why did you flee there in the first place? It's not known for glamor." Jemma motioned towards the deceased forests in the distance and the smog touting the night sky.

"Because Knoll has the tools to defeat demons."

"You mean the Yellow Storm that Elder An Drew mentioned?"

"Precisely. You have witnessed such a storm before."

"Yes…" Jemma tried not to remember the Storm of Nightmares in Newbird's Arm. A demon tore through town, and while Brent Harley and Bria Smidt appeared to stop the monster in its tracks, the destruction remained. Nightmares haunted everyone's sleep for months.

If another storm, or demon, was out there…would the nightmares ever stop?

Senator Cordova explained, "We received information that these storms are all over the globe now after an outburst in the Independent City of Mert. We have an informant that tells us the storms are born of magic. The monsters that live in them feed on magic, and nothing can destroy them."

"But what does that have to do with Knoll's Gully?"

"Ah, Sister Jey Ma." Senator Cordova patted her hand. "You have much to learn. How do you kill an invincible monster?"

"I…don't know, sir."

"You destroy its food source, Sister."

Jemma stiffened. "You do not mean—"

"Yes. It is what we have always stood by: magic attracts demons. Magic is born out of stories and lack of faith. We destroy magic, we rid our lives of stories, and then the demons have nowhere to go. They starve to death." Senator Cordova straightened his spine. "And we, dear Sister, rid ourselves of pestilence. Dangerous Magii have ceased, demons are extinct, and no one ever tells a falsehood again. This is my goal."

Jemma knew most of this deep in her core, but hearing it out loud chilled her bones.

She asked the next question in a squeaky whisper: "But what means do we have to do such a thing?"

"Give it time, Sister. You have much to learn. I have already set you up to be Elder Un Dine's mentee. She is a wise sister, and I think she will prove a valuable guide in your quest to become one with the Effluvium. While you train, I hope you will consider the answer to the following question: how can we make the Order a home for young people like yourself? You are our future. I think your insight will be most valuable."

Jemma bowed her head. "I will consider it, Senator."

"I trust you will succeed as the Effluvium shall guide you." The senator kissed the tips of his fingers, then placed them to Jemma's head in prayer. He still carried that same composure as when he was an Elder.

As he left the room, it was as if the Effluvium followed behind him, untethering Jemma so she could once again breathe. Once alone beneath the Year Glass, vertigo set in her mind. With her feet wobbling, she made it to the nearby chair, dark splotches decorating her vision.

Jemma wasn't even sure what caused it. Nothing Senator Cordova said was entirely new to her. She knew of the Order's distaste for magic—after all, Magii and Storytellers always ended up in the Pit. But part of it was in abstract only. This was more; this was Senator Cordova confirming the Order's desire to rid the world of magic once and for all.

Jemma had seen firsthand the detriment of magic. The Storm of Nightmares first ravaged Newbird's Arm. Beneath it, Bria Smidt conjured plants and left the town in disarray. Yet, when she traveled with Micca, Jemma also bore witness to the happiness magic brought. The tricks and elements of a magical circus brought smiles to patrons' faces. Could even simple tricks attract this horror-ridden storm?

This is your chance to change the Order, Jemma. Even Senator Cordova said he wants your input. You could change everything for the better. Her attention drifted back to Knoll's skyline. *Perhaps this is the Effluvium's plan.*

She kept her gaze on the horizon, only flinching when the door opened on the far side of the atrium. Cadet

Christof Carver strode in with a platter of food. Despite his burned face, he was still attractive. He had deep green eyes, lush blonde hair, and a strong stature fit for any guard. His personality tainted him, though; obsessive, rude, and pugnacious, Jemma often avoided him back in Newbird's Arm. But here in Ab Aeterno, there was a softness to him she hadn't seen. Without his father, the notorious Captain Glenndal Carver, present, Christof did not try to match any expectations. He performed each of his duties with dignity and loyalty.

Jemma hoped his heart had opened after the events in Newbird's Arm. Was it possible he came to terms with knowing that Bria never loved him back?

Jemma never pressed the issue. The only time they spent together was during these meals, where they sat in meditative silence.

"Thank you, Cadet." Jemma bowed to him as he placed the food on the table. She took her place at the table while Christof took the other side. He never asked if he could stay, but it never bothered Jemma. She liked the company, especially from someone close in age to her. Senator Cordova and Elder An Drew's presence bled with age.

Christof never said much, nor did he eat. Often, he just stared at the Year Glass with an empty look in his eye.

Today, though, Christof spoke. "Are you looking forward to Knoll, Sister?"

"It will be an interesting change of pace," Jemma said as she cut a piece of chicken. "The last year had many surprises."

"Yeah …" Christof glared at the skyline. "I think you'll learn a lot there."

"Did you spend a lot of time in Knoll?"

"We fled to Knoll after the Storm of Nightmares," he stated.

"Oh. Right." Jemma knew that. Christof and his father had left Newbird's Arm in disgrace, disappearing into the night as the Storm of Nightmares dissipated. No one missed them. Not even Christof's uncle, Brother Roy Al.

She had hoped for more details, but Christof kept his silence. She opened her mouth to say something else but had nothing more to inquire. Jemma supposed she wouldn't have much to say either.

For now, all she could do was watch as Knoll approached, greeting her with a putrid embrace.

She prayed it wouldn't swallow her whole.

A CARNIVAL OF TWO

Micca led Bria and Brent over to a small café on the edge of the park, just past the train station. While Bria was certain that Brent caught most of Micca's story in the air, he didn't say a word. Instead, he listened to Micca, taking in how Micca traveled across Rosada with none other than Jemma Reds. That had been the last person Bria imagined taking a voyage like that. Bria spoke little with Jemma growing up, and after her betrothal to Brent, it only furthered their differences. Not that Bria ever blamed Jemma. Overall, it had just been a difficult situation. The Order offered Brent a chance to be secured by a union to a woman, pious and pure.

Yet before they left Newbird's Arm, Jemma showed a new spark.

Perhaps she was changing.

Once Micca finished his story, Brent filled him in on the past few months, weaving a story of half-truths that took them from Mert back to Rosada. He left out the part about the Diabolo as well as everything about the Mist Keepers.

A smart move, in Bria's opinion. The less they had to explain, the better.

"That's bonkers! Really! I honestly didn't think I'd see you two again!" Micca said with a mouthful of rice and beans. Beside him, his partner, Timothée, ate silently. Micca described him as a gentle giant who'd won his heart with a single smile.

"It's been...a long couple of months." Bria glanced at Brent.

Micca smirked. "Yeah, I'm sure. But I hope you two have time to get reacquainted if you catch me? You know..." He leaned forward. "I'm sure you gotta be married by now."

Brent's face reddened. "Um, well...um...well..."

"We've been dealing with a lot," Bria interjected, taking Brent's hand under the table and squeezing between his knuckles. "We haven't had time for marriage."

"Ah, you gotta fix that. Brenty-boy, you've been talking about this since—"

"Micca, enough." Timothée shot a glare.

Bria relaxed her shoulders, but tension remained in her throat and stomach. *Marriage.* She and Brent had talked about their life together but never about formalizing it. Now, with the world churning just out of reach, the mere thought seemed preposterous.

Micca wiped his mouth. "Right. Yeah, right. Sorry. Got overexcited, but yeah…I still can't believe this! You two should come to the carnival tonight! It's a blast and so much fun, and…yeah! Timothée is amazing!"

"Carnival?" Bria cast a glance between Brent and Micca.

"Oh, yeah. I saw it in the newspaper and with the…I mean…yeah, the flyers and the newspaper." Brent shifted in his seat. "Didn't think we had the time to check it out."

Bria mumbled, "I don't know if we have time. We need to leave here soon."

"Ah! C'mon! Just one night!" Micca pressed. "Please! It's been so long, and you all owe me!"

"Why do we owe you?" Brent asked.

"I take full responsibility for your little romance. You two wouldn't ever have been friends if it wasn't for me. And I definitely pushed you two together." Micca smirked. "It's my fault. No denying it. You owe me!"

Brent exchanged a glance with Bria. "It's not like we're gonna leave tonight, right? We still gotta figure out everything and all. Might as well have some fun before causing mayhem?"

Brent was right, of course. Bria knew that. When would they have fun again? But did they have time to have fun? Every moment, Bria swore someone watched them. One wrong move, and wouldn't they be found out? Ningursu could be watching…anyone could be watching. They didn't have time for *fun*.

Yet, she also wanted a moment of normalcy. She dreamt of being able to spend time alone with Brent, her friends, and her family, laughing without sadness in her steps.

A few hours of fun didn't hurt anyone, right?

She replied with a soft whisper, "I guess so."

"C'mon, Beebelle! It'll be fun!" Micca grabbed her hands. "Don't you know how to have fun anymore?"

"Of course!" Bria yanked her hands back. Why was Micca's heartbeat so loud?

"Then stop being a downer! C'mon. Where's that smile, girly?" Micca insisted.

Bria's lips twitched.

"There it is!"

It was hard not to smile around Micca. Sure, he didn't have magic in the traditional sense, but he'd always had a way to lighten a room. When she first moved to New-bird's Arm, Micca caught her eye quickly. He always got her to smile, always welcomed newcomers, and invited them to play.

And she wouldn't have become friends with Brent without him. She supposed they owed him, in a way.

Really, in all of this, it was strange sitting here with Micca and Timothée. It was almost like she and Brent were...well, normal. They weren't facing a war; they didn't carry the weight of truth on their shoulders. They were just some young adults trying to navigate life in a confusing world.

Bria gave in to his pleas. "Okay, we can go. Sounds like fun."

"Yes! Atta girl!" Micca shot up from his seat. "C'mon! You can ride with us!"

Exchanging a glance with Brent, she noticed the light filling his eyes. It seemed childish and carefree. After all this time, he still smiled. It was easy to forget that he had been a monster's vessel for six months or how he used to sit in town defeated by his black stamp. Despite every-thing, he flourished.

You're so much stronger than you know, Brent. If I were in your shoes, I would have fallen apart a long time ago. She couldn't bring herself to say those words to him, but she wore them close to her heart.

So for tonight, she would give him a chance to be care-free again. They would go to the carnival. It'd be like a date. Just for a little while, they could pretend they were like any other couple.

No brand.

No magic.

No Order.

No Mist.

Just them.

Bria and Brent rode with Micca and Timothée to the circus in the back of a cramped buggy. Nix hopped between them, her ears back, drooling on the armrest in the front of the car. Yet, while the dog bounced with excitement, Bria fell into that same silence as before, smiling at Micca's jokes but mostly staring out the window. Her attention remained locked on the dead landscape, listening to the trees cry. Did they judge her for riding in a buggy, poisoning the air with profuse smoke? Or did it not care?

Did the earth know she existed?

Brent said little either, and he kept his gaze distant. Surely, he witnessed stories in the air. How many did he push back each day? How many were in this car alone?

Micca didn't stop rambling the entire trip. "I've been checking every day since Jemma went and vanished on us in Aeterno. I'd hate to leave her behind, but we're packing up tomorrow. Heading north and all. Where we heading again, Timothée?"

"Siskin, then Juno, then back towards the east coast, I think. Gotta ask Mr. Santiago."

"Right. We're doing a loop around Rosada. The normal loop and all…then possibly head south to Volfium or some shite like that."

Micca kept rambling, and Bria nodded, watching as the multicolored tents came into view. Beside her, Brent shifted, his face pale, eyes distant. She assumed it was the stories getting to his head. Only when the buggy stopped and Brent stumbled out after Nix, gagging off to the side, did Bria realize the motion of the car made him sick.

"You okay?" she asked as Brent heaved one last time.

"Yeah. Don't like that." Brent shook his head. "I'm a'ight."

Micca hopped over to them, grinning. "Never took you for having a weak stomach."

Bria placed her hand on Brent's back and glanced around the border of the circus. Lights flickered throughout the tents with performers in masks and colorful outfits greeting patrons. All Aeterno might have been at the carnival, crowds bustling and laughing, gathering around makeshift stages.

Brent flinched as he watched the performers. "So many damn stories…" he mumbled.

"Just focus on one at a time," Bria whispered.

"Yeah, a'ight."

Micca teasingly slapped Brent's shoulder, causing him to jump back. "Listen, mate! You and Bria outta enjoy yourself and shite! Timothée and I will be around, but we got jobs to do. Otherwise, Lolli and Mr. Santiago might get up our arses, y'know?"

"Here." Timothée removed two tickets from his pocket. "Our treat. Got a few of these on hand for guests."

Bria took them. Across them, the words *Santiago's Cirque Sunrise* peered back at him. "Thank you," she said.

"Now go have fun, you two kiddos! And be safe! We'll catch up more tomorrow before the carnival goes and leaves here. So you best not go vanishing from Aeterno, y'hear me?" Micca winked.

"C'mon. No more dilly dallying. Don't want Santiago to have your head." Timothée grumbled, and before any-one else spoke, he dragged Micca away into the crowds of performers.

"Meet us at the same café, a'ight!?" Micca called over his shoulder as he and Timothée vanished into the com-motion of the carnival.

Bria took Brent's clammy hand. "I forgot how…intense Micca can be."

"Yeah, he's a character," Brent whispered, stealing another glance around the carnival. "Guess since we're here, we might as well explore, yeah?"

"You still up to it?"

"Sometimes the stories come like a cyclone, and it's hard to beat them down or whatever. I'm...I'll be a'ight."

Bria squeezed his fingers. With Nix in the lead, they wandered through the crowds. Brent continued to flinch at every story, but Bria kept a grip on him, squeezing his fingers every time he began to slip.

The further they moved away from the entrance of the carnival, the more relaxed Brent grew. His attention drifted to the makeshift stages where various performances enamored the patrons: a man juggling multicolored fire, a small pink-haired woman displaying feats of strength, and a tattooed artist whose body paint moved like the sea.

Bria followed his attention. She watched the tattooed artist spin, the different images on their skin changing. Around them, it was almost as though the earth pulsed with a silent song that only she could hear. It gathered on the performer's skin.

And it wasn't just the tattooed artist, but the strong woman, the juggler, and all the rest. The earth called.

Or was it something else?

"It's magic," Bria whispered.

"Huh?" Brent glanced at her.

"The performers…they're using real magic. I can feel it."

"You can…feel it?"

Bria stared at her hands for a moment. "It's like an itch on my skin. I don't understand it. Whatever Ningursu did…it's igniting something."

Brent glanced at the performers. "Are you sure? I mean…the stories show fantastic things, but…are you absolutely sure?"

"Positive."

"But we're in Rosada."

"I don't know how they're getting away with it…" Bria hugged herself. "But I feel it. There's definitely magic."

"Are you a'ight? Do you want to leave?"

"No…I'm okay. Really."

She laced her arm through his arm again and followed him along the path. The magic clawed at her back as she walked. Were these the demons the Order feared? Why did she sense it now?

She shook it off as they walked away from the stages, slowing outside the striped big-top tent bordering the train tracks. Vendors sold an array of goods and odd sweets and candies. Others called for them to "step right up" to play their ring-toss and dart games, to win a cheap porcelain or plush prize. Young couples gathered at the games, one always trying to woo the other with their skills and strength while the other cheered on with utter delight.

Bria's heart sank watching them. That was the life she yearned for more than anything—to have a day without care. No magic, no Mist Keepers, just laughter.

I almost want to see Brent try to win a prize. He has no coordination. She glanced over her shoulder. Brent had wandered over to one of the animal exhibits, standing face-to-face with a llama. He jutted out his jaw, mimicking the llama's disinterested expression.

Bria joined his side. "What're you doing?"

"Trying to turn into a llama." Brent shook back his head.

"I don't think it works that way."

"Yeah, it does." Brent produced a gurgling laugh. Moments later, the llama responded with a similar noise. "See!"

"Come on." Bria tugged him away from the petting zoo.

Despite the odor of manure and hay, Brent seemed more at peace as they wrapped around the big top.

"Animals have stories," Brent told her, "but they're...they're not the same as human tales. I dunno...they are less heavy. Guess it's just how they perceive the world or something. Makes it easier on my head. Sometimes."

Bria clenched Brent's fingers as Nix darted ahead of them to bark at a goat.

At every couple of exhibits—from the mist squirrels to the smokey anteaters—Brent stopped and marveled. There was something childlike about Brent's curiosity; he'd told stories about animals like these all his life. This circus was more than just a performance. It was a museum of oddities and carnival of obscurity. No one would notice a Magii and a Mist Keeper amid the commotion.

A line of people gathered on the opposite end of the big top, babbling with excitement. Acrobats performed in circles around the patrons while a clown bumbled by, squirting water from his fingertips.

"Bri, look." Brent pointed at a vendor selling a colorful assortment of masks. "Maybe we could use those as a disguise or something."

"Good thinking."

While Brent ventured over to purchase the masks, Bria joined the line of patrons. *This circus is a great place to hide. No one notices us here at all.*

It didn't take Brent long to return with two wooden masks: one in the shape of a bear and the other that took the form of a llama. He placed the latter on his face with a big grin. "Told you I would turn into a llama."

"Goof." Bria took the bear mask and pulled it over her face.

The line moved slowly. Nix kept bolting off, returning with either a stick in her mouth or disappearing into the crowds. Bria didn't worry about the dog; she always returned to them.

"What's this line for?" Brent asked, his eyes darting about the area.

Bria shrugged. "Something magical?"

The woman in front of them glared. "What? You don't know?"

"I'm sorry?"

She scoffed. "How do you not know? This is the main attraction!"

"We're not from around here," Brent mumbled in response.

"Neither is the dragon in the tent!" The woman tossed back her hair and returned to her partner.

*A dragon…*Bria tried to peer over the heads of the people in line. She had seen the smaller relatives of the legendary creatures flittering around parts of the western continent; they dominated the landscape in Spinoza and the Region Delilah. But by the sounds of this, the beast in the tent was far larger than those lizards.

The line moved at a snail's pace. Bria occupied herself by listening to the forest and the magic of the circus. She still didn't dare reach out to it, but it pulsated beneath her. She stared at her fingers. A few pieces of moss still occupied her skin, marking her as more than human.

"In the circus…no one notices," she whispered.

"Hm?" Brent tilted his head to the side.

"It's just…we'd blend in well with the circus. And didn't Micca say they were heading north?"

"And if we want to get to Knoll, then they could take us," Brent finished her thought.

"We'll have to talk with Micca and Timothée later. The sooner we can leave Aeterno, the better." Bria eyed a few of the small guard towers in the distance. There was no way they matched the beauty of Ab Aeterno, but they existed as dominant forces, ready to take away vagrants and Magii.

The line moved again. A few more steps and they entered the tent.

The tent wreaked of dung, sea salt, and straw. Bria wrinkled her nose while people around her gagged and marveled at the cage glowing with lanterns. Mist pulsed from the bars.

Inside, a beast with dark scales, translucent wings, and silver eyes lay curled on the floor of the cage. As each person approached the bars, it flared its nostrils, sending mist out through the room in plumes. It recoiled as children shouted at it, and a man nearby whined about the animal's hygiene. At every negative comment, the creature's morale shattered, its head falling closer to the ground. Bria swore it frowned.

"This is boring, Daddy!" one child exclaimed, bouncing on a sugar high from staying up far too late. "Can we go back to the games?"

"Don't you want to see the dragon?" the child's father inquired.

"It's doing nothing!"

Others continued to complain, demanding the dragon perform a silly trick. The beast remained curled up, unmoved.

Bria raised her mask, unable to take her eyes off it. She never imagined that she would see such a glorious dragon. Its black scales glimmered in the lantern light, producing a fool's aura of gold. What would it look like flying across the sky?

"It doesn't want to be here..." Brent mumbled as they approached the cage. He removed his mask for a better look. He scanned the cage, leaning forward as if listening to a story. "*She's* trapped. She...she's a prisoner."

"How do you know?" Bria asked.

"Her story is strong...almost human. I think it means that...I mean, I think...she's...she's sentient." Brent reached his hand towards the cage. The dragon leaned her snout towards Brent's hand. Mist caught his fingers, dancing around them. A story formed at his fingertips of a dragon flying through the sky, reaching for the clouds, and eclipsing the sun with its wings. Freedom and victory marked the dragon's wings.

Until she fell from the sky.

And—

A voice sliced through the air. "What are you doing to my Zephyr?"

Bria pulled her mask back over her face as she turned. A man in a golden suit stood in front of the tent, watching Brent with narrow eyes. As soon as he spoke, the mist vanished.

The man peered down at Bria, then at Brent, then back at Bria. "You gonna answer me?"

"We were just looking at the dragon...like everyone else," Bria squeaked.

"You were messing with her," the golden suit man approached them, eyes narrow and sharp. "Didn't you read the sign?"

"What sign?" Brent asked.

The man glanced around the room, then cursed under his breath. "Fuckers must've forgotten to put it out! Well, no matter. The sign says don't touch the dragon, y'hear me?"

"Yes, of course." Bria took Brent by the arm. "We'll be leaving now."

"Good. I better not find you two around here anymore, understand?"

Bria didn't reply, dragging Brent out of the tent and into the droves of patrons. She swore the man in the golden suit continued to stare after her, eyes stern and unmoving.

No, it wasn't just him. It was every single patron. They all saw *her*.

Bria gulped and clutched Brent's hand tighter. *My mask was only off for a minute. There's no way they recognized me. Not with the blurry pictures.*

She shook off the worries, hurrying through the droves of patrons. Nix continued to trot along at their side. Beside her, Brent seemed distant, sucked into another story.

Once they reached the fence bordering the carnival, Brent finally spoke, his voice thick with trepidation. "I should have...I mean...why did I use my magic? What if he saw? Bri...magic...it's...illegal...and...I mean..." He wrung his hands behind his head, pacing back and forth along the fence. "Shite, I feel like I need a smoke. I could've gotten us caught or shite or...or...shite!"

"Brent! Relax!" Bria forced him to sit. "We're at a magic circus. I doubt anyone cares you did a bit of magic. That man just hated that we were messing with his dragon is all."

"That man was Mr. Santiago, the ringleader. I saw a glimpse of his story, and he…he's not the kindest, Bri. He…he has…I mean…I saw things that…he runs everything for profit, and it's just…shite." He leaned his head back. "This wasn't supposed to happen. I fucked up a perfectly good evening and—"

"Stop it. You got over this self-deprecating nature. Don't start again." She removed his mask and placed a hand on his cheek. "The evening was wonderful. But I'm tired. It's been a long day. Let's head back to the tavern, okay?"

"You sure?"

"Positive."

"Micca might not be happy if we leave without saying goodbye." Brent glanced back towards the carnival.

"We'll see him tomorrow."

"A'ight, yeah. A'ight." Brent clamored to his feet.

They strolled in silence along the perimeter of the circus, watching as the lights danced in multicolored hues. People laughed with drinks in their hands while performers used their magic to capture the eyes of many. It was quite a sight, really. While the magic flew through Bria's body, sending her head spinning, she also couldn't help but marvel at the talent. She admired the performer's different abilities, the way they could lead a crowd.

It's a different life. I'll never have anything like this.

But at least tonight, she could try to pretend that the world wasn't burning.

At least tonight, she could try to smile.

CHAPTER NINE

QUARANTINED

Morning light flooded the train car through the open doors. Lex blinked a few times, squinting towards the entrance, with Garrett held tight to her chest. She hadn't slept since she saw Toddle, her anger steady and unwavering.

How could he rejoin the Guard after everything? *By Luna and Sol of Yilk, I swear,* she cursed to herself, selecting her deity of the day. If Toddle was standing on the other side of that doorway, she might claw off his face.

Madame Owiti told her anger in this situation was valid but to not completely disregard Toddle. *Life is a rainbow. Sometimes, you fail to select the right color. But if he continues along this path, he may find the right one.*

But how long could she wait for Toddle to find the right color? It'd been ten years; could she wait another ten?

It wasn't Toddle but the captain waiting on the other side of the door. His smirk matched his curly mustache. "Hello, ladies."

No one dared look as the captain strode through the car. Lex held Garrett tighter. Beside her, Madame Owiti kept her arm positioned in a way that meant she held Preston close.

"Listen up, you damn heathens!" the captain shouted as he circled back to the front of the boxcar. "When you get outside, don't you go thinking about escape, y'hear me? We got guards, and they're ready to fire. No special magic or none of that bullshite, y'understand?"

"Yes, sir," Lex said with the others.

One at a time, they all slumped out of the boxcar, heads down, hearts weighed heavy. The line diverged into sets of three, as dictated by the Guard. The protests of the women and shrieks of the children muffled the instructions. What was happening up ahead? Lex reached for Madame Owiti's free hand as they strode, unable to speak, a tension building in her throat.

"It will be alright, my deary dear," Madame Owiti said. "Keep your head tall."

They approached the front of the line, where the captain spewed orders. "Please hand your children over to Elder Un Dine and Elder An Drew. They will make sure all is well while we complete further testing."

Lex clenched Garrett tighter. He squirmed.

"You can't take our kiddies away! They've done nothing wrong!" one mother screamed at the captain. "Please don't do this!"

"And they'll be safe away from you."

"Fuck you!"

The captain unfurled a whip from his side and shot it through the air. The woman let out a scream. Her child wailed as she hit the ground with a thud. A guard dragged her away while the Sister standing beside the captain lifted the disheartened child into a covered truck.

Lex rocked Garrett. *They can't take him away. Where's Toddle? He'll stop this!*

Toddle was nowhere to be seen. The only guards wore sneers and distaste, not a fraction of heart remaining. At least Toddle had a heart, however misguided.

"Garr-bear." Lex brushed back Garrett's dark hair. "Don't be scared, okay? Mama loves you and will always protect you. But...but we might be apart for a bit. Do you understand?"

Garrett blinked at her, wide-eyed, then reached to where Preston most certainly sat in Madame Owiti's arms.

Lex choked down the tears as they marched a few steps forward.

The captain glared as she reached the front. "Children to Elder Un Dine and Elder An Drew, please."

Lex kissed Garrett's brow. Fighting would only make it worse, but everything crumbled around her as she passed her squirming son to the Sister. Perhaps if she were stronger, if she were actually magic, she might have fought for Garrett.

But she couldn't.

It would only risk his life.

Madame Owiti placed Preston on the ground, not that Lex saw him, and ushered him to follow his brother.

It was only after a few steps did Garrett register what was happening.

"Mama!" He reached out as Elder Un Dine started carrying him away.

"Be strong, Garrett. Be good. I'll see you soon."

"Mama!"

Lex's world fractured as she watched the Sister load her son into the truck. She wanted to scream, to beg, to plea, but she knew from her years in the Pit that it would change nothing. Compliance meant giving in without compromising morals. She had to remind herself that this wasn't a choice.

Toddle had a choice.

Dear Luna and Sol, am I being a hypocrite? Lex's eyes welled as she watched Garrett vanish in the truck. *What if I never see him again? Either of them? Should I have fought harder? Am I as bad as the rest?*

Her knees shook. In the end, she knew she had no choice. There was no way to fight.

"Come along, deary dear. Everything will work as fate intended, yes, yes?" Madame Owiti wrapped her arm around Lex's shoulder and began leading her towards the other woman.

"Halt!" The captain stopped Lex from walking away. "Come with me."

Lex's head began spinning. First Toddle, then Garrett, and now Madame Owiti? How much more could she take?

"You damn pig! You've taken everything from her today! Don't take her away from me!" Madame Owiti shouted.

"She goes where she is told!"

"Why is she going with you?!"

"That is none of your business, Madame!"

"I think it is!"

The captain cracked his whip, hitting the old woman across the arm.

"Madame!" Lex reached out as the old woman hit the ground, writhing in pain.

"I am okay, deary dear. Don't worry." She smiled.

"No...please!" She wanted to hit something. After all of this, they were being dragged back into this nightmare! Instead, her knees gave out, and sobs rippled through her body. She cried out for Garrett, cried out for Madame Owiti, and even cried out for Toddle.

The captain didn't care. With little effort, he tugged Lex off the ground and towards a truck on the far side of the train tracks.

Lex was the only one in the truck. She stared out the window in silence, her hands and feet chained together. The captain was kind enough to at least allow her a bit of sunlight.

She would have preferred not seeing anything.

As they rounded the bend from the train tracks, past the dead forest of bone trees and gray leaves, Knoll's Gully dominated the landscape. The city's towers acted as shadow-ridden beacons, circling the downtrodden shacks that bordered the city center, creating a wall just along the outside of the Pit. The tall stone walls and decrepit tenement halls of Knoll's Pit called to her. They haunted her, reminding her of the years she spent wasting away in squalor. Often, Knoll's Pit haunted her memories: guards came to pleasure themselves, vagrants exchanged the darkest substances for coin and food, children slept in the streets with naught a blanket or pillow to be seen. Even though the degradation hid behind a stone wall, nothing could truly hide it.

Knoll was nothing like Mert. While her old home dazzled with color and magic, Knoll itself sank in death and dismay. Every building reeked of dust. No trees flourished. Those who walked along the side of the road never looked up, wearing tattered clothes, holding their satchels close and children closer.

The city didn't improve as they neared the tower in the center of the city. She didn't recognize this tower; she had long grown familiar with the tall stone tower in the distance, the prison tower known as the Aviary, during her first time in Knoll. From her narrow window, she memorized the other towers: the different moving guard towers, Knoll's Temple with its decrepit walls, and the Dispensary Tower, which had often been her home. Sickly, weak, it offered her solace.

But there was no solace in Knoll. Even beneath the gaze of this glorious now tower, guards marched, and workers gathered in chains. Malnourished and pale, they behaved only as ghosts, fading into the dusty landscape.

The captain continued his drive to the windowless Dispensary Tower. It glared like a shadow, with dead ivy wrapped around the stones and a polluted river thrashing waves against the foundation.

"Out," the captain ordered after parking the truck. "Now."

Lex kept her head low as she climbed out of the truck and stumbled over her chains. The captain pulled on them once.

"You're a quiet lassie, aren't you? Prefer them that way. Means fewer problems."

Lex stared at her feet as they approached the tower.

"Good girl. You know your place, don't ya?"

"Yes, sir," Lex whispered.

"Ah! You speak. You ain't as stupid as you let on, yeah?"

"No, sir."

"Good girl." The captain guided Lex into the tower.

Memories inundated her thoughts as she stepped into the dimly hit hallway. Lex closed her eyes tight, but they had already assaulted her with a vengeance. She'd walked this same path years ago as a child, almost too small for her chains. They led her into a dark room, where she waited, yearning for food. She cried for her mother and father until she had no more tears. Darkness was her only friend.

How many lights are in the room? they asked her way back then.

I don't see any lights!

There are three.

No, there aren't!

She never could fight away the darkness. Eventually, she learned it was best to say nothing at all.

This time, the captain didn't lead her into one of the dark rooms, though. They wound up the stairs, past cells of moans and cries, where lights flickered and danced with shadows. The vivid smell of iron pulled at her nostrils.

Where is he taking me? Why am I alone?

He opened a towering metal door and ushered Lex inside, where a single cot sat in an otherwise barren room. On top of it lay a single beige gown.

Lex shivered. The room radiated with a stale but frigid aura.

"Sit down," the captain ordered.

"What are you going to do to me?" Lex squeaked.

"That is for Professor Gratz to decide. Now get changed. She'll be with you shortly." The captain pushed Lex into the room, then shut the door behind him, leaving only one lantern waving back and forth on the ceiling.

Lex changed into the new gown. It hugged her stomach a little too tight, and the material scratched at her already sensitive skin. She was sure her eczema would flare up after all of this, although that was the least of her worries. As she sat on the bed, it creaked, and Lex flinched.

With no windows in the room, Lex watched the shadows flicker on the wall.

As she counted the shadows, her mind wandered. Just a few days ago, she was safe in Mert. The last few months had been quite crazy; between Brent's arrival in her shop, followed by Bria's outburst that resulted in Lex's Phantom Rot, life hadn't been normal. But she was safe then.

Her only solace now came from the lack of magic in Rosada. During the train ride, she felt the nausea of Phantom Rot encase her, the strength of magic pulsing through her fellow travelers. Now, alone with nothing but her thoughts, she could breathe without fear of collapse.

But she would trade all of that to be with her son again. Was he okay? Was he staying strong? Did he even know what was happening? She clutched the edge of the bed, tears welling in her eyes. Why did they take him from her? What had he ever done?

And what about Madame Owiti? Where was she now?

A noise escaped Lex's lips that sounded like a horse, and she broke down into tears. What could she do now? Once again, they left her to rot in a cell.

Stay strong, Garr-bear. I'll find you. She clutched the sheet and returned to watching the shadows.

Lex didn't know how much time passed when the doors finally opened again. A middle-aged woman with wire-rim glasses, auburn hair, and rosy cheeks entered, wheeling a covered cart in behind her.

"Oh fooey," the woman grumbled as the cart got stuck in the doorway. After a few tugs, she freed it and pushed it into the room. With a flustered sigh, she shut the door and turned to Lex. "Ah! Hello! You must be Elexis Dray, yes?"

Lex nodded.

"My name is Professor Etta Gratz. You can call me Etta." She smiled widely. It almost made her look kind.

Lex always believed in the best of people, but she had to keep her skepticism alive with this woman. This woman was not a friend.

"I understand you are probably scared, Elexis. That Captain Carver can be frightening. But I want you to trust me. I am only here to help."

"What do you want to help me with?" Lex glared. "You took me away from my son."

"Oh, that silly captain didn't tell you anything, did he?"

Lex shook her head.

"It's quite simple. Do you know that blood test we did out in Chelidae's Mark?"

Lex glanced at where they had pricked her fingers a few days earlier. "Yes."

"My superior developed that test to identify those with magical inclinations. If your blood turns gold, it means you have magic. If nothing happens, it means you are untainted. But...your blood turned black."

Lex looked at her hands. She didn't dare mention her Phantom Rot to this woman. Not yet.

"The Guard sent a telegraph to me immediately. I am a leading professional in my field, and they thought my expertise would be beneficial."

"Leading professional in what?" Lex asked.

Professor Etta Gratz's smile still did not falter. "I am the leading magepidemiologist at the Academy in the Capitol Rosada. I study magical based diseases such as Shadow Drip, Totemic Blisters, Séance Disorder..." She continued listing off ailments.

But she did not mention Phantom Rot.

"What does that have to do with me?" Lex feigned cluelessness.

"I won't know until we run more blood tests." She giggled. "Truthfully, I'm ecstatic! I haven't seen a magical ailment in practice in over fifteen years! With magic technically eliminated in Rosada, being a magepidemiologist is so *boring*. I considered going to Mert, but my boss said, 'No, Etta! We need you here, Etta!' And I guess that's true."

Etta fumbled with the cart and removed a few syringes. "You could just have a very mild case of Mystic Ache, but we won't know until I run the tests. Although, I think this is something way more intriguing than that. I am sure plenty of people from Mert come over with Mystic Ache, and it goes undetected! Oh, I can't wait to study you!"

Lex looked at her feet. Once again, she was an anomaly. They initially took her away from her parents because of her white hair and paper skin. Back then, they tested her for magic and curses, trying to uncover why she had no color. It became a search for magic, convinced more than anything that she was the product of a demon's revenge.

Now, she was back here again. An experiment.

She dropped her head in shame.

"Hey! Hey now!" Professor Gratz plopped on the bed beside her. "We're going to treat you great! We just want to see what is wrong and cure you...and make sure no one else suffers the same fate. Alrighty?"

"Will I be allowed to see my son?" Lex whispered.

"Once we know you're not contagious. Not that the Guard did a good job at that, cramming you in with all those others. We could have a pandemic on our hands!"

Professor Gratz patted Lex's leg. "But I don't think that is the case. You're the only one to register any sort of reaction from our test. You were on an airship for over a day! No one else showed those signs. I think this is something a bit more genetic. Oh, I hope I don't need to get our geneticist. He's a piece of work if I say so myself. But that's enough about that." Professor Gratz raised a syringe and eyed it. "I need to draw blood now and report back to the captain. We'll bring you food shortly after."

Lex didn't fight as Professor Gratz rolled up her sleeve and stuck the first needle into her vein.

CHAPTER TEN

RECLAIMED

Bria walked with Brent back to the tavern, holding his arm tight, leaving the fear and oddities of the carnival behind them. It was a quiet walk back, whisked away under the stars without a care. A few guards glanced their way, but it was easy enough to play the role of drunken lovers out for a midnight stroll hiding beneath their masks.

Music greeted them upon arriving at the tavern. Brent spun Bria in his arms as they entered, his goofy smile lighting up his face. The music took them away to a moment of paradise, dressed in their carnival masks, laughter mingling with drinks. It looked ridiculous, but she didn't care.

They danced, they drank, and they laughed. It was as if all worries left Bria's body, if only for a minute.

She kept her sobriety, though. After two drinks, she led a drunken Brent upstairs before he launched into a ridiculous mist-laden tale. They didn't need the Guard to discover them because of irresponsibility.

Their rendezvous beneath the covers left Bria's heart pounding for an hour. As Brent sobered, he kissed her softly, telling stories with each kiss and weaving sagas with his fingers.

They fell asleep in each other's arms, breathing with each other sighs of relief.

Yet despite the drinks and romance, Bria did not sleep well. She tossed and turned, pulling the covers off Brent in the process and clutching the blanket tight. Nightmares remained from the Library. Every time she closed her eyes, she heard the earth calling to her.

The fibers of the blanket tickled her skin.

The walls closed in around her.

Everything screamed.

And she woke gasping for air.

Sleep never returned, and at the crack of dawn, she left the bed and snuck down the hall for the lavatory. A few drunkards stood in the hall, their gaze firm on her body. She refused to pay them attention as she entered the lavatory, locking the bolt behind her.

Head high. You can protect yourself. She hugged herself as she stepped into the cold shower.

Each drop of water gave her life. Her heartbeat increased, and her shoulders loosened. Bria traced the drops of water on the concrete wall. Why did it seem like even the walls called to her? The building. Everything.

What was she supposed to do?

I can control this. I controlled it for years. She dressed in one of Brent's shirts and stepped out of the shower, weaving her damp hair into a braid. Water dripped across the floor with humidity thick in the air as she exited the lavatory. It seemed to follow her back through the now empty hallways, louder than the catcalls on the lips of the drunk patrons.

Brent still slept when she returned to the bedroom, his long arm hanging over the bed, brushing the floor. Even in his sleep, his brow furrowed as if he told a story. Yet she wondered how many of his dreams belonged to him. Brent was usually one to talk about his feelings, but he had said little about Nedo's story since he killed the ghost.

Killed? Was that the right word?

Helped? That sounded better.

The bed creaked as Bria sat beside Brent and Nix. The dog placed her head on Bria's lap, her ears back and eyes wide open. If Bria closed her eyes, just for a bit, she could pretend that everything was normal.

A banging from down the hallway broke her reverie.

"Bri...be quiet," Brent grumbled.

"That wasn't me," She whispered.

"Still." Brent rubbed his eyes and glanced at her. "Oh...you're already wet."

"What?"

"You bathed, I mean."

"Oh, yes...I did."

"Couldn't sleep?" He fiddled with a strand of her hair.

Bria frowned. Did he catch a whiff of her story again? She hated how he read her like an open book. As much as he tried to avoid them, she knew his magic always acted, catching stories and telling him tales.

Brent seemed to read her mind here as well. "I don't see your story. You were tossing and turning a lot last night, and it's early. I mean, I figured you couldn't...I mean...I use my brain sometimes."

"It's okay if you see my story," Bria replied as another bang echoed from outside. "It's not like you can control it."

"Yeah, but I want to. I don't want to live life knowing everything about everyone. It's headache-inducing. I have enough in my head as it is."

Bria smiled. "You're a good man, Brenton Harley."

"I try." He leaned in to kiss her.

Bria pushed him away, wrinkling her nose as his breath hit her face. "Ew! Go freshen up!"

"Ah, you love it."

"Go!" She shoved him from the bed.

Brent stumbled to his feet, grinning as he pulled on his clothes and meandered to the door. He opened the door—

Then slammed it in an instant.

If he could turn any whiter, Bria swore he would have just then. His eyes were wide as he mouthed a single word: "Guards."

Bria reacted automatically, grabbing their bag from the floor and tossing it to Brent. As he scrambled to pull on his shoes, Bria found her bowler hat and stuffed her hair inside, then pulled on her bear mask before pushing up the collar of her jacket.

Bang.

The knock sounded off against the neighbor's door. Nix barked from her spot on the bed.

"Shite!" Brent cursed under his breath.

"Do they know we're here?"

"I dunno. They might be doing their usual rounds in slums like this. I didn't catch the story or anything."

Bria glanced towards the window. Snow continued to fall against the windowsill while a gentle breeze rocked the lifeless tree beside the tavern. "They're after me…"

"We don't know—"

"I'm the most wanted person in Rosada! Even if they're not after me, they'll recognize me."

"Yeah, but—"

"But we're better safe than sorry. Just meet me down by the train station. Micca might already be there. We can either leave with him or on a train or something…but we can't stay here. We've already stayed too long."

He followed her gaze to the window, then nodded. "A'ight. Yeah. I understand."

Bria pressed her fingers to her lips and held them out to him. "I'll see you in a minute."

Before Brent replied, Bria forced the window open. She hopped into the embrace of the dead tree, balancing on the branch as she closed the windowsill behind her. Her eyes locked once with Brent.

I'll see him soon. Don't worry. We're going to be okay.

She leapt from the tree, glancing back over her shoulder one last time at the tavern. The tree didn't speak to her as she left. It didn't call to her. And rather than lying dormant, its soul had vanished. Lifeless.

Dead.

Bria snuck through narrow roads, head down, trying her best not to draw attention to herself while avoiding the calls of the trees. The early morning snowfall grazed her skin. All was quiet. If her heart didn't beat like a drum in her ears, she might have thought it beautiful. But she didn't dare take a moment to marvel at the quiet village of Aeterno.

Once she reunited with Brent, she didn't care where they traveled. Knoll. Newbird. Opal. Or out of Rosada entirely. It didn't matter. They could reconvene in a safer location and begin hunting the pools from there.

The narrow road took her on a disorienting path towards the train station. She prayed her detour gave her enough time to escape the Guard and allowed Brent to leave the tavern in peace. No one knew about Brent Harley; he was a tragedy of the Storm of Nightmares, not a villain. She made sure of that as she took his limp body away that night almost a year earlier.

He'd already suffered too much to be treated as a terrorist.

She slowed at the edge of the road. Her stomach churned as the train station came into view.

A tower brooded over the train tracks. Its stone body was reminiscent of a storm cloud, its dark windows like a starless night. It stood with authority and animosity.

Guards marched along the grassy square, dragging individuals towards the mouth of the beast.

Bria's heart broke at the sight.

One guard led a group of children towards the tower. Covered in soot, with charred clothes and empty gazes, the children didn't even seem phased, as though they'd accepted their fate long ago.

And all the prisoners had one thing in common: the black stamp on their wrists.

*They're taking everyone…*Bria leaned against the wall to stay upright. Moss climbed along her arm. Watching the children, she momentarily envisioned a younger Brent Harley, yelled at by the guard for his stamp and eyes. She would watch in horror and do nothing, the obedient daughter of a basket weaver.

Bria would never be that person again.

She continued watching from the shadows as the guards tugged their prisoners towards the tower. Something about the chains struck a chord with Bria, though. From a distance, they looked like normal, metallic chains. But, subtle as ever, sparks bounced, and a hum buzzed from them.

Louder.

And louder.

Buzzing.

Bria clenched her fist. *It can't be.*

As a child stumbled to the ground, the guard turned with fire in their eyes. They wrapped the chain in their hand and slammed it into the child's face. That alone carried a wave of pain with it as the child let out a scream.

When the Guard lifted the chain again, a red burn coated the child's cheek.

Electricity. Bria almost felt it coursing across the green space towards her. Electricity ran through the earth; often, she felt it in the storms and in the rhythm of her own heart. But the only time Bria had connected with it was under Ningursu's guise. She refused to risk the lives of children.

Except their lives were already at risk.

Since the Storm of Nightmares, Bria had heard the Order of the Effluvium's role in the government had grown stronger. All thanks to Elder Don Van—or Senator Cordova, as he went by nowadays. Now, guards filled the streets of what Bria assumed had been a peaceful town.

Well, as peaceful as anywhere in Rosada could ever be.

No, Rosada always held a distaste for the unique. Stories, magic, and oddities had no legal foot to stand.

Her grandmama used to say it was getting better. Bria remembered sitting on her grandmama's lap, listening to stories of years long ago, when guards would round up storytellers on the street just to be executed.

Or worse.

In some ways, at least those horrid pits provided protection, some said. Bria disagreed. She saw the way those people suffered, the way they carried themselves with heads lowered and mouths quivering.

But it didn't matter now; the Guard was taking everyone.

Young. Old.

Everyone.

Why now?

Did it matter?

She knew what had to happen.

I'm sorry, Brent. I hope you forgive me. Bria removed her hat and mask, letting her braid fall against her shoulder as she walked into the plaza. The snow-speckled grass hit the edges of her pants, and with each footstep, flurries bellowed around her. No one noticed her.

You will see me. Bria raised her hands above her head. As she marched, the snow continued to pick up, the grass grew around her feet, and the trees bowed.

I am the Forest Queen.

You will see me.

She stroked the side of a nearby tree. Its dormant heartbeat sped up, and at her touch, the leaves grew.

The roots spread.

And a touch of spring mingled with the winter.

The roots wrapped around the ankles of guards, causing them to fall forward, dropping the chains holding the children in place.

The children didn't move at first, stunned.

No one moved.

No one spoke.

A few more guards fell.

Bria glanced again at the children. She didn't know where they belonged. Did they have a home? Or did they come from the Pit? Surely whatever fate awaited them in the tower was worse.

Brent would know what to do in a heartbeat. He'd see their stories and know where they belong. She glanced over her shoulder. *I hope he's okay.*

She sent another wave of roots after the guard, then shouted over the now bellowing wind towards the children, "Go! Run! Now!"

Her voice broke the paralysis. With chains in tow, the children darted off into the alleyways. The guards screamed as they writhed against the roots.

Bria clenched her fists, ordering the roots to tighten. Around her, the earth reached for her. It wanted more; it yearned for more.

I'm dying, it called.

I don't have enough to give. I'm sorry. Bria bowed her head. She didn't know how much longer the distraction would continue. Soon, something would give.

Soon, the earth might just reclaim her.

CHAPTER ELEVEN

Mist and Masks

B rent double-checked the window was closed after Bria left, trying his best to keep his head together as the guard yelled next door. He rushed to find one of his silver pills and popped it in his mouth as he sat on the bed. *Pretend you're just here mulling about here. No big deal. Just pretend.*

Pah. Good luck. You're a pathetic sap. His Diabolo cackled.

How many times do I have to tell you to be quiet?

It doesn't matter if you act like a twat or not. You still have the face of a vagrant.

Brent touched his cheek. The Diabolo was right. He had silver eyes and a black stamp. The Guard would notice him at once.

It was best for Bria to flee; right now wasn't the time to put up a fight. No one needed to know they had returned to Rosada.

Another bang sounded off down the hall. Nix barked, zooming back and forth across the room. Any moment now, the door would swing open.

He glanced at the llama mask on the floor. The Guard would ask him to remove it if he wore it.

A mask... Brent touched his face again. He'd never considered everything the mist could do for him. Yet, in the short time he spent with the Mist Keepers many months ago, he learned a few things. The mist operated under multiple guises: the mist of the surrounding played into the world, the mist of the mind played into the psyche, and the mist of the soul played into the imagination. His old teacher, Caroline, used the mist to create masks. She hid her true face and disguised herself as others, the ultimate illusion of self.

Isn't it just another story hiding my face? He held out his hand, letting the mist drift over his skin. Like painting a picture, he let the tale of a crooked man who once stayed in the same room take over his body. It hid his stamp, and his reflection in the mirror turned unrecognizable. Only his curls remained on his head, poking out in every direction.

Just as his façade stabilized, the door flew open. A guard walked in, a scowl on his face, nothing remarkable in appearance. Every guard really looked the same in the end. Wide shoulders, a clenched jaw, narrow eyes…They reminded Brent of Christof Carver back home or his deceased friend Cadet Chet Lawry. Sometimes, if Brent focused enough, he heard Cadet Lawry in the Diabolo's voice.

Was that man's demon part of him now?

The guard glowered at Brent. "Up."

Brent rose.

"Name?"

"Um…" Brent searched the room for a story. He found one in the floorboards. "Gull. Joshua Gull."

The Guard wrote the name down in his book. "Thank you, Mr. Gull. We're currently looking for someone spotted yesterday at the circus in town."

"Oh—oh?" Brent stammered.

"You may have seen the posters. There are rumors that one of our most wanted, Briannabella Smidt, from the Newbird Region, is in town. Do you know anything about that?"

"Oh, um, no. I don't know a Briannabella or Smidt or anything."

"Are you sure? Take a gander." The guard handed him a flyer with the blurry photo of Bria.

He stared at it for a moment. To think this flyer might be the only photograph of Bria broke his heart; they never had any photographs taken, always taken aback by the price. Now, a blurry wanted picture marked her face across Rosada.

"No. Ain't seen her." Brent caught the story's accent in his voice. If he stayed too long under this man's guise, he might lose himself.

"A'ight then. Keep a look out then. Have a good stay."

Much to Brent's surprise, the Guard left the room, closing the door behind him.

Brent stared, then turned to the mirror again. The mist dripped away from his face, giving him a chance to be himself.

The guard had never treated him with such courtesy— ever! They'd always looked at him as wrong; his silver eyes, his black stamp, and his stories all marked him. But to be someone else, with a different face, an identity, made him feel...human.

It would be so easy to leave behind his true identity.

But my name is Brent Harley. And I'm not going anywhere.

Life would be easier if you weren't.

But I'm happy to be me.

Brent glanced at Nix, who sat obediently at his side. His pulse hadn't stopped racing since the Guard left.

Once the tavern fell quiet, he left a handful of coins on the nightstand, grabbed his bag, and with Nix at his side, raced out into the village. The guards stood as mere specks in the distance, disinterested in Brent as he hurried down the path towards the train station.

The wind picked up as he walked, snow flurries attacking his face. Nix ran a few paces ahead, stopped, then rejoined him every few paces.

As he neared the plaza, hidden under the shadow of a guard tower, screams caught his attention. Brent bolted into a run, pushing through a few villagers as they walked with their heads low, bags held tight, eyes downcast.

Guards filled the plaza. A snowstorm had localized right in the center of the field beneath the tower. Children fled the scene while villagers gathered and guards shouted.

Brent pushed through the crowd. He already knew what waited for him in the plaza, but his heart dropped all the same at the sight. He should have known she would do this; he would have done the same thing.

There stood Bria, creating a diversion with her magic, giving the prisoners a chance to escape. Children darted away from the guards while a few adult prisoners garnering the black stamp used that moment to escape. Some guards hung from the trees, others fell to the ground, but Bria controlled the whole situation.

It came with a statement:

The Forest Queen had returned to Rosada.

Guards rushed from the tower, pistols loaded, all aimed at Bria. She kept her hands above her head, and as the final child fled, she turned to face them. Everything was silent. Brent swore, not even hearts beat. Everyone waited. What would happen next?

Bria caught Brent's attention with a sad smile. He knew that smile; he read her like a book. *Don't move*, she said. *It won't do us any good if you're in jail too.*

Brent gulped, then nodded once. Her name sank on his lips like a prayer. He would hold it close, his one constant, to ground him.

Around them, the snowstorm slowed, the vines and roots rescinded, and the trees let go of the guards. Bria held her hands higher as she turned to the Guards surrounding her.

Brent read her lips. "Don't take anyone else. I surrender."

It was on her terms; no one else decided for her.

Yet, it didn't stop one guard from shooting in her direction.

The gunshot ripped through the air. Brent threw his hands over his ears.

Bria toppled backwards. Blood pooled from her right arm. Did he scream her name? He wasn't sure. Everything buzzed. His head. The sky.

Bria! No! Bria!

Another guard rushed over, yanking her from the ground by her braid. Her face contorted in pain as he lifted her over his shoulder.

Finally, Brent broke his trance. "Bri!"

He reached the front of the crowd. His eyes stung, snot running down his nose. Nix barked at his side, but the guards didn't care. He was just a face in the crowd, hidden by the mist, a nobody with a black stamp.

"No!" he cried out again, watching as they carried Bria away into the tower. She didn't fight; she just closed her eyes in defeat.

Acceptance.

This was her choice.

But Brent didn't have to like it.

"Shite!" He ran forward.

Only to have a set of arms pull him back.

"Brent! Mate! You gotta calm down! You look like you're having a fit or something!"

Brent spun. Micca stared at him, wide-eyed and paled.

"They got her! They...I mean...they..." Brent stammered.

Micca pressed his hand onto Brent's shoulder. "Yeah. I saw. We all saw. It's gonna be a'ight, a'ight? Just don't draw attention. C'mon. I got an idea."

Brent glanced back over his shoulder at the tower, his hands riddled with sweat. The door to the tower slammed shut.

All was still.

Until a horn blared from the top of the tower.

Bwaaamp.

Bwaaamp.

Brent covered his ears.

"C'mon! We gotta hurry!" Micca grabbed Brent by his arm and tugged him away from the plaza.

Brent had never seen Micca move so fast. He stopped twice to catch his breath, then continued, not bothering to explain to Brent where they were headed or why. Brent didn't care, his own mind racing. Why would Bria turn herself into the Guard?

The children?

*Dammit, Bri. We were doing okay. We were together, and now...*Brent shook his head. He couldn't be mad at her. If he was in her situation, he would do the same exact thing. Children didn't deserve whatever fate the Guard handed them.

And Bria was the Forest Queen, a queen of life and compassion.

She would not turn her back on suffering.

So Brent would not turn his back on her.

Micca led Brent to a wide field on the outskirts of Aeterno Village. Lines of buggies, trucks, and automobiles waited for them, dusted with snow and ice. Micca stalked along them until coming to an unremarkable gray truck with dirt along its wheels. He removed a pin from his long hair and began toying with the lock, sticking his tongue out and chewing on it while he worked.

"You gonna tell me what you're thinking?" Brent panted. His voice sounded shrill and out of practice.

"Obviously, we can follow the tower." Micca pressed the pin deeper into the lock. "Gotcha!"

"Yeah, but stealing a buggy is gonna cause more problems!"

"Since when are you all high and mighty? C'mon. I got Jem to steal an auto with me."

"We don't know where the tower's going, though."

"Where do you think it's going, Brenty-Boy? It's gonna head to Knoll to turn Beebelle over to the Order or some maniacal shite like that. C'mon! Get in!" Micca pulled open the door and shoved Brent inside the vehicle.

He landed face-first in the front seat. Groaning, he sat up, brushing his hair out of his eyes as Nix leapt onto his lap.

Micca climbed into the driver's seat and fidgeted with the ignition. Cursing under his breath, he tore wires out of the compartment. After a few shocks, the car engine burst to life.

"Ha! Still got it!"

"Still got what?" another voice cut into their conversation.

Brent glanced over his shoulder.

In the back seat of the car sat the man in the golden suit from the circus the previous night with a pistol in hand.

"Neither of you better move, or I'll shoot," the man hissed.

"Mr. Santiago!" Micca exclaimed. "I didn't know you were napping in the back!"

"I don't think it's any of your business what I do in my automobile. If I want to take a nap, I'll take a damn nap if I please. You and Timmy were s'posed to file the permit with the captain so we can get a move on. That's it."

The man glowered, aiming the gun straight at Micca.

Brent gulped, clutching the seat cushions, afraid to speak.

"Pray tell, Mr. Fein, what are you doing here with this man? Wait..." The man's eyes narrowed at Brent. "You were in the tent with my Zephyr last night!"

"I...um..."

"What're you playing at, boy? And you—" Mr. Santiago spun back around to Micca. "I never did like you. Just kept you around 'cause you were good with a wrench and Timmy liked you, but now you're trying to steal my car? Pathetic. I should throw you both to the Guard right now."

"Is that what you did with Bria?" Brent snapped, eyeing Mr. Santiago. He tried his best to collect the man's story, but it bounced around the automobile. It told a tale of a petty man counting coin with a smile on his face. He brought girls back in this car with him, his greed knowing no bounds as he paved a path in gold.

With all the harrowing stories in the truck, Brent struggled to delve deeper into Mr. Santiago's story with only a glance.

"Who the fuck is Bria?" Mr. Santiago asked.

"The young woman who was with me last night!"

"Her? Oh, yeah. Pretty thing, isn't she?" Mr. Santiago shrugged. "Don't know anything about that."

"Bullshite!" Micca interjected. "You'd do anything for a quick coin! She had a bounty on her head!"

"If I knew that, trust me, I wouldn't be napping in this old piece of junk." Mr. Santiago leaned forward. "But that leads to my question. What're you doing trying to jump start one of my automobiles, Mr. Fein?"

From what Brent could tell, Mr. Santiago was telling the truth. Stories had a way of revealing lies, hovering on the surface of the skin and dancing with the mist. But in this case, the mist remained calm.

Micca wiggled his way into a lie, though. "I just wanted to show Brenty-Boy here the ropes with automobiles and everything. He's a good old friend of mine!"

"That's not what it looked like," Mr. Santiago snapped.

Micca squirmed. "You're right...you're right. I just..." He sighed dramatically. "I didn't want dear Timmy to find out. Brent and I...we're madly in love."

"Enough with the lies!" Mr. Santiago raised his hand.

Suddenly, Micca's lips fell shut as if sewn together by pieces of thread. Micca yanked at his lips, but they refused to part.

Mr. Santiago turned back to Brent. "You have an honest face. Now tell me, boy. What're you doing in my auto?"

Brent placed a hand on Nix's back, running his fingers through her soft fur. "The Guard took my friend...Bria. The girl we mentioned. She, um...she has magic...like your circus and everything. We were hiding from the guard. Micca found me as she was getting taken, and we were gonna follow the tower, but...now it's gone, so...It doesn't matter. I...I lost her."

Mr. Santiago scoffed. "Ain't my problem, kid. Find yourself another way to Knoll. I got a show to run."

"Yes, I know. I'm sorry," Brent mumbled.

He could take the tunnels, or hop on the back of a caravan, or walk. No matter what, Brent would find a way to Knoll.

"Mmf! Mmf!!" Micca waved his hands above his head.

"What?" Mr. Santiago snapped his fingers.

Micca's mouth flew open. "We can take Brent to Knoll! The circus is heading just south of there to Juno's Den! Can't he stick around? He can help around the train with me and—"

"Why should I even let you back in my circus? You tried to steal from me!"

"Cause I'm Timothée's beau?" Micca smiled. "You wouldn't want to lose your shadow artist, would you?"

Mr. Santiago's nostrils flared. "I don't got room for two lazy bums lying around."

"But Brent can perform!"

"I don't got room for some juggler or shit. I hardly have room for you."

Brent squared his shoulders, finding a chance to speak. "I have magic."

The words surprised him after exiting his mouth. His whole life, magic had been illegal in Rosada. Now he said it to some stranger? Could Mr. Santiago even be trusted?

The confession got Mr. Santiago to pause. He studied Brent again, waving the gun in his face. "What type?"

"Illusions…mirages…I tell stories with them. I can…I can show you. It…it isn't hard. I…" Brent stroked Nix's fur again. "I can perform with it, I mean."

Mr. Santiago said nothing at first, continuing to scan Brent. No matter how hard Brent tried to read the man's story, he couldn't; it bounced between different events, as erratic as a child or a confused animal. Perhaps it was his own exhaustion; every second that passed, his heart grew heavier, his eyelids hung, and his mind ached. He had to find a way to Bria without alerting the Council, or Kek, or anyone. This was their fight now.

"You perform tonight. In the show. Ain't gonna be able to leave with the Tower on the tracks as it is," Mr. Santiago said.

"Tonight?"

"Tonight. If you're lying, you'll at least be amusing to watch."

"Can't I—"

"It's tonight or not at all. It's our last show in Aeterno before we head to Siskin. I don't want you taking up space on my train, eating my food, or any of that bull unless you're worth it. You earn your keep in my circus. Is that understood?"

"Um, yeah…a'ight."

As Brent said the words, his throat tightened with the promise. *Tonight. Or not at all.*

"Very good. And as for you, Mr. Fein." Mr. Santiago turned to Micca. "I think manure duty for the next fortnight is an appropriate punishment, don't you?"

CHAPTER TWELVE

ROSE AND ADA

As soon as Jemma arrived in Knoll, Elder Un Dine assigned her to a small room in the cloister in the Temple of Knoll and put her to work reciting the daily prayer. She didn't see any familiar faces during those first couple of days, keeping to her routine and only stopping her prayer to eat and sleep. At night, she stared at the Tower of Ab Aeterno in the distance, all while listening as the Brothers and Sisters paired up, dissolving into intimacy in the hall and behind closed doors.

At first, their behavior came as a shock to Jemma. When she approached Elder Un Dine on the matter, she said celibacy did not show loyalty to the Effluvium, only the expectation of not bearing children. For children, she decreed, took away their attention; with attention divided, Brothers and Sisters might lose their way, falling victim to the demons hidden in the Effluvium.

"Over the years, many Sisters of the Order avoided romantic inclinations because of the risks. Modern medicine is magnificent, though, if I do say so myself," Elder Un Dine remarked as she walked with Jemma one day. "Love, when acted upon with honesty and safety, helps the Effluvium thrive."

This was never quite something Jemma considered. Brother Roy Al kept his personal life quiet. Perhaps if Jemma had taken a room in the Newbird Cloister, she might have been more aware. Then again, Newbird's Arm had such a small congregation of Brothers and Sisters that perhaps it didn't have the same prevalence.

She had much to learn.

Despite Elder Un Dine's pointed statements, she was a kind woman with dark gray eyes that did not harbor demons and a smile that bore too much lipstick. Lines of age wore down on her face, but she continued to walk with grace as she completed her cleansings and offered food to those who needed.

How could such a kindly woman be one of the leaders in Knoll? Jemma had long heard the rumors of the city: this was a place of horror, where towers watched and vagrants cried, where Guards took women by their waists and sliced open their virginity with a scowl and cackle.

Elder Un Dine represented only kindness and the firm guiding hand of the Order.

High above the temple, in the atrium, elders and captains with far more sinister plans waited. Jemma often saw them come and go during the day, heading to the Tower of Ab Aeterno with their eyes dark and foreboding. They spent their days talking with Senator Cordova and Elder An Drew, making plans that Jemma couldn't even fathom.

After a couple of days, Senator Cordova approached her as she and Elder Un Dine finished offering a prayer of the morning sun to a pair of newlyweds.

"Oh, good day, Senator!" Elder Un Dine lowered her head. "You look as proud as a sunbeam."

Senator Cordova bowed his head. "Thank you, good Sister. You look as shiny as the moon."

Elder Un Dine waved her hand, her already pink powdered cheeks flushing. "You're so kind, Donovan. But an old dame like me doesn't deserve such words."

"Alas," the senator laughed. "I am actually here to talk with young Sister Jey Ma if you can free her from duties."

"Ah, yes, of course."

Jemma bowed to the senator. "I am ready to learn whatever you have to offer."

"Excellent. Please follow me, Sister. We have much to discuss." The senator beckoned Jemma out of the

Temple, away from Ab Aeterno, and down the broken road towards a windowless fixture where Guards marched in unison.

She'd spent her days gazing from the Temple into the city of Knoll's Gully. Over the past few days, she hoped that being away from the senator would help her decide her next course of action. Instead, she spent her days examining her thoughts on magic, storytelling, cleansings, and silver eyes. On one hand, she had seen the lives of vagrants in Opal's Canyon; on the other, she'd seen destruction lay waste to Newbird's Arm. Part of her adored the stories she heard Brent teach, but then the other half feared the magic that, by a rumor, destroyed Aeterno a couple weeks earlier.

If an individual represents hypocrisy, it is me. She wanted change more than anything, but every movement brought her deeper into the Order's fray. Perhaps Senator Cordova would offer her clarity over the next few weeks; perhaps she would finally decide where her heart belonged.

But where to begin her questioning?

Jemma bit her tongue, waiting for the senator to speak.

His words eventually hissed like the wind. "Do you know why we hate magic, Sister Jey Ma?"

"It taints the Effluvium." Jemma recited.

"Yes, but do you understand why it taints it?"

Jemma shook her head. "I only learned as the scripture says."

Senator Cordova eyed the windowless tower. "It started centuries ago with the armies of the Fleeing Princesses, Rose and Ada. Have you heard of them?"

"Our founders, yes? They came to Rosada many years ago and established the Order."

"I knew you paid attention." Senator Cordova smirked, his deep blue eyes twinkling.

"I only ever wanted to understand."

"And now you shall." Senator Cordova paused again, filling the air with a pregnant silence, before continuing, "What do you know about the Fleeing Princesses?"

Fleeing Princesses? Jemma wracked her brain. "I learned that hundreds upon hundreds of years ago, they left their home in Yilk after their father went mad with power—"

"No. With magic. It was not power, I fear. Teachers often beat around that topic when discussing our true history. But indeed, their father, a pernicious man with glaring silver eyes, tainted his kingdom with magic and hatred."

"So they fled?"

"Indeed. The story goes their father wasn't always a bad man, but after their mother passed away in childbirth, he remarried, and his new wife turned him to the demons. It may not be the truth, but it doesn't matter. Their father turned quite wicked and did much damage. Magic poisoned their kingdom and the Effluvium. Even though they did not know of the Effluvium's prowess, the damage remained. We still bear its damage today. Do you remember the Storm of Nightmares in Newbird's Arm?"

"Of course I do."

"While the sorcerer and his wife didn't create the first storm of such terror, history says they are the ones who amplified it. Since then, as you have seen, they have not ceased. Tamed, perhaps, by the slow fall of magic. But as long as magic exists, the storm will return." Senator Cordova gazed towards the sky. A yellow tinge danced on the top of the bare trees. "Rose and Ada, after leaving their father, poked their own eyes out. They believed their equally silver eyes bore the curse of magic. And they'd seen too much; people had fallen apart because of magic. It was a plague across their kingdom. They also pledged to never have children out of fear of spreading their own disease. So, with their eyes gone and their vows made, they left with an army, crossing the sea to what would become Rosada, to find a haven from the plague brought on by magic."

"You mean the Storm of Nightmares?" Jemma asked.

"While that is a far more…clear plague, we believe that magic has tainted humanity, leaving people ill because of its impact."

"What? I've seen nothing like that—"

"The Magii keep it a secret. We believe Magii often kill those who go ill…or they flee. But the Order aims to cleanse it from the world," Senator Cordova said. "Some call it Midnight Lattice, as their veins turned black with dark magic. Others called it Phantom Rot, as it ate away at the insides of others. And a few others call it Enigmatic Cancer because of its puzzling nature. Magepidemiologists have studied it for many years, but the records are old and tattered, so no one knows the true history behind it. But one thing is certain: magic is the culprit."

"And the plague has returned?"

"As with the Yellow Storms of Nightmares." His eyes flickered. "Now, we have evidence, too. Come along."

Senator Cordova led Jemma into the windowless tower. It reminded her of the crevasses below Newbird's Temple, dark with only the lanterns flickering and shadows dancing on the walls. Brothers, Sisters, and Guards hurried about the stairwells, traveling in and out of different rooms. People shouted. Children cried.

This is a prison. Not a Temple.

Jemma glanced at her feet. How many towers throughout Knoll were like this? She'd seen more windowless towers towards the edge of the city, where the Pit walls stood with no pride. Were they just as horrible? Did these people really deserve this treatment?

After hearing a whip snap as she walked past the crevasses, she knew that wasn't the case. This tower was home to not the first three levels of the Cleanse—a fast, a cold bath, and humility—but the two more terror-ridden levels.

Jemma had only witnessed Levels Four and Five back in Newbird's Arm after Brent confessed to causing the destruction in Newbird's Arm. They whipped him, but she saved him before they could pursue Level Five: the Buzzing.

Here, in Knoll, these Levels were more common. Wires buzzed on the walls as she walked by, and people screamed in terror. Were they undergoing the Buzzing right now? Was their whole personality being dragged out of them by electricity?

Jemma followed Senator Cordova up the stairs until they stopped at a door on the third story. He knocked on the door, and not even a second later, it swung open. A stout woman with auburn hair and round glasses greeted them.

"Ah! Senator! Hello!" She bowed, then glanced at Jemma. "Oh! This must be the young sister you told me about! Hello! My name is Professor Etta Gratz, magiepidemiologist."

"Sister Jey Ma." Jemma bowed her head.

"How wonderful!" The professor clapped in giddy excitement.

"Etta, how is our patient doing?" Senator Cordova inquired.

"Ah yes. Ms. Dray…" The professor's face grew solemn. "Come. I'll show you."

She led them out of her small office and up another flight of stairs. She continued to babble to Jemma the entire way.

"Ms. Dray came to us from Mert. When she arrived, her magic test had an odd reaction. Typically, we either get someone who has a magical response to our test or not…but Ms. Dray's test results came back as inconclusive. We ran more tests which confirmed she has some magical ailment. While there are plenty of ailments as simple as the common cold, this one proved more drastic. For the past few days, and with each test, she has gotten much, *much* worse. My team and I aren't sure what to do." The professor removed her glasses and cleaned them. "We are trying our best, though."

"Have you determined if she is contagious?" Senator Cordova asked.

"Not in the traditional sense. It has to do with her exposure to magic, we think. She must have been exposed to it more than any of us here in Rosada—a clear warning about the dangers posed by a society like Mert."

"I shall vocalize that to my contact in Mert, then. It is imperative we stop the practice of magic there at once."

"Until we understand this disease, yes, I agree." The professor removed a key from her belt and unlocked a door.

The room bled with mist. Disoriented, Jemma gripped the wall, waiting for a second for everything to stabilize.

Once it cleared, her vision stabilized, focusing on a woman sitting on a bed in the corner of the room. She was striking, with paper-white skin, snow-white hair, and red eyes. Her veins and arteries pulsed on her skin like shadows.

"Hello, Ms. Dray. I am here to take a few more blood samples if that's okay." Professor Gratz beamed.

"Can I see my son yet?" the woman begged. Her voice sliced through the air like a wire cutting into clay. "It's been almost a week, and I haven't gotten an update. Please, can I see him? Please, in the name of the Saints and Devils?" The woman turned to Jemma as if staring into her soul. "Please?"

"I am sure your son is fine, Ms. Dray." Professor Gratz removed a needle and placed it into the woman's arm.

Ms. Dray didn't even flinch. "I need to see him. My poor Garrett. Please. He's only a toddler. Please let me see him."

"Once we know you cannot infect him, then I'll see what I can do."

"I can't infect him. This is just..." The woman seemed to give up any sense of fight all at once. "I have Phantom Rot. It's a magical degenerative disorder. It's not contagious. Please. You can contact the Mertoni Sanitorium. They have records!" Tears welled in the woman's eyes. "Please! My son...He's all I have. Please. By the grace of the Saints, please."

"Phantom Rot..." Professor Gratz stepped away, clutching the vials of blood to her chest. "Then that is all the more reason for us to be concerned."

"There's a treatment...they gave me a treatment in Mert. Please...please..." The woman got to her knees. "Please."

Professor Gratz turned back to Senator Cordova. "I must conduct more tests."

"Please!" the woman begged again.

"I'm sorry, Ms. Dray. Please stay here. I'll bring you food shortly." Before the woman could reply, Professor Gratz left in a hurry, with her fists clenched at her side.

Senator Cordova followed, but Jemma stared at the woman long and hard for a moment. She held her body as if it would break any second.

"I'm so sorry," Jemma whispered.

"Please…my son…"

"I'll—"

Before Jemma could reply, the senator called, "Sister! Come along! We have much work to do!"

Jemma glanced back at Ms. Dray one last time. "I really am sorry."

Ms. Dray only hung her head in defeat.

CHAPTER THIRTEEN

THE GREEN TENT

Brent loitered in the Green Tent. It sat on the edge of the Big Top, quiet and undisturbed, waiting for the performers to occupy the vanities and chairs. Mr. Santiago told him to take a seat as soon as they arrived, then left, a swagger in his step, while dragging Micca out towards the Husbandry Carts. Nix lay at Brent's feet, waiting for someone—anyone—to come into the tent.

He could easily leave, find passage to Knoll without the help of Mr. Santiago and the circus. But he didn't know where to begin. A train? Perhaps it would get him there, but then what?

What would he do once he arrived? How would he find Bria?

Was she okay?

He let his imagination wander, each terrible thought worse than the one before it; the Diabolo didn't help quell his thoughts, putting in ideas of rape, torture, and murder. *She can take care of herself,* he reminded himself. He trusted Bria gave herself over to the Guard with reason. She calculated every more, every thought; she wasn't erratic.

Brent tried to refocus on the performance approaching. He didn't worry about coming up with a story; he'd done so hundreds of times. But so much rode on this performance! If he failed, would Mr. Santiago turn him into the Guard?

It's a'ight. It's a'ight...I'm a'ight.

He flinched as a few performers waltzed into the tents, decked out in iridescent outfits. The short, strong woman with pink hair led the pack, commanding the room as she walked past him. She didn't even steal a glance in his direction.

A narrow-faced performer sat themselves down on the bench beside Brent and rummaged through the vanity. They didn't acknowledge Brent at first, tugging a large wig out from a chest as well as a gorgeous red dress.

Once they put on their wig cap, they spun around to face Brent. "You must be the new kid, aren't you, hun?"

"Mr. Santiago's testing me out tonight..."

"Yeah, Salazar does that to all the newbies. You'll be fine, you'll be fine. He asked me to make you look stunning, though." They held out their hand. "My name's Horton, but my performance name is Ms. Honey, so call me whatever you like, alright? I'm the one here to kinda get the crowd ready for some entertainment. Tell a few jokes. Show off my skills. But I'm no clown, so don't mess around. You understand?"

Brent took their hand and shook it.

Ms. Honey scowled. "Well, you look like you've been living in squalor, don't you? We don't have time to get you all cleaned, but let's see what I can do."

Brent fidgeted. "I was, um...today's been kind of a mess. I mean—"

"Relax, relax. You'll be fine and dandy soon." Ms. Honey patted his cheek. "Now let's get to work with you, alright? The better you are, the more you'll shine...and then Santiago will be happy. No one wants to be on Mr. Santiago's bad side. "

Before Brent could say anything, Ms. Honey pulled out a pallet of colors and a hairbrush. They powdered Brent's face, hiding his exhausted eyes and pale cheeks, and forced the comb through Brent's mangled curls. After a few minutes of work, Brent couldn't believe he'd been running through the streets of Aeterno hours earlier.

Damn, I need a haircut. Brent tugged on a curl hanging down the side of his face.

As Ms. Honey touched him up, Brent caught whiffs of their story. It was a happy story, one that Brent clung to with every part of his body, filled with a loving family and a child expressing artistry in multiple forms. They supported Ms. Honey. It was the way the world should have behaved.

"Here you go, hun. This should be your size." Ms. Honey removed a purple sequined suit from their wardrobe. "Might show your ankles a bit, but close enough."

Brent dressed, fidgeting with the buttons on his shirt for a good couple minutes before getting the outfit looking right. With the cosmetics hiding his face, his combed-back hair, and the suit, he had to admit he looked like a performer.

I don't even know what they want me to do.

Yeah, you're a worthless twat, if you ask me, his Diabolo whispered.

Go away, Frankie.

Nah. Without your medication, I'm just going to get stronger.

I won't let you.

You can't stop me.

Brent gulped down the anxiety clawing at his throat. Everything rode on this performance; he had to succeed for Bria's sake.

He wiped the sweat from his brow as he glanced around the tent at the different tales. *One story. That's all.*

He finished getting dressed, then returned to Ms. Honey. They looked like a new person, with a large purple wig framing their face and a cinched waist. Brent wouldn't have recognized them if not for their purple polished nails. Timothée stood beside them, arms crossed, his skirt like an incandescent rainbow and mustache perfectly trimmed.

"Micca told me what happened. You doing okay?" Timothée asked as Brent approached.

Brent shrugged.

"That's what I thought. But don't worry, tonight will go fine, okay? Let me give you the rundown since there wasn't a show last night..." Timothée glanced at Ms. Honey, then back at Brent. "A few performers are already out there, getting the audience excited. Then Mr. Santiago's gonna lead a parade around the stage. He put you as the first act, so be ready to put on a show. If you fail...well, he won't be happy. You're what warms up everyone else for the other magic."

"Isn't it risky to put on a show like this?" Brent asked. "With the guard, I mean..."

"Salazar has enough money to keep the guard placated," Ms. Honey said as they painted their lips.

"Exactly," Timothée agreed. "The circus is one of the safest places to have magic in Rosada. Patrons think it's illusions and fantasy. Only we know the truth."

Brent glanced at his trembling fingers. Could he do this?

It's just a story with a big audience. You've done this many times.

"You'll be alright, hun. Just follow orders and do your best." Ms. Honey placed a hand on his shoulder.

"A'ight. Yeah. A'ight," Brent sucked in his lips and exhaled. "I can do this."

Ms. Honey squeezed his shoulder, then strode out of the tent towards the Big Top with poise and grace. Brent caught a glimpse of them waving to a few patrons, cracking a joke, or mingling amongst the other performers. Brent had to admit, with Ms. Honey gone, he felt out of place, like another cog in the machine.

"C'mon, boy. Get behind me in line. We're all gonna march in. Smile and wave, be a performer. A'ight?" Timothée motioned Brent towards where all the other performers gathered. Mr. Santiago stood at the helm, garnished in his signature yellow suit. Timothée positioned Brent a few steps behind Mr. Santiago. All the performers dazzled and glistened with animals and magic on their heels. Timothée wrapped his hands through the air, capturing colors in a state of pure melancholy. The pink-haired strong woman bore two hundred-pound weights over her head as if carrying a twig. Anywhere else, at any other time, Brent might have looked on in awe.

A horn blared.

Mr. Santiago's scowling demeanor transformed, a smile gathering across his lips as he cartwheeled out of the small tent and into the Big Top. The other performers followed, the music jingling about, and the audience roared. Brent squinted as he walked into the tent, ignoring the flickering array of colorful lights. He held up his hand as if to wave, following close behind Timothée and the other performers, wielding magic and prowess. Fire, water, sparklers, and dancing—they entertained with their powers. Brent's mind raced. How could he match this vivid introduction?

His head roared as he continued his loop around the Big Top. Acrobats completed flips in the air, and Ms. Honey entertained the crowds in the stands. The jeering and applause grew louder with each step. And their stories followed. Who was real? Who was a story?

Don't get lost. You can do this. Don't get lost.

Mr. Santiago centered himself in the middle of the ring, then held his finger up to his mouth. The entire tent grew so silent, Brent swore he could hear a pin drop.

Then, Mr. Santiago's voice boomed, "Hello, my pretties! We have a wonderful show for you tonight! A show filled with the new, the old, and everything in between! So, sit down, relax, and let us take away your worries for a while. Tomorrow the sunrise will look brighter with our magic in your heart."

He snapped his fingers, and applause roared.

"So let us begin!" Mr. Santiago held his hand out. Timothée stepped forward, and with a single wave of his arm, the color black filled the room like smoke.

When the color cleared, leaving a pink residue sifting through the air, Brent stood alone amid the Big Top. All eyes stared at him.

Just a story.

The silence dripped around Brent.

A single story.

He stepped forward. His hands grew clammy, his vision entirely encumbered by the surrounding tales.

"Let me tell you a story..." His voice echoed.

And with an open palm, a story climbed into the surrounding air about an airship soaring through the sky.

The applause still echoed in Brent's ears as he waited outside the Big Top, watching the array of acts in the ring. For over a minute, the crowd gave him a standing ovation, demanding an encore. But before he reacted, a wave of blue washed over the tent, and someone ushered Brent outside, where the other performers waited.

Yet, despite the reprieve from his performance, Brent couldn't pull himself away from the spectacle—nor from the stories. Timothée commanded curtains of color between each act, Mr. Santiago's voice boomed, and the performers moved with such fluidness that Brent sometimes didn't know where one act started and the other ended. The pink-haired woman, Lolli, performed feats of strength; acrobats flipped in the air; a woman set herself on fire and harbored not a scratch...and more! Brent couldn't imagine it getting any better.

Until the final performance.

The tent filled with a silver glow, and out of it emerged a beast-like creature. It stomped forward, unfurling its wide wingspan, its nostrils permeating with mist.

"It's the dragon," Brent whispered to himself.

"Now, our star performer!" Mr. Santiago roared. "Zephyr the Dragon!"

The dragon huffed once, then took flight towards the top of the Big Top, stopping before hitting the canvas. A true spectacle. Mr. Santiago's voice raved about the beautiful beast while music played to a gentle hum. Zephyr the Dragon captured the audience with her radiant wings, sailing through the air on the back of misty stories.

Brent refused to turn away. The dragon's stories permeated the air, sad and broken, like a human's story. He saw a creature begging for freedom, longing for home.

Instead, the beast flew and performed as another puppet in Mr. Santiago's game.

As Zephyr descended in her final bow, Timothée sent a rainbow of colors through the circus tent. Brent got caught up in the performers, and in a flurry of excitement, he followed them back into the Big Top.

Mr. Santiago stood in the center of the ring. With the grace and poise of any ringmaster, he motioned to each of the performers. When it was Brent's turn to take a bow, the audience exploded with excitement. Blood rushed to Brent's ears in embarrassment. He did his best to stay focused on the spinning audience. It was a strange feeling; sure, he'd told stories in Newbird's Arm or in the streets of Mert, but here...people wanted more. He put on more than a story.

He put on a show.

The applause continued ringing as he ventured out of the Big Top and back into the Green Tent. A few of the acrobats somersaulted by, congratulating Brent on the stellar performance. Timothée patted Brent on the shoulder, while even the staid pink-haired Lolli tossed him a smile.

"Hun!" Ms. Honey ran over to him. "That was fantastic! I saw Salazar for a second, and he was thrilled. You were fabulous!"

"I just...I told a story." Brent picked at his fingernails.

"C'mon, hun, be happy! I was in the audience collecting tips, and when you were out there, hun, they were throwing coin upon coin in the jar! Salazar is going to be so infatuated with you, he'll be kissing your feet."

I don't know if that's good or bad.

Brent forced a pained smile at Ms. Honey. More of the performers came by to congratulate him once Ms. Honey walked away, welcoming him into the family. For a moment, Brent almost felt like he belonged. But when his thoughts traveled to Bria, he knew that as much as the audience's applause excited him, this could never be his home.

"Ah! There you are!" Mr. Santiago pushed through the performers and smacked Brent on the back. "Amazing! Absolutely amazing! You've earned yourself a place with us! But here, have a bit of the goods. You earned it." He removed coins from his pocket and placed them in Brent's hand. "We'll discuss the terms of your contract tomorrow, kid. Absolutely brilliant!"

Brent rolled the coins over in his hand, watching the coins glisten. "My...contract?"

Mr. Santiago's eyes narrowed. "This ain't no free ride, kid. But don't worry about that tonight! Go! Celebrate! The crew always gets together for some drinks and songs under the moon. They're gonna wanna meet you! Already no one can stop talking about you! What you've got is something quite special. You're going to be my new star!"

Before Brent could protest, Mr. Santiago spun out of the tent, his laughter booming like thunder.

FALLEN QUEEN

Bria fought back the urge to scream as they chained her against the wall like a rag doll. Her arm pulsed as the bullet wound in her forearm gushed with blood. Only when she saw spots and when her skin went pale did they wind a dirty rag around it to prevent blood loss. Then they left her to wither against a cold wall, arms chained above her head, a gag over her mouth.

She drifted in and out of consciousness, unable to focus on the world outside the tower wall. The building rocked back and forth, marching across the landscape, breathing of stone and metal. A slight twinge of electricity buzzed through the air, but after the chaos in the plaza, Bria didn't fixate on it.

Irrationality took advantage of her when she saw the children. She couldn't let it continue. It started in Newbird's Arm after the monster, after they blamed her for the destruction...but now, it was across Rosada. Children taken into towers; the Order dictating the land. The only thing Bria could do was stop it.

But that wasn't all. When she saw Brent standing in the crowd, watching the Guard beat her down, she realized the other reason she gave up her freedom. This was how she would get to Knoll and find the Order's pools.

She just wished she'd told Brent her plan.

Bria trusted Brent already knew; even without his magic, he had decent intuition.

Sometimes.

Usually.

Not always.

But he'd gotten better. And when she met his gaze, she felt like he at least somewhat understood her plight.

I'm sorry, Brent. Stay safe.

Her exhaustion settled, and she hung her head, only to be woken by the door opening.

"Wake up!" a voice commanded.

Bria lifted her head. Two gas lamps lit the room, creating a fiery glow around a tall woman with pale skin, slick black hair, and steel eyes in a captain's uniform. On her chest, she bore the insignia of the Black Stamp with the last name "Palmer" inscribed above it.

Two other young guards stood behind her like shadows beneath the lanterns.

Captain Palmer spoke with dignity equal to her appearance, "Well, well. When I heard the elusive Briannabella Smidt appeared in Aeterno, I thought it was a joke! You've stayed hidden for quite a long time, haven't you, girl?"

Bria pulled against the chains. Her wounded arm screamed, and as much as she tried to summon her magic, the pain prevented her from acting. Even the bits of magic she managed to muster fizzled out, resulting in a dull shock from the restraints on her wrists and hands.

She flinched.

"Don't try using your magic. It's not gonna work, a'ight?" Captain Palmer leaned forward.

Bria glared.

"You're a lame looking one, aren't you? Glenndal told me all about you—stubborn as a mule, more whorish than a rabbit. Didn't think you'd be so tiny, though. His son described you like you were some sort of terrifying goddess or something." Captain Palmer patted Bria's cheek. "Ah, well. You're mine now."

Bria tried to shake off the gag, but it remained tight over her lips.

"Aw, you want to speak? Very well..." Captain Palmer ripped the gag from Bria's mouth. "It's not like you'll have a tongue much longer."

Bria flared her nostrils.

"Go on...speak!"

Bria forced out her question. "How did you know I was here?"

"Who says I knew? You revealed yourself, remember?"

"Because you were searching for me."

Captain Palmer glanced at her two guards, then back at Bria. "Let's just say some people don't know how to stay quiet. Choose your friends better next time, dear."

Her stomach dropped. The only two people who knew she was in Aeterno were Micca and Timothée. They didn't tell anyone...right?

She didn't have time to ponder it.

Bria shook her head. "I only wanted to protect the people I care about. I'm not a terrorist. I'm not trying to cause an uprising."

"We have all seen what you did in Newbird's Arm. The vagrant population chants for you, their Forest Queen. Magic is reemerging. There are rumors you even murdered a fine young man. Well, no more. Their victor will fall."

Some of that was true. But Bria had to keep her head high. That was what her grandmama told her. "What are you going to do to me?"

"Oh, that would spoil the surprise. Besides, I think you've had enough answers for today." Captain Palmer raised the gag back to Bria's lips, patted her cheek again, then turned to her two guards. "Dumont. Pollard. Take her to the boiler level."

"Yes, ma'am," the two guards said in unison.

Captain Palmer strode out of the room.

Bria didn't fight as the two cadets unshackled her from the wall. The chains continued to pulse with electricity as they led her from the small room and into the belly of the tower, where heat and steam dominated the air.

Cells lined the walls deep in the tower, lights flickering, while the engine hummed above her. Bria squinted in the darkness, counting each light as she walked. *One…two…three…four…five… Five in the hallway.*

Flickering.

Not four.

Not seven.

Five.

A guard opened a cell that wreaked of human excrement. Three other individuals occupied the same cell, each chained to the wall, their heads bowed in shame.

The guards wasted no time. They chained Bria to the wall, casing her hands in steel. Electricity pulsed from every piece of metal, each buzz equal to Bria's own heartbeat, each shock equal to her fear. While Bria felt the way the electricity moved, she didn't have the energy to enhance it. At least, not like she did back in the Library. Even if she tried, she had no clue how to control electricity. It was by pure chance, pure rage, nothing more.

Instead, her arm continued to wither, begging for some form of relief.

It took all her willpower to not start crying.

"Y'know, if Captain Palmer wasn't in charge, I'd fuck you and beat you for dead," the guard grunted as he finished chaining her up, pressing his hand to her thigh. "Shame you're a fucking demon. You ain't half bad looking."

Bria glowered.

"Aw, what? Can't speak?" The guard ripped the fabric from her mouth. "We could probably make you scream."

"You don't know what I can do," Bria hissed.

"We'll have to see about that later." He leaned forward, mere inches from her face.

Bria spat at him.

"You fucking bitch!" The guard slammed a fist into Bria's face. Spots filled her vision, and blood seeped into her mouth. She squirmed as the guard pressed his hand against her throat.

"Cadet Dumont! Enough!" the other guard shouted. "Captain Palmer wants her alive."

"Doesn't mean I can't fuck her up a little," Cadet Dumont growled.

"You think Captain Palmer will like that?"

Cadet Dumont dropped his hand, backing away from Bria. "Very well. But if she gets on my wrong nerve again, I'm gonna beat her to a bloody pulp."

The two guards left the cell, locking the door behind them. Bria watched them, struggling against her restraints.

With the door shut, only one lantern lit the room, but it was enough to illuminate Bria's fellow prisoners on the wall.

She blinked a few times, taking stock of them. Three others hung from similar restraints: an old man with glassy silver eyes, a young woman with long black hair, and an adolescent boy with club feet.

Bria didn't expect anyone to speak.

But the young woman broke the silence with a high-pitched nervous laugh. "Wowee! I haven't seen Cadet Dumont so angry since Mr. Gorge bit him! He really doesn't like you!"

Bria stared at the young woman. "What?"

"Cadet Dumont! He never chains someone up like they chained you! Not since Mr. Gorge here! Right, mister?" The young woman turned her head to the blind old man. "I don't got my arms strung up like that, but Mr. Gorge here does! He bit Cadet Dumont, and they was so angry."

"It's all because Cadet Dumont thinks I'm a vampire. Decided to give him a run for his money," Mr. Gorge chuckled.

"Are you a vampire? You've never told me!"

"No. That's just a story, Marisol." Mr. Gorge sighed. "A story lost long ago."

"You're a storyteller?" Bria asked.

"Ay. Didn't want a stop. Used to go to those storytelling taverns, but when you get old and blind like me, it doesn't happen as much."

Her thoughts traveled back to Brent, and she stifled back the knot in her throat. Was he safe? Or did the Guard find him too? Was he already searching for her story in the landscape?

"So what're you in for?" the woman, Marisol, continued blathering.

"Now, Marisol, let the girl breathe for a moment or so. She only just joined our little family," Mr. Gorge chided.

"I'm trying to get to know her!"

Bria looked away, focusing her attention on the boy with club feet. He didn't speak, didn't look up at her; all the childhood in his gaze had vanished.

Marisol continued talking. "Well, if you won't tell me, I'll tell you! I got no shame about it, and I would rather people hear the truth. That way, people can talk about me. See, I'm here 'cause I got magic." The girl leaned forward as much as her chains allowed. "I can make anyone tell the truth with a single touch. It's not very helpful in here; I can't touch any of you. But out there? On the streets? I angered a bunch of people!"

"Oh, that's…interesting," Bria murmured.

"Interesting? It's awesome!"

"How'd they figure it out, though?"

"They started doing tests in all the different major cities. Blood tests or something. I was already on their radar, though, 'cause I could get so many truths out. Became a little obvious. I wasn't the smartest with my magic. Not like Chander over here," Marisol nodded towards the little boy. "He's able to see through the eyes of the last person he touched. Isn't that cool? It's why he doesn't say much. I think it's hard for him to focus on where he is right now when he's seeing double."

See through their eyes… Bria stared at Chander. His distant expression reminded her so much of Brent.

"So? What about you? C'mon! You gotta have something cool if they threw you in our little cell!" It was hard to ignore Marisol, with her grin so wide, her eyes pleading.

The truth pulled at Bria's heart. Bria sensed the way Marisol's magic knit through the air. Although it surely was stronger with a touch, the sensation remained.

Bria tugged on the chains again, her right arm roaring in defiance. What did she have to lose? She was already in jail.

Perhaps her story could spark something greater.

After taking a deep breath, Bria raised her gaze to meet her fellow prisoners. "My name is Briannabella Smidt. And I'm Rhodana, the Forest Queen."

CHAPTER FIFTEEN

THE TALKING SKULL

Yaz refused to leave her room for two days, hiding beneath her covers and playing with her dollies and skulls. Sir Jama sat on her end table, except whenever Mr. Nasr or Ms. Kai came to visit. Whenever they opened the door, the skull vanished from its spot, leaving Yaz flustered. Surely, Mr. Nasr and Ms. Kai thought she was going mad!

On the morning of the third day of her self-isolation, Yaz woke to the tower skidding to a halt. From her small lookout window, she watched as a steam-riddled town came into view. Factories dotted the skyline. Yaz gripped her windowsill as she stared out at the sight.

It reminded her of the nightmares, where ghosts riddled her memories and chilled her core. In those dreams, she walked for hours and days, calling out names. No one ever responded.

Yet Ms. Kai still called for her now. "Yasmin? Do you want something to eat?"

"No!" Yaz snapped.

"Yasmin...you can't hide in there forever."

"If I come out, I'm not allowed to have any fun! Leave me alone!"

Ms. Kai sighed, then walked away, her footsteps echoing down the hall.

Yaz collapsed back on her bed and glanced at Sir Jama. "Ms. Kai isn't my mommy, Sir Jama. Nor is Mr. Nasr my daddy. They took me from a home when I was a baby and said they were gonna show me the world and protect me and have fun. But they make me work in their shop all day. Sometimes, I dream about my mommy. She gave me this." Yaz rummaged in her drawers and pulled out a simple cloth doll with a scarf wrapped around its head. "Back in Jrin Ayl, they made these dollies. My mommy made me one before she gave me up and told Ms. Kai that it was my devoted protector."

Yaz stared at her dolly. She never kept her dolly's name consistent. For a long time, she called it Gisela—Ms. Kai's first name. Part of her believed that Mr. Nasr and Ms. Kai were her devoted protectors. But in the last year, they'd become more like her bosses. There was no fun.

Only chores.

Only work.

They never let her explore.

"I don't know her name…" Yaz stroked back the doll's hair. "But maybe she isn't my protector. Maybe you are, Sir Jama! I found you all on my own! You hid from Ms. Kai and Mr. Nasr! You're probably my protector."

The skull didn't move.

"I know, I know, it's silly." She put her doll back in the drawer. "I stopped believing in that when I was seven. I'm almost nine now! Gotta grow up, right?"

Yaz placed her hand over the doll, then glanced back over at her skulls and stones. She might have moved on from her dolly, but she still adored games and stories. Even though Ms. Kai told her Rosada prohibited story-telling, Yaz couldn't help but make up tales with these toys.

She still had a few years before she had to move on from her silly toys.

Yaz's stomach growled. After two days of eating only the snacks she hid in her drawers, her hunger had caught up with her.

A low voice interrupted her thoughts. "I don't think you need a devoted protector, Yasmin. You are quite good at protecting yourself."

Yaz jumped, glancing around the room. *Ghosts?*

"Do not fret, Yasmin. You are safe."

Yaz followed the voice. *Sir Jama?*

She lifted the skull in her hands. Sir Jama's eyelid twitched.

"Sir Jama? Are you listening to me?"

A smile worked its way over his half-lipped mouth.

"SIR JAMA?"

The skull shifted, blinking one last time, then opened its eye. It had no iris, completely white like its skin.

"You're alive!" Yaz gasped.

"Hello, Yasmin of Jrin Ayl, daughter of Suri and Omar Issa. It is nice to speak with you," his deep voice cooed.

"You speak! Do all skulls speak? Are you a magic skull?" Yaz hopped between her knees in excitement. She could hardly contain herself.

"I had to let the water from the lake you found me in exit my cavity before I could speak to you. You are a curious young woman, aren't you?"

Yaz giggled. No one had ever called her a young woman! "Most skulls don't talk, though."

"Ah, well, I am honored to be the first talking skull to grace your presence." His odd white eye dazzled like a pearl as he spoke.

"This is so special! I gotta show you to Ms. Kai and Mr. Nasr!"

"Now, now, Yasmin, do not act in haste. Not everyone can see me like you. Besides, even if they could, they might take me away and sell me. Then you'll lose me. That's why I hid."

"But how did you know they might take you away from me?"

"Well, I have been watching you for a long while."

"You've been watching me? Like a devoted protector?"

"I told you, you don't need a protector. Think of me more as...a guardian."

"A guardian? Is that why you know my name? And my parents? I don't even remember my parents..." Yaz frowned. "Suri and Omar?"

"They would be proud of you." Sir Jama tilted his chin as if he were leaning forward. "You're a very special young woman. After all, you are one of the very few people who can see me. Your powers would amaze them."

"But if no one else can see you...does that mean you are imaginary?" Yaz picked at a loose thread on her shirt. The last thing she needed was another ghost haunting her. Already Ms. Kai claimed they were only voices in her head.

"I am not imaginary, Yasmin. Trust me." There was that glimmer in his eye again.

"Then what are you?" Yaz pressed.

"I am a Mist Keeper."

"A what?"

"A Mist Keeper. What if I told you, Yasmin dear, that there is a group of special people who collect the souls of the living after death?"

"You mean like the Final Protector?" Yaz recalled a story about a protector who would come to pick the souls of the dead and carry them away to paradise. Did her mother tell her that story? It was such a distant memory, sometimes Yaz wondered if she dreamt it.

Sir Jama reaffirmed her belief, though. "Yes, like the Final Protector."

"But the stories say that the Final Protector is a woman." Yaz crossed her arms.

Sir Jama grinned. "Some are. I've trained many. I'm their leader, after all."

"That means you're the Ultimate Final Protector!" Yaz scooted back slightly. "Does that mean I'm dead?!"

"No, Yasmin, no. Not yet."

"But why can I see you?"

"Because I wanted you to meet me. You would make a wonderful Mist Keeper. After all, you saved me from drowning," Sir Jama said.

"I saved you? But death can't die!"

"Everything ends."

"So you drowned?" Yaz scowled. "But why were you drowning? You're the Ultimate Protector!"

"Oh, Yasmin, that is a long story. Let's just say that bad people tried to hurt me."

"Is that how you lost your head?"

"In a way."

"Can you tell me what happened?"

"Hm. How about a trade? A game, if you will. You like games, right, Yasmin?"

"Sometimes..." Yaz pulled at her fingernails. "I don't get to play much anymore."

"Well, now you get to play with me. You tell me a secret, and I'll tell you one of mine. Is that a fair game?"

Yaz glanced at Sir Jama, then back at her other skulls and toys. She leaned forward on her hands and knees, her attention solely on the skull. "A'ight. You go first!"

"Yes, where to begin...ah, yes. This is a good place to start." Sir Jama closed his eyes. "My name is Ningursu, the Head of the Council of Mist Keepers, God of Death."

MARKED BY THE SUNRISE

Brent woke in a pile of straw, his head pounding, while Nix snored against his leg. The night came back to him like a subtle dream: the performers danced, drank, and sang together, exchanging vials of liquid they injected into their arms. Brent watched from the sidelines until Micca pulled him over with a drink and a crazed dance. Stories flew from his fingers, and his laughter mixed with tears until he finally collapsed in the straw.

I shouldn't have been partying like this. Bria's in trouble, and I was getting drunk. He held his head and groaned.

I'm rubbing off on you, his Diabolo cawed.

"I told you to shut up!" Brent said aloud.

"Hmph. I see how it is," a high-pitched voice replied.

Brent sat up and glanced around the area.

The small, strong woman with pink hair stood behind him, arms crossed, eyes narrow.

"Sorry," Brent mumbled. "I was…I mean, the…I woke up from a bad dream is all."

She rolled her eyes. "Whatever. Salazar wants to see you."

"Oh, a'ight. Thanks."

The woman led Brent through the groggy workers cleaning the carnival. Everything moved like a well-oiled machine. Micca shoveled away at the piles of manure near the petting zoo, scowling to himself, while Timothée helped load a few of the tents onto the train. Brent waved at them before following the woman into one of the train cars.

As they entered, Brent caught quick glimpses of the carnival's story; a fire breather accidentally setting his room ablaze, affairs ignited in the hallways, and…a sister of the Order with her red hair bowed low.

Jemma? He blinked, swearing he saw his old betrothed's story. Then he remembered. *Right. Micca said she was here.*

Before he absorbed the story, the woman led him into another train car.

Mr. Santiago's suite sat in the center of the winding train. If Brent didn't know any better, he would have thought he'd entered a house. Artifacts, coupled with dim lighting, a satin rug, and scattered mahogany furniture pushed forward a sense of regality Brent had only witnessed in the Library of the Council. A carved desk sat in the far corner, with curtains hanging over the doorways of the bedroom. Dim morning light trickled in through the sprawling windows.

"Sit. Salazar will be out soon." The woman motioned to the bench, then took a stance on the far wall like a loyal soldier.

Brent thanked her and took a seat, futzing with his tight, sparkly pants. He hadn't changed out of his attire from the night before, and now he regretted it. Sweat dampened his skin, and even the brisk late winter air did little to cool him.

It didn't take long for Mr. Santiago to waltz into the room towards his desk, humming to himself. Upon seeing Brent, his eyes glimmered. "Ah! Good! Thank you for bringing him in, Lolli."

Lolli bowed her head and left the room without another word.

"Don't mind her," Mr. Santiago said. "She's the quiet type. Hates newcomers. Don't trust them. But who would? So many fucking vags and criminals here…and magic. You know?"

"Yeah. Guess so. But…how do you get away with it in Rosada? Surely the Order notices you…or something…" Brent fidgeted.

"Money." Mr. Santiago winked. With the wink, Brent saw the man's story. A young fellow leaving Perennes with only a subtle bit of magic. He wooed patrons across the continent, acquired a small fortune, and used the same talent to make sure the guard looked away from his misdeeds. He bathed in gold and mounted silver on his walls.

One goal highlighted his endeavors: wealth.

"I understand," Brent mumbled.

"Of course you do! Because now you've got yourself a job, my boy! I've got you booked for ten shows." Mr. Santiago leaned across his desk and patted Brent's cheeks. "We've got to get ya all together now, don't we? We need to give ya a show name and get ya branded and a cabin, but oh yes, indeed, you will be a fine addition! I'll have Timothée get you over to Hortense and Horton to get you branded—"

Brent interjected, "I'm sorry…branded?"

"Your contract, of course! All of my performers get it branded on their skin."

"Sir, sorry, but isn't this…this is a temporary arrangement, right? I'm not…this isn't…I can't…"

"You already agreed, kid. Any agreement you made with me is binding." Mr. Santiago tapped Brent's lips. His magic spread over Brent's lips, and they pulled back into a fake smile.

Brent forced it back into a frown.

Mr. Santiago chuckled. "As I said, you get ten shows for two weeks. More if you like after that. The brand guarantees you don't run off with some showgirl or boy or anything."

"But I…I didn't want *this*. I need to get to Bria as soon as possible. Two weeks is…it's too long, and—"

Mr. Santiago gripped Brent's cheeks and squeezed his face. "Listen up, kid. This is our little arrangement. You've got talent, you've got skill, and you'll make this show proud. But if you're gonna be a twat about it and try to get out, listen to this. You were messing with my Zephyr, you were colluding with the so-called Forest Queen terrorist girl, you were trying to steal my car, and you got a black stamp. I've seen it on your wrist there. There is no reason for me to not turn you into the Guard. So the way I see it…this is your only chance to save your girl. Got it?"

Brent shrunk in on himself.

"Ten shows. That's it. I say that's a fair arrangement."

"Is it really ten shows, though?" Brent asked.

"As long as you behave yourself."

"...a'ight."

"Good kid." Mr. Santiago placed a hand on Brent's shoulder. His stories caused Brent to flinch. "You're gonna fit in just fine here. We'll get you a nice, comfy room and come up with your next show. But first, Timothée will take you to see Hortense and Horton. Then you can get to work cleaning up the site with the others. Ya won't get paid if ya just sit around, understood? Fifty percent of all performance tips go to the circus; thirty percent covers your lodging. If ya want that last twenty to line your pockets, be on your best behavior. Understood?"

"I get paid?" Brent recalled the few coins now lining his pockets.

"This isn't a slave trade, boy." Mr. Santiago walked over to his desk. "I'd hate to have unhappy performers on my hands."

Paid. Brent only ever had one paid job. For just a few weeks, he served as Madame Gonzo's apprentice in the market square back home. After vendors began to leave, Brent backed out. His black stamp and silver eyes left too much of a negative reputation on the old woman's empire. He couldn't be responsible for her failing.

Brent picked at the brand on his wrist. He had no better options.

"Got it."

"Good. I'll go get Timothée. You're part of our little Cirque Sunrise family now."

Brent fidgeted as he followed Timothée out of Mr. Santiago's car and towards the front of the train. His mind wavered with possibilities. Two weeks! Would Bria even still be in Knoll in two weeks? He trusted she could protect herself. She calculated every action, but he couldn't be certain.

He needed to get to her. If she destroyed the Pool, she might be weak. If the Guard tortured her, she might be suffering. And if she used too much of her magic, she might wither. But if he ran, how far could he get before the Guard caught him?

Santiago's Cirque Sunrise provided the best opportunity.

Yet, as Brent followed Timothée, he couldn't help but notice how the performers, including Timothée, operated like tin soldiers. They followed each of Mr. Santiago's orders without question as if controlled by an invisible hand.

Like the way Ningursu has control over the Council, Brent realized. Governed by fear, governed by control...Mr. Santiago reigned.

Timothée guided Brent through the sleeping cabins to a curtained room dotted with beadwork. "Hortense is right through here. She'll get you all marked up and everything, then you'll be one of us."

"Marked…" Brent's fingers went to the black stamp on his wrist.

"Yeah, sorry kid," Timothée said as he opened the door to the next train cabin. "Hortense and Horton—err, you know 'em as Ms. Honey—live in here."

"Oh, um, thanks."

Timothée smiled, curling his mustache around his finger, before taking his leave.

Brent ducked into the cabin, nearly hitting his head on the molding.

Ms. Honey greeted Brent with exuberance. "Darling! I'm so glad you are staying!"

Brent forced an uncomfortable smile back at Ms. Honey.

Outside of their theatrical costume, Ms. Honey was almost unrecognizable. They bore mousy brown hair with a face that easily blended into the stories in the small cabin. Their sister was nearly identical to them, with longer brown hair and a round face that made her look small. She sat upright in a wheelchair, dabbling with a rusted tattoo gun on the table.

Ms. Honey took no time in throwing together a wardrobe for Brent while babbling on about the different shades of purple that complemented Brent's skin. They even found a pair of casual trousers, suspenders, and a lilac tunic. Brent gathered all the clothes in his arm, but as he was turning to leave, Hortense grabbed Brent's wrist.

"Sorry, love." Hortense kept her voice low. "I gotta do this too."

Brent's stomach flipped. "Right..."

"Salazar brands all his employees. Keeps you in line. Sorry."

Employee. Yeah. Okay. He rolled up his sleeve, stopping just before the Reaper scar was visible. "Just add it to the collection."

He turned away as Hortense grazed his skin with the needle, humming to herself as if painting a picture. Brent remembered seeing the stories of the shopkeeper Todd in Mert tattooing people. He couldn't help wondering what had become of that city. Yet the thoughts of Mert caused the Reaper scar on his arm to ache with yellow-tinted memories.

He tried not to think about his time with Edith. She tortured him, hate and bloodlust in her gaze. With her mangy hair brushing his face, she carved away at his skin, treating him lower than a vagrant.

Brent tossed the memory away and glanced at the tattoo on his forearm. A simple etching in the shape of a sun branded his skin. Hortense pressed a cloth down on the tender area and waved her hand over the skin. Sparks of magic caught the edge of the tattoo, then settled.

"There. Done." Hortense frowned. "I do apologize."

"What'd you do?"

"Barred you to the carnival."

"I'm...a prisoner?"

"You are bound to your contract."

Brent poked at the sun-shaped tattoo. "Is there any way to escape?"

"Hm?"

"Santiago. Will I ever be allowed to leave?"

"Once the contract is over. Yours is only ten performances. Behave, and it'll be over soon. I know you want to leave." Hortense turned Brent's hand over once. "Your partner is waiting, I'm sure."

"Huh?"

"The betrothal brand." Hortense traced the triangle on the back of Brent's hand. "It was poorly done. I can fix it up if you want."

Brent traced the stenciled triangle. "Oh, uh...no. It's a'ight. This one...it's not a real one. I mean...the person I was betrothed to…we called it off. My real partner…she and I…we don't have them. We're just…we're together. That's all."

Hortense shrugged. "Doesn't matter to me. If you want to update it, though, you know where to find me."

"Oh, um, thank you. I'll let you know."

"Yeah, that's what they all say."

Before Brent responded, Hortense rolled herself into the other room.

"Hortense!" Ms. Honey called after their sister. "Ugh. She always gets like this after branding someone. Just…bitter."

"Then why does she do it?"

"She doesn't have a choice in the matter. Father branded her with Santiago's insignia years ago, and if she fails…she pays the price."

"Your father was part of the circus?"

"My father and mother. Mother taught me to sew, and Father taught Hortense to tattoo with her magic. Such is life." Ms. Honey walked over to the window and tugged at the blinds. Their story floated in the air for a moment, and Brent followed along as they told their tale. "We've always known this life. It's hard to change. *I* could leave, but I love my sister too dearly. We're best friends. So, I stay and provide hospitality to ones like you."

"I…appreciate it. Thank you."

"Of course. If you need anything, don't hesitate to ask."

"Yeah, a'ight. Thanks."

Ms. Honey patted Brent's shoulder. "I'll get your quarters assembled. You best be going and help clean up the circus. Otherwise, Lolli will have a fit. She hates when people dilly dally."

Brent thanked Ms. Honey again and ducked out of the train car and into the sunlight. He blinked a few times, holding his newly branded arm up to his face. The performers and laborers all worked together in rhythm, disassembling the circus and loading it onto the train. They were completely unphased by Brent's arrival.

"Brenty-Boy!" Micca waved from on top of the boxes. Nix sat beside him, watching as Micca wound up a couple tin toys. The toys walked a few paces forward before teetering on their side.

Brent joined his friend. He wrinkled his nose as a horrid smell bounced off Micca's body.

"Oi! You wouldn't smell all that wonderful if you were picking up manure all night like me."

"Yeah, still. Um...sorry about that," Brent breathed out through his mouth. "You shouldn't have gotten into trouble for me. I could have figured out a way to find Bria on my own."

"You were a fucking mess. Knowing you, you woulda ended up doing something dumb. Like trying to swim there or something. Really, it ain't no problem. Santiago always finds a reason to put me on manure duty. Hasn't liked me since we met."

"Wasn't that only a week ago?"

"Something like that. I leave an impression."

"Yeah, but you have protection, don't you? Timothée, I mean."

"Yeah, but not many people like me, Brenty-Boy. I'm a bit of a twat. Besides, Tim's not too happy with me at the moment. Wouldn't talk to me last night." Micca shrugged. "Ah well, he'll get over it. He's just in a mood or something. Probably cause I pissed off Santiago."

"Sorry," Brent mumbled.

"All good. We'll be in Knoll soon, and you can go fulfill that hero complex of yours."

"Yeah, as long as I stay on Santiago's good side, I guess. I'm part of this mess for now, though," Brent lifted his sleeve, revealing the new brand above his black stamp.

"Shite! Santiago gave that to you?" Micca poked Brent's skin. "Shite, sorry man. I didn't know."

"It's fine. I mean, just gotta behave, right? Santiago said if I behave, it'll just be ten performances."

"No...it's not just for ten performances." Micca continued to stare at the brand. "Santiago...he finds ways to keep people. You could be an angel, and he'll say you breached contract or some shite. That's why Timothée is still here." Micca lifted his gaze. "Mr. Santiago owns you now."

Brent froze as a gong rang in his head. For a moment, everything stood still. *He owns you.* Those words twisted around Brent's heart and suffocated him. He couldn't move; he couldn't blink.

No.

Mr. Santiago couldn't own him. He'd spent months trying to escape, trying to be his own person.

He owns you.

The words dragged Brent forward. Each step weighed heavily.

Owned.

"No," Brent mumbled as he reached the threshold of the carnival. He took a step past one of the last tents towards the trees.

Thud.

Brent stumbled backwards, his forehead aching as if an imperceptible wall prevented him from leaving.

Trapped.

Owned.

Micca joined him. "You a'ight there?"

No anger or sorrow filled Brent's chest. Only emptiness, resting on the cornerstones of his heart, remained.

This is where you belong, the Diabolo chided. *A prisoner.*

"Yeah," Brent responded to both Micca and the Diabolo. "Guess so."

"You sure?"

"It's just...I dunno...I dunno what to do. I...I feel useless."

"Well, lying here in the mud ain't gonna help you. C'mon. Up you go. We'll figure out how to find Beebelle, a'ight? I can do some poking and prodding if you like while you stay on Santiago's good side so you can get outta this contract."

"You can?"

"Yeah, I got them street smarts. I can get some information from guards with the right charm. Find out where exactly they're taking her and when and such." Micca winked.

"You? Charm?" Brent laughed.

"Just cause it ain't worked on you don't mean I don't have it." Micca hoisted Brent to his feet, arm laced around Brent's waist. "Not for lack of trying, though."

Brent grimaced.

"Beebelle is tough. She'll be a'ight. You, on the other hand, are gonna get a ripe old beating if you don't get your head together. Come on now, let's head on over to work before Lolli throws another fit today, a'ight?"

"Yeah, a'ight."

As they left the perimeter of the circus, Brent stared back into the forest. He swore the trees watched him, begging for his attention, with hints of fog trickling over their branches.

In another world.

Suffocating.

Alone.

CHAPTER SEVENTEEN

OXIDATION

B ria didn't sleep.

She couldn't.

Not while an electric current pulsated with her every movement.

Not while her right arm screamed in pain.

Not while Mr. Gorge snored, Marisol talked, and Chander stared at her with curiosity.

Instead, she focused inward, listening to the way the electric current moved through her, from her feet to the little branch behind her ear. Even when she didn't move, it was there.

Had it always been? Did everyone have this pulsing through them?

Did the leaves? Did the trees?

Wasn't every element linked? Wasn't everything part of the world?

She winced as another shock roared through her skin. Her head pounded with the electricity. She worried sleep would cause her to lose track of the current.

Captain Palmer only came to visit her once as the Tower rumbled across the landscape, a posse of cadets on her heels. She paced the cell, eyes on Bria, a scowl on her lips. Behind her, Mr. Gorge listened while Marisol and Chander watched.

No one spoke.

The bitter taste of fear hung in the air.

Captain Palmer's voice fueled the tension, her first question slicing open the air as she rested her gaze on Bria. "Tell me, how many prisoners are in the room?"

Bria didn't respond.

Captain Palmer took Bria's cheeks in her hand, squeezing. "Listen, little girl. We can do this the easy or the hard way. I can have my men break every bone in your body. You might think that would kill you, but oh no...we won't let you die. You'll feel the pain of every bone snapping. And if that doesn't motivate you enough, I am sure we can find your family and do the same to them. So I suggest you answer my question."

Bria glowered.

"How many prisoners?"

Bria shook Captain Palmer's hand away with her response. "Four including me."

"What if I said there were no prisoners?"

"I'd say you are a liar. Just like if you told me there are four lights. There is only one in the room." Bria stared straight at Captain Palmer. "I know where I am. I know who I am. You can't change that."

Bria didn't recognize the confidence in her own voice. It belonged to the girl who used to rule the tunnels; the girl who believed the world could stay pretty; the girl who had hope. Where had she gone?

She's still here. Keep holding tight to your convictions— that's what Grandmama would say.

"Hm." Captain Palmer turned away. A beat passed. Then she pivoted back with full force and slammed her first into Bria's nose. "Don't you dare belittle me, girl!"

Bria winced as blood trickled down to her lip.

"Let's skip these games and cut straight to the point." Captain Palmer rubbed her hands together. "What are you planning?"

"What I'm planning?" Bria repeated.

"Are you intending to overthrow the government? Destroy the Order? The world? Tell me!" Captain Palmer leaned forward, her breath wreaking of coffee.

Bria furrowed her brow. "I don't have any plans. I'm only trying to survive—"

Another smack.

Bria whimpered.

"Pathetic." Captain Palmer stepped back. "You won't be able to hide when Captain Carver begins his interrogation. We'll get the truth out of you yet."

Bria didn't reply, watching as Captain Palmer left. As she passed Chander, the boy threw out his leg, causing Captain Palmer to stumble once. She cursed at him before slamming the door.

Bria glowered after her. "Captain Carver doesn't scare me..."

To her relief, Captain Palmer nor her guards didn't hear.

Silence reigned, and Bria sank back into the suffocating embrace of the pulsating electricity on her skin. None of the other prisoners spoke, letting the silence drizzle over the room.

Marisol finally broke the silence. "You really don't have a plan or anything?"

Bria glanced at her. "No."

"I thought you said you were the Forest Queen, though? Everyone heard about what happened in Newbird's Arm!"

"I didn't plan everything. The riot happened by accident." Bria sighed. "I wanted to save Brent. It was a selfish reason...that's all."

"Brent?"

"My...boyfriend." Bria's cheeks warmed.

"You've got a beau? How sweet! I guess love makes us blind, and we do silly things, huh?" Marisol giggled. Her voice infected the room, and for a moment, Bria swore her own pain lifted.

But only for a moment.

Bria looked away, shutting down the conversation. She fell back into focusing on the currents, the metals, the stone, and the earth. Her head spun as she tried to follow each piece. She needed time to analyze the way each element behaved. But her heart thudded with exhaustion, her muscles seared with pain, and her head screamed in terror.

When she closed her eyes, she dreamt of Brent; she missed his smile, his gentle touch, and the way he laughed. If he was with her right now, he'd help her investigate her magic. They were a team; they always had been. Before all of this happened, Bria used to bounce ideas off him in the garden. They solved problems together.

I can't do this alone.

She glanced back at her fellow prisoners. Marisol continued to babble away about her recent romantic partners, her favorite flowers, and meals she missed the most. It helped bring light to the room otherwise left in a dark glow.

One conversation caught Bria's attention.

"Chander!" Marisol turned to the boy. "Was Captain Palmer the last person to touch you?"

Chander gawked. "Um, I…um…"

"C'mon, Chan! You can't lie to me! We saw you trip her."

"Yeah, um, she was." The boy looked away.

"So does that mean you can see what she is up to right now?"

The boy shrugged. "Yeah. But when I do, I get shocked like the rest of you."

Bria glanced at the chains on the boy's wrists. She hadn't noticed earlier the copper wires attached to the metal nor the way it seemed to glow every time the boy moved. She tugged at her own chains. *That must be why it's nonstop for me. I'm always connected to the earth.*

The electricity pulsed through the metallic chains. Iron. Straight from the earth. Iron existed in plants, in blood, in everything. She'd learned that long ago in school. At the time, it meant nothing, a non sequitur fact. But now, it meant the world.

"Can you try looking briefly? Hm?" Marisol prodded the boy. "I really want to know what she's up to!"

"It hurts to look," Chander mumbled.

"Please!"

"No!" Chander turned his head away from Marisol. "I don't want to!"

Mr. Gorge groaned, "Can you two shut up? Some of us wanna sleep."

To Bria's surprise, even Marisol grew quiet out of respect for the old man. Silence became their companion, followed by the gentle breaths of sleep.

Bria continued staring into the darkness, feeling along her chains, learning the different crevasses of the iron and the pattern of the electric pulse. It did not differ from plants. No different from creating sinkholes. No different from being a conduit for a storm.

She just had to focus.

Bria drew in on herself, listening to the creaking tower and popping furnace. She couldn't feel the earth beyond her stone chamber. It was like she existed only in a vacuum. She instead expanded her senses outward, reaching for air pockets in the stone, mold growing beneath the pipes…

Anything.

She focused her energy on her chains. With a jolt of electricity climbing through her body and a flinch of her wrist, years of wear passed by in a minute, and the iron chains rusted.

Then they snapped.

Bria smiled. *I'm more than just a gardener.*

Her knees shook as she tiptoed across the prison cell, holding her injured arm close to her chest. She debated waking her fellow prisoners but stopped. It was best to let them be; if the guards caught her, the last thing she wanted was for the others to bear the burden of her actions.

She placed her good hand against her little branch. A camellia flower bloomed, then wilted, leaving behind a seed pod. Bria placed each of the seeds into the lock and ordered them to grow.

With a snap, the lock gave out.

No one in the cell woke.

Bria snuck out into the corridor, using the dark space between each flickering lantern as a cloak. She held her breath at each step, listening as the shadows moved or as pipes snarled. The wires above shrieked.

Multiple cells lined the hallway. Bria slid open the panel over the first door.

Her heart sank at the sight.

On the floor slept seven children, fresh brands on their wrists, huddled beneath thin blankets. None woke as she looked inside the cell.

Shit. Bria checked the next one. The same scene graced her presence. They were younger than her own cellmate, Chander, no older than ten years of age. Who were these children? Did they have magic? Silver eyes? Or did they end up in the wrong place at the wrong time?

Bria restrained a sob. She couldn't leave them. None of them belonged here.

Stick to the shadows. Once you get your bearings, you can figure out an escape plan. Okay? She tapped her little branch and let it expand out from behind her ear. Moving nimbly on her feet, she continued along the hallway, checking each corner for the guards.

No one.

They must not have expected someone to break out. Bria smirked. *They're going to need to increase security after I'm done.*

A stairwell out of the belly of the Guard Tower greeted her with lights. The bellows and drunken laughter of guards echoed down to her. With care, Bria started up the stairs only to freeze.

"I don't get why Captain Palmer doesn't let us near any of those damn girls. It ain't like they're gonna get shite as good as us soon," one guard ranted. "I kinda like that one with the black hair. The truth seeker girl? She's a doll."

"Yeah, but she'll make you tell all your secrets," another guard responded.

"But ya seen that ass?"

"Eh. I think I like that little forest queen girl."

"The terrorist?"

"That little thing, a terrorist? No!" The guard chuckled. "I think she'd be a fun time."

Bria gripped the wall. The stones rumbled beneath her fingers. She'd grown up hearing the catcalls and disgusting remarks of guards; her grandmama told her to ignore it and never react. She always took the high ground and never once gave them affection. How had she been able to ignore it for so long? Perhaps it was the part of her that saw the captain's son, Christof Carver, as the young man in school with her. Perhaps it was the small piece of her that remembered her first kiss long ago with that despicable man.

No more.

She dug her fingers deeper into the stone.

The Guards looked up as the walls shook.

"The fuck is going on?" one asked.

"I dunno, but…shite! Look at the stairs!"

The stairs gave out, crumbling at Bria's command. Her magic wrapped around her fingers and transported to the stone, seeking every element of life in the stone and pulling them apart.

"It's that forest bitch!" a guard screamed.

Bria glanced up at them, smirked, then waved a hand.

The last stone fell, blocking the entrance to the prison chamber at the base of the tower.

Bria raced back to her cell. She didn't know how long they had until the Guard alerted their captain. Was there another way into the bottom of the tower than that terrible stairwell? Surely, right? It wouldn't make any sense to have *one* entrance.

She had to act fast.

Marisol, Mr. Gorge, and Chander all turned when she entered.

"Rhodana!" Marisol gasped in amazement. "I thought they took you! You were just...gone! What happened? You can't lie to me! Tell me the truth!"

Bria walked over to Marisol and placed her good hand on the chains. They broke apart.

Marisol gasped again. "How did you do that!?!"

"Magic," Bria whispered as she approached Chander. The boy recoiled but didn't reject Bria's help. Last, she walked over to Mr. Gorge and aided him down from the wall.

"Yeah, but I've never seen magic like that!" Marisol continued.

"Shush! The guards might hear!" Mr. Gorge hissed.

Bria interjected, "I trapped the guards upstairs. I don't know how long we have until they get back down here, but we need to free everyone else. Together, we might have a fighting chance."

"Everyone else?" Marisol echoed.

"The children." Bria turned to the door.

"The children?!"

Chander spoke, "They took all the younger children from Maedee's Outlook with me. They said some of us got an evil magic or demons or something. I was older, so they threw me in this cell, but my sister and friends are all trapped and scared and…it's dark and cold. I saw what they could see, then couldn't see anymore. I'm not sure if they're safe."

Right! His magic! Bria pivoted back to Chander. "You touched Captain Palmer, right?"

"Yeah…"

"Can you see what she's up to?"

"It…it hurts."

Bria approached the boy. There was something about him that felt similar to Brent—the way he flinched, his downcast gaze. For a moment, she swore mist swirled around the boy's fingertips. *But he can't be a Mist Keeper. Brent's the current apprentice. Can't there only be one apprentice?*

"I know it hurts," Bria said to him, "and I understand it's hard. You don't have to do this if you don't want to. If it really hurts so much, we'll find another way. But…if you can do it, we might get out of here faster."

The boy licked his lips before nodding. "A'ight."

The mist moved over the boy's body, only for a blink, then he settled into a trance.

"About eight guards are there with her. I think that's most of them," Chander mumbled.

"Only eight?" Bria asked.

Mr. Gorge replied, "They don't keep a big group when the tower is moving. No more than ten, usually. Not likely anyone will get out. They'd have a bigger welcome wagon in Knoll or wherever they're heading next."

"Right...that makes sense." Bria glanced down the hallway. "If we all work together, we can take them."

"The three of us will not be able to handle all those guards! You're the only super magical person!" Marisol exclaimed.

"No. All of us." Bria motioned to the doors. "All the prisoners. We can work together."

"But how are we going to get them out?" Marisol placed her hands on her hips. "It's not like we have a key!"

"The same way I got out of here before..." Bria tapped behind her ear. A few camellias bloomed, depositing seed pods in her hands. "I just need to make something a little pretty."

ON THE BACKS OF PEONIES

The last prison door fell with a clank, and Bria let her remaining seed pods fall to the floor. Prisoners tiptoed out of their holding cells, squinting in the dim light, pale and frayed. Mostly adolescents, they huddled against the wall, afraid to look in her direction but too fearful to turn away.

Footsteps pounded on the floor above them. Bria shot a glance at Chander. wobbling beside a younger girl with a near-identical face.

"They're using the air shafts to get down, I think. She sent five down here." Chander blinked a few times. "I can't tell. The captain isn't with them."

Bria turned towards the fallen stones. The group of prisoners could theoretically take on five guards. But could they fend off firepower? Did the guard have pistols? Would they risk a misfire?

"Okay..." Bria turned back to the prisoners. They gazed at her attentively, searching for a form of leadership. Bria's stomach churned; she never wanted to be a leader. Not like this. Sure, she'd always admired her grand-mama's ability to fight and conquer, but she saw herself as a shadow. Even as the supposed forest queen, part of her sought guidance.

Yet here, deep in the belly of the tower, she stood as the sole leader.

And she had to find the solution.

Her mind raced as she scanned over the prisoners. "Who has magic?"

Twelve uncertain hands rose.

"Right...okay..." Bria counted to herself. "There are twelve of us with magic. Twelve of us who scare the guard. Together, without bloodshed, we can lure them into the prison cells. Lock them up, throw away the key. We'll make a statement that we don't want to do any harm. Or at least we can try. Then the rest of you..." She glanced at the others. "Well, really, all of you. I'm only asking you to do what feels right. Hide if you're scared;

fight if you are bold. But together, we can prove to the Guard that we are not weak."

Murmurs from the group responded. A few children whimpered.

Bria lowered her head. "I'm sorry. I know this isn't a great plan, but it's all I can offer. I'm not a leader."

Mr. Gorge smiled in Bria's direction. "You're doing great, lass. Most leaders don't have their heads together."

Before Bria could respond, a banging sounded from the pipes. Footsteps roared.

"Shit, they're here! Stand your ground!" Bria shouted.

The prisoners operated like a machine. In a blur, children ducked behind the rubble, Magii took ready stances in corners, and teenagers and adults manned themselves with rocks and sticks. After scanning the room once, Bria joined Marisol behind a door.

A shaft opened from the ceiling. Bria held her breath as five guards dropped into the crypt. Their steel-toed boots landed with a thud, wreaking of alcohol and smoke.

None of the prisoners made a noise.

"Lieutenant!" one cadet shouted. "The cells! They're open!"

"What? How?!" the lieutenant asked.

Their pause gave them a chance to act.

"Now!" Bria hissed.

The prisoners attacked. Children cried out as they rushed at the guards with rocks. Lashes of magic followed, capturing Bria's awe. While neither Marisol nor Chander had offensive talents, others attacked with magic beyond Bria's imagination. One child sang a song and lulled a guard to sleep, while another attracted the Guards' pistols like magnets. If the danger wasn't imminent, Bria might have spent hours talking with the children, learning about their abilities. Did Kek know that magic like this existed? Did these children understand the importance of their skills? Did they understand the common link?

Was this why the Order feared Magii?

Bria didn't ponder the answers. She sprang into action with the rest, dodging rocks and blasts of broken glass. She summoned the seed pods sleeping on the floor, letting bloom and lace their way around the ankles of the guards. Rocks spun. The air screamed. What part of it was her magic? She didn't know. Everything attacked, and she was one with the earth.

Gunshots mingled with the magic. Screams and cries overpowered the booming engine. And through it all, the guards fell.

One at a time.

The first fell to the child's song. Another tripped over a wad of roots. One tripped over the stone. As they fell, locked and cuffed by Bria's own plants, the older prisoners moved the bodies into the cells. Bria locked each door with vines, just like the ones she used to create her hideaway in the tunnels all those years ago.

She stepped back to count. *One...two...three...four...*

"Gotcha!" Like a shadow, the last guard emerged, snatching Bria's arm and pulling her close. "Think you can cause more shite, don'tcha?"

Bria glared, but before she could react, Marisol threw a rock at the guard. It hit him on the shoulder, and he dropped Bria in fury.

Using the window to her advantage, Bria summoned a twisted round of branches around the guard's ankles. They dragged him across the floor and into a cell, stringing him upside from the ceiling.

"Bye fuckface!" Marisol slammed the door in the guard's face.

Bria twisted branches over the door, then slid to the wall. Other than the banging on the door matching her heartbeat and the creaking of the tower, all else sat silent.

Except for a child's tears.

Chander knelt on the ground over Mr. Gorge. "No! Grandpa!"

Her knees shaking, Bria neared the man. Blood seeped from Mr. Gorge's chest. His eyes stared vacantly, mouth hung ajar.

"Grandpa!" Chander sobbed into the old man's chest. "No..."

Bria approached him. *If Brent were here, he could release Mr. Gorge's soul. Hopefully a Mist Keeper will come soon to help him.* All she could offer were soft words. "I'm so sorry, Chander..."

"Rho," Marisol whispered. "There are still more guards. They'll be here soon, probably."

Bria paused, then nodded. "Right. Can you stay here and deal with...this? I'll take a group upstairs."

"Of course. Good luck."

Bria wrangled nine people to come with her upstairs. Any more, and they'd become an easy target. Other teams would join them within the next quarter-hour, but only in small groups. They had to take the tower by surprise. It gave them the stealth and upper hand over Captain Palmer and her guards.

Most of the individuals in Bria's group were teenagers, no older than sixteen, with a few children on their heels. Most of the team had their own arsenal of magic: songs of sleep, flying glass, agility, and perfect aim, just to name a few.

They followed Bria up through the utility shaft with wide eyes and eager ears. No one spoke. Breaths came in uneven beats. Yet, unlike the crypts below, the Tower itself resembled a maze of zigzagging floors, crisscrossed stairs, and locked doors. A siren blared from above as they reached the top of the shaft, echoing through the metal.

Bria helped the children out of the shaft, then squinted in the flickering lights. Over the siren, she yelled, "Chander said there are a few guards remaining. It's not a big group, just a prison transport. Let's form teams and split up. Act with stealth. Take them by surprise."

They clumped into three groups of three; every team had one older teenager as their leader. Bria ventured off on her own, leaving the others to fend for themselves. She wasn't quite a fan of leaving these kids to their own devices, but after witnessing them in the crypts below, she knew their strengths.

"Okay, good. We need to take control of this tower soon—before they can radio for backup!" Bria continued shouting while adjusting he bad arm. "Split up, and find the control room. Try to avoid conflict. The rest will be up here soon to help. Okay?"

The group agreed with a silent nod.

She knew it wasn't a cohesive plan, but it was the best option she could conjure through the pain and the confusion. *I'm not designed for something like this. Everything I do is on a whim. Brent is rubbing off on me.*

With a final "good luck," the teams split, leaving Bria alone as she navigated along the tower, nimble and capable as she hopped between each of the catwalks. Just as she moved between the trees, she hopped from one side to another, letting the heat from the furnace guide her into the heart of the engine room. She kept her breaths even and her emotions in tow; she didn't need the metal to bend at her whim or for electricity to eject itself from her core. Those were elements she couldn't control.

Why? What made them different from plants?

And why did they react now?

Copper wires jolting with electricity and a boiling furnace greeted her in the center of the tower. Gears droned around her, twisting and twirling, creaking and roaring. She moved towards the edge of the catwalk and stared into the mechanisms beneath her.

Then she stumbled backwards.

A basin oozing with silver liquid sat amid the gears, laced with wires. With each jolt of electricity, the Pool gurgled, and the gears turned. Sparks flew from the Pool, flitting with magic in the air.

Why is there a Pool? Bria leaned over the edge to get a better look. *This doesn't make any sense.*

"Halt!" a voice tugged Bria's attention away from the Pool.

She spun, turning face-to-face with Captain Palmer.

"Ah, so it is the little terrorist." Captain Palmer hit the railing with her club as she walked towards Bria. "I suppose you're the one who started this insurrection?"

Bria didn't reply.

"No matter. At least there is nowhere for you to go." Captain Palmer stood mere inches from Bria now. She was a tall woman with a narrow face, towering over Bria so her back arched. She poked Bria's chest. "Well, except down."

Bria gripped the railing tight with her right hand, stumbling over her feet.

"So why don't you come with me? I would hate to return you to Knoll dead."

"I won't be much value dead," Bria snapped.

"Oh, that doesn't matter to me. What matters is my tower returns to Knoll in one piece." Captain Palmer shoved Bria.

Clenching tighter to the railing, Bria felt the iron beginning to rust. She glared straight into Captain Palmer's eyes. "What is that down there?"

"What is what?"

"The silver pool."

"Fuel."

And with that single word, Captain Palmer pushed Bria over the edge.

Bria acted fast. As she fell, she grabbed Captain Palmer's hand, tugging her over the edge…

Down…

Down…

Down…

And into the heart of the engine.

She landed on her bad arm, sending another crack from her elbow to her shoulder. Bria resisted the urge to cry out, wincing as she rolled over on her back.

Captain Palmer crawled to her feet, blood dripping from her face. A sneer decorated her lips as she stumbled over to Bria.

Bria backed up until her head hit the basin.

Captain Palmer removed the club from her belt. "Before I beat the living shite out of you, I have one question, girly. Answer wisely." She pointed to the two lanterns hanging from the catwalk. "How many lanterns are there?"

"Two," Bria said without hesitation.

"And what if I said there were three?"

"You'd be wrong."

Captain Palmer shrugged. "Very well."

She raised her club and hit Bria.

Once.

Twice.

And again.

Bria didn't scream. She took each blow, holding back the tears and tasting blood as it poured from her nose. Between each blow, she lifted her already injured arm higher, up the side of the basin and into the silver pool. The liquid burned her fingers, charged with lightning and volts. Her skin cried. As the club slammed into her head again, Bria used her last bit of consciousness to reach for the peony heart in the basin.

The pool bubbled. Electricity sparked in the air. The currents climbed through Bria's skin.

As the peonies exploded from the pool, the electricity rocked from Bria's body. It shorted the wires, froze the gears, and burst the lighting. With a wave of flowers and electricity, Captain Palmer flew backwards, her club falling to the floor. Bria couldn't see where she landed.

She couldn't see anything.

The electricity continued to burn from her arm and sizzle through her body, riding on the backs of peonies in the air.

As the final petals settled on the ground, Bria closed her eyes and drifted away on the back of peonies.

POWER AND ORDER

Jemma assisted Elder Un Dine in her tasks to pass the time in the Temple over the next few days. She saw little of Senator Cordova, as expected, nor did any other familiar faces pay any visits.

Had she become only a cog in the machine, wasting away like the others? Senator Cordova promised her more, didn't he? Why had they reduced her to one of many?

In Newbird's Arm, she glowed like a flame.

Here, she'd diminished.

I'm doing what's best, Jemma reminded herself as she led a few individuals into the crevices beneath Knoll's Temple. The mirrors reflecting on the walls swirled with each of her steps. As beautiful as they were, after spending so much time in the Tower of Ab Aeterno, the Temple of Knoll lacked luster. When could she go back? Anxiety over the possibility rumbled in her stomach and tightened in her throat.

She assigned the last patron to a crevice, then marched back up the stairs with her head bowed. Above, Elder Un Dine's voice dazzled as she led the congregation in a prayer of spring.

> *So it goes, so it goes,*
> *She will come with vengeance,*
> *Don't you know?*
> *The world is brown, the soul it sighs,*
> *But green she will bleed,*
> *And the Effluvium shall never die.*

"And the Effluvium shall never die," Jemma recited with the congregation. But the prayer left a frozen dagger in her heart. Something felt different about it.

The year before, when Brother Roy Al said the same prayer, her heart pulsed with happiness and pride.

That was before the Storm of Nightmares.

That was before Brother Roy Al died.

She remained against the wall, watching as the congregation filed out, her head bowed. No one noticed her;

she was one of many. Back home, she was a protégé. On the road, at least she was the recluse sister of the Order.

Here…was she only a pawn?

Elder Un Dine approached her after the ceremony concluded. "Sister Jey Ma. How are you this fine afternoon?"

"I am fine, dear Sister."

"Are you sure? You have been quiet lately, dear."

"It is nothing, really." Jemma sighed. "Part of me is…yearning for more. But I suppose the Effluvium has its way."

"That it does. But it only has its way if you speak to it. So pray tell, dear Sister, where did this yearning begin?"

Jemma glanced at the elderly sister. Her eyes gleamed with her aged smile.

She then said, "Back home, in Newbird's Arm, I was a prodigy; people listened to me. Elder Don—I mean, Senator Cordova—said that here in Knoll, I would be more. But I have just been conducting cleansings and prayers like any other Brother or Sister of the Order. Most patrons don't even know my name. It has been wonderful working with you, Sister, but…I hoped that I'd learn under Senator Cordova. He seemed to insinuate that he would be my mentor." Jemma stared up at the Year Glass above the pews. "If I can't do anything here to change the world, I might as well go home."

"I see." Elder Un Dine nodded. "I've known many like you before; some go home or travel to Ab Aeterno. Granted, Ab Aeterno is here now...so I can see why you hoped for something greater. And after your journey. I would want to do more as well."

Jemma bowed her head. "I am glad you understand, Sister."

"I think most of us do. It can be a fruitless job, this cleansing and praying, yes?" Elder Un Dine smiled sadly.

Jemma didn't want to agree, but her heart thudded with an affirmative response.

The Elder glanced towards the window. "If you would like, I can send you over to the Dispensary Tower today. I am supposed to lead the ill in prayer, but it's cumbersome for someone of my age. Perhaps you can lead a new charge there."

"Are you sure?"

"Absolutely. You've gone with me before, so I expect you know what to do. Your talent and leadership are unmatched. Besides, I would much rather stay here and help with the low-profile cleansings."

Jemma thanked the old Sister, and without taking a moment to delay, she exited Knoll's Temple and took the walk towards the Dispensary Tower. Although the air warmed her skin with hints of spring, the landscape still echoed with the voice of winter. Dust cradled her skirt as she walked, and while a thin film of sweat coated her brow, there was still a feeling of death in the air.

Jemma took comfort as she walked in the presence of the Effluvium, shifting about at her feet, collecting the dust and watching with curiosity. Wherever she went, Jemma knew the Effluvium would follow. She saw it when she gazed out at sea; now, she saw it everywhere. While she continued to question Senator Cordova and his motives, she couldn't deny he had opened her eyes.

Her faith in the Effluvium remained, even when all else seemed dusty and bleak.

It didn't take long to walk to the Dispensary Tower, and the Guard welcomed her with the same respect they gave Elder Un Dine. Most days, she entered the infirmary in a fog-like trance, blessing those fulfilling their cleanses and those healing from wounds that no one could explain. This time, she tried to keep her head higher, walking with purpose up the stairs to the Cleansing Crevices.

Her confidence wavered as she walked past the room where they kept the woman with white hair and red eyes whom she'd met a few days earlier. Ms. Dray continued to haunt Jemma's memories, and curiosity lured her to peer through the slit-like window in the door. The woman sat on the bed, her hair cut short, two round burns on the top of her head. Her strange red eyes kept shifting back and forth as if watching something on the wall. Black and blue bruises coated her already translucent skin, elevating the stretch marks on her thighs and the pimple scars on her cheeks.

"Interesting, isn't it? What this disease can do?"

Jemma hadn't heard Senator Cordova approach. But like a snake, he slithered in, hissing in her ear. How long had he been watching?

"Has Professor Gratz determined if it is contagious?" Jemma asked, trying to keep her poise.

"We believe that any overexposure to magic causes negative effects. Hopefully, by cleansing Ms. Dray, we will rid her of magic and begin the cure. We plan to start the final levels soon." Senator Cordova nodded to himself. "If it works, and she is free, then we think the best road to cleansing our great nation is through a mass five-level cleanse of everyone. If we can capture the magic, harness it, then we no longer have to fear it."

Jemma narrowed her eyes at Senator Cordova. "Pardon...*harness* it?"

"Did I say harness?"

"You did, Senator."

"I knew you were an observant one, Miss Reds. I saw it back in Newbird's Arm, and I see it now. Come with me. I think it is time we talk more about Rose and Ada."

Jemma glanced back one last time at Ms. Dray in her room. The woman had curled up on the bed, resting her chin against her knees, still hardly blinking, still with her eyes wide open. Jemma pressed her fingers to her lips and raised them towards the woman. *I hope the Effluvium guides you to safety.*

Senator Cordova led Jemma up the stairwell towards the top of the Dispensary Tower, past where wires buzzed and muffled voices echoed through the halls. The Senator's voice rang out as he spoke with each confident stride. "Where did we leave off in our story? Do you remember Miss Reds?"

"I believe the sisters arrived in what would become Rosada and poked their eyes out," Jemma recalled.

"Ah yes. Their arrival, indeed." Senator Cordova stroked his finger along the dusty railing. "They arrived here after a harrowing journey, blinded and with only a small army. The locals welcomed them—who wouldn't? Rose and Ada were kindly and beautiful and wise as well. But soon, they learned a terrible secret: the locals had magic still. They had not escaped their father's curse."

Senator Cordova paused, glancing over his shoulder at Jemma. She nodded, hanging on to each of his words. The Senator in no way captured a story like Brent Harley ever did, but this wasn't a story.

The words of the Senator and the Order had to be history.

Right?

Senator Cordova continued, "At first, the sisters tried to make do, but to put it bluntly, the locals were demons. They used their magic for everything, and slowly, Rose and Ada's armies left, distraught by the magic.

"But Rose and Ada weren't stupid. A great sorcerer had raised them, and even if he was evil, they learned many things...such as the power within magic. They could not just wave it all away. Even if someone with magic died, their magic had to go somewhere.

"This was something their father had been experimenting with for years, but rather than using it to help society, he took the Magii and their magic. He powered his own being, as well as monsters beyond our wildest dreams, according to the history books. But Rose and Ada never realized the benefit.

"That is until one day when their army got into a skirmish with some locals and killed one of their powerful Magii. They burned the body, and one of Rose and Ada's soldiers noticed the flames did not extinguish. The magic provided fuel to the flame, and they soon realized they could use it to power their new nation."

Senator Cordova stopped at the last stair before a door. Wires and pipes skirted over it, pulsating with a rainbow of color.

Jemma met the Senator's gaze, a lump forming in her throat and toppling down into her chest as she waited for him to speak.

"The Order believes that while magic can be detrimental, under the right guise...we can build a sparkling utopia where no one is without light or heat or a bed. We will have order. We will cleanse the world." Senator Cordova laced his fingers around the doorknob. "Is that not what you want, Miss Reds?"

Jemma's throat tightened, but she squeaked, "That's the reason I became a sister."

"And you want to do more?"

"I want my home to be safe."

Senator Cordova smiled. "That is what I thought. Perhaps it is time I give you a bigger role."

"I would like that." Jemma swallowed down her eagerness.

"I shall discuss it with Elder An Drew and Elder Un Dine. I believe there is a grander role for you yet, as promised." Senator Cordova turned the doorknob. "Especially as our plan comes to fruition."

The door creaked open before them, revealing a Year Glass. At first glance, nothing about it seemed peculiar, but as Jemma walked into the atrium, she noticed the wires and pipes zigzagging along the ceiling, connecting to the top half of the Year Glass. Puffs of smoke filled the glass from the tub, mingling with the chartreuse metallic liquid in the glass chamber. Sparks of magic and electricity danced on the liquid's surface.

Senator Cordova placed his hand on the glass. "Before I left Newbird's Arm, I had hoped to implement a Year Glass like this. It was something I trained on when I was a young brother in the Order. This Year Glass alone powers this entire building as well as some of the neighboring houses. It provides tranquility, happiness...and order. Think about how many towns we could power, how many people we could save, if we put a Year Glass like this in every Temple across Rosada. We would finally have not a worry about the world; no Magii, no reason for stories, and no needless deaths."

Jemma walked over and placed her own hand against the Year Glass. A shock rippled up her arm as she touched it but not enough to throw her off her feet. Part of her wanted to stare at it forever, to know all its secrets, and to share it with the world.

But the other half wanted to break open the glass and let the liquid pour over her, to absorb all its knowledge and power.

She snatched her hand away, staring at her burned fingertips. Her voice came out as an inaudible gasp. "I want to help."

A smile worked its way over Senator Cordova's face. Before he could speak, though, the door behind them swung open. Cadet Christof Carver raced in, his eyes wide in fear and sweat pressing his golden hair to his face.

Senator Cordova kept his poise. "Ah, Cadet. What brings you racing in here unannounced? I am sure your father wouldn't be happy."

"My...my father—" He gasped for air. "My father sent me, sir. He knew you were here. I apologize, but...well..."

"Go on."

Christof straightened his back, trying his best to keep poised. "Captain Palmer returned an hour ago."

"Captain Palmer? I am unfamiliar with him."

"Her. It's a...her." Christof wiped his brow and glanced at Jemma. "We stationed her out in Aeterno Village after we left. She sent a telegraph that she found..." His voice lowered. "Bria."

Jemma's stomach knotted at the name. *Bria's back?*

She didn't expect the queasiness. Months ago, excitement warmed her whenever someone mentioned Bria Smidt. The so-called terrorist of Newbird's Arm had left a strange feeling of warmth throughout the region. Now, nausea replaced that excitement. If Bria hadn't caused the uprising, would any of this be taking place? Would Jemma be home with Brother Roy Al leading the Temple, and her teddy bear, Ms. Porridge, to keep her company?

It didn't feel right to blame Bria for all of this. But Jemma had seen what magic had done. Bria left them and let demons dominate the country.

Had she?

Or was that a story?

Confusion nestled in her head, and another bout of nausea raced through Jemma's body. She shook it away, redirecting her attention to Senator Cordova and Christof.

"So this Captain Palmer claims she found Miss Smidt? The terrorist?" Senator Cordova recited.

"Well, she did, yeah, but...here's the thing. The vagrants and Magii and demon and shite they had in the tower...well, they overtook it! Some kids found Captain Palmer disoriented along the edge of the Necrowood. They took her to the Guard's Barracks to clean her up, but she kept saying that the damn girl took the tower."

"You mean Miss Smidt?"

"Ay, that's correct, sir."

Senator Cordova stared out the window towards the city, but Jemma couldn't bring herself to move. *Bria took a tower. And I thought Micca was insane for taking a truck!*

Senator Cordova asked, "And what became of her tower?"

"The Necrowood claimed it, sir. No one can find it. They found half her guards wandering in the forest, but the others…they don't know where they are." Christof fidgeted. "No one has found the prisoners either."

Senator Cordova bowed his head. "Very well. Thank you for the information. Please take Sister Jey Ma back to her cloister. I must speak with the Elders and Captains."

"Ay, sir." Christof turned to Jemma. "You a'ight there, Sister?"

Jemma blinked. It was as if she'd become a mere fly on the wall listening to the conversation. Her mind raced, and her head ached.

She could only respond by nodding her head.

"A'ight. C'mon. I'll take you back." Christof offered her an arm.

Trembling, Jemma took it, her hands pale like paper against the black sleeve of Christof's uniform. She glanced once back at the Year Glass and Senator Cordova, then repositioned her shoulders and raised her head high.

For the Effluvium's sake, she couldn't show weakness to magic, to stories, or to demons. She had to stay tall. She had to fight.

If only she knew what she fought for…and why.

THE MELTING WOMAN

Yaz spent the next couple of days immersed in Sir Jama's story.

No. Ningursu. His name was Ningursu.

But to her, the skull was still her Sir Jama.

Whatever his name, Yaz clung to his stories, hardly leaving her room except to get food. She didn't even watch as their tower left Aeterno Village and traveled across the gray wooded landscape towards a nearby industrial town. There, Mr. Nasr and Ms. Kai parked the tower, and they remained for days. The itch to explore continued to nag Yaz, but she couldn't risk Sir Jama being discovered...especially now that she knew he could talk!

For days, Sir Jama told her about the Mist Keepers. He said it was his duty to save the dead from burning in their minds, in Hell, as he called it. While he alone tackled this 'Hell' for centuries, he soon found other Mist Keepers. So, he created a council of seven others, all of whom had been alive for hundreds of years, with the goal of protecting the dead.

But according to Sir Jama, an evil alchemist, a disruptive storyteller, and a crazy plant witch had compromised their reign. The story sounded preposterous...but so was a talking skull!

"You see, Yasmin, I need to get back to my Library," Sir Jama said. "It is where I am at my safest and most powerful."

"But I don't know how to get there," Yaz whispered.

"That is all okay, Yasmin. The others will come. I am sure of it."

"But they haven't come yet."

"That is why tonight, you will leave a window open. I will summon them forth. They will meet you, and you will help us become heroes again. Does that sound good?"

"You mean I get to be a hero?"

"Yes, of course."

"But...how?"

"All in due time, dear Yasmin."

Sir Jama didn't speak for the rest of the night, leaving Yaz to pace her room. She wanted to ask more questions, but Sir Jama seemed locked in a stupor that reminded Yaz of Mr. Nasr's meditative trances.

Yaz resorted to sitting on her bed to play with her dolly and her skulls. Her growling stomach pulled her from her games, though. Despite her grudge against Mr. Nasr and Ms. Kai, she really was hungry.

After exchanging a quiet glance with Sir Jama, she snuck out of her bedroom and headed upstairs to the kitchen. All remained dark and quiet, except for the bustle of visitors in the shop on the ground floor. Yaz listened to their laughter. She could picture the scene; Ms. Kai had a way of luring the crowd into their shop while Mr. Nasr's knowledge ranged far and wide over an array of products. They would drink, laugh, and whisper secrets into the shadows.

With all the commotion, they never noticed their young ward slip into the kitchen.

Once the door shut, Yaz squeezed between the counters and found a jar of pickled tomatoes in a drawer. She wrestled with the top, smiling to herself as a loud click pulled the scent into the heart of the kitchen.

As she reached in to grab a tomato, footsteps entered the room.

Yaz spun.

Behind her stood a woman in a black cloak, her dark hair falling over her face, hiding melting skin and a piercing blue gaze.

"Oh, sorry, ma'am. Customers aren't allowed up here," Yaz said.

The woman opened her mouth to speak, then closed it.

Yaz held out the jar. "Do you want a tomato before you leave?"

The woman gawked.

"Oh. Okay. More for me." Yaz brought a tomato to her mouth.

The woman blinked a few times, then asked, "You can see me?"

"Why couldn't I..." Yaz burst into a smile. "Are you one of Sir Jama's friends? Is that why you're so surprised I can see you?"

"Sir Jama?"

"Sorry, Nin...Nin-ger...Ningursu? That's his name, I think. Yeah, Ningursu. Are you his friend?"

The woman's mouth hung open. For a moment, she stood there like a statue before recomposing herself and saying, "I feel like I am dealing with Brent all over again. I must speak with Ningursu at once!"

Yaz put down the jar. "A'ight. I can show you him. But be quiet! I don't want you getting in trouble with Ms. Kai and Mr. Nasr."

The woman in black followed Yaz back to her bedroom, her long black cloak sweeping across the floor as if she were a shadow. Yaz resisted the urge to glance back at the woman multiple times. While she had to be human, without a doubt, she also reminded Yaz of a sea witch. Her skin drooped from her bones, and blotches of dark blue hung about her neck and chin. Would she melt if she took one wrong step?

Yaz held back her questions and opened the door.

Ningursu's voice boomed, "Ah! Caroline! Alas!"

"Ningursu, sir…" The woman stepped forward. "I did not expect to see you again. You disappeared. I have been working, and I received a pull of the dead, so I thought…What are you doing here, sir?"

A smile worked its way over Ningursu's lips. "I called you here, Caroline."

"As I am aware now. But what of this girl?"

"Yasmin has helped me in this time of crisis. She mended my wounds and cared for me deeply." Ningursu squinted behind the woman called Caroline. "Do you know if the others received my message?"

The woman, Caroline, spoke with poise and elegance. Yaz hung onto every word as she slid onto the floor beside

Sir Jama. "I am sorry, sir, I do not know. We were separated. Kek took the Library once you vanished, and we were too discombobulated to fight their armies. Tomás, Julietta, and I were together for a time, but they disappeared somewhere in Spinoza. I tried to follow them, but we separated..." Caroline wiped her eye and continued. "I apologize. It has been a strange couple of weeks. With the tunnels misbehaving, the Diabolo rampant...I have struggled quite a bit."

"That is fine, Caroline. We shall regroup."

"Will we?" Caroline asked. "To be frank, sir, we thought you died. What happened to you?"

"My brother made a decision, and I ended up floating in a lake. But that is not important. What is important is that we are on our way to restoring the Council as the pillar of the Second World."

Caroline shifted and twiddled her thumbs. "And what of Brent?"

"Brenton Harley is no longer a part of this Council. He is a rogue player who needs to be snuffed out before all the balance and order in the world collapses." Sir Jama paused and eyed Yaz in the corner. "But in the meantime, I have found a new apprentice for you to focus on...with my guiding help, of course."

Apprentice?! Yaz perked up in her spot; Ningursu had mentioned nothing about being an apprentice!

Caroline turned towards Yaz. Her eyes grew wide, like two enormous sapphire gems. "She is a child."

"She has the mist's blessing; therefore, she is the next apprentice."

"But Brent is still...functional! There cannot be two apprentices at the same time...can there?"

"As I said, Brent is a rogue player. He does not harbor the mist's blessing."

Caroline waved her arms towards Yaz again. "But she cannot be older than eight years!"

Yaz shrunk. She didn't quite understand what Caroline and Sir Jama said. Who was Brent? What did it mean that she was an apprentice? Was she going to become a Mist Keeper?

As Sir Jama and the woman argued, mist pummeled against the walls. Yaz brought her hands to her ears and rocked. She hated when adults argued.

Especially when there was nothing she could do to help.

"I refuse to teach a child how to be a Mist Keeper!" Caroline raved. "Brent is irrational on all counts, and he is already in his twenties! Imagine teaching a child?!"

"A child can be shaped. Yasmin is willing to learn. Isn't that right, Yasmin?" Sir Jama glanced at Yaz.

"I want to learn and help," Yaz whispered. At least Sir Jama kept a level head. She would rather have him as her teacher than this crazy-eyed woman!

"But child...it is a big sacrifice. A tremendous sacrifice!"

"Caroline, that will come in due time."

She looked at Yaz and continued, "You will lose contact with your mother and father and all your friends! It is not an easy path."

"I don't have a mama or papa...or any friends." Yaz shuffled her feet. "I just ride around the world with Mr. Nasr and Ms. Kai, but they don't love me or anything."

"See, Caroline? Yasmin is a perfect addition to the Council. We are here to help lost souls, after all. Yasmin is as lost as anyone we take under our wing."

"Sir, I don't think it is wise—"

A knock on the door ended the conversation. In a blink of an eye, mist encompassed Caroline, and she vanished. Sir Jama fell silent on the floor.

"Yasmin?" Ms. Kai's voice cooed, dragging a heavy cloak of reality back over the room.

Yaz kicked Sir Jama under the bed and took out her toys, scattering them across the floor, then rushed to the door. Ms. Kai stood there, holding the jar of pickled tomatoes.

"Hi, Ms. Kai," Yaz said. "I was just playing with my toys."

"What have I told you about leaving jars on the counter?"

"Don't…"

"And you left this one on the counter why?"

"I forgot. I'm sorry." Yaz kicked the ground.

Ms. Kai sighed and placed the jar on the end table. She walked across Yaz's room, stepping over a few of the toys, before taking a seat on the bed. "Come sit with me, Yaz. Let's talk."

Yaz approached the bed. "About what?"

"Sit." Ms. Kai patted the mattress.

Yaz hopped up beside her.

Ms. Kai glanced around the room, then sighed. "Yaz, talk to me, please. You've been acting aloof since we left Aeterno."

Yaz shrugged.

"Is it because we didn't let you go explore? You know we have your best interest at heart."

"Yeah, guess so…" Yaz kicked her feet in the air.

"Yeshua and I—Mr. Nasr and I, I mean…we've been talking, and I think we have been hard on you." She glanced towards the window. "It has been a very long time since we were children. It is easy to forget that you need to have…fun."

"I have fun with my toys." Yaz glanced at her skulls on the ground again. The bird skulls and dolly seemed boring compared to the world Sir Jama had unlocked for her, but she wouldn't dare tell Ms. Kai that.

"Yes, I know, but you need to see the world as well." Her face lit up with a smile as she turned back to Yaz. "That's why Mr. Nasr and I bought tickets to Santiago's Cirque Sunrise. We're going to be in Siskin for a couple days to meet with a potential client, so we thought why not? The circus will be here for a couple of days, and they have a new performer. Doesn't that sound fun?"

"A circus?" Yaz's heart pattered. Before they entered Rosada, she would often try to sneak out to the circuses and carnivals in the cities. Most nights, she never made it far before Mr. Nasr found her, and then she had to watch the carnival from a distance as the colors lit the sky. Her imagination sparked with the possibilities hidden behind the tents. What sort of magical acts awaited her?

Now she might find out!

Ms. Kai removed a flyer from her coat and handed it to Yaz. On the front, an image of a dragon filled the advertisement, hovering above the list of performances scheduled for the day.

"Wowee!" Yaz exclaimed. "Is there really a dragon?"

"We'll have to find out, right? Unless you don't want to go..."

"I do! Please!"

"We'll go once you finish your chores."

"A'ight!"

Ms. Kai planted a kiss on Yaz's head before leaving with a smile on her face.

After the door closed, Yaz pulled Sir Jama out from under her bed and showed him the flyer. "Look! A circus Sir Jama! Do you think there is magic there?"

Sir Jama stared at the flyer. His lips turned upwards, his single white eye glistening. "Oh yes, Yasmin. I think there is more than just magic there. I cannot wait to see what it has to offer."

"You wanna come?!"

"Of course. I want to go wherever you are, child."

CHAPTER TWENTY-ONE

Trapped in the Circus

Brent popped one of his silver pills into his mouth as he sat on his bunk with Nix. They couped him up with two quiet jugglers, both of whom woke before the sun rose and fell asleep by the time the moon nestled over the trees. Brent spoke little with either of them as the train chugged along the countryside towards Siskin's Corner over the next couple days. Instead, he absorbed the stories, trying to catch wisps of truth. When those grew too strong, he turned his attention to the outside world.

As he watched the countryside pass by the window, stories wavered with intensity. It was hard to ignore the call of the dead on the landscape, begging for his attention, crying for a release. Brent placed his fingers to the glass, trying to call forth their stories. The train moved too fast for him to act, though.

I have a job to do, but I can't do it. I hope Caroline hasn't fully given up her duties.

Thinking of his old mentor left a strange sadness in Brent's heart. She'd screamed at him during their last encounter. He couldn't save her friend, Julietta, the Memory Painter and Fourth Mist Keeper, after being attacked by a Pool in the Library. She became a vessel for a Diabolo, like he had, but rather than helping her escape its clutches, he left her as an empty shell. Caroline blamed him, and despite Brent begging her forgiveness, it had been for naught.

He once thought that Caroline could be his confidant and friend in the Council. Now? He wasn't sure.

On the dawn of the third day, Brent woke to the train chugging into a field outside of Siskin's Corner after passing out with a story-riddled headache. He peered through the window, taking in the industrial town. Smoke gathered over the factory's steam stacks. In the distance, towers moved across the landscape.

His thoughts immediately went to Bria. Was she in one of those towers? Was she nearby?

The train's whistle blew, pulling Brent away from the window. With that signal, all the performers and workers left their rooms, moving like a well-oiled machine to get the carnival up and running. It was almost like its own form of magic; each worker erected the tents with ease, creating a world hidden amongst the trees where magic reigned and stories sang.

Brent limped from the train car with Nix at his heels. Hortense sat in her chair outside, injecting a silver fluid into her veins. As it entered her skin, she tilted her head back and sighed. The tattoos on her arms shimmered, moving in intricate patterns as if alive.

"Want any?" Hortense held up a vial.

Brent shook his head.

"It helps the magic be stronger. Good performance, y'know. Santiago likes it." Hortense waved the vial again.

"I can't. I mean...no." Brent scratched at his wrist. "It wouldn't be...no."

You're scared, the Diabolo taunted.

I don't want to lose control.

But it's such fun.

Go away.

"Suit yourself." Hortense chuckled to herself. Her tattoos moved with her laughter.

As Brent left Hortense, he noticed other performers sitting in circles and injecting themselves with similar vials. Stories of similar vices shone around the site.

"Brenty-Boy! My man!" Micca slammed a hand on Brent's back. "You done hiding away in your room like some hermit?"

"I wasn't being…I mean…I…"

"You moping about Bria?" Micca prodded.

Brent bowed his head.

"Of course you are. You're a lovesick sap. Always have been. I remember when you were too shy to tell her how you felt. Damn, those were some shitty days if you ask me." Micca frowned slightly. "But she'll be a'ight. She's a tough one. "

"Yeah, I know…" Brent scratched at the brand on his wrist, not daring to meet Micca's gaze.

"And once you find her, you stop dillydallying and ask to marry her already. It's ridiculous that the two of you are still beating around the bush about that."

"I—"

Micca poked Brent's forehead. "Don't give me that bullshite. You were gonna propose to her years ago. Stop waiting and just do it already!"

Brent rubbed his wrist again. "One thing at a time."

"Yeah, like you gotta get ready for the show so you stay on Santiago's good side!"

"I am—"

"You take any of the Silver Dew yet?"

"The what?"

"Silver Dew. The good drug. The stuff everyone has." Micca motioned to the fire-breathing performer sitting on the bench with a silver vial. "You see? Won't let me have none of it. Says it's cause I don't got magic."

"I...no." Brent looked away. "I don't need it."

"Santiago gives it to everyone. Makes 'em perform good or some shite."

"I can perform without it. I really don't...I already take a lot of...I mean...no thanks. I'm trying to be...I haven't even smoked recently. I can't risk it."

"Well, don't blame me if Santiago gives you shite. I just know everyone takes it." Micca shrugged. "Well, good luck tonight. Gotta go get off Santiago's shitlist...literally."

"Good luck."

Brent watched his friend leave. Once alone, he turned to help some workers set up a game booth. He smiled at them, then continued his work, placing the oddly shaped jars on the table and exchanging small talk. He watched their stories: an old acrobat who broke an ankle, a tightrope walker with vertigo, and a juggler who burned half their face. They all moved together in a confusing conglomerate gnawing at Brent's psyche.

The stories blended through the work, causing time to pass in a strange rhythmic beat. Workers spent most of the day constructing the carnival. The colors, the noises, the performers—all of them created a wonderland that would enchant any child. Brent immersed himself in the tasks, trying his best to cast aside his worries and focus on the night ahead of him.

Despite the chilled air, sweat battered Brent's forehead. He wiped it with his sleeve as he finished hammering in the last nail in the booth. He then hung a plush rabbit on the nail, a prize to be won, and bid the others goodbye.

As he left, Nix jumped from where she napped in the hay and joined him with a steady trot. Brent brushed his fingers over her head. *At least I have someone to lean on here.*

He walked with his head down over to the water pump at the edge of the site, far from the stories, the laughter, and the jeers. Silence. He yearned for silence. Yet the new brand on his arm tightened around him like a noose, reminding him he wasn't alone. For now, he still belonged to Santiago.

Of that much, Brent was certain.

He splashed water on his face. It'd been five days since the Guard captured Bria; he could only hope she had managed to fight. Perhaps she'd already escaped. He had to believe she was fighting her way through the towers, leading a rebellion, being the Forest Queen.

Brent raised his hand to the invisible wall, gazing out across the rail yard towards the industrial center of Siskin's Corner. Growing up in Newbird's Arm, he'd heard about Siskin, Aeterno, and many cities past the mountain ranges of his home. Once introduced to the tunnels, he could explore the world. But now, here he was, a prisoner to a magical carnival...trying to fight against powers beyond his control.

Trapped. Always trapped.

He was ready to escape and pave his own destiny.

Mist gathered around his fingers.

How could he escape? How could he find Bria?

How?

That was the word he always pondered.

What if he no longer asked how? What if he just...did?

He let the mist fall from his fingers as he took a step forward.

And another one.

And another.

And...

Pow!

Despite no clear barrier, it was as if he had hit a solid wall. He toppled backwards, hitting the ground. Nix barked behind him.

"Shite," he grumbled. The sun-shaped brand on his arm seared as if an electric current was wrapped around his tendons, locking him tight in place.

His sight blurred as he lay there. He had one other option that he hadn't wanted to try. The Mist Keeper's tunnels still held a weight of fear over him. Yet...could they break Santiago's magic?

He reached forward to a nearby tree root and tugged at it.

It didn't budge.

Cursing, Brent tried another one.

This time, it opened, but only a crack. Brent smiled, then stuck his hand through the crack. Within seconds, heat scorched through his arm. He cried out, then rolled onto his back, holding his arm close to his chest.

Guess that won't work.

Brent lay there, his chest rising and falling, in utter pain. Stories spun around his head. He struggled to focus again, but each tale proved as cumbersome as the next.

No. I'm here. Don't do this. Shite. He blinked a few more times.

A shadow entered his field of vision, draped in black, as he lay on the ground.

He squinted. "Caroline?"

"I think staying here is your safest option, Brent," the figure replied.

It sounded like Caroline. But he couldn't be certain.

"Why? I need to…Bria…she's…"

"You need to stay out of sight. It is for your own protection. Trust me."

"But—"

Then, with a blink of mist, she vanished.

Brent parsed through the stories in the air. His head spun; his heart raced.

I need…I need…shite. What do I need?

Maybe a bit of fluids to get your mind clear. The Diabolo cackled.

I'm not taking any of that fucking drug.

It'll give you strength to do what needs to be done.

No.

The Diabolo's cackling continued.

Go away!

He focused on what Caroline had said. Was it a warning? Why would she care?

Last time he saw her, she hollered at him; she called him useless, pathetic, and worthless. Why would she want to protect him?

Or was it a false warning?

An illusion?

They didn't call her the illusionist for nothing.

Brent hoisted himself off the ground with a groan, staring out at Siskin's Corner, past Santiago's invisible barrier.

He swore that in the distance, the sky flickered with yellow.

Or was it red?

HE WHO FEARS HORSES

The performance that night ended with a victory. Brent put together a wild tale about three sisters taking over the tyrannical rule of a ruthless king. Each character marched through the mist, and with their detailed faces and magic armor, the tale transported everyone to a world far away. The audience cheered, and when Brent returned to his seat in the green tent, he found a jar of tips waiting for him.

Brent counted the gold coins to himself. He'd never had so much money to his name; growing up, if he was lucky, his mom gave him one gold coin a week—enough to buy a loaf of bread if anyone dared sell to him. He saved for years but ended up giving most of it back to his mother and younger sister, Alexandria.

Now, he had enough in one jar to make them comfortable.

If this kept up, he might even find a small cabin in the woods, away from society, to hide with Bria...just like they dreamed.

Although the mere thought seemed preposterous.

Ms. Honey squeezed Brent's shoulder with a smile as they reentered the tent. "Fantastic as always! Mr. Santiago loves you!"

Brent shrugged and pocketed his coins. "I'm only telling a story."

"Yeah, but you've really got a way to charm the audience."

Brent flushed. Isn't this what he always dreamt of doing? Telling stories freely, making people smile?

Well, he wasn't free. That was the problem.

"I'm surprised you didn't take any of the Silver Dew," Ms. Honey said as they removed their wig.

"I...I don't want to. I'm...It wouldn't be good."

"It isn't that bad. Makes you touch base with your magic."

"Really, I'm fine." Brent wasn't about to explain the circumstances of his condition to Ms. Honey. The mere thought of tainting his head with some sort of drug, awakening the Diabolo inside him, caused a knot to form in his chest.

He would keep taking his pills, but all the substances that once made his head relax scared him.

As more performers piled into the tent, Brent took his leave to avoid their stories, joining Nix outside by the fence. The patrons left the carnival without a care, their stories whisking through the air. Brent kept his head down, hoping that he'd be unrecognizable without his purple suit and combed hair.

If anyone noticed him, they didn't say a word.

He didn't even wave to Micca and Timothée where they sat on a bench, hands clenched, smiles on their face. Brent half-grinned. They were an odd couple, but Brent was happy to see his long-time friend find someone who understood him.

Stories thickened around him as he strolled to the furthest edge of the carnival, beckoning to him, whispering his name. There was a deeper tug from these stories, like children crying.

Or the dead pleading.

They clawed at his psyche, suffocating his thoughts, more powerful than the Diabolo's thud on his forehead.

Groaning, Brent sat down on a nearby log and removed another silver pill from his pocket. He swallowed it and let the clarity wash over him for a moment.

Still, the stories pulsated more than usual. They called for him, rallying in the sky, breathing in the air. Why were they so loud? Had his performance been too much? It didn't feel like anything out of the ordinary.

He glanced around his surroundings. These were more than just history. The stories of the dead called to him, begging for a chance to be free.

Often, Brent forgot his true role as a Mist Keeper. Perhaps it was because of the way the Council behaved; they didn't act in the best interest of releasing souls. Rather, his focus was more on staying alive.

But being a Mist Keeper is about being more than just a god of Death. It's about helping the stories of the deceased survive. How could I forget that?

His Diabolo cackled. *Because you're a selfish, useless Mist Keeper.*

I never finished my training.

Useless.

I'm not even sure if these are stories that belong to the dead.

Well, use your head and figure it out!

Brent shook his head. He was a Mist Keeper, but how could one person oversee all of this? How many souls still screamed alone in the forest because Caroline or Alojzy or any of the other Mist Keepers had failed to find them?

He focused on the stories but watching them brought tears to his eyes. They had grown more vivid in the past few minutes, more alive than the forest and louder than the chugging gears of the nearby train. He saw a boy running across the hill, a hunter chasing down a rabbit, a woman building a nest in a tree. The stories captured his surroundings, not telling the single story of one person but of the wooded border of Siskin's corner.

No...not only the woods.

The more Brent watched, the more clearly he realized that he saw the story of Siskin's Corner taking form around him.

Each story knitted into the next. It reminded him of a time a year ago when the Sixth Mist Keeper, Malaika, found him in the woods and brought him in her airship to Spinoza. Brent released three souls at once. Their stories entwined together like a blanket. Surely that was no accident. He just needed to find the heart of all these stories.

This tapestry of stories weaved through the woods, and Brent used his invisible and mental tools to unravel the threads one by one. From the rabbit hunters to the children, all the stories came together mere steps away from the carnival, beyond the invisible barrier he couldn't cross. The hunter chased the rabbit beneath a nearby tree; the young boy played a game of come-find-me beneath the brush where he found the rabbit hiding; the tree-climber was none other than the boy's neighbor.

Each piece wove together. Every person, no matter the circumstances of their death, belonged to the fabric of humanity.

Some threads extended beyond the hill, pulsating within the industrial town at the foot of the hill. It didn't matter how far away the body lay; their stories brought the souls back. That much Brent knew.

But Caroline had shown him, long ago, how close he had to be to release a soul. She stuck her own hand into fire and grazed a dead woman's skin to introduce Brent to the Release, only for Brent to inherit the woman's hatred of cats.

But was that the only way?

Ningursu wants control. Nedo's story spoke, clear and direct, for the first time. *He doesn't want things to be easy, or stronger, or better. He wants to control the outcome.*

So there is another way? Brent asked.

Nedo did not reply.

What could go wrong? All Brent had to do was try.

He opened his palms to the truths of the hillside. The stories washed over him, and with a pull of semi-consciousness, he yanked a handful of souls along the stream of their stories and out of their Hells. It differed from times when he'd released each soul individually or when he eradicated Nedo. This time, the focus was on the everlasting stories; tranquility followed as the souls fled around him. A whirlwind of color, a heartbeat of death, and a moment of clarity encased him.

He was momentarily part of the world's story, and he would carry the burden of telling the stories of the dead.

His guard fell, and the Diabolo, deep in the confines of his mind, clawed at each tale.

Wrong choice.

Brent stumbled back. "Shite...shite," he breathed out. His mouth tasted of blood.

He couldn't control his body. While his mind faltered under the weight of the stories, the Diabolo pushed his consciousness down into darkness.

The hillside left his view, masked by fog.

He choked.

He tried to scream.

But he was falling...

Trembling...

Forgetting...

No! No! Stop! He lashed out. *My name is Brent Harley, and I just released souls from Hell. I am a fucking Mist Keeper. You need to stop this bullshite, Frankie! This is my mind!*

Yellow clouded his vision as the Diabolo cackled.

Stop it! He shook his head, trying to regain his footing. But he couldn't see or feel his body; he fell further into a dark abyss.

Falling...

Falling...

Falling...

And he hit the ground with a thud.

Still strong enough to knock back the Diabolo, Brent regained control of his body. He landed on his hands, but the impact still set tenderness through his arms and shoulders. The shock silenced the Diabolo.

"Shite..." Brent laughed and pressed his forehead into the dirt, allowing the stories to whisk him away like a dream.

Brent woke to Nix licking his face. The carnival's lights still danced in the distance, mingling with the stories. No one had noticed his collapse.

He hoisted himself up from the ground. Mist decorated the carnival. It contained no stories, no ghosts. Just pure, undeniable mist.

Brent reached forward to touch it. As he extended his fingers, the mist clasped his hand and tugged him forward into its embrace.

Brent fell again into the dirt. Fear stroked its fingers along his back. His first thoughts went to the Diabolo; had it gotten free again? Was he wrapped again in its misty grip?

No. I'm still here.

A voice boomed out, answering all of Brent's questions. "Brenton!"

Brent raised his head and stared through the mist. This voice didn't belong to the Diabolo.

No. He knew that voice.

"Brenton! Look at me!"

Gulping down fear, Brent turned. Hovering in the air with mist wrapped around what would have been his body was nothing other than Ningursu's skull. His white eye stared directly at Brent, his skin drooping to one side.

I didn't know he could float.

Brent squinted. He swore for a moment that a shadow held Ningursu's skull, but then the mist grew thicker, and he only saw the head.

"Nin-Ningursu!" Brent stammered. "What…how…how are you…you're floating!"

"What a god complex you have, dear boy. You couldn't stop to think about the repercussions of releasing that many souls at once. It attracts the wrong people, Brenton."

"You mean people like you?"

"The job of a Mist Keeper is to be invisible, not save the world!" Ningursu bellowed.

"Invisible? You're…you're manipulating the world!"

Ningursu snarled. "Enough with the tomfoolery, young man! It is time to end this!"

Brent crawled backwards with Nix on his heels. "You…you don't have any power here! You're…you're just a head! I'm not…I mean…you can't control me!"

"Stupid child. You don't even know the reach of my powers." Ningursu opened his mouth. A chain of mist poured from his jaw. It raced towards Brent and knocked him into a tree. "We can do this the easy way or the hard way."

Brent lifted his head, pushing away his fears and pulling at the seeds of courage in his stomach. "You should know by now that I don't…I don't go out without a fight."

"You are merely a boy."

"Yeah, but you're scared of me." Brent turned his attention to the tales whisking around Ningursu's head. They were vague, distant, but he had Nedo's story laced into his own soul. It told him a tale of a man with a passion, with a mission, only to return home with a fear. That same fear haunted him, even now, as a mere head.

Horses.

Brent smirked and gathered the mist on his fingertips, allowing the story to wash over him. "Once there was a man…who left his home in search of riches—"

"This is no time for stories, Brenton!" Ningursu hollered, sending another tendril of mist out of his mouth.

Brent lifted his hand. To his shock, he caught the ringlet of mist as if it were a piece of rope. He stared at it. *How did I do that?*

With a shrug, he laced the mist around his fingers, continuing his tale. "He thought he'd make a name for himself and promised his brother he'd return. But all he did was return with one thing...and that was fear of *them*."

"BRENTON!" Ningursu shouted again.

Brent ignored him, continuing to mold the mist like clay in his hands. "Nedo never understood why you were so fearful of them. I mean, really, Ningursu; they're just horses. What happened? You get kicked by one or something?"

Another wave of mist exploded from Ningursu's mouth, sending the head flying backwards into the dirt. As the head fell, Brent caught a whiff of horror from Ningursu. He smiled as the story revealed itself to the mist.

"Oh...I see. It kicked you and left you, didn't it? Your own horse abandoned you? I...that's...yeah, that's no fun. Sorry about that. I...you shouldn't be afraid of all horses, though. I mean...one bad person doesn't mean everyone's bad."

"You do not understand, Brenton. You have not seen what I have."

"I've seen enough. I...I'm not powerless against you!"

Brent turned the mist over in his hands. Out of them, he released a story of horses stampeding towards Ningursu. The ground rumbled. The horses whinnied.

And as the horses raced towards Ningursu, the mist thickened. Brent couldn't see in front of him, nor could he hear. All became white.

When it cleared, Ningursu had vanished. All that remained were hoof prints in the dirt.

Brent stared at the space where Ningursu had hovered, then at his own hands. What had happened? He'd created stories out of the mist for a while now...but never before had he used the mist to interact with the real world!

He closed his hands. The mist disappeared, the stories nothing more than a gentle hum around the carnival again.

This isn't possible. It's an illusion, nothing more.

Brent rose from his spot. His knees shook as he turned to face a handful of performers standing mere feet away from him, gawking in amazement.

"Oh, um, hi..." Brent shrunk as he spoke. "I, um...was practicing and—"

Mr. Santiago pushed through the crowd. "Brent!"

"I...I'm sorry. I mean...I...sorry." Brent winced, bracing for Mr. Santiago's fury.

"That was AMAZING!" He ran over and embraced Brent tight. "You, my boy, you're going to be rich! Rich!"

"I...um...but...I—"

"Rich!"

Before Brent knew what was happening, applause ripped through the performers. They surrounded him, brimming with excitement. Words of enthusiasm, of success, and of pride crossed before him. Even Lolli, the grouchy strong woman, offered a brief smile.

The stories tightened around Brent as he tried to focus. Every story suffocated him. Patches of black filled his vision. Everything spun.

Then his body hit the ground, and he was drifting again.

CHAPTER TWENTY-THREE

FALLING

Yaz fell.

Everything had happened so fast, she hadn't the time to react. Mr. Nasr and Ms. Kai took her to the circus with smiles on their lips and pep in their step. Yaz followed behind them with Sir Jama in her bag. She opened the bag just enough so Sir Jama could watch the circus. While he said little, the starting act caught Sir Jama's attention: a storyteller who created illusions out of thin air.

While Yaz marveled at the entire show, that storyteller stuck in her mind as well, even more than the dragon who ascended to the sky in pure glory. As she followed Mr. Nasr and Ms. Kai out of the tent, she kept thinking about what stories he held in his palms.

Her mind wandered, as did her feet, taking her far away from Mr. Nasr and Ms. Kai, like an invisible rope tugged her away from the carnival.

That rope guided her to the edge of the carnival, where the storyteller from the circus held his hands out to the woods. Mist gathered at his fingertips, then shot out as he stumbled to the ground.

She didn't know why she removed Sir Jama, but suddenly he was in her hands, beckoning her to confront the storyteller.

The storyteller woke as she approached and said Sir Jama's name.

He can see Sir Jama. Yaz held her breath. Sir Jama mentioned an evil storyteller. Was this man that storyteller? Yaz thought he seemed so nice...but was he responsible for Sir Jama's demise?

The storyteller didn't acknowledge Yaz, only Sir Jama.

And they argued like two warriors in battle.

Mist pummeled around them. The storyteller's eyes kept changing color. Even his face transformed with the passing mist.

As the mist thickened, the storyteller raised his hands, his voice echoing, his words confusing. With a single flick of his hand, the mist moved like a stampede of horses towards Yaz and Sir Jama. Beneath Yaz's feet, the ground rocked as if actual horses raced towards her.

Closer…

Closer…

Closer…

She screamed as the horses neared her. Sir Jama cursed at the top of his lungs.

Then the mist spun around them both, encasing Yaz in a blanket of white.

And she fell…

Down…

Down…

When she opened her eyes, she saw black instead of white. Her fingers remained locked around Sir Jama's head.

Yaz lurched forward. Had the storyteller kidnapped them? Where were they? What happened? The last thing she saw were the horses galloping towards her. Then mist. Then white. And she was falling.

What happened? Had the storyteller seen her?

Before Yaz said anything, Sir Jama unhinged his jaw, and a bright light flooded around them, riding on the back of the fog.

They had landed in a tunnel that extended deep into blackness. Stalactites dripped, and stalagmites pricked. Ghost-like individuals moved about the tunnel before vanishing.

She marveled. *I always knew ghosts were real.*

"There," Sir Jama whispered.

"Sir Jama? Are you a'ight?"

"I am fine, Yasmin. We are safe. I saved us," the head replied.

"You...saved us? From what? What happened?"

"Remember the evil storyteller I told you about? The flawed apprentice?"

Yaz nodded.

"You just met him."

"But he was so powerful! He created horses!" Yaz shrieked. "I didn't know you could create horses!"

"It was a powerful illusion from the mist. He has more control over it than I thought. We must reorganize with the other Mist Keepers to understand our full predicament. This is quite dangerous, dear Yasmin, quite dangerous."

"Am I able to help you?"

"Oh, dear Yasmin." Sir Jama pulled a lopsided smile. "You have already done so much. I would not have been able to get us here without you as my conduit."

"What? Where are we?" Yaz wracked her brain. Some of what Sir Jama said made little sense!

"We're in the Tunnels of the Mist Keepers...the magical network that allows us to transverse across the world. Now come. We must join with the others in haste."

Yaz paced in the dark cave. Sir Jama had her carry him through the tunnels to a dark cavern decorated by crystalized stones and dripping water. Throughout the stroll, he explained to her how she would join the Council of Mist Keepers. In due time, he promised, she would understand how. But she was important, and that was all that mattered.

Her stomach groaned with hunger. They hadn't given her much food. Without much to do, she was left listening to her stomach's complaints while watching the occasional bought of colorful mist surrounding Sir Jama's head.

Each time she opened her mouth to speak, it was as if a hand clasped her lips shut. Her throat tightened, and she swallowed her words.

I wish I had my skulls. Or my dolly. Why didn't I pack my dolly? She pouted to herself and picked at a nail. *I wonder if Mr. Nasr or Ms. Kai noticed? They might be happy to get rid of me.*

Footsteps pulled her from her thoughts. She squinted into the mist. Sir Jama still sat in the center of the room, but a figure approached him.

Yaz shot to her feet. Was it the evil storyteller? Had he followed them?

No.

Caroline, the woman in black, strode forward with poise, her melting face flickering in the light.

"Ah, Caroline," Sir Jama boomed. "Did you find the others?"

"Yes, sir. They shall be here in a moment," Caroline glanced at Yaz but didn't address her.

Sir Jama closed his one eye. "Excellent."

The pattering of more footsteps down the tunnel confirmed Caroline's statement.

A bird-like woman and a balding man emerged from down the path. Yaz stiffened. While she flinched at Caroline, these two were terrifying. Their eyes pierced the air, and when they looked at Yaz, she wanted to shrink into the mist just like Sir Jama.

They greeted Sir Jama with less excitement than Caroline. The man wore a garnet robe, while the woman bore a long dress beneath a petticoat, her hair combed back to the point of prestige. Yaz pulled at her own hair and frowned. She didn't look anywhere near as sophisticated as these Mist Keepers.

"It is wonderful to see all of you again. Our family will soon be whole again, and the terrors of this past year will end." Sir Jama smiled and turned to the newcomers. "Aelia, Alojzy, perhaps you know where the others are? Caroline has been little help."

The bird-like woman, Aelia, responded first. "Malaika vanished from Mert before the Battle of the Library even occurred. I tried to track her down, but it was for naught. She is erratic as ever."

"I would not be surprised if Tomás went to find her, the traitor," Alojzy spat.

"Most likely, that is the case," Aelia replied. "Jiang has been to Mert a few times, though, with his own updates; he has been trying his best to track down the droves of Diabolo for our army."

"Wonderful. And Julietta?" Sir Jama pressed.

Caroline spoke in a hoarse whisper, "Does it matter? She is gone."

Aelia glared at Caroline, then added, "It is of concern that we do not know where she is. Some of my contacts believe they saw her with Tomás, though."

"And you have inquired with the Mertoni Authorities to see if Tomás is staying with his old flame?" Sir Jama asked.

Yaz's attention darted between each of the Mist Keepers, trying her best to keep track of the conversation. She had no clue who or what they were talking about, but she didn't dare ask a question.

Living in the tower, she'd been in the middle of enough conversations to know when to blend into the wall. The constant barrage of questions, followed by both negative and affirmative responses, made her head spin. Why did Sir Jama talk like they were at war? Where was Mert? Who were all these other people?

At last, Sir Jama redirected his attention to Yaz. He smiled. "Ah, Yaz, I apologize. This must be a lot for you. Let me introduce my friends. This is Aelia, my apprentice from long ago, and Alojzy, Caroline's teacher from many years past. We're only a small part of the Council of Mist Keepers."

"That I am supposed to join?" Yaz asked.

"Correct. Smart girl. You learn quickly. Yes, you'll be number nine. And as our ninth member, you'll play a crucial role in helping us defeat the Evil Alchemist who has taken our Library. They led an army of powerful people into *our* home. The storyteller did nothing to stop them. But you, Yasmin...I see something special in you that will help us take control of this predicament. Do you not want to help your Sir Jama?" A twinkle filled Sir Jama's eye—one that reminded Yaz of Mr. Nasr when he was in a trance.

"I wanna help," Yaz mumbled.

"What was that?"

"I wanna help!"

"As I expected." Sir Jama raised his chin, grinning. "Alojzy, please prepare the accommodations for Yasmin and me. We will need a proper place to prepare."

Alojzy bowed. "Of course, sire."

"Accommodations? You mean I'm not going back to the tower?" Yaz asked.

"No. This is your home now," Sir Jama replied.

"But what about Ms. Kai and Mr. Nasr? And my dollies and—"

"That's a part of your petty past, Yasmin. The future is bright with me now."

Yaz glanced over her shoulder down the tunnel. She didn't even say goodbye to the people who had taken care of her. Despite everything, they gave her a good home. If they hadn't, where would she be now? Her mother couldn't take care of her; she would have ended up on the streets.

She at least owed Mr. Nasr and Ms. Kai a goodbye.

Didn't she?

"Remember, Yasmin," Sir Jama continued, "you said it yourself: Mr. Nasr and Ms. Kai weren't letting you have fun anymore. I'll treat you right."

"Really?" Yaz asked.

"Really."

Yaz bit her lip and glanced between Sir Jama and the other Mist Keepers. He hadn't lied to her yet; everything he'd said was true. There had been an evil storyteller. There was a Council of Mist Keepers. Why should she believe he was lying now?

"A'ight. I believe you."

Sir Jama beamed. "Perfect. While we prepare, I am sure you are hungry, aren't you, Yasmin?"

As if on cue, Yaz's stomach gurgled as she lifted Sir Jama from the ground.

"As I thought," Sir Jama laughed. "What do you want to eat?"

"Um..." Yaz pondered for a second. "Apple pie! Mr. Nasr and Ms. Kai never let me have apple pie!"

"Caroline! Go fetch your apprentice an apple pie!"

"Sir, that is not my—"

Sir Jama shot a glare at Caroline.

"Yes, sir. Sorry, sir."

One at a time, each Mist Keeper vanished down the tunnel, leaving Yaz alone once more with Sir Jama to save the world.

TRUE COLORS

Lex lost track of time. Professor Gratz visited her irregularly, sometimes with a red-headed Sister of the Order in tow, other times with a member of the Guard. The red-headed sister often tried to make small talk, but Lex had none of it. They were all the same.

No matter who conducted the experiments, they never told her what they were doing; they came in, pricked at her skin, tested her blood, and ran different tests. Sometimes her skin screamed as they dotted her arm with a silver liquid, and other times the room filled with a profuse mist. What were they doing? They never said.

At night, terrors haunted Lex. In some of them, she was nothing more than a little girl, traded between men and women with black slits for eyes. Other times, she had chains on her wrists, screaming and crying as her world deteriorated. But most often, she dreamt of the guard as they tore her away from safety.

At first, the guards in the nightmare were only faceless men.

As time moved on, they all became Toddle.

She woke up each time praying to a different god, goddess, or entity. Yet soon, her faith in the above wavered. Lex only held onto one belief and one belief alone: Garrett was okay.

Lex would sense if her son wasn't okay. He had to be, right?

He had to be.

Lex didn't know if it was night or day when Professor Gratz next arrived with Captain Carver. The scientist smiled, as she always did, extending an olive branch of friendliness. But the energy she shed held no trust. Only fear.

Still, Lex returned the smile, holding her teeth tight.

"How are you feeling today, Ms. Dray?" Professor Gratz asked.

"I am alive," Lex replied. "But I would feel better if I could see my son."

"Your son is safe, Ms. Dray. Do not fret."

"Then may I see him please?"

"I don't believe you are in a place to ask for favors, are you, Ms. Dray?" Captain Carver glared.

Professor Gratz raised her hand. "Captain Carver, please. She is in duress. She is allowed to ask questions."

"Fuck off, ya annoying broad!"

"Oh, it's no wonder Senator Cordova put me in charge of you. You have no respect."

The captain snarled.

If Lex wasn't Professor Gratz's prisoner, she might have admired how she shut down the captain. But her heart only continued to ache, and she repeated the same question as before: "Can I see my son?"

Professor Gratz frowned. "We must complete our tests so we can understand your disease."

"I told you, it's Phantom Rot. It's not contagious."

"We know, but the question is this: why do you have Phantom Rot in the first place? If you know why you have this disease, then our investigation may end."

Lex stared ahead. It'd be so easy to lie. To say it ran in her family or that black magic left her insides rotting. But she didn't speak. Instead, she bowed her head in defeat.

"It's okay if you don't quite know! Really! We'll find the answers." Professor Gratz took Lex's hand. "It's not your fault magic has assaulted you. That's those silly Magii's fault! We'll end it yet. We promise."

By the gods, I don't want you to end it, though! Lex wanted to scream. But she remained silent, complacent.

Had she always been this scared?

Captain Carver finally interjected, "You're forgetting the caveat, Professor."

"Ah yes. I apologize, Ms. Dray, but our tests have been inconclusive as to *what* triggers your rot. So we believe it is necessary for you to be cleansed of demons and magic prior to us continuing."

"Cleansed?" Lex's stomach turned. Memories tugged at her thoughts, demanding attention with their incessant and rude remarks. She shook them away. "Haven't you been cleansing me for the past week? I've been fasting, taking ice baths…humiliated. What more is there?"

"Levels Four and Five," Captain Carver remarked.

"Lashing out the demons and buzzing away their thoughts," Professor Gratz explained, "but because of your fragile circumstances, we shall skip the lashings. The Buzzing, though…yes, that should shake your body free of magic. It will give us a clean slate so we can help *cure* you."

"Why are you telling me all this?" Lex asked.

"Because we want to help you, dearest Lex. As your caregiver, it is my responsibility to be transparent, even if some parties"—Professor Gratz stole a glare at Captain Carver—"disagree."

Lex stared at her feet, refusing to meet the Professor's gaze. Her heart and mind fell into a state of rapid prayer, begging that someone there would protect her. She had to keep fighting for Garrett, even if it took every bit of her energy. "If I go willingly, can I see my family?"

Professor Gratz eyed the captain, then nodded.

With that simple affirmation, anxious excitement replaced her fearful dread. Lex's footsteps felt like feathers as she stood. The clouds had parted in her head, and even the chains Captain Carver applied to her wrists did not weigh her. Each step bore no consequence.

Captain Carver and Professor Gratz led her up the stairwell to the chamber beneath the tower's steel Year Glass. A single white bed, with straps on both sides and a clanking metal helmet hanging over it, waited in the room. Heat passed over Lex's face as she walked through the doorway.

Why did it all feel familiar?

It was like reentering a dream. Hazy. Dreary. All with a hint of memory.

Professor Gratz motioned for Lex to sit in the chair by the wall. "We'll start with a weak buzzing, just enough to rid the magic from your mind and soul. If we must go more extreme, we shall. But not yet. Not yet."

Lex took a seat in the chair. Vertigo seeped into her vision. The room spun.

Hadn't she sat here years ago in Knoll? Wasn't she just a little girl then? The shadows of guards stood over her, one with a pair of shears, and they cut away at her long locks, just like Professor Gratz sheared her head now.

The hair fell like snow upon the ground.

Why? she wondered then.

She wondered now.

Perhaps it had never happened; perhaps it was a figment of her imagination.

But she had been a prisoner for years.

Why?

Why couldn't she remember?

As they led her to the bed and placed the metal hat on her head, the question screamed louder.

Why did they take her?

Why did she spend her life running?

Why did she have Phantom Rot?

The questions continued to spin as the hat buzzed.

Was she a child now, waking from a long dream beneath an electric helmet?

Was everything else but a dream?

Who was she?

It didn't matter. The buzzing in her ears grew. Her head seared.

And a fog washed over her.

The forest moved past the train windows in a blur. Lex stared out, pressing her fingers to the glass before turning to the faceless woman with an aura of red coasting over her face.

"Mama?" she asked. "Where are we going?"

"Someplace better," the faceless woman replied.

Lex screamed as electricity coursed through her body. Her mouth tasted of blood.

Mama walked her across a field, far away from the train tracks.

Two figures approached them from the fog. Once again, faceless, but she could see the collection of tools and trinkets hanging from their waists.

"My daughter...she is ill. It is too much for me to handle. Can you help me?" Mama told the stranger.

Lex looked at the strangers. The color purple blocked their faces, coating their bodies in an eerie aura that wreaked of deception.

The shorter stranger chuckled, full and hearty. "I can rid your daughter of her demons."

"What is the cost?"

"One hundred gold for my services."

"Mama?" Lex pulled at her faceless mother's sleeve. "I told you I'm not sick. I like seeing the colors!"

Her mother didn't reply, only pulling out a pouch of gold and handing it to the stranger.

Spots covered Lex's vision. She couldn't breathe. She couldn't see.

Except for a rainbow of colors performing somersaults around the room.

At the top of the stairs to the basement, the taller stranger turned to Mama. "If this doesn't work, we'll need to take more drastic measures."

"I understand."

Lex asked, "What's happening, Mama?"

"We're going to make you better, so no one dares to harm you again. Okie-doke?"

"Okie-doke..."

Color didn't fill the basement. All was dark. Mama waited on the stairs, watching as the faceless stranger led Lex down the steps. A chair sat, waiting, with a crown of wires hanging above, producing an odd electric hum.

"Sit," the stranger ordered.

Lex shook her head. The stranger's aura had turned black in the dim candlelight.

"Elexis, do as she says!" Mama ordered.

"I don't want to! I'm not sick!"

Lex's eyes fluttered open. Spots of purples, reds, and grays caught her vision. She raised her hand up to block the light, catching sight of black and blue bruises on her fingers. Her veins lay visible on her translucent skin.

Someone moved about the room, but she didn't have the energy to lift her head. She wanted to sleep again, to be wrapped in a blanket of dreamless nights.

But the colors invaded her eyes. If she slept, would the glow disappear?

The person in the room moved. Bronze pulsated around their body, almost like a ghostly mist.

"Lex, love, it's me." Toddle knelt beside her and took her hand. "You're a'ight now."

"Where's Garrett?" She blinked, squinting towards the other side of the room. "I want to see Garrett. They said I could see Garrett."

"They said you wanted your family. I'm here now, Lex. Don't worry."

Toddle reached for her cheek, but Lex pushed him back. "I didn't want to see you! Not after everything—"

"I'm trying to protect you and Garrett!"

"That's what you always say!" Lex sat up slightly. Her hands trembled, tears streaking down her face. "You always say that, but look at me, Toddle! Look at me! And where's our son? Have you found him? You haven't even visited me!"

"It's more complicated than that, Lex."

"Is it? Don't talk to me like I am a confounded child. I'm not!"

"Lex," Toddle begged.

She withdrew. "Leave me alone, Toddle. If you are trying to protect us, find our son. I can take care of myself, but our son can't. Find him."

"I wouldn't know how..."

Lex stared. "Why would you think that's the appropriate response?"

"It's the truth. Isn't that what you want?"

"He's your son! Find. Him."

The color vibrating from his skin turned from bronze to a putrid gray as Toddle spoke. "I've searched...but it isn't like they're really giving me a lot of free rein or nothing."

"Bull."

Todd sighed. "Fine...fine. I'll...I'll try."

"Do not try, Toddle. Do."

Lex closed her eyes. Her headache battered her temples, leaving her with only a subtle desire to sleep. She did not say another word, listening as Toddle whispered affirmations of love and promise before leaving the room.

She wasn't sure she could believe him anymore.

Especially now that she understood the true colors of his aura.

AMPUTATED

Bria remembered the pain.

It shot through her arm, up her body, and rippled through her like electric currents.

She remembered falling.

The aching of her body against the ground.

She even remembered voices as they spoke above her.

They spoke nonsense.

When she opened her eyes a few times, all she saw were shadows.

Then came the gag to her mouth, the burning of whiskey, the feeling of leather on her arms.

But she still couldn't see. Her head kept spinning.

Only a few sentences made any sense as she writhed and pleaded for freedom.

"She's septic."

"Is it worth saving her?"

"She's so young."

"You know who this is, right? *Rhodana*."

"That's a myth."

Bria tried to wake, but each time she dared, sleep grabbed her and pulled her back into its embrace.

She dreamt of Brent, Nix, her father, Mr. West, and her grandmama. They were mere steps away from her, calling her name. Would it be so bad to go to sleep forever? To forget the weight of Rhodana, of her mother's attempt to suffocate her magic, and of the parties trying to use her…or destroy her? Would it be so bad to concede?

She'd be one with the earth again, finally at peace.

But she only slept, woken by a trickle of light through her eyelids and a burning sensation on her right arm. She blinked a few times and glanced to her left, where a woman crouched beside her. The woman applied a topical ointment to Bria's upper arm, humming to herself.

"Where…" Bria choked.

The woman looked up, a wide smile filling her round face. "Oh, good! You're awake!"

Bria tried again. "Where…"

"Shhh. Shh. Relax. My name is Hue. I've been your doctor here the past week."

"Where…"

"You're safe here." Hue placed a hand on Bria's forehead. "You had quite the ride in the tower, didn't you? Your friend, Marisol, told me all about it."

"But…where?" Bria repeated.

"Knoll's Pit."

"But…"

"Relax. You'll understand soon. Let's get some food into you, though. You need it. Stay here." Hue rose, her long black hair falling like a curtain behind her as she left.

Bria sank into the cot and looked around the room. She lay alone in a small ward beneath a dilapidated ceiling. Cots lined the walls with decrepit machinery and old vials on the far side of the room. The intravenous line in her left arm tugged at her, a clear fluid dripping into her veins. She reached over to itch where the needle dug into her skin.

But upon lifting her right arm, she nearly screamed.

Her shoulder, her upper arm—they moved fine. But beneath it, her lower arm and hand had disappeared.

"Wha…what?" Bria choked on bile in her throat.

Nausea pushed her onto her side, and she hurled over the edge of the cot.

She continued gagging as footsteps approached.

"Well, that's riveting," a new voice said.

Bria glanced over her shoulder. A woman in a red jumpsuit carried a bowl of soup and a glass of water. A black stamp garnished her cheek, blending in with her already dark skin.

"My…my arm," Bria squeaked.

"Yes, it's gone. Hue had to remove it."

"But…my…I…" Bria tried to sit up in the bed. Waves of vertigo wrapped around her.

"Don't," the woman ordered as she dropped a tray of food on the end table. "Save your strength."

Bria sank back into the bed, trembling. The woman arranged a few pillows behind Bria, then sat on the side of the bed with a bowl of porridge.

"Eat." She spooned a wad of the gruel into Bria's mouth.

It didn't matter that the food tasted like sawdust. Bria inhaled each spoonful, her hunger clawing at her like a beast. A bit of strength returned with each swallow.

Bria tried to grab the spoon from the woman after the second wad but caught herself off balance. Without her right hand, she struggled to balance the bowl, and it nearly toppled from the bed twice before she gave up and succumbed to being spoon fed.

As Bria ate, she tore her gaze away from the woman and out the window, accepting each spoonful of gruel with a grumble. A dusty morning light nestled over the dirt road. Decrepit buildings lined the street where vagrants marched in different colored jumpsuits. They walked with an emptiness in their gaze and black stamps garnishing different parts of their bodies: shoulders, wrists, necks, and cheeks.

If I'm in Knoll's Pit, it's far larger than I realized. This is more like a miniature city.

Bria swallowed another bite of gruel. She didn't want to believe she ended up in the Pit, despite everything. But the signs were there; the Black Stamp ravaged the civilians, the homes knew no cleanliness, and towers cast shadows in the distance.

So much for freedom.

"You really got yourself messed up here, didn't you?" the woman said after Bria polished off the bowl. "Captain Palmer's not one to fuck with. You've got three broken ribs, bruised up face, and now no hand. Hue fixed you up well, but it was a struggle there for a bit."

"But...how did I get here?" Bria asked.

"According to your friend Marisol, you took control of the tower. They found you unconscious in the engine room after the tower just sort of...stopped. Got you on a gurney and brought you here." The woman took the bowl from Bria and raised both her eyebrows. "So I'm curious...how did you do it?"

"Do what?"

"Take the tower."

"I…um…" Bria shook her head. "I don't know."

"You're among friends here."

"Am I…am I actually in…am I in the Pit? I…I was trying to escape…and you said I did and…" Bria choked on her words.

"Knoll's Pit doesn't operate like the rest of Rosada. We're our own city, in a way. Trust me, you are safest here."

Bria stared at the woman. Could Bria trust her? Could she trust any of them? If Brent was by her side, he would know in an instant. Instead, she had to trust her own gut.

The woman seemed to have no real reason to hurt her. There was a familiar kindness in her dark eyes, despite the scowl on her lips.

"We saved your life, girl. I think you owe us some sort of explanation."

"I…"

"Start with your name."

Bria stared hard at the woman. "It's…um…Rho—"

"Don't lie to me. *Rhodana* isn't your name. That's just an alias, a story children sing while playing. Ridiculous, if you ask me." The woman scoffed.

She paused, pondering whether to give her real name to the woman.

Did it matter if she did? The Guard already plastered her face across Rosada.

"Bria."

"Bria," the woman recited. "Now that's better. Much better."

Bria eyed the woman. The black stamp on her face glistened, a constant visible reminder of her vagrancy.

The woman continued, "Now tell me, Bria. How did you destroy that tower? Those towers are impenetrable weapons. So what did you do?"

"Do we have to do this right now? I...I lost my..." Her throat tightened. She couldn't even look at her right side or so much as think the words.

"You owe us, girl."

Bria closed her eyes, pondering what to say. She could easily tell this woman that she was the terrorist of New-bird's Arm. But what if the Order was watching? How likely was it that a vagrant might overhear and turn her over to the Guard? Wouldn't someone jump on the chance for freedom?

"I don't know if I can trust you," Bria whispered.

"You can, though."

"How do I know you won't tell the Guard?"

"What would that do for me? I'm here for life. Doesn't matter what I say to them." She pointed to the brand on her face. "This won't ever go away."

Bria held back on her words for a moment. The woman was clearly smart, undeterred, and unafraid. One wrong move and Bria worried her life in the Pit might be permanent, too.

She settled on a half-truth. "I used my magic to break out of the cells and destroy the prison. That's all."

"Magic. Hmph." The woman glowered at her. "You must be quite strong if you could do all that."

Bria shrugged, wincing at the delicacy of her right side, before sinking back into the pillows. Her head pounded again with phantom pains shooting from her missing right hand into her shoulder.

The woman rose. "You must have more to tell. But I won't press further until you're better. Get some rest. Sleep. You'll feel better soon."

"I'm fine."

"You lost your arm."

"I'll be fine then."

"That's a lie."

"What—"

"I say it, too. It's an easy phrase to say. You're able to convince yourself that everything is okay. But it isn't, is it?" The woman turned. "Get some rest."

"Wait!" Bria lifted her head again. "Who are you?"

The woman stared for a moment before saying, "You can call me Lana."

And without further explanation, Lana left, leaving
Bria alone with her thoughts.

CHAPTER TWENTY-SIX

LIQUID CONVICTION

The next few performances in Siskin's Corner blended into each other. Brent woke up, helped prepare the tents, then found his place in the Green Tent, where Ms. Honey helped him get ready. His stories came naturally, and despite multiple performers offering him a hit of the narcotic they injected into their veins, Brent declined. He could create stories without a thought.

And now, it seemed, he could do more.

Ningursu haunted his thoughts day and night. The story of the horses pounding on the ground continued to rock his footsteps. Had he actually made the illusions...something more?

Or was it a mere game with the mist? A ploy?

He was the only one to bear witness to its true prowess. Sure, the other performers watched in awe, but what did they see? Did they only witness a story of battle? Or did they feel the horses? No one quite said, instead helping him back to his room on the train. When he came to his senses the next morning, only his skinned knees provided reassurance that he wasn't going crazy.

So as the days passed, Brent performed. He made small talk with Ms. Honey, Hortense, and Timothée. The strong woman, Lolli, glowered at him whenever she passed, often then disappearing into the heart of Mr. Santiago's cabin. Brent would catch whiffs of their romance in the hallways, but he trained his eye not to look.

After each performance, Mr. Santiago left a pile of coins on Brent's bed. He'd never imagined collecting so much money for himself, and he sat in his lower bunk with Nix curled against his leg, counting each coin thrice.

Brent knew the game Mr. Santiago played. He gave coins to his performers to satisfy them, keep them happy, make them believe they wanted to be here. But it was just an illusion.

Brent collapsed on the bed after his third performance in Siskin and stared at the ceiling. His head roared from the stories. Each audience member cheered, and their stories unraveled. He saw the tales of women in heavy coats shopping in the capital, of men in pristine suits searching for shoes, and of children in summer shorts playing in the streets. While the mundane stories blended, sometimes one stuck out, and it took all of Brent's willpower not to get absorbed.

Now, all Brent wanted was to sleep.

He unlaced his boots and undressed while the room was empty, tossing his sparkly purple coat to the floor and dressing down into his pajama pants. Nix lay across his dirty clothes, watching Brent as he picked up a gazette from one of his bunkmates' beds and skimmed through it. His heart pounded, searching for any sign of Bria.

After scouring the gazette, he paused on one article deep in the pages. Only a paragraph, but it was enough to make his stomach churn.

A tower scheduled to return to Knoll a week ago has yet to resurface after being seen in the Necrowood. Captain Palmer, leader of Squadron 3678 and herald of Tower A-89, emerged from the forest disoriented and bloodied. Tower A-89 remains missing.

Brent's heart twisted—though whether with relief or terror, he wasn't sure. If only his magic allowed him to pull stories out of print, read into the details, and find the truth. But the gazette wasn't a novel; it only provided the facts.

Well, at least those sanctioned by the government.

Brent placed the gazette back on the bed just as the door to his room slid open. He turned, covering his chest with his hands.

"What're you doing? You've got the flattest chest ever," Micca scoffed as he entered the room, carrying a bottle of whiskey.

"I...um..." Brent lowered his arms. For a moment, he *was* a woman surprised by an intruder entering her bathroom. But the story faded from his mind at once, leaving him standing there face-to-face with Micca.

"Eh, whatever. At least you got pants on this time. Though I don't mind seeing that either." Micca winked.

Brent ignored him. "What do you want?"

"What? I can't come see my best buddy." Micca waltzed over and threw an arm around Brent's shoulder. "We were best buds, weren't we, back in Newbird's Arm? Pfft. *Newbird*. What type of name is that? Birds don't got arms!"

"Aren't birds' arms their wings?"

"Then shouldn't it be Newbird's Wing?"

"Point," Brent laughed, whiffs of Micca's stories infecting his persona. As a wave of desire for the whiskey washed over Brent, he shrugged Micca's arm away and shook his head.

"We missed you down at the celebration thing, Brent. Timothée sat in the dunk tank for a bit, and he exploded with color when someone hit his target!" Micca spun in a circle before sitting on the floor. "It was a world of fun, y'know."

"Yeah, well, I'm tired." *And I had to get away from the stories.*

"Eh, you've gotten boring. No smoking, no silver dew...you're an old man now." Micca nudged Brent. "Well, no matter, I got you some whiskey! You should celebrate. You're gonna be rich with how much Santiago fondles his piglet over you."

"That's not an image I want."

"C'mon, Brenty-Boy! One drink! Like old times. Remember? We used to drink by that disgusting fountain back home, and you made up stories about people that made shite sense? That was such fun." Micca shook Brent's arm. "We should be doing that still. Not this...not this bullshite! C'mon, man. C'mon!"

Brent pulled on his shirt and took the bottle of whiskey. He rolled it over in his hand.

The Diabolo whispered, *Drink it.*

I can't.

You want to, though.

Brent stared at the bottle. One drink wouldn't do any harm, would it?

He took a swig and passed it back to Micca, gagging at the taste. Almost at once, the liquor polished his mind with aplomb and solace.

Micca took another gulp of the whiskey and collapsed onto one of the bunks. "Y'know, I used to joke we'd end up someplace like this. Both of us, running away with the circus. Didn't think I'd find Timothée or nothing..."

"I haven't seen you with Timothée lately."

"He's been kind of a twat lately. I dunno, busy running around doing things for Santiago and shite. Doesn't wanna talk much or nothing. Like, c'mon mate, if you don't wanna be with me anymore, just say it. Not like we been committed to each other for long or nothing. I only met him like a month ago or something, so it won't break my heart if he don't like me anymore." Micca sighed. "You're so lucky to have found your soulmate."

"Soulmate?" Brent scoffed. "I don't believe in that shite."

"Eh, well, I like the idea of it. That someone is meant for me. No matter how fucked up in the head...they'll love me. You said you went to hell and back, and Bria was still there. If that ain't a soulmate, I dunno what is. You two are stuck together like two magnets. Sometimes you just face the wrong way, and...bam! You get thrown apart. But you come back together, and that's so sweet to me."

"She's my constant. But I mean, we just...we've been through a lot and...I mean..." Brent trailed off, eyeing the whiskey again as panic trembled through his core.

"You gotta marry her already, man."

"Huh?"

"Marry her. You were going to, back before the whole Jemma bullshite or whatever. Just ask her already."

"It's not the right time..." Brent scratched at his brand.

"Well, when is the right time? Think about it! You've got all this bullshite going on or whatever it is. Like she turned herself into Knoll, and you're in a circus. It ain't gonna change much! Just ask her. She'll say yes."

"First, I have to find her!" Brent's voice carried louder than he intended. "She could be dead!"

"Beebelle? Dead? Nah. You'd know."

Brent didn't know what Micca intended by that, but he was right. He would feel her story reverberate through the earth if she died. It would destroy every other tale, all of them replaced only with the song of Rhodana the Forest Queen.

His forest queen.

Brent fidgeted with the edge of his shirt. "I'm worried is all. I mean...I just don't know what happened...and there is that missing tower or...or something..."

"Yeah, well, don't worry much, a'ight? You'll find her. Then you marry her."

"Yeah, I know. I just...I..."

"Just do it. Ask her the moment you see her next time."

"Might not be the right time."

"Well, soon. Otherwise, I'll go do it for you." Micca winked.

They continued circumnavigating the topic of marriage for a time while Micca poured two more glasses of whiskey. A false sense of euphoria wrapped its arms around Brent, whisking him away into a misleading reality. A haze entered his vision, blocking all the negatives of the world. He thought of Bria, and he laughed loud, the guffaw rising in the center of his stomach.

Micca was right. He needed to ask for Bria's hand in marriage. He loved her more than anything, and as much as Bria would tell him it was ridiculous, he would risk his life to save her.

Who was he kidding? She would save him first.

"I'm thinking," Brent slurred, waving his hand through the mist. "Maybe I'll go ride off on...you know...the dragon. The dragon thing. The thing that belongs to Santiago. Ride off into the sunset and, you know...I mean...Bria and me. We would...I mean...I mean..." He started laughing, unable to finish the sentence.

"Where'd you go?" Micca rolled over on the bed, his brown hair floating in his face.

"The sun. Or maybe the moon. Or both." Brent closed his eyes. "The universe. We'll fly to the end of the universe, and we won't look back."

Rose-colored glasses and spinning laughter marked the evening. Brent and Micca laughed, drinking and bantering just like old times. In a drunken stupor, they talked about their past, laughing over old school jokes and childhood melodies. Micca pulled out his army of tin wind-up toys, set them running in circles around the cabin, and threw out wild theories about how the "little fellas" could destroy the Order. Brent laughed with liquid amusement, supporting his friend's endeavors, before diving into his own outlandish tales. Filters gone, emotions unleashed, Brent flitted between happiness and despair, unable to understand the function of his legs as he watched stories spin around the room. With each passing moment, he let his mind fall deeper into the stories' embrace, confusing shadows with acrobats and Micca with a flying donkey. Brent ranted about Bria as if she were a goddess in a way that he knew would cause her to flush in embarrassment. He didn't care. He let the alcohol whisk over him.

Until he lay on the floor shouting about his inability to walk.

The door slid open. Timothée slinked in, a hearty smile on their lips. "So this is where you went off to, eh Micca?"

"Timmy!" Micca crawled to his lover's feet and hugged him around the ankles. "I missed you. You keep being distant and not saying things. You were gone!"

"Told you I was dealing with Zephyr."

"But I had to drink with Brent! You know what Brent does? That!" Micca motioned to Brent.

Brent cocked his eyebrow, only to realize he lay with his legs pressed against the wall, his arms outstretched on the floor like a bird.

"I think you both had too much to drink. C'mon." Timothée hoisted Micca off the ground and positioned him over their shoulder. "You should get some sleep too, Brent. We got an early morning tomorrow."

Brent grunted and pulled himself onto his bed beside Nix. His eyes shut with the door.

Dreams started almost immediately. His head spun. His mind wandered. The Diabolo called for him.

She's gone...

She's gone...

You'll never find her...

Brent woke with a jolt, the front of his head searing. He brought his knees to his forehead and produced a wheeze reminiscent of an elephant. He had to have faith; in both Bria and himself.

I've gotten so used to being near her. But we're too separate people. If she can fight, so can I. We'll find each other again…it's not like we're that discreet.

To his shock, the Diabolo didn't reply.

Brent pushed himself off the bed, taking slow steps over to the pitcher of water by the door. His knees and feet trembled with every step, only for him to jump at a sharp pain entering his foot.

"Fuck!"

A piece of glass from the broken whiskey bottle had cut into his foot. He picked it up, wincing, before gathering a cup in his hand and taking a long gulp of water.

You're okay. You're okay. Breathe. He inhaled again. *Can't do much about anything now.*

He settled back onto his bed and pressed the back of his head to the wall. Dreams of Bria already filled his eyes.

Only for Mr. Santiago's shouts to stop him from falling back to sleep.

"EVERYONE OUT. NOW!"

Brent groaned and climbed onto the bed again. Mr. Santiago waited in the hallway, marching up and down the train car, his nose pointed and eyes narrow. He passed a glare from one person to the next, nostrils flaring, mouth quivering in utter disgust. Lolli marched beside him, arms crossed, a perfect minion to whatever Mr. Santiago had up his sleeve.

The sun-shaped brand on Brent's forearm burned as the ringmaster walked past him.

"I don't tolerate theft lightly." Mr. Santiago glared at the performers. "So, let's just be honest now, why don't we, hm? Who stole my liquor?"

No one spoke. Brent's stomach churned as he glanced down the aisle. Micca leaned against Timothée, jaw slack, half awake.

Mr. Santiago continued down the row. "Was it you, George?" he spat at a graying old man. The man winced and looked away. "No, didn't think so. You ain't got the guts." Mr. Santiago continued pacing. Each question came with a hard point-and-fact, causing the recipient of his lambast to quiver in fear. Lolli proved to be the strength of the interrogation, holding a few of the performers by the collars of their shirts, daring to punch them in the face.

This isn't the first time... Brent blinked away a few stories. Mr. Santiago had roamed these halls on more than one occasion, shouting over minuscule "crimes," as he so decreed. He ran the circus with fear, branding those threatening to run. This was no colorful paradise; this was a prison on wheels.

Mr. Santiago stopped in front of Micca. "Was it you, Mr. Fein? This wouldn't be the first time ya stole from my liquor cabinet."

Micca chuckled and threw back his head, still leaning on Timothée's side. "So what if it was me? What'cha gonna do about it?"

Lolli grabbed Micca by the collar of his shirt, despite Timothée's screams, and led him over to the car door. "We can throw you out there!"

"It ain't even moving!"

"It can be!" she hissed.

Mr. Santiago stopped Lolli. "What say you, Mr. Fein? Did you steal it? I've had just about enough of you and your vagrant ways. I can send you back to the Pit from whence you came if you like that. Or worse. Hm?"

Micca opened his mouth. Timothée gawked in shock.

Courage swooped into Brent's soul. He snuck back into his bedroom where the broken whiskey bottle lay, scooped it up in his hands, then reemerged into the hallway. Confidence budding, he stared down at Mr. Santiago. "Sir!"

Mr. Santiago pivoted. "Please don't come to the aid of your friend. I've seen the two of you spending time together; it ain't worth it."

"But he didn't steal it…" Brent held out shards from the bottle. "I did."

Manure Duty

Mr. Santiago assigned Brent manure duty after yelling at him for a good five minutes about his absolute disgust. His star performer stole from him! Brent held his breath, anticipating a beating reminiscent of Captain Carver, but no such onslaught occurred. What came next was far worse, though: without a beat, Mr. Santiago glared right at Brent and said, "Your contract has been extended."

No elaboration followed. Instead, he dragged Brent to the back of the car to spend the morning shoveling manure.

Brent stayed quiet in his corner of the husbandry car, holding his breath as each pile of dung hit the bucket. The laborers bickered behind him. *Focus on your favorite smell,* he recalled Caroline telling him during the early days of his apprenticeship. *Keep it right in your mind. That is your essence of death.*

So, Brent imagined the smell of the swamp, watching Bria surrounded by the forest, commanding it with a mere flick of her fingers. It was easy to get lost in the story, but soon the tales in the husbandry car jabbed at him, whisking him away to years of animal dung.

For years, laborers of all shapes and sizes shoveled away manure, demoted from classy performers to mere slaves. Death and wealth offered a path to escape; otherwise, the dung surrounded them for years.

"We need fresh labor like ya, y'know," an old man sat on the crate beside Brent. "I've been working here for Mr. Santiago for almost my whole life. Used to be an acrobat, but then I broke my ankle, and Santiago threw a damn fit. Gave me an option: get better or start shoveling doo. Guess I'm shoveling doo now."

Brent stopped and glanced at the old man. "You were an acrobat?"

"Ay. Was a long time ago."

"But Mr. Santiago—"

"You were gonna say he's younger than me, eh? Used to think he and his father looked the same, but nah, he's the same man. Guess magic's a fickle thing. He's got some years under his belt and all. Think that's why he gets away with running this thing. Some deal with the guard or something."

Brent's eyes widened. *He's one of Kek's immortals. Damn bastard.*

"Ain't ever seen him age a day. Wish I could get ahold of whatever fancy-schmancy elixir he uses…but it ain't with his liquor or nothing. Trust me, I looked." The man winked. "I'm sure I got some trapezes and twists in me, I bet, but I don't think I wanna try. Will probably break something or other."

"So you're stuck here shoveling shite?" Brent watched as the old man leaned back.

"Ay. Hard to break the bond with Mr. Santiago less you got the money or something." The man picked up his shovel. "Don't mind it. Gives me a warm bed and such, but sometimes I dream of a bit more. Just, y'know, to enjoy myself a bit before Death comes knocking."

Brent scratched at the sun-shaped brand on his arm. It stung as he dug into the skin, retaining its control over his location at all costs. The old acrobat was just like the other three individuals shoveling away debris and animal feces: stuck. Brent had landed himself in a prison once again: sure, he could make his own money and do what he loved, but just because he was an animal performing tricks didn't mean he was happy.

He moved towards the cage where Zephyr, the dragon, slept curled up in a ball, her silver eyes flinching every few moments as Brent shuffled around her. Mist pooled from her pores, and with each breath, Brent drew on the edges of the beast's story. They branded her just like him, a sun-shaped scar at the bridge of her nose.

Brent cleaned the area around her, piling the dragon dung in the corner, watching her with the same intensity as her own stare. There was something different about the dragon compared to the other animals. Sentient.

After placing the shovel down, he knelt on the floor beside the dragon and extended his palm. The beast gently brought her snout to his skin and pressed into it, her eyes shutting. Her skin was smooth, her scales pulsing with heat. The mist bound everyone, but more than anything, it bound the dragons to Mist Keepers. He saw her story—and not just her story, but thousands of years of stories about dragons soaring through the sky, defending those who needed it most. The dragon shared a continuous story. It was one that Brent could not even fathom.

But he tried.

He sank into the story, letting its song swarm around his head. It ate at his thoughts, and in those few moments, he was nothing more than a dragon, soaring.

A beast in the air,

Flying,

Flying,

Flying free.

Coated in mist, a plume of smoke,

It follows it,

Down.

Down.

Down.

A metallic beast runs across the mountains,

Chug,

Chug,

Chug.

The sky beast descends,

An introduction.

A landing.

On the tracks.

Crash,

Crash.

Crash!

The beast awakens,

Dark.

Alone.

Cold.

Caged.

A man in gold walks forward.

A whip in hand.

Crack.

Snap.

Crack!

The beast screamed.

Then fell to sleep.

Awoken again, decked in glistening golds,

Forced to fly,

A broken wing unfolds.

Cheers,

Lights,

Shouting,

Falling.

Fall.

It shrieked and spiraled down.

Smoke pouring from its skin.

Teeth bared.

Eyes narrow.

Down.

Down.

Down.

A gunshot.

Another wound.

The man in gold returned

To prey on the beast again.

Brent gasped as he pulled himself out of the dragon's story, still trying to understand what happened. It wasn't as vivid as a human's story, but it was there, masked in the confusion of a beast over a man.

Brent roared as if a beast, then covered his mouth, counting down and reciting his name before meeting Zephyr's sad stare. "So he didn't just capture you? He maimed you...made you...made you fragile to mold you."

Zephyr closed her eyes, seeming to nod.

Brent backed away, his heart breaking not just for this poor dragon but for the men shoveling manure and for all those held prisoner by Mr. Santiago's greed. *Mr. Santiago doesn't want Zephyr to fly. He doesn't give her free movement. Why?*

He glanced at the sun-shaped brand. Thoughts of flight and dreams of soaring bubbled at the top of his thoughts. *He can't keep us from the sky.*

Brent turned back to the dragon. "I'm gonna figure out a way to get you out of here...just give me a few days, a'ight?"

The dragon produced a puff of smoke as a response.

After Brent finished manure duty, Santiago let him continue his usual duties to prepare for the last show in Siskin's Corner without a fuss. Mr. Santiago didn't say a word to him, but the implications were there. As the sun rose high in the sky, the sun-shaped brand on his arm burned, tugging deeper at the contract, tying him tighter to the circus.

He settled down in the grass with Nix near where the performers took their smoke breaks. The scent of tobacco and leaves reached out to him, begging for him to come back to the old habit. It had stopped naturally back when he and Bria ran off to Mert, long before the Diabolo assaulted his mind.

He yearned for a smoke more than anything. It'd be so easy to go back to it, to let it take away his worries.

Brent dug his fingers deeper into Nix's fur and peered out into the forest. The stories had grown quiet.

It made it all the easier for him to hear the footsteps approaching.

"May I sit?" Timothée's deep voice rumbled.

"Yeah, go ahead."

Timothée sat across from him and offered a piece of bread. "You hungry at all? I know manure duty can destroy anyone's appetite."

"Yeah, I'm fine. I've smelt worse." Brent broke the bread and tore it to pieces before bringing the crust to his mouth. Timothée watched, brow furrowed, nose creased.

"You don't have to watch me. It's not like I'm gonna do something with a loaf of bread," Brent said with his mouth full.

"I know. I just…I wanted to thank you is all." Timothée squirmed. "For what you did for Micca."

"He's a good friend of mine. I wasn't gonna let him get the brunt of it when I drank half that bottle. He would've done the same for me."

"Yeah. I'm sure…you're a good kid," Timothée replied.

Brent shrugged and took a swig of water. "It's nothing."

Timothée shook his head in disagreement. "No. You don't understand, do ya? You don't belong here. Can't help but feel like this is my fault."

"It's not your fault."

"No, listen," Timothée sighed. "I've wanted to leave this madhouse since I was a kid, but when you're raised in this mess, it's kind of hard to get out. Yeah, you get tips, but it's not enough to escape the permanent hold Santiago has over you. He's given me more freedom than most, letting me travel into town. But if I strayed, the brand brought yanked me back to the circus. I'm stuck. Thought I found a way to get out of here a week ago…a nice sum of cash…but…"

Brent stared at Timothée as his story emerged from the mist. He saw Timothée approach the guard at night, pointing to a couple in a tent in a llama and bear mask.

Time stopped. The mist, usually so soft and calm, turned dark with anger.

And Brent's next statement sliced the air in two. "You turned Bria into the Guard."

Timothée didn't respond.

Brent rose. The mist flew around him, sending debris flying and stories racing. "You...you turned her in! Why!?"

"I could have left the circus. That bounty...it was more than I could dream of."

"Does Micca know?" Brent felt the Diabolo bubbling in his stomach, with Nedo's story of betrayal roaring in his heart. If he wasn't careful, he would lose himself.

"No." Timothée's eyes watered. "Please don't tell him. I...love him. Fell in love with him as soon as he and that prudish sister snuck onto our train. I thought...getting that money...I thought it would help us. We could go live our dream. I didn't know that the Terrorist...Bria...that she was just a girl. I only saw the person on the poster."

Brent clenched his fists tighter. Anger swelled in his chest while a gong rang in his head. His entire body shook. He couldn't even find the words to describe his emotions.

But the mist showed it.

Reds, yellows, and oranges filled the surrounding area, detailing the mist like flames.

Give into the anger.

Set it loose.

No. Brent released his fingers, and the mist fell to the ground. Would he have done the same thing? If he didn't know Bria, if he had a chance for freedom by turning in a criminal…would he take it?

Probably.

Especially if it meant a better life for the ones he loved.

"I…would like to be alone," Brent whispered.

"I apologize. Really." Timothée started to leave.

As he rose, a group approached from the city of tents. Lolli walked at the front of it, her eyes shifting over the landscape. Timothée froze, his demeanor changing almost instantly from the meek apologetic man to the performer Brent watched in the tents. A smile burst out over his lips, causing his mustache to curl.

"Ah, Lolli! What goes on here?" Timothée boomed.

"We're looking for a child," Lolli said.

"Our ward," a woman with heterochromatic eyes spoke behind Lolli. "She disappeared the other night. We've been looking all over Siskin for her, but she's nowhere to be seen. She's made us late for our rendezvous for our next job."

The man beside the woman, a dark, stout fellow with red eyes, nodded. Brent's stomach churned as their eyes met. *He's a seer.* Brent didn't know if the seer had anything to do with Kek's Palaver of Immortals, but Brent had no desire to find out.

The man continued to eye Brent as he spoke, his voice softer than Brent expected. "You're the Storyteller, right?"

"Uh, yeah." Brent fidgeted.

"Can you help find her? It is quite important."

"I just, um, I mean…I tell stories. How would that help?"

"You see them too, though," the man stated. "I'm sure you already know my name."

Brent watched the story mingle around the man's head: a man shrouded in secrecy for hundreds of years, burning away an old identity assigned to him at birth. He loved many but kept one by his side. Nomads. Wanderers. Entrepreneurs. Together they thrived, with a goal of prosperity in grasp.

"Yeshua Nasr…" Brent glanced between the two. "And Gisela Kai…"

"As I thought."

Lolli and Timothée exchanged a look that made Brent's stomach churn. He hadn't displayed the full extent of his abilities to Mr. Santiago or anyone else in the circus. The only one who might have known was Zephyr.

Fool, his Diabolo cackled.

Shut up, Frankie.

"We need to find her." Gisela, the woman with mono-chromatic eyes, begged. "We made a promise to protect her."

"There are...there are a lot of children..." Brent glanced over the carnival. To pinpoint one child's story would be difficult, the stories so interwoven with the fabric of booths and games. He searched it all, feeling the twinge of death in the distance, but not of a missing girl. As his mind wandered over the mist, the stories solidified around him. Hundreds of stories, with children tossing balls in rigged games and marveling over the exotic ani-mals, detailed the area. But of their misty and repetitive exteriors, they might have been patrons any other day.

Brent crooned his neck. How long could he keep this story going without getting lost? Already, the pull of childhood pattered in his chest. If he closed his eyes just long enough, he was no more than the children playing games or laughing. What voices came from his own throat now?

Nix nudged her head against his knee. He'd forgotten about the dog, sleeping by his foot, but her fur brought him back.

The stories continued to pulse.

Gisela and Yeshua immediately took stock in the story, not fazed by the sudden change or by Brent's demeanor. They scanned the stories of children, pushing aside the mist.

"There she is!" Gisela called.

The story of a girl with round glasses and short, tousled hair walked past Brent. Mist wrapped around her, thick and defensive. She strode away from the games and attractions.

With Nix on his heels, Brent followed the story towards the edge of the carnival where he had encountered Ningursu nights earlier. The story of their encounter trumped all else. The mist gasped and roared, blocking the interaction so no mortal eyes could watch. Brent tried to push farther past it, but the brand on his arm seared, tethering him to the circus.

Here, at the threshold of the circus, near the forest, the girl's story ended. Where did it go? Brent couldn't see.

Did she get caught up in the commotion with Ningursu and me? Did we harm her? His mind raced as the stories faded around them.

Perhaps you are too stuck in your own head to notice a little girl.

No. I would've known she was there.

Kid, you're in your own head most of the time.

Only because you don't be quiet.

"Where'd she go?" Gisela asked, pulling Brent from the dreamlike state brought on by the stories.

Brent blinked a few times. Sweat dripped from his brow. Mist continued to gather on his fingers. Yet, the stories had ceased, only a gentle hum demanding his attention.

"I, um..." Brent licked his lip before continuing. "I dunno. The stories got weird here. I couldn't make them stable."

"Might be because of the magical perimeter around the circus, maybe?" Timothée asked a few paces back.

"Salazar doesn't like people snooping. Wouldn't want anyone's magic to mess around here either," Lolli added.

"She can't have just...vanished!" Gisela exclaimed. "She's a good girl. She wouldn't have run away. This is...horrific!"

"We'll find her, love. Don't worry," Yeshua touched Gisela's arm.

Brent glanced towards the trees again. "She definitely went into the forest, I think. If that helps?"

Yeshua nodded. "Yes, it does. Thank you."

Gisela kept shaking her head. "What are we going to do?"

"We'll find her. She shan't have gone far."

"I hope so."

The two walked away. Lolli shrugged, then followed them.

Brent watched them leave, his heart pounding in his ears. He swore something more was going on with the couple and their missing ward. The story was there, just pleading for him to listen.

But the stories, from the dragon to the carnival, tore away at his attention. His head spun, his eyes watered. He couldn't focus.

All he wanted was to lie down and cry for his mother, for his father, and to play...carnival games?

"I need...I can't...I want...I mean..." Brent sputtered. His head spun. Everything from the last twelve hours came to a front: Zephyr's stories, Timothée's truth, and now these stories. The Diabolo in his head prayed on them, cradled them, and fed on them. His own heart ached from fighting.

"Come on, kid. Let's get you back to your cabin." Timothée placed a hand on Brent's shoulder, guiding him away from the perimeter of the carnival as the stories sang their nightmarish songs.

CHAPTER TWENTY-EIGHT

THE CAPTAIN'S SON

Magic and demons loomed overhead as Jemma dove into each day, assisting Senator Cordova with his goals at hand. Each day brought new vagrants into the Towers, and each day, Jemma helped with the cleansings before escorting hundreds of prisoners to high-security vaults in the Aviary. The Guard brought those determined to have little-to-no risks to the Pit under the guise of Captain Carver.

She occasionally visited the pale, sick woman, Ms. Dray, bringing with her a gift of prayer. Professor Gratz rarely provided Jemma with an update on the woman's condition, only mentioning how the woman did not seem to improve over the course of her treatment. Ms. Dray, on all counts, refused prayer. She even refused to see her husband, a guard with tattoos strewn up his arms. Every effort to get her to speak resulted in silence. Jemma never pressed, focused only on her duty: the cleanse.

Day after day, she returned to the Technology-Ridden Year Glass in the Dispensary Tower. After multi-level cleanses, and with the heart and soul of hundreds of Magii, the Year Glass pattered with more life, just as Rose and Ada would have wanted. Clean, true energy; Rosada could reign. Everyone would thrive.

Just as Jemma wanted.

Some nights though, Jemma lay in bed, questions pouring over her thoughts. Were they harming innocent civilians? Had all Magii done wrong? She didn't know. Plus, there had been no news about Bria or the prisoners from the tower. They had accounted for all of Captain Palmer's guards, but not a single prisoner had turned up anywhere in Knoll or the surrounding towns. Jemma couldn't let Bria's presence taunt her, though. She had one duty, and it remained all the same: she had to help Rosada. If she could protect the nation from terror and fear, then surely she served the Effluvium with pride.

Knoll held a promise of peace over her. Riots didn't exist. The Pit operated in the distance like its own society, with vagrants rarely venturing beyond its walls. Those who attended services did so with the Effluvium in their soul. This was what Senator Cordova wanted in

Newbird's Arm, but their reining Senator Heartz prevented it.

Perhaps Brother Roy Al had been wrong.

Her heart fell. Would he be proud of her?

One day after a service, Jemma returned to the cloister, her head bowed. While Elder Un Dine still did not let her lead any services, her role in the Temple had significantly increased. Some patrons knew her name, no longer a mere fixture on the wall. Senator Cordova promised that with each day, her role would surely increase.

As she walked down into the cloister, she nearly fell straight into Cadet Christof Carver as he stood watch at the edge of the stairwell.

"Oh. Christof!" she lowered her head. "I hope the Effluvium has welcomed you with wide and open arms today."

Christof saluted. "As to you, Sister Jey Ma."

"You can call me Jemma." She smiled. "The formalities are a little excessive. We've known each other for years now."

Christof nodded, but his posture did not relax. A quiet sadness sank over his face, sitting in the center of the burned side of his face. It was a brutal scar, extending from his chin up to his hairline. He had buzzed his once lush blonde hair to a frizz, revealing where the burn stopped at the top of his head.

Jemma held her hands to her chest, tempted to reach up and touch it.

"Forgive me for staring, Christof, but what happened to you?" Jemma asked.

His face contorted in visible frustration.

Jemma recoiled. "I apologize. That is out of line for me to ask."

"You know, a year ago, I probably woulda hit you for asking something like that. I guess I ain't as tough as I used to be." He sighed.

"You don't need to respond—"

"Nah. It's a'ight. You outta know. Was during the Storm of Nightmares, y'know. There was that fire in the Temple and all. Got caught up in it trying to chase down Harley and wasn't paying much attention. Was angry, I guess. I mean...my best friend *died*."

"You mean Cadet Lawry?"

Christof nodded. "He was an ass, but y'know, we trained together and shite. He was a good guard and all. Woulda been a great captain."

"It's okay to be sad about the loss of your friend," Jemma whispered. "We all lost something during that storm. Some more than others."

"Hmph." Christof shrugged, walking in stride with Jemma as they ventured further into the cloister.

Jemma chose not to press Christof as they continued down into the belly of the Tower. She glanced at the faded betrothal mark on his hand. Of course she had heard the rumors: Bria Smidt had killed Cadet Chet Lawry in the forest right before the Storm of Nightmares. While Madame Gonzo and Senator Heartz held onto the premise that it was an accident, what if it wasn't? What if Bria's magic had made her do the unthinkable?

Did it break Christof's heart?

Jemma chose her next words carefully. "You don't seem happy here."

"I'm doing my duty. That's why I became a guard, ain't it?" He didn't meet her gaze.

"But I am sure you want something more."

"The Effluvium doesn't have that path for me."

"How do you now?" Jemma raised her eyebrows. "The Effluvium's paths are not set in stone, after all."

Christof paused outside of Jemma's chamber, gazing down at her with that perpetual sadness. She reached out, taking his hands, and squeezed them, a silent prayer exiting her lips as she traced the coarse skin on his palms and around his wrist. As she stared up into his face, she found her own heart fluttering for a moment, a strange warmth settling in her lower abdomen.

"I didn't think I'd be in this shithole, if that's what you're wondering..." Christof pulled away. "Thought I'd be married, expecting my first child. Shoulda been, actually. Was betrothed and everything to the girl of my dreams…" He clenched his jaw. "Or thought I was at least."

"You mean Bria Smidt?"

Christof sighed. "Been stuck on her for years. Finally got her to agree to a betrothal, and she ran off with Harley. Guess that means you and I got something in common."

Jemma shook her head. "I ended things with Brent far before they ran off. We would never work out. Perhaps that is the case with you and Bria? The Effluvium might have other plans."

"I loved her."

"Did you? Or was it lust?"

Christof scowled.

"The Effluvium has a way of working its fingers through our destinies. I think Ms. Smidt was never meant to lie in bed with you, so you ended up here instead." Jemma stared up at Christof. "You will find whatever destiny the Effluvium holds for you."

"And what do you believe it holds for you?"

Jemma paused. What did the Effluvium hold for her? She was helping rid the world of evil, but then what else? What life was she destined to live? "I am still figuring that out. A few months ago, I would have told you I would bring peace to Newbird's Arm as a devout sister of the Order. Now…I think it is more, but only time will tell." She opened the door to her cloister room. "If you wish, Cadet Carver, we can explore our destinies together through scripture and prayer. Perhaps with companionship and discourse, we may discover our purpose."

Christof smiled, a glimmer in his otherwise stern eyes. "That would be most favorable, Sister. Tomorrow, though. I'm running late, and my dad's gonna have my head otherwise."

Jemma bowed. "Very well then. I look forward to exploring the One Scripture with you, Cadet."

"As do I." His smirk remained. "But didn't you say we should drop formalities?"

"Yes, I apologize, Christof. Force of habit." Her cheeks flushed.

"It's a'ight, Jemma. I can't wait for our…discussions."

Jemma exchanged a bow with Christof, then watched as he turned away, cracking his neck as he walked. There was something about his stride, filled with determination but shyness, that warmed her inner core. She'd always admired Christof's aesthetic; his broad shoulders, his square jaw, and his hazel eyes often came to her dreams. Like so many other girls growing up, they used to point at him and swoon in his presence. Many had been lucky enough to kiss him. But Jemma held to her pious nature even then, determined to serve the Order.

But who was to say her heart had to belong to the Effluvium alone? As Elder Un Dine told her, love did not tarnish the Effluvium. Her mind wandered as she walked back into her bunk, where the other sisters knelt in prayer. She was human, like everyone else; her body yearned for touches, longed for affection.

Whether it came from Christof Carver or someone else didn't matter.

But as she closed her eyes to recite a prayer of mist and prosperity, all she saw was Christof Carver's face.

She could not wait until their first prayer session.

AURAS

Ever since the auras took over Lex's sight, she feared opening her eyes. They sheathed everything in her sight. People glowed colors she'd never seen before, and each time the Guard brought her for another round of cleansing, the auras only grew stronger. She didn't quite know what they were doing: with every buzz and consequence, Professor Gratz commented on Lex's condition getting worse.

But they continued, no matter what the Professor said.

They didn't bring her back to the cell, leaving her in the prisoner's infirmary to heal after her third buzzing. Her head spun in circles. For a moment, Lex swore she even forgot her own name until memories of Garrett, Madame Owiti, and Toddle rushed back to her.

Whenever Toddle asked to visit, she would turn him away, focusing instead on the noises and sounds of the room. The Guard occasionally brought in other victims of the cleansing, but Lex never dared to look at the drab colors encapsulating their bodies. They reminded her far too much of blood, and hatred, and death. What if they brought Garrett in, and he bore the same aura?

She didn't speak when Professor Gratz came to visit her. Most days, the professor checked Lex's pulse and drew blood before continuing on her way.

Some days, though, she spoke to Lex with a calmness that pricked through the air like wasps.

"Hm..." Professor Gratz muttered one day as she looked over Lex's chart. Her aura, Lex discovered, glowed with a blinding white light of false purity.

"You've been running these tests for far too long," the captain grumbled beside her. His aura dripped red. "Can we throw her away now? She's taking up valuable space."

"Captain Carver, may I remind you that these tests take time? We won't have answers for quite a few weeks if the buzzing is working." Professor Gratz scribbled on her clipboard.

"Clearly, it isn't! She is displaying signs of magic!"

"We are rooting out the core of her problem."

"Bullshite! You're causing her to fall back into the arms of demons!"

Professor Gratz chuckled. "Captain Carver...do you not have somewhere else to be or someone else to deal with? I can handle Ms. Dray myself."

"I'm giving you only one more week, Etta. Then we're putting her back in a cell. You understand?" Captain Carver glared at the Professor.

"If you insist." Professor Gratz returned to her clipboard.

Lex closed her eyes again as Captain Carver stormed from the room. The Professor continued her work, drawing a few vials of blood while humming to herself. Lex didn't want to speak to the woman, yearning that sleep would whisk her away.

But it never came.

"You are quite an interesting case, Ms. Dray," Professor Gratz told her. "I thought that the buzzing would remove all that pesky magic from your soul, but it seems to have ignited something hidden deep down."

Lex opened her eyes. "What do you mean?"

"I am unsure. That is what I'm trying to understand. This routine is supposed to rid you of magic, help with your phantom rot, and purify the world. Instead, your soul has somehow turned darker." Professor Gratz placed the vials of blood in her storage container and marked one last thing on her clipboard. "I trust you never knew about this?"

Lex wracked her mind. Memories flitted through her head from her early life; there'd been buzzing, there'd been torture, but she remembered no magic.

Not until recently.

But it could have just been a dream.

"No. I wanted to have magic but never did," Lex said.

"I see. Well…I will continue conducting my tests and let you know what I uncover, okay?"

"Thank you, Professor Gratz. I appreciate all your hard work."

The Professor left with a smile. Lex wasn't lying. She appreciated whatever work Professor Gratz was putting into this. Even if Lex remained their prisoner, at least the Professor seemed to want answers…despite her methods.

No matter how often she asked, Professor Gratz didn't bring her to see Garrett or Madame Owiti. All Lex had was the pitter-pattering promise in their heart that told her they were alive. So she held onto that with both hands and hugged it every day as she ignored the flitting colors in the infirmary.

She didn't know when or how she fell back to sleep, but without realizing it, her eyelids flickered open to the sound of the doorway opening. Lex glanced over, watching as a young guard marched over a few prisoners and sat them down on the examination tables. Chains looped around their ankles. The young guard's aura reminded Lex of browning leaves, while the different prisoners bore faded colors upon their souls. One caught her eye: a hunched-over figure with a silver aura that still dazzled like the stars. The figure held its head up and smiled in Lex's direction.

She blinked, letting her own vision stabilize. For the first time in days, Lex climbed to her feet and called, "Madame Owiti!"

The old woman limped to her feet, dragging the chain across the floor. Her usually tightly woven hair lay matted on her head, gray frizz sticking out from all directions, while dark circles traced her red eyes. Her skin hung from her bones, emancipated and broken after weeks of obvious torture.

"Sit down, fucking hag!" the young guard shouted at her.

Madame Owiti glared at him, eyes like daggers. The young man eyed her, nostrils flaring, and reached for the club on his belt. "Don't make me hurt you, hag. I will!"

"No, you won't. Madame Owiti sees you won't," the seer said with poise. "You never do, Cadet Carver."

"I-I will! I can!" the guard stammered.

No, Lex realized, he was only a boy. Was he related to the captain who often visited? Was he just trying to impress his father? Their auras were similar.

Madame Owiti bellowed, "No, you won't. You will let Madame Owiti go over to her friend now without causing issues."

The cadet remained frozen in place as Madame Owiti met Lex in the middle of the room. Even the other prisoners stared in awe. But their auras had diminished far too much; the idea of rebelling probably didn't even cross their minds.

Lex threw her arms around Madame Owiti, tears flooding her eyes as she pulled the old woman into a hug.

"I was so worried for you, dear Lex." Madame Owiti stroked back her hair and cupped her face. "I wasn't sure what they were doing with you. But now I know..." The old woman touched the scars on Lex's temples. "Why would they even consider doing something like this to you?"

"They're trying to cure me of my phantom rot..." Lex whispered as she kept hold of the old woman.

"I can see by your aura that they have failed."

"No. They've done something else. I can see colors now. Auras. Just like I always dreamed of! This is a dream come true, but I cannot celebrate. Instead, I wake up every day praying to a different god, hoping to be back home with Garrett." Lex sniffled. "Back home in Mert…where everything felt right and safe."

"You will return one day to peace. I have no doubt. You, Garrett, and Preston shall return."

"But I don't even know where Garrett is…" Lex caught another sob in her throat. "I've failed as a mother…I lost him."

"I sense he is safe, dearest Elexis. He is safe and alive." Madame Owiti squeezed her fingers. "Scared, but alive. You will find him. I have faith."

"I can't do it alone…" Lex glanced over Madame Owiti's shoulder at the young guard. The boy remained in place, his scarred face in a state of shock and horror. "Please…help me, Madame Owiti."

"I cannot, dear. I cannot. You will find him. Just have faith. My road is ending soon."

"What are you saying, my friend?" Lex clung to Madame Owiti's hands.

"Follow your path, Elexis, not Madame Owiti's. You will find your son. I promise."

Madame Owiti stepped back just as the door opened. Her aura sparked with gold for a moment, her premonitions settling onto her face in contentment.

In stormed Captain Carver moments later. He glared at the cadet. "What're you doing letting the prisoners up and about? I told you! Just fix up their wounds and get 'em loaded onto the cart. We ain't got time for this bull-shite!" The captain grabbed Madame Owiti by the wrist and dragged her back towards the other prisoners.

Lex recoiled, holding herself against the wall in fear as the captain continued his rant.

"Dad!" the cadet protested. "I'm sorry! I didn't want to hit an old woman. It didn't seem right or nothing—"

"I don't give a damn! You hit 'em when they misbe-have! Watch."

Lex shut her eyes tight. She didn't need to watch as Captain Carver removed his whip. She didn't need to see Madame Owiti's body crumple beneath the assault.

Snap. The whip crackled.

Madame Owiti shrieked.

The screams were enough to plant a vision in Lex's head. They painted red on the back of her eyelids. *Please don't let this be the end for her…* Lex sobbed to herself.

The lashing stopped. Silence eased its way into the room.

"That is how you do this bullshite!" Captain Carver snapped.

Lex opened her eyes again. Madame Owiti lay curled on the floor, uneven breaths rocking her body. Captain Carver forced the woman to her feet while his son stared at the ground.

"What're you looking at?" the captain snapped in Lex's direction. "If you weren't Etta's little pet, I'd have you beaten and thrown in the darkest brig, y'know!"

Lex sank onto her bed.

"That's what I thought!" the captain spat. "C'mon, Christof."

"Dad—" the cadet objected.

"Stop fucking around!"

The cadet bowed his head, and moving just like the prisoners in his grasp, he slumped out of the room. Madame Owiti glanced one last time at Lex.

They didn't need to exchange words. Lex understood. This was it.

Goodbye, Madame Owiti. I love you. Holding back her tears, Lex climbed into the bed and pulled the blanket up to her chin. *We'll meet again someday in the arms of the Effluvium.*

Edge of the Necrowood

Almost a week passed before Bria managed more than a few steps from her bed. Her body continued to ache, and she found herself unable to shake the feeling of her missing right hand. She'd reach out to clench a glass of water, only for it to shatter on the floor. She sucked back the urge to cry. Why cry over such a ridiculous thing? She could still pick up the cup with her other hand.

But she'd never be able to use her right hand again.

Marisol often came to visit, chatting away about the goings in the Pit. She kept a peppy demeanor, bringing Bria flowers and meals, all with a smile on her face. Yet,

Bria spent most of her time staring out the window as Marisol rambled. Knoll's Pit operated somewhat differently from Newbird's Pit; it behaved like a miniature city, with vagrants filling the streets, exchanging goods and services, performing jobs, and offering other pleasantries. While some performed vices, most vagrants held close to their virtues. These could be people in a market square or in any city across Rosada. Not vagrants.

Once she was well enough to walk, Dr. Hue assigned her a room inside a tenement house near the center of the Pit. The room consisted of only a narrow cot and a small end table. Bria smiled to herself as she stepped inside the room; something about it reminded her of Brent's small bedroom back in Newbird's Arm. She used to sneak into that room at night, where they would lie in their innocence, wrapped in each other's arms. That had been back before Brent knew of her magic; back when their love was a secret from all but a few. They kept to chastity for a long time, only succumbing to the deeper emotions after Bria unveiled her powers.

She ran her fingers over the end table; *I hope Brent is okay.* While she knew Brent had the smarts to take care of himself, he always found his way into an armload of trouble. Once she had her energy back, she would find him.

Over the past week, her imagination wandered. What if the Council found him? Or the Guard? What if he couldn't leave Aeterno?

No. He was probably trying his best to find her. Brent Harley wasn't the type to sit idly.

Not anymore.

A tap on her doorframe tore Bria from her reverie.

Lana waited in the entranceway, her black eyes scanning the room. The woman visited Bria a few other times while she was in the infirmary, keeping her questions to the point: how did Bria stop the Tower? Could she do it again?

In contrast, Dr. Hue always spoke with a smile, caring more for Bria's well-being. She helped Bria get used to her missing arm. While tending to the wound with such care and precision, Bria wondered if the woman had magic of her own.

Lana glanced around the room, then stole a glance at Bria. "You adjusting?"

Bria reached for her missing arm. "I'll be okay."

"Thought I told you that's a shit answer."

"It's the truth."

"Yeah, but that's not an answer. How do you feel now?"

Bria glanced at the floor. "Tired. Scared. I lost my arm...it's kind of bizarre. I keep trying to grab things, keep trying to do things...but I can't. It's...it's just gone."

She flexed her good hand. "But...I also feel antsy. I don't want to sit here doing nothing."

"Well, lucky for you, no one gets by for free around here. Actually, you can, but then you'll be living in tents rather than these homes." Lana tapped on the doorframe again. "We assign new jobs every morning by the bonfire. If you're feeling healed up, we would love more help and all. Might make you feel a little better."

"Oh. Okay." Bria said. She had full intentions of leaving the Pit, but the aches and pains from her ordeal made it hard to walk more than a few paces without rest. She kept dropping objects or losing balance as she walked. For now, the best thing she could do was stay and wait. She would find Brent, then together, they could destroy the Pools used by the Order.

If her inclination was correct, those Pools couldn't be far away.

But she had to be ready to fight.

Lana placed a green jumpsuit on Bria's bed. "Well, be down in thirty minutes if you wanna help. If not, that's your prerogative."

"I'll try to be there," Bria replied.

"Good...I'll see you soon." Lana left without another word.

Bria slowly changed into the jumpsuit, struggling to get her legs in while using only one hand. It would take time to get used to doing, well, anything. Her right hand had always been her dominant one. With that hand stolen, it left her with a bitter reminder of her left hand: the hand branded with a betrothal that Bria never meant. She did it to protect Brent. *I should have just whacked Christof with a branch.*

Once she got the jumpsuit on, Bria stumbled back outside, taking in the wind on her face. Dead trees, the stragglers from the graying forest on the far end of the Pit, called for her. She heard their voices, as thick as the mist and desperate as babes; they wanted her help.

Her heart yearned to obey.

But her body said no.

She kept her head down as she walked along the path towards the center of the Pit. Marked by an everlasting bonfire, the heat danced in the springtime air, dripping sweat on Bria's forehead and nose. She rolled up the sleeves of her jumpsuit to breathe, nodding slightly to a few of the vagrants as they hurried by with their assigned duties. Unlike those in Newbird's Pit, no one hollered in her direction. Everyone nodded towards her with respect.

Lana sat by the bonfire with her arms crossed, the early spring breeze catching wisps of her hair. A few other individuals stood beside her, assigning jobs and maintaining a poise of leadership.

Marisol glowered at them with her hands on her hips. "I don't want sewer duty!"

"We all exchange roles," one vagrant in a red jumpsuit said. "Today is sewer duty for yellow jumpsuits."

Bria hadn't noticed how each person wore a different jumpsuit. While Lana bore red, Marisol bore a yellow one like the vagrant with whom she spoke. Another vagrant walked by in black. A few children ran past, each wearing a white jumpsuit stained in dirt.

"But that's gross!" Marisol protested.

"It's sewer duty or manure duty. Take your pick." The vagrant didn't look up from his clipboard.

"Fine! But I'm not happy about it!" Marisol stormed off, not even noticing Bria as she raced by, her eyes wild with fury.

Lana followed Marisol with her gaze before drawing her attention to Bria. "Ah. Good. You're here."

"Am I on sewer duty too?" Bria half-smiled.

"No, no. You're in green."

"What does that mean?"

"You're with me is what it means."

"But...you're in red."

"Red means I get to do whatever I want." Lana waved for Bria to follow. "C'mon. I want you with me today. We're not done talking."

Bria followed in stride beside Lana, glancing back once at Marisol as she joined the other yellow jumpsuits. Marisol glowered at the red jumpsuits. They were in charge, the ones who made the rules, the leaders of the pack, but why?

She didn't ask, instead continuing in step with Lana, trying not to succumb to the weakness in her knees. "What are we doing?"

"Guards are bringing a new group in today. Gotta get them situated and all." Lana said without hesitation.

"You mean vagrants?"

"I mean people." Lana waved her hand in the air. "Come on. Hue and the others will meet us there."

Bria followed Lana away from the fire. She passed by a few people from the towers, all decked out in different colored jumpsuits. The boy from the Tower, Chander, sat with his sister and a few other children, all dressed in white. She went to raise her right hand but then pulled back, forcing herself to use her left hand to wave at the boy. He didn't respond, his eyes heavy with loss.

Lana wasn't much for words. She brushed her short black hair back as she walked, her black stamp glimmering on her cheek like a badge. She kept a type of pride while wearing it, as if reminding everyone that she had no shame. Whatever caused her to end up in the Pit, she didn't regret it. What was it, though? Did she have magic? Or did she do something else? Was it her career? A cold-hearted murder? Or nothing but the Guards' prejudice?

Bria didn't dare ask.

The Pit's city-like fantasy disappeared as they approached the wall. A tall fixture with barbed wire fencing and guards lining the gate. Beside it, the dead forest glowered down at the Pit. It called for Bria, demanding her magic and attention. She tore her gaze away and hugged her stomach with her good arm.

"That's the Necrowood," Lana stated, motioning to the forest with her chin. "Where we found you."

"Isn't there a fence?"

"Nah."

"Then why wouldn't people just…leave? It's only a forest…" Bria asked. Yet the way the forest beckoned her already answered her question.

"No one has ever escaped through the Necrowood. It's got some sort of magic. Makes it hard to leave. Towers seem to be able to navigate it…like a path was made for them or something…but people? Nah." Lana scowled. "Some have gotten close, but they always end up back in the Pit."

"Oh." Bria stared at the Necrowood. It pulsated with death and mist. *It reminds me of the Library.*

Its glare followed as Lana led Bria over to a group of beige jumpsuits. Hue also stood among them in her doctor whites, eyeing the gate. She smiled when Bria approached.

"Good to see you up and about." Hue said.

"Yeah, I feel better." The lie tasted sour on Bria's lips. Already exhausted from her trip across the Pit, she wanted to curl up and hide, to sob into her pillows, or to fly away in reveries.

Lana held up her hand as the gate opened. "Stay here. I'm sure the Guard will have some questions about their missing tower. They've already inquired multiple times, but they're relentless, I swear."

Bria inhaled. *Right. The Tower.* She hadn't even considered what became of the Tower after their insurrection. Did it still stand in the Necrowood? Did the Guard find it and release Captain Palmer and her men?

As Lana approached the wagon by the gate, Bria slipped behind one of the nearby trees. The bark laced its way onto her skin, mingling with her little branch and hiding her from the Guards and other wandering eyes. In the trees, it didn't matter that she'd lost her arm. Still, she could be the Forest Queen.

Hidden away, she could just make out what Lana and the Guards said.

A guard climbed out of the driver's seat to greet Lana.

Bria's stomach dropped.

"Good afternoon, Captain Carver." Lana saluted.

"Lana," the captain glowered. He still bore the same narrow face, with beady eyes and a permanent scowl. A new mustache sat fixated on his upper lip, curling at the edges. Otherwise, he still had the same presence he did back in Newbird's Arm—a caricature of hatred, dripping with petulance.

"Looks like you got a big shipment coming in today, don't you?" Lana kept her kittenish poise.

"A bunch of damn Magii arrived from Mert couple weeks back. Got what we needed. They're your problem now." The captain walked to the back of the truck. A cadet joined him.

Bria held her breath.

"Christof, get these fuckers outta here and then we gotta go, you understand?" The captain shouted.

Cadet Christof Carver bowed his head in submission. Bria wouldn't have recognized him if not for his father; burns and cuts adorned half his face, scraping away at his once unblemished skin. The mere thought of him made the betrothal mark on her right-hand itch. He had dragged her to the Temple one day after almost killing Brent in the forest; she agreed out of necessity. Then Elder Don Van placed the iron on her skin and branded her.

Yet Christof haunted other memories; he brought her back to when Cadet Chet Lawry attacked her in the forest, and her magic acted out of necessity. She could easily do the same to Christof now.

But instead, she kept to the shadows, watching.

Waiting.

Christof and his father unlocked the truck. One at a time, emancipated prisoners stepped out of the truck. Each person bore the same haircut, with burns crisscrossing their temples, hallow expressions haunting their faces. None of them glanced at Lana as they exited the truck, submitting to their new life in the Pit.

"Anyone causing trouble now, Lana?" Captain Carver asked.

"No, sir."

"You sure? We're looking for some fugitives, you know. Sure you didn't see no one coming out of the Necrowood?"

"No one survives the Necrowood, Captain. I know that better than anyone."

"Hm..." Captain Carver stared down at Lana, eyes narrow. "Very well. I think the senator is gonna wanna send some people out to the Aviary for a cleanse."

"You know I would report anything suspicious, Captain. No need to send anyone to that hideous prison tower."

"I am quite aware, Lana. My interests are aligned with yours; I'd hate to do the paperwork required. But Senator Cordova has his fixations."

"I know, sir."

"So, I'd highly consider speaking up if anything abnormal occurs. I know you like to keep this shite-hole orderly."

"Yes, sir," Lana said again. Bria admired the way the woman stood against Captain Carver. There was a determination in her dark eyes. It reminded Bria of her grandmama. She held her guard, held no fear.

No wonder she is the de facto leader here. Bria nearly smiled.

The last of the new prisoners emerged from the caravan. Lana exchanged a nod with Captain Carver, and without another word, the captain and his son left the Pit as if finishing just a standard delivery of goods.

Bria hurried back over to the others, nearly losing her balance as she approached. A few of them peered at her while Hue commented quietly to the old man beside her. No one said a word otherwise.

Lana led the newcomers over to the welcoming committee. Hue removed a bundle of clean clothes from her bag, and like a well-oiled machine, handed each person a different colored jumpsuit. A few of the prisoners returned the smile before the next person in their brigade offered the prisoners food and water. Bria stayed to the side, waiting for someone to give her orders.

Bria glanced towards Lana, who helped an elderly woman approach the group. The elder stumbled to the side, long coarse hair hanging over her face, hands trembling. Bria raced over to help catch the woman as she fell forward.

Only to be greeted with another familiar face.

"Madame Owiti!?!" Bria exclaimed, gripping the old woman's arm with her hand. "What're you doing here?!?"

"I can ask you the same thing, Rho, but Madame Owiti already knows." The woman's red eyes shimmered. "I can see you've been a very busy girl indeed. Your aura is the color of the earth, wind, sky, and sun. It's quite alive, indeed."

"We've been up to a lot..."

"Yes, yes, of course." Madame Owiti waved off the statement. "You'll have to tell Madame Owiti all the details. For now, I must rest. Yes, yes. I need rest. Like you must rest." She turned her attention to Lana. "Where can I go to rest my head? That silly captain did a number on dear old me."

"Hue will set you up in the infirmary," Lana said.

"Yes, yes, that'll be nice." Madame Owiti eyed Lana for a moment. "Your aura is quite stunning too, deary dear. Actually..." She glanced between Lana and Bria. Her eyes opened a tad wider. "You both have very similar auras. Very similar indeed. You must have similar magic, yes?"

Lana froze, closing her hands tight as she glared at Madame Owiti. "I don't have magic."

"Yes, you do. Yes, oh yes! I can see it! I always know!" With each word, life returned to Madame Owiti's face. The old woman clung to the prospect of magic like any other. In a way, wasn't the Pit a haven for magic and storytelling?

"Listen here, I don't have magic. The Order has messed up your head, that's all!" Lana snapped. "Hue! Madame Owiti here needs someone to care for her! You going to handle it or what?"

Hue rushed over, offering an arm to Madame Owiti, while Lana turned on her heels, storming off along the fence towards the edge of the Necrowood.

"Temperamental one, that one is, yes, yes?" Madame Owiti chuckled to herself, then smiled back at Bria. "We shall catch up once my head no longer spins, yes, yes? For now, go after Lana. I think you'll be quite interested in what you find."

"I don't know about that." Bria scratched at the nub of her arm. "I don't want to get on her bad side."

"With auras so similar, I don't think you could." Madame Owiti winked, then followed behind the group of new arrivals with Hue, back into the heart of the Pit.

Bria stared. Only once had she met someone with similar magic to her: Yusef, on an island far away from here, while hunting for the copper periwinkles for Brent's medication. Yusef's powers were far milder, though; he could track different plants no matter the location. He didn't exhibit the connection Bria had to the core of the world; no one did.

Could Lana?

Or was it just Madame Owiti picking on a single strand of color, linking the two women together?

I guess there's only one way to find out.

CHAPTER THIRTY-ONE

SHADES OF GREEN

Bria walked along the side of the fence towards the Necrowood. The trees moaned for her, reciting the name *Rhodana* like a prayer. Mist hovered around their hollow trunks, painting the coarse landscape gray. Only a few oaks and pines maintained their drab greenery, their trunks bowed in defeat.

Or to her.

Didn't the trees understand? Just because her grandmama first gave her the name Rhodana, it didn't mean she was the Forest Queen. It was a coincidence. The song predated her. It wasn't a prophecy.

It couldn't be.

Others had magic, just like her. There had to be others stronger, better, and wiser.

Would Lana have answers? Bria didn't want to get excited; Madame Owiti had just gone through a horrific ordeal, after all. For all Bria knew, perhaps Madame Owiti wasn't even perceiving auras correctly. She'd been in the Guard's custody for who-knew-how-long. *I only saw her a little over a month ago. What has become of Mert since I left?* The Order was coming to take the city, but Bria fled to fight the Council only to hide away in the Library. Was there anything she could have done to stop them?

Probably not.

Part of her wish she'd tried.

The trees grew denser as she walked, their hollow trunks humming in her direction. She kept her head tall, listening as the wind directed her towards Lana. Every time she lost balance, the forest caught her. Here, at least, foliage could be an extension of herself.

At least in the forest, she still had some form of control.

As she walked, she checked a few tree roots for an entrance to the tunnels. While she still intended to avoid the tunnels at all costs, it would be good to have an escape if things took a wrong turn. No roots budged, and no tunnels emerged in the trees.

Strange. Bria stroked the bark of a tree. Usually, she found the entrances to the tunnels without a problem.

She didn't focus on it, returning to the wind as it guided her to Lana.

Bria found Lana sitting beneath a dead sequoia tree, her eyes closed, fingers dug deep into the ground. Around her fingers, small blades of grass sprouted.

Only to disappear moments later.

Lana cursed and leaned her head back against the tree. She still didn't open her eyes.

Without speaking, Bria shuffled over to Lana and sat on the ground across from her. She stroked her own fingers into the dirt, giving way to clovers and wildflowers beneath the sequoia tree.

"Why did you follow me, Bria?" Lana said without opening her eyes.

"How did you—"

"Because no one could enter the Necrowood without getting lost." Lana picked a dandelion from the grass and raised it to her face. "We have the same aura, so I know your magic well."

"So, you have magic then?" Bria inquired.

"Used to. The Order squelched it out of me. Can barely get a flower to bloom now…" She raised the dandelion in the air. It wilted beneath the sunlight, left with only a bright white fluff. Lana blew on it. The seeds caught the air. A few even attempted blooming before falling to the dirt.

Bria caught one on her left hand. Within seconds, the plant burst to life on her skin.

Lana narrowed her eyes. "Even before though...my magic was never as...alive as yours."

"What do you mean?"

"It's no secret what you did in the Tower. Breaking open cells, destroying the fuel source..." Lana shook her head in disbelief. "Giving life to plants is just second nature for you, isn't it?"

Bria stared at one of the dandelion seeds on her finger. She didn't even need to think anymore. The flowers, the saplings, and the roots all obeyed her whim without a thought. But here was Lana, struggling to even get the grass to grow.

"What did the Order do to your powers?" Bria asked.

"Buzzed them away." Lana shrugged and pressed her head against the tree.

The Buzzing. Brent talked about that... She glanced towards the smog-ridden sky. They had threatened Brent with the same fate as well back in Newbird's Arm. Here in Knoll, the Buzzing was a reality. Not a legend. Not a story. A truth.

Lana closed her eyes again as if listening to the forest. "Even when my magic was stronger...it wasn't second nature to me. I could grow a fantastic garden, give life to small plots of land...but you, Bria. It's more like the earth obeys you. There is something about your magic that shines."

"I don't know why…I'm just a gardener." Bria kicked her feet. Kek said the same thing those months ago. Everyone admired the prowess of her magic. But why? What made her special?

"Did someone train you as a child?" Lana asked.

Bria shook her head. "No. My grandmama wanted me to keep it hidden. My father didn't like it either. I…didn't listen. It was almost like I needed to use my magic to survive. Without it, I withered…" Bria raised her left hand behind her right ear and touched her little branch. "It's who I am."

"Hm." Lana regarded.

Bria shifted the conversation back to Lana. "How long ago did the Order…buzz away your magic?"

"Oh, over twenty years ago. They got a hold of me during the Smoke Riots."

The Smoke Riots, of course. Bria's grandmama had talked about the Smoke Riots with her. It left so many people disoriented and masked by hatred. The Order's radicals took hold of Knoll, where she now saw clearly they never left. The Smoke Riots were a precursor of the days to come. Not that Bria saw them. She was born out of the Smoke Riots, a product of malice and discontent.

Born with a flower from her head, planted into the earth by her mother, perhaps Bria was born with her destiny scribbled on her skin.

Lana continued babbling, "In some ways, I'm glad it's gone. I don't deserve it. Not after everything I've done."

Lana lowered her head. She didn't cry, her face worn away by years in the Pit. But Bria understood the woman's own heartbreak. She could only imagine the stories spiraling around her head.

Brent would see them; Brent would sink into the heartbreaking pain.

Pushing the thoughts of Brent from her mind, Bria refocused on Lana. "Is there any way for you to get your magic back?"

"I told you, I don't deserve it," Lana replied.

"Why?"

"I am in the Pit for a reason…far worse than just having magic." Lana raised her hand to her cheek and traced along her black stamp. "But I can help you." Lana rose and paced across the forest floor, kicking up a few leaves. She met the trees with a glare. "Over the years, I've seen many Magii come and go through the Pit. One thing they all have in common is this: they don't know their potential. They don't see the way their magic connects. I help them unwind it, so they can see the spaces. But none of them had magic like yours."

Bria said nothing, waiting for Lana to elaborate.

"My life in the Pit has been a waiting game. I don't have a choice. So, I wait. I learn about magic. And I help others explore theirs. I think, initially, I did it to reclaim my magic. But that has proven unsuccessful. But since, as the old woman said, our auras are similar. I might be able to help you more than anyone else." Lana offered Bria a hand. "Come with me. It might be best to show you what I am thinking."

Bria hesitated, then accepted Lana's hand.

The woman led Bria away from the trees and deeper into the Necrowood. As they walked, she ignored the phantom pangs where her right hand used to be; it would take a while to shake off its ghost, a constant reminder of the events under Captain Palmer's reign.

And a constant reminder of everything stolen from her.

An old stone building sat in the center of the forest, with skeletal bushes and yellowed ferns guarding its entrance. Lana ran her fingers over the stone exterior, her eyes heavy and mouth pursed. Bria shivered, the area pulsating and begging for a cure. A plague of dust and smoke had ravaged this land heartless, a remnant of the Smoke Riots.

Or something worse.

Lana led her into the building. A sinkhole ate away at the wooden floors, bubbling with none other than the silver liquid that haunted Bria's dreams.

She skidded back, pressing her back into the stone wall.

"So you've seen this stuff?" Lana asked.

"Everywhere," Bria whispered.

"It's all throughout the Necrowood. I call it the Earth's Blood." Lana shrugged. "We're not here for that, though. We're here to see what you can do."

"I don't understand…" Bria glanced around the dilapidated building.

"I've worked with a handful of Magii here. Well, only the Elemental ones. I don't know how to help those Body and Mist Magii. Outside of my purview."

"Body and Mist?"

"That's what I call them. Probably isn't the right terminology, but it's not like I have any way to find out. I call them that, though, cause Body Magii use their internal source to produce their magic—like your friend Marisol. Mist Magii, I haven't had a lot of encounters with…but they use the Order's so-called Effluvium. Tend to vanish, though." Lana glanced back at Bria. "Then there's Elemental Magii. Like you."

Bria nodded.

"But your magic…it's special, isn't it?"

"No special than anyone else."

"Most people don't have a lot of potential. They taper out. You flourish. And it's not just plants, correct?"

"Yes, you know that."

"Elaborate."

Bria glanced around nervously. The woman shared similar magic. She had to trust her...right? They were all in this horrible pit together, after all. "I've made sinkholes...storms...destroy stone...harness electricity. I don't know how. It just...links together."

"Let's try this." Lana picked up a handful of dirt from the ground. She sifted through it until only a pinch remained, then brought it over to Bria and dropped it into her hand. "My father once told me when I was a young girl that soil contains all the nutrients we need for life. The same elements that exist in the air, in the leaves of plants, in humans, and in these stones. We're all connected to the earth."

Bria shuffled the dirt in her hand, sensing as it buzzed in her palm.

"It sounds like you're connected to Earth. Plants are your direct link—like how others can manipulate stone and fire. Most Element Magii have a link to one element or one aspect of the earth...but you have managed to tap into all of it." Lana scratched the bridge of her nose. "It is only conjecture, but I've been watching a lot of Magii in the Pit now."

"But why would I be the only one to uncover this?" Bria squeezed the dirt between her fingers. It reminded her of something Kek said on the island months earlier. They had caused Bria to bring the forest back to life while reaching into the dead core of the earth. Bria had no time to explore it, though, soon caught in the commotion brought on by the Council of Mist Keepers.

Lana shrugged. "Circumstances are always helpful. Or maybe fate. Whatever you want to believe in. Why bother wondering when you could explore?"

"So, what do you want me to do?"

"As I tell all the Magii I meet, all the girls who want to dabble in the streets, and all those suffering in the hospital sheets...whatever you want. But if you wish to test your magic, my recommendation is this: focus on the soil in your hand and see where the magic takes you. That's what my father used to say. Can't give you much more help than that. I don't have much magic anymore...remember?"

Bria stared down at the dirt again. Lana's instructions reminded her of a teacher, words level and direction clear. This was a woman who had tried for years to harness her own magic again. What horrors had plagued her mind, preventing her from daring to delve deeper into her abilities? *Is it as bad as me killing a guard? Is it as bad as all the harm I've done?* Bria shuddered. It was for protection. She had to remind herself of that. She only did what she needed to survive.

That's what Brent had told her.

That's what Bria knew was true.

She let the soil drift off her fingertips. With each grain, she listened and sensed the way it pulsed. The soil hummed with the essence of life; air to breathe, nutrients to eat, and compost to seed. While the song was softer than in plants, she still felt it there. Each piece played a different instrument, all winding together in the craziness called life.

Bria let the song wrap her in its embrace. Each beat expanded out of her, touching the stone wall, lacing its way through the skeletal bushes, and rising into the stale air. The elements in the soil were everywhere. Not only did the trees and bushes call for her, everything whispered her name.

She was more than a forest. More than a gardener.

She could taste the very essence of life.

Bria let the last few grains of soil fall from her fingers. The Earth's vibrations flowed through her, sending waves of hot and cold through the core of her body. She closed her eyes tight, allowing her magic to take hold. She felt everything: the way the silver pool in the sinkhole bubbled, the way the rocks moaned, and the way the trees begged for life. All from a few pieces of soil; she could connect herself to them all.

They sang to her.

Her name.

Loud.

Proud.

Incessant.

Rhodana,
The forest queen,
She loves to laugh,
She hates to scream,
She promised the world a reverie,
Rhodana.

Rhodana,
Your promise is true,
Rhodana,
Your screams are due,
Rhodana,
Give into us,
Rhodana

She gasped and hurdled to the ground. Her eyes flung open.

Around her, green replaced the drab atmosphere, wrapping around the stones and turning them to soil and dust. Peonies bloomed where the silver pool once stood.

And the clouds above had parted, letting the sun shine upon her.

Bria stared at her hands in amazement, glanced at Lana, then looked back at her hands one more time.

Hands.

While her left hand still looked the same, on her right side, her little branch wove its way from her ear and down her shoulder. It formed a bark-covered appendage from the nub of her arm to form a shape of a hand.

It wasn't perfect. But it was there.

She had a hand again. Her little branch was no longer a scar or a mask.

Now, it was truly part of her.

She smiled at her new hand, opening and closing it so leaves and flowers blossomed and wilted at her command. *I'm going to be okay. It's not the same, but it'll work.*

"I knew there was something special about you. Not every day that I see someone with that kind of magic." Lana grinned, her dark eyes shining with pride.

"I can't believe it..." Bria mumbled. "I never thought..."

She stepped forward, meeting Lana's smile. A bout of dizziness caught hold of her, and Bria took a knee.

Lana helped her stand. "Very good. Come now, let's get you back. You look like you need some food and a rest."

"Okay. Thank you."

With Lana's arm around Bria's shoulders, they headed back towards the Pit, leaving the Necrowood crying out for life as a whisper to the winds.

.

CHAPTER THIRTY-TWO

BITTER TASTE

Ropes dug into Brent's wrists. Squinting, he took in his surroundings. He lay on a cot, a single glowing lamp hanging overhead. His head pounded. Nix slept beside him. As Brent opened his mouth, the taste of blood wasted away on his tongue while the soreness of his throat roared.

What happened?

Memories returned to him after a few minutes. The stories of children at the carnival flooded his memory. In an instant, he forgot his name; at once, he was not just a single child but all the children, playing games, crying for their parents, and yearning for an endless day. But behind their smiles, their stories bore fears, and those fears fed the Diabolo...

With a bitter taste…

A sour drink…

Yes.

"No! Fuck off, Frankie!" Brent cursed at the Diabolo, pulling himself from its terrible claws. It never went away. He had controlled Frankie for such a long time, but now he lay here on the cot, trying to fight it.

How long had he been out? What had he done?

What if he lost himself for weeks? Would Bria find him again?

He inhaled once and glanced at Nix beside him. *No. I'm still on the train. I haven't left the circus. It can't have been that long.*

Every time he closed his eyes, the stories returned. No matter how hard he tried, fighting them seemed impossible. He had to keep his head together.

He couldn't fall back into the Diabolo's grip.

My name is Brent Harley.

The door slid open as he recited his mantra to himself. Mr. Santiago walked in with Lolli behind him. He held a cane in one hand, his golden suit glowing around him as he approached Brent. His eyes narrowed.

"Ah, good. You're awake," Mr. Santiago snapped.

"Yeah…" Brent grunted, lifting his head slightly to glance between Mr. Santiago and Lolli. "Sorry about that."

"You made quite an issue of yourself. Started summoning stories. We wouldn't calm you down at all. Luckily, Lolli here could restrain you," Mr. Santiago smiled back at Lolli, then glowered down at Brent. "You've been hiding some of your magic from me."

"What?" Brent blinked. *Right. The stories...*

"You made the past come to life!" Lolli said.

"You're more than a mere illusionist, ain't ya?" Mr. Santiago pried. "You can see the past; you can play with your surroundings. I ain't seen any magic like yours...well...ever!"

So you don't know about the Mist Keepers. Brent stayed quiet, watching the stories behind Mr. Santiago and Lolli. The stories acted on emotion, toying with excitement and rage. Stronger.

More vibrant.

Ever more alive.

Mr. Santiago continued, "Surprised I didn't see it sooner. You've been taking the silver dew, haven't you?"

"No," Brent mumbled. "Stuff wouldn't be good for me..."

"Everyone's supposed to take it! Part of the carnival rules!" Lolli snapped.

"Now, Lolli, hang on there." Mr. Santiago paced around Brent. "Clearly, he doesn't need it...he's just been holding back. So, we can overlook that for now. I've got an offer for you, kid."

Brent raised his head. "An...offer?" That was the last thing he expected to hear. Why wouldn't Santiago turn him over to the Guard right now? Or if the man had immortality, as he saw in Zephyr's story, wouldn't he want to hand him over to Kek? Or was this a different ploy? Was this a rebellion born from years of dislike?

"When we arrive in Juno's Den in a couple of hours, I want you to be my lead act. Wasn't going to offer that to you yet, but you got potential. I saw what you did with those horses. Now you can be a full-fledged fortune teller or something! I dunno, kid, but you've got talent."

"What? Salazar!" Lolli protested.

"Lead act? I can't. I...Bria...she...I..." Brent shook his head.

"We can reevaluate your contract before we get to Knoll."

"But—"

"Listen, kid. The lead gets all the dough. You'll be a rich lad by the night's end. Think of what you can offer that girl."

Lolli interrupted, "Salazar, you said that I could be a lead act in Juno."

"No one gives a flying shit if you can lift fifty tons, Lolli. They want to see illusions and grandeur!"

Brent ignored Frankie chuckling in his head, ignoring the constant worry that someone was out to get him. He asked, "What do you want me to do, though?"

Mr. Santiago leaned forward. "I want to know everything you have to offer, kid. Don't hold back. Show the world your magic."

"But what about the Guard—"

"Forget about them. I have ways of silencing them."

Brent stared at the ceiling, writhing against the ropes again. The boy in him reveled with delight. A lead act! He always wanted to tell stories to the largest audiences, gather smiles on their faces, and hear their applause.

But he couldn't delay finding Bria any longer. His contract still stood; he continued to feel the push of the circus's walls on his skin, and he carried the burden of Zephyr's story close to his heart. Every other tale that he cradled pushed him to do the noble deed. Free the dragon; find the girl; be the hero.

From Nedo's story of saving the world to Zephyr's story of torture to Santiago's story of greed...every story pushed him.

Every tale begged for his attention.

Brent nodded, the cogs in his head turning as he began piecing together an act. "Okay...I'll do it. I'll be your lead act."

"Excellent. Tomorrow will be your trial run. If that works…I'm gonna pair you up with Zephyr!"

"Salazar!" Lolli protested.

"Shush!" he spat.

Brent said nothing. His mind continued to race over possibilities. This was the perfect opportunity to free Zephyr. But how?

The Diabolo asked the same question. *How are you going to do it, kid? Freeing the dragon won't be easy.*

I'll figure it out.

Or you'll be eaten. Yum.

I doubt I'm all that tasty. Don't have any meat on me.

Mr. Santiago's voice tugged Brent away from his Diabolo. "Lolli…cut him loose. I think he's safe now. He has a performance to prepare."

Brent rubbed his wrists as he walked through the shaking train cabins with Nix on his heels. The rope left painful burns on his wrists. *Just another mark for the pile.* He didn't even care about all the scars anymore. Each one held a story hidden in his skin.

He'd be able to work with Zephyr later once the train had reached its destination. Mr. Santiago discussed all the details with him; tomorrow night, give a usual performance with more grandeur. If that drew in the audience, he could perform with Zephyr the next night.

But what would he do with the dragon? Would the dragon even obey?

How could he use the story to his advantage?

Brent pondered each possibility as the train screeched as it chugged to a halt. He placed a hand on the wall to keep himself from falling forward. No one spoke to him as they hurried past, some even looking at him with concern. His magic, his mist, it wasn't like the other tricks in the circus.

But years ago, he would have found these tricks unbelievable.

Now, he'd seen the impossible in a blink of an eye.

Nix bounded into the room as he opened the door to his bunk. Micca sat there, waiting on the bed, snacking away on a platter of fruit.

"Brenty-Boy! There you are." Micca flung a piece of pineapple in Brent's face.

Brent gagged. "You really throwing pineapple at me?"

"I can throw a grape too." He flicked a grape in Brent's general direction.

Brent groaned as it hit his forehead and collapsed on the bed across from Micca.

"Do you live in my room now?" Brent asked.

"Nah. The two acrobats...don't know their names. They're never here, so I thought I'd welcome you back."

"Hmph." Brent closed his eyes, ignoring the gentle hum of his roommates' stories.

"Oi!" Micca threw another piece of pineapple at him. "Don't go sleeping now. You've been asleep for a day!"

"I don't really call having my mind implode sleeping."

Micca tossed more pineapple in his general direction.

"Can you stop hitting me with that demon fruit?!"

"Demon fruit? Pineapple is a fucking gem, and you know it."

"Then why are you wasting it?"

"Cause your reaction is priceless!" More pineapple flew across the room. "Why do you hate it, anyway? You ever even tried it?"

"Yes, I tried it. And it's like…it's like…" Brent glared at the piece of fruit on the floor. "You know ostriches?"

"What do ostriches have to do with pineapples?"

"They look like they taste weird."

"Ostriches don't taste like pineapple."

"Yeah, but they got weird heads that have fuzz on them like pineapples and…I'm sure it's repulsive. No one would lick an ostrich head, but that's what it's like to eat pineapple."

"Yeah, that sounds fucking ridiculous."

"Nope. It's final. Pineapples taste like ostriches."

Micca snorted. "I don't wanna know what goes on in that head of yours."

"You really don't—oi!" Brent glowered as once more, a piece of pineapple hit him square in the jaw.

After snatching the tray of food away from Micca and picking out a few pieces of apple, Brent settled back into the bed. The stories remained strong of the chef cutting the apples and of the little boy who picked them in the field. If he looked hard enough, would he see the story of who planted the tree?

He pulled away before it dared take hold of him. Instead, he reached into his bag under the bunk and pulled out his jar of silver pills. They burned going down, but as soon as he swallowed, a weight lifted from his shoulders.

And the stories became only a gentle hum.

Micca watched Brent from across the room, arms crossed. He broke the silence. "Y'know…Timothée said you had some crazy fit. Everyone's been talking about it."

"Yeah. I do that sometimes." Brent stroked back Nix's ears. "My magic isn't necessarily as nice as it seems. Kinda…misbehaves. I mean…yeah. Misbehaves. That's the word."

"But you were showing stories. Like the past. Like the things that happened."

"Mmhm."

"Wait…so wait!" Micca jumped up. "If Timothée isn't lying about that…then that means you can see stories and shite? You can you see mine?"

"I see everything," Brent said without flinching. "I've been blessed with the burden of seeing the stories of…everything. Living. Dead. Everything."

"Shite!"

Brent waited if Micca would say anything else. It was easy enough to say he could create illusions, but his magic extended far beyond anything in the circus.

But Micca didn't flinch.

"Damn. So I guess nothing gets past you, huh?" Micca asked.

"I wouldn't say that."

"But you could use this to find out who turned Bria in! Or where she went! Or…or…I dunno…learn Santiago's schedule so you can cover his office in feathers!"

"I'm not decorating his office with feathers."

"C'mon!"

"I don't want to get on manure duty again."

"Right…" Micca glanced at his shoes. "I never thanked you for covering for me. That was something special there. Always knew you liked me."

"Yeah, well, you're one of my oldest friends. Wasn't gonna let you fall."

"Y'know, if I wasn't in a committed relationship right now, I'd come over and smooch ya right on the lips. But I got Timothée, and you got Beebelle. And we're gonna find her so I can be there for your wedding because, dammit, I wanna get you in a tailored suit."

Blood rushed to Brent's ears. It wasn't easy to talk about Bria, to imagine her in his arms again, but Micca spoke like it was just any other day. *I'll find her. I have to find her.* But then he recalled what Timothée said to him, right before he helped search for the child. *She's gone because of him.*

Tell him. The Diabolo hissed.

He's happy.

You know it's right.

I can't hate Timothée for what he did.

But you do.

I'm upset. Hate is a strong word.

Give into it.

"Fuck off..." Brent grunted.

Micca raised his brow. "Huh?"

"Sorry, um…just there's something…I mean…I need to…I…" He stared at Micca. Despite the squalor of the circus, Micca held relaxation on his shoulders and a smile on his lips. Even Brent could tell, without the stories, that after years in the Pit and living in vagrancy, here…Micca Fein was at home.

It's how Bria makes me feel. I can't break his heart.

Instead, Brent redirected the conversation. "I need to get out of here."

"Don't you got a deal with Santiago, though?"

"Yeah, and he's not letting me go anytime soon. But I…I gotta find her. I can't stay here…" Brent pressed the back of his head against the wall. "And there's so much I can't even describe. I've been through so much shite, Micca…and I think I have a responsibility to deal with it. Cause dammit, I don't want this world to get turned to even more shite. "

"So what're you thinking?" Micca asked.

Brent glanced at his friend. "I think I gotta steal a dragon."

CHAPTER THIRTY-THREE

A YELLOW SHADOW

Yaz felt like a shadow on the wall, listening as Sir Jama bellowed orders at Caroline, Alojzy, and Aelia. They arrived a day earlier at the dusty snow-covered cliffs of Spinoza, a place that Yaz had only heard about in stories. In the distance, shadows of small dragons fluttered about like birds swooping in and out of the water below the cliff. The cavern in which they resided looked like a home, with a bed for Yaz to sleep in and a small kitchen. No one cooked, opting to bring in food, while a Giant Mist Keeper named Jiang carried in a large basin of silver liquid. Once it was there, Sir Jama spent most of his time gazing into the basin for hours, almost never flinching. The Mist Keepers fed her and kept her warm, but otherwise, Yaz might have been their new pet.

She sat against the wall most days, hugging her knees, watching Sir Jama stare into the odd silver basin. It reminded her of the lakes where she'd found Sir Jama; was he searching for his body? Or something else?

"May I sit with you?" Caroline approached Yaz. Half her face still appeared melted to one side, her lipstick dripping down her chin.

Yaz nodded.

Caroline crouched beside Yaz and twiddled her thumbs. She said nothing for a few minutes. Were the Mist Keepers always so…strange?

"You can still go home, Yaz," Caroline whispered. "You have not been impacted by the curse yet."

"Curse?" Yaz gawked. Sir Jama hadn't mentioned a curse!

"This is fundamental to your understanding of becoming a Mist Keeper, Yaz. I failed to tell this to my first apprentice, but you have a choice in the matter. Because, in order to become a Mist Keeper, you have to—"

"Caroline, enough of that!" Sir Jama barked from his perch without looking away from the silver liquid. "Yasmin, please come join me by the basin."

Yaz hustled over to Sir Jama's side, excited to be more than a fly on the wall in their secret hideaway. She had so many questions to ask Sir Jama! How did they get to the mythical land of Spinoza? Were the tunnels magic? What was the curse that Caroline just mentioned? When would she get to see the Library? What about learning more about her Mist Keeper abilities? Her mind raced with possibilities.

But Sir Jama spoke before she inquired. "What do you see in the basin, Yasmin?"

Yaz peered inside the basin. It was as if she was looking up at the sky but from inside the water. But it wasn't just the sky she was looking at, but a monster gliding through the clouds. It oozed yellow, its face inhuman, body like a spider. Each movement came with unease, erratic almost, and the monster crashed through the air. *What's the matter with it?* Yaz touched the top of the liquid. Like a magnet, it moved towards her fingers, then climbed up her arm.

She screamed, "What's happening, Sir Jama!?! Make it stop!"

Sir Jama said nothing.

"SIR JAMA?!"

"Ningursu, what is happening?" Caroline sounded far away, her voice like an echo.

The silver liquid had reached Yaz's shoulder, clawing for her neck and chin. She wanted to cry, but every movement caused the liquid to slither forward more, almost like a serpent.

Without warning, Yaz fell backward, and the silver liquid dissipated. Caroline enveloped her in a hug, dragging her into the corner of the room. Yaz's head spun. What just happened?

"WHY WOULD YOU DARE LET HER BE CONSUMED BY IT?" Caroline shrieked. "YOU SAW WHAT HAPPENED TO JULIETTA!"

Yaz curled up on the ground. Her arm ached, and her head buzzed. While Caroline continued to yell, each of her words seemed farther and farther away. Every time Yaz closed her eyes, she saw the yellow monster; she swore she could even hear it. What was it? Where was it?

Where was she?

Why was she here?

Yaz squeaked and hugged herself tighter.

"Yasmin," Sir Jama's voice cooed.

Yaz shook her head.

"Yasmin, listen to me."

She glanced at Sir Jama. Caroline sat on the opposite wall, her arms crossed, mouth closed tight.

Sir Jama smiled. "I understand. It was quite scary, was it not?"

Yaz nodded.

"I wanted to see if you could help the monster. You are so kind and innocent; I thought you would be able to guide the monster to safety. I did not expect it to attack you." Sir Jama spoke with tenderness and care, luring Yaz in like a fish on a hook. Why would Sir Jama lie to her? He continued, "The monster is suffering. You see, the monsters used to be good people like you and me. But they succumbed to evil magic. Like the storyteller you met. Over time, they grew corrupt and immoral. I thought you might free the monster from its anger since you're such a good girl."

Yaz pouted and looked at her feet. "I'm sorry, Sir Jama. I didn't know what to do—"

"Of course, of course. It was foolish of me to think otherwise. We need to prepare you for such an endeavor."

"But what do you want me to do, Sir Jama? Defeat the monster?"

"No, dear Yasmin, not at all." Sir Jama prodded his chin forward as he spoke, a smile across his skinned face. "No, I want you, dear Yasmin, to help the monster. I believe the monster wants what's best: to rid the world of evil, evil magic. With you as the guide to this monster and many, I think we can be saviors. Is that not what you want, Yasmin?"

"I guess so..."

"SIR! This is preposterous!" Caroline rose again from her spot. Yaz didn't understand why Caroline always seemed to protest; did she not trust Sir Jama?

"Caroline, do you not have work to do?"

Caroline continued, "Should I not be training *my* apprentice? She needs to learn how to be a Mist Keeper, not how to—"

"Enough!"

Mist exploded from Sir Jama's mouth, wrapping around Caroline and chaining her to the wall. The woman fought against it, then bowed her head in defeat, her face drooping to one side as she bowed her head.

"I know what is best for the Council and for Yasmin," Sir Jama continued. "Once everything is in order again, we can deal with Yasmin's proper training."

"But—"

"NO!"

Yaz brought her hands to her ears. Why did grown-ups always fight? Why couldn't they just get along with each other?

Why did she go with Sir Jama?

Why? That was the question, wasn't it? Why did her mother give her to Ms. Kai and Mr. Nasr? Why did they keep her in the tower? Why?

Why?

Why?!

Yaz rose from her spot, holding her hands over her ears as Ningursu's voice continued melding into the walls, bouncing and booming. She raced to the front of the cave and stared out at the clouds dancing over the landscape. The dragons continued to rise and fall. Free. Without a care in the world. Yaz couldn't help but wonder what she'd be doing if she never found Sir Jama's head; would she be cleaning the shop? Or would she be having a tea party with her skeleton collection? What became of her collection?

She had too many questions.

And no answers.

The whole predicament made Yaz's head spin. She believed in Sir Jama, but some of what he said was odd.

I need to keep trusting him. Besides, I don't even know how to get home. Or if Ms. Kai or Mr. Nasr care. I was just annoying to them. Yaz hugged herself, watching as a dragon in the distance spun into the air. She imagined she rode on the dragon's back, seeing the world from above the ground. Perhaps if being a Mist Keeper didn't work out, she could be a dragon rider in Spinoza! That seemed like fun.

But she wanted to make Sir Jama proud.

No.

She had to make him proud.

Yaz eventually turned back to face Sir Jama just as the sky turned a shade of purple. Caroline had left the cave without saying goodbye, but in her place stood Aelia, helping Sir Jama perch himself upon the table.

Sir Jama grinned as Yaz approached them.

"I wanna help," Yaz mumbled. "I wanna defeat the evil magic and help."

"I knew you would, Yasmin," Sir Jama replied.

"What can I do to help, though? I'm just a kid…"

"I was just speaking with Aelia about that. She has concocted a special potion that will strengthen you."

Aelia nodded and approached the basin at the far end of the room. She never seemed to smile, always serious with her brow furrowed, so wrinkles formed on her head. Being careful not to stain her dress, Aelia ducked a cup into the basin. Instead of silver, the liquid inside looked like gold.

"You must drink this." Aelia brought it over to Yaz. "It will help."

Yaz sniffed it and scowled. "It stinks!"

"Just because it stinks doesn't imply it is bad for you."

"Now, Aelia, be nice to dear Yasmin. She is our key to winning this after all." Sir Jama's lips curled into a smile.

Aelia nodded again, but her scowl remained.

Slowly, Yaz brought the potion to her lips. It slid down her throat like oil, clogging her throat and rocking her stomach in a pathway to nausea. As she tried to keep it down, clouds descended over her mind. Her vision turned yellow and red. Inside, her veins and arteries throbbed.

And with each passing second, she forgot her name, her past, and her identity.

All she knew was blood.

CHAPTER THIRTY-FOUR

RULES OF THE APOTHECARY

Bria still struggled with her new arm. When she woke in the morning, the branches and vines lay withered at her side. She had to will the arm back into existence after letting the old branches wither away. It required her full attention to move, and if she forgot it existed, sometimes the branches would wilt throughout the day.

Lana didn't come to visit her, leaving Bria to perform odd jobs throughout the Pit. Often, Bria worked alongside Marisol, cleaning waste on the side of the road or helping to serve meals to other vagrants. Twice, she visited the infirmary to see Madame Owiti, but Dr. Hue turned her away. The old woman wanted no visitors, only rest.

So, Bria left it alone.

At night, she huddled in the bed in the tenement hall, listening as moans and laughter seeped through the walls. From her window, she saw harlots stand on the edge of the Pit, pleasing guards, while junkies sold good-feeling substances through the cracks in the wall. A couple of times, she swore Lana walked among them, offering similar vices.

Or perhaps it was a trick of the light.

In the back of it all, the Necrowood sang to her, begging for her magic. Even from her window, Bria could feel it, with its subtle peony heart beating. The Pool poured out through all the Necrowood, but Bria knew her magic wasn't strong enough to destroy it all.

Not yet, at least.

She still barely had the strength to keep her new arm alive.

After a couple of days without seeing Lana, the woman knocked on Bria's door.

"Come in," Bria called over her shoulder as she pulled on her sweater. Her branched arm caught on the sleeve, and after a few attempts, she pushed it through the arm-hole.

Lana walked in carrying a thick old book in her arms. She glanced around the room, scowling, then dropped the book on the bed. "Here, brought you a present."

Bria glanced at the dust-riddled cover. "A book?"

"It's a bit dated, but Hue brought it with her from the Rosadian Academy." Lana shrugged. "Thought you might find it interesting."

Bria glanced over at the cover. *Rules of the Apothecary.* She traced the words with trembling root-made fingers, then glanced at Lana. "Oh, um, thank you."

"Read it when you have a moment." Lana glanced towards the window. "Or don't. It is up to you."

"I'll take a look."

"Hm." Lana didn't say another word for a few minutes. Bria watched the woman. She held herself steady like a tree, her dark eyes narrow.

Lana broke the silence with another statement. "I look out of these windows, and I don't see vagrants. I've been in here for so long that most of their crimes seem petty. Stealing? Pah. Murdering a guard? Deserved. Telling stories? Ridiculous. Imagine what Rosada would be like if the Order didn't lock away those it deemed scum. We'd be like—"

"Mert?" Bria finished the woman's sentence.

"Mert, Spinoza, Delilah, and so many more. At least, from what I've heard. I've been trapped in this pit since I was twenty. Hard to see the world that way." Lana crossed her arms, still glowering out the window. "But someday soon, we will be free of this pit."

"I hope so," Bria said.

"Don't hope. Do."

"I will."

"Good. Cause we—Hue, me, and some of the other leaders here—we've been putting together a plan to escape this hellhole. I don't think it will work, but it's worth listening to, I guess. You're welcome to join…you'd be a good addition."

Bria stepped back. Kek had wanted her to be part of something; even the Council wanted to use her magic for something. There was always that caveat.

"Because of my magic?" Bria asked, not daring to look Lana in the eyes.

"Nah," Lana replied. "Your magic is fantastic, but I see something else. You are the Terrorist from Newbird's Arm. Pits across the province are chanting your name, even if it's in some foolish song. You've survived this long. I think you would make a fantastic addition to our planning." Lana walked across the room, pausing in the doorway. "Plus, I like you. You're a smart girl."

Bria didn't respond.

"Just think about it. If you're interested, come to the old barn by the Necrowood."

"Okay."

"I'll see you around." Lana glanced back at her one last time, then left Bria alone in her room.

Once Lana disappeared down the hall, Bria extended her hand, using the edge of the branch to shut the door. She didn't quite know what to make of Lana's request. On one hand, she wanted to help fight; joining forces with the vagrants might get her to Knoll to destroy the way the Order communicated with the Council...and hopefully get one step closer to peace. Yet, on the other hand, she hated the idea of putting other lives at risk. Her plan was simple enough in her head: leave the Pit, sneak into Knoll, destroy the Pool, and find Brent. But could she really do it alone? Especially now that she stood out, with a branched arm teetering from her shoulder and her face plastered throughout the nation. By now, rumors would have spread that the Terrorist of Newbird's Arm returned to Knoll.

She parsed through the book Lana left her as she mulled over her options. A single passage caught her eye in the preface:

The world is made of more than just earth, wind, fire, and water. While these base elements are the home to both science and magic alike, this is just a broad category of their behavior. All four elements hold subgroups - true elements, if you will.

For instance, air comprises more than only air. Multiple elements compose it. The first that comes to mind is oxygen. It is what sustains life, what we use to breathe.

But fire needs oxygen to live as well. Water needs it to exist. And everything on the earth needs it as well.

The world is not just made of earth, wind, fire, and water...but so much more.

Alchemists try to control these elements for their own use, and apothecaries try to use them in the name of science. What else can we do with this knowledge? How can we grow from it? This book will discuss every known element of humanity and more.

Bria stared at the words, running her fingers over the page again. She never thought of the world like that; earth, wind, fire, and water were all interrelated. But how?

She let her magic gather on her fingertips, stroking the edge of the page. *I've made the earth obey. I've made the sky listen. And I've made water react. They're all related.*

Bria shook her head. It was a preposterous idea.

Yet Lana handed her this book. She'd seen Bria's potential.

Perhaps she'd seen more than even Kek did on the island.

Bria placed her good hand against the brass doorknob. Rather than turning it, she tugged inward on the elements inside it. They quivered, a dull thud on her fingertips. As she focused, her branched arm flourished, pulsating with its photosynthesized breath.

Every element works together to create life. Bria tightened her grip around the doorknob. *Plants use whatever composes this brass knob. That's why I can feel it...*

She focused harder, listening to the heartbeats of the elements. The book on her bed would help her with the names.

As she turned the knob, the brass beneath her fingers vibrated.

And the doorknob snapped into twelve pieces.

Bria spent the rest of the morning trying to reassemble the doorknob. Despite the way the elements called to her, unlike with her plant magic, she could not reunite the pieces. Instead, she formed a new handle out of a few of the seeds she brought back from the forest, giving life to them with a wave of her fingers.

Her gurgling stomach dragged her from the room and out into the Pit. The springtime air tasted stale, dead almost, and it weighed on her chest as she walked barefoot across the dirt. In her wake, grass gathered at her feet, blessing the world with at least a sprinkle of spring. Yet, despite the mere prayer of spring, death continued to hang in the air. A thick smog gathered over the smokestacks of the towers in the distance. The midday sun hung in the sky, creating a halo of yellow through the fog resembling a Diabolo.

Bria shook away the fear as she joined the line for food. She said nothing, instead keeping her head down and gaze far from those she knew. Marisol sat on a bench talking with exuberance to Chander and his sister. A few other vagrants gathered around them, listening as Marisol spoke about how they took down the tower. She described it with gratuitous details, making it seem like a magical battle filled with a spark of lights and glam.

Bria only recalled terror.

But she wouldn't deny Marisol the chance to tell an exciting story.

Though Brent would have told it better… Bria's heart sank. She wanted his arms around her more than anything, his lips against her forehead and his heartbeat against her skin.

It did not do her well to dwell on it, though, so she shook the feeling off as she took her food.

She avoided Marisol and the others as she trudged away from the food line with a bowl in her hands. Part of her wanted to go back to her room and hide. Instead, her feet carried her away from the bonfire in the center of the Pit and towards the dilapidated barn on the border of the Necrowood.

Bria tapped on the barn door with her branched fingers, trying to become familiar with the way they moved.

"Who is it?" Lana called.

"It's Bria."

"Come in."

Bria gripped her bowl of stew as she entered the barn. She didn't know what to expect, half imagining a bunch of warlords gathered around a table, plotting the demise of Knoll.

Instead, she found a small gathering of individuals sitting on piles of straw. A tattered old map hung from the wall, marked with fresh red and black streaks. Hue stood before it with her arms crossed and her thin lips pursed into a frown.

Lana rose from her spot. "I am glad you could come."

Bria nodded. "I...want to help."

"Hm. Sit."

Bria sat down next to an elderly couple and picked at her food.

Hue led the discussion as she walked back across the room. "The Guard has been cleansing more individuals. Over the past week, at least a hundred new patients have arrived at my ward. I fear what they are doing across Rosada."

"There's a rumor spreading they are expanding their troops," one man said. "They're gonna head into Kainan to recruit…and we all know they're a bunch of ruthless fuckers."

Another woman interjected, "It's not like we can stop them. We're better staying here, safe and all. Wait out this fucking war until the end."

"Then why have we been meeting?" Someone else added. "We're all here cause we're sick of this. We got forces. We have strong Magii!" They glanced at Bria. "We can take 'em down."

"We might have Magii, but the Guard has ammunition," Lana said with poise. "Even if we send the Magii to attack, the Guard will shoot on sight. They're always in those towers…watching."

*Towers…*Bria placed her bowl down and glanced towards the muggy window. Yes, the Guard always watched in their towers. They would shoot any Magii on sight. But…

Bria spoke, "What if we go through the Necrowood?"

"You don't think we've tried that, girl?" One vagrant asked. "No one ever comes back. The Necrowood belongs to Death. We can't survive."

"Bria has magic that might help," Lana said.

"With all due respect Lana," Hue interjected. "Don't you think the Guard would notice if the Necrowood came back to life with Bria's magic?"

"I don't think I could bring the woods back to life even if I wanted. My powers are still...weak from my ordeal," Bria replied. "But obviously, the Guard can make it through the woods."

"Yeah, 'cause they got towers," one vagrant stated.

"So do we."

A confused silence settled in the air.

Bria continued, "Unless the Guard went to retrieve it, the tower that took me here is probably still in the Necrowood. If we find it and get it working, we can escape. No one would suspect us at first glance."

Still, no one spoke, eyes wide, mouths open. Bria waited. Perhaps they'd already ruled it out.

Lana's smile confirmed that wasn't the case. "I knew there was a reason I liked you. Let's go find ourselves a tower."

CHAPTER THIRTY-FIVE

THE FINAL BOW

Brent paced inside the Green Tent, picking at the brands on his arm. His head pounded, his mind raced, going through his plan for that night. Micca waited outside the tent, ready with Nix at the edge of the circus with his bag; if all went according to plan, he'd retrieve the dog on his escape with his belongings in tow. Not that he had much: a quarter-bottle of pills, Bria's cowl, his old clothes, and, of course, more coins than he ever thought possible.

He'd worked with the dragon for only one and a half days. She listened to each of Brent's instructions with a nodding gaze. Whether she would obey was a different issue entirely.

Brent kept promising himself it would work, as long as Micca told no one. He even had Micca promise not to tell Timothée. After what happened with Bria, he didn't fully trust the man, even if he hadn't told Micca why. Tonight couldn't fail. He would escape this prison.

After all, the sky offered the only method of escape. Mr. Santiago had maimed Zephyr for that reason. Could a simple story be enough to give her back flight?

Brent didn't know.

Fears continued to mount and circle in Brent's mind. He'd already taken two of his silver pills, despite the shortage in his supply, but the Diabolo laced its fingers into his self-deprecating thoughts. *This is stupid. It's going to fail.*

Then why are you doing it?

Because that dragon is suffering…and so is everyone else here. This is a prison.

You owe them nothing.

I need to get out.

Just to find that bitch? There are better things.

"Fuck off!" Brent cursed and pulled at his hair. Without a doubt, the medication worked—it kept his head together and mind in check—but the Diabolo would never leave. Its story was potent, weaving its way into his personality, just like all the others.

"Ah! There you are! Are you ready for your big show tonight?" Mr. Santiago intercepted Brent's thoughts as he walked into the room decked out in his classic golden suit. After Brent headlined the show the night before, garnering excitement throughout Juno's Den, Mr. Santiago welcomed Brent back into his family with open arms and a handful of coins. Brent never expected his ridiculous story of a gorilla named Mr. G to ignite such excitement, but it wrapped the audience in delight and laughter. Mr. Santiago raved about Brent's talents to anyone who would listen, promoting the new act all the following morning, Brent and Zephyr performing side-by-side.

Yet, despite Mr. Santiago's sudden change of heart, it was hard to ignore the ongoing persecution riddling the train. Brent watched from his room as Mr. Santiago yelled at the laborers when they took a break or forced the performers to practice all day.

All bore the sun-shaped brand.

All remained prisoners.

No contract. No freedom.

Brent didn't know how many shows he had left. But he couldn't wait any longer.

"Yeah, I'm ready." Brent smiled slightly. He met Mr. Santiago's determined smile with one of his own, though his nerves went rampant in his heart. "It's gonna be a good show."

"Good. Cause y'know, if it ain't, I might not be able to hide ya from the Guards when they come a'knocking," Mr. Santiago smacked Brent's shoulder. "But I don't think I gotta worry about that."

Brent gulped. "Yeah, of course not."

One wrong move, and you'll end up a prisoner, you know. The Diabolo cackled with his insecurities.

Brent didn't reply, exchanging one more smile with Mr. Santiago, joining the droves of performers in line. A few people congratulated him, but both never spoke. They wore their stories close; sad stories, heartbreaking stories, and stories of capture. Their lives were a continuation of their performances.

He took his position at the back of the line and held his breath. The music began with Mr. Santiago at the helm.

This was it.

His final bow.

The circus continued in its usual rhythm. Transitions of color, heralded by Timothée, wove their way through the audience. Yellows to oranges to reds to purples signified a change in each act. Even after seeing countless performances, exchanging slight smiles with most of the performers, and sometimes a few drinks, the mere acts continued to whisk Brent away. He lost track of time watching each of the performances. Only when Timothée took to the stage and transformed the area beneath the Big Top transformed from the orange of a fire to a soft lilac did Brent know it was time.

Brent glanced at Timothée as he took center stage. He closed his hands, smiled at Brent once, and the lilac color dissipated. Alone, Brent stood before the audience.

Let me tell you a story…

He opened his palms and let the story wrap around him.

It was a simple story, at least at first. Out of his palms, hundreds of misty dragons took flight, soaring through the Big Top and past the audience. The patrons clapped and jeered, pointing at the different mist-made creatures flittering about the air. Their smiles reminded Brent why he told the story, but he couldn't lose focus now.

Thousands of dragons flew across the world… He waved his hands, and the illusions disappeared, but for one sitting in the center of the room. It grew and grew, taking the form of a dragon grooming itself. It almost looked real.

The story took a sad turn, and with his heart on edge, Brent wrapped himself in Zephyr's tale. He let the audience see as a golden knight shot the dragon from the sky, maimed and beat her, and took her far away and wide.

The patrons booed at the golden knight and cried as the dragon begged for freedom. Brent's own heart broke as the story itself washed over his soul; in that moment, he wasn't just the storyteller. He was the dragon.

And his tears were true.

But he changed the story's end this time. As the golden knight loaded the dragon onto the train, a hundred dragons descended from the sky. The illusions were smaller than the main character but still just as vicious and on point. They swarmed the golden knight, tackled him to the ground, and let their companion go free.

The audience burst with applause as the mist-dragons flew into the ceiling of the Big Top. Brent clenched his hand shut but did not pull back on the mist. The stories would continue to bolster in the striped canvas, waiting...

Waiting...

He took a bow and stepped back into the shadows to allow for Zephyr's grand entrance.

Mr. Santiago cartwheeled out into the center ring, winking once at Brent, before his voice echoed. "And now, let's welcome to our act...the one you've all been waiting for...Zephyr the Dragon!"

Rather than returning to the green tent, Brent stayed hidden in the shadows. He let the mist and stories wrap around him, shielding him from any curious gazes. The entrance to the tent opened, and Zephyr plodded to the heart of the stage, ropes tied around each of her appendages. A few laborers held tight to the ropes, their heads bowed as the beast roared.

The audience applauded at her anger.

"Zephyr has been traveling with me for many years," Mr. Santiago boomed. "Just watch what she can do..."

Brent watched. He knew the routine well enough by now. Mr. Santiago had Zephyr breathe fire and mist, igniting hoops that the performers juggled. Zephyr's body swayed with the loud music, but her silver eyes did not show any light.

Waiting for the right moment, Brent watched the act in awe and horror. When he first saw Zephyr perform, it had been in a state of total amazement. Now he saw—and felt—her struggles.

"Now, Zephyr, show us what you can do!" Mr. Santiago called.

Zephyr huffed and lifted into the air. The spotlight shone on her, three laborers with tranquilizer guns aimed at her body as she flew. One wrong move, and she'd come crumbling to the ground.

Brent held his hand up as he watched. Zephyr circled the tent once.

Twice.

Three times.

The mist thickened in plumes behind her.

As Mr. Santiago expected.

He didn't expect the story that followed.

Once it cleared, a hundred dragons followed behind Zephyr. But these were not part of the act.

Mr. Santiago gaped. "What the—"

Zephyr's shrill caw drowned out Mr. Santiago's voice.

Brent laughed, racing into the center of the tent, directing the fake dragons to take to all sides. There was no longer just one dragon in the tent: now, there were hundreds.

The audience continued to applaud, completely unaware of the sudden change in the agenda. More and more fake dragons spawned from the mist, the story itself taking on a life of its own. Brent kept his attention on Zephyr as the story continued, approaching her as she landed on the ground with a few other illusions in tow.

Brent approached her and held out his hand.

The dragon sniffed it and roared.

"Boy!" Mr. Santiago shrieked. "What are you doing?"

Brent glanced over his shoulder at Mr. Santiago. "I gotta leave. Sorry, sir."

"No, you ain't!" Mr. Santiago barked. "You're my property!"

Brent placed his hand on Zephyr's neck. "No. Not anymore."

"I'll throw ya to the Guard right now, boy!" Mr. Santiago glared towards his tranquilizers. "Stop him!"

Zephyr lowered her body, allowing Brent to throw his leg over the beast's back. The dragon roared, and with a single heartbeat, took to the sky. Brent hung on, closing his eyes tight as Zephyr spiraled into the air. His stomach performed acrobatics, and his head spun. In the distance, Mr. Santiago's voice grew softer as Zephyr continued her wild ascent.

"Aim for the one with him on it! That's the real one! The rest are fake!" Mr. Santiago's voice boomed.

Shite! Brent thought for a moment. He held out his hand, and around him, the dragon-filled stories reshaped. Mirror images of himself, mere shadows, appeared on the faux-dragon's backs. Confusion provided a clear shield. The shots rang out from below, but rather than hitting Zephyr, they soared through the mist and into the canvas tent.

Brent laughed and returned to Zephyr's harness. The dragon circled the tent once, then forced her way out of the Big Top entrance, sending concession stands flying and patrons hiding.

A yellow tinge filled the sky outside the tent.

"Listen, we gotta pick up my dog and stuff. She's right outside," Brent whispered to the dragon.

Zephyr purred and hovered close to the ground, circling towards the far end of the circus where Micca waited with Nix. The dragon skidded to a halt just at the end of the carnival, though, screeching as she hit an invisible barrier. Brent toppled to the ground only a few paces away from where Micca and Nix waited.

The dog barked in excitement as Brent took her tether.

"Good girl!" Brent took the tether in his hand and his bag in the other and guided Nix over to Zephyr.

Nix growled at the dragon, and Zephyr responded with the same snarl.

"Hey, hey, now's not the time, a'ight?" He glared at Nix.

The dog whimpered again.

Brent glanced at Micca. "Thanks for all your help with this."

"Yeah, I'm always down for making an issue of myself. You know that." Micca winked. "You better get out of here. Listen to that mess."

Shouts echoed from the edge of the carnival.

Brent glanced back at Micca. "You sure you wanna stay here?"

"I ain't leaving Timothée behind."

"A'ight. I understand."

"Good luck, man. Go find Bria and save the world or some shite. And get married, or I'mma force-feed you pineapple."

Brent placed a hand on Micca's shoulder and squeezed it. "A'ight, I'll try."

"Go, you dumbass!"

With a final wave, Brent wrapped an arm around Nix and mounted on Zephyr once again. He tugged at the dragon's harness. She threw herself against the invisible barrier again and shrieked. This time, Brent felt a jolt of electricity rip through him, starting at the center of his arm and through his chest.

"We have to go up! Understand?" Brent called over the dragon's shrieks.

With one open arm, Brent tugged up on the dragon's harness. She screamed again, then shot into the air.

Up and up and up she climbed, high above the carnival until it looked like nothing more but a child's toy sparkling below them. The colors wove together, sighing against the breaths of the yellow sunset. It was almost beautiful. But Brent held his breath.

They had yet to break through the barrier.

He gripped the reins around Zephyr as they neared the perimeter, bracing for impact.

Bam!

Zephyr screeched, spiraling down towards the ground again. Nix howled.

"C'mon, Zephyr! You can do it!" Brent pleaded. His arm burned and head spun. They had to break through this. *Surely there must be a weak spot.*

He scanned the circus below him for a story. Dots of people moved about with Mr. Santiago's gold coat glistening like a beacon. Brent had seen the man's stories in waves—a man controlling a circus, barking orders, and reveling in golden coins.

That tale held no answers, so instead, he turned to the circus. It arrived in the night in a blanket of steam pouring from the smokestack on the locomotive. When it settled, the steam parsed out in a dome, forming a momentary wall before dissipating.

Brent glanced to the front of the train, then called out to Zephyr, "Go to the engine! Right above the smokestack…then go up! A'ight?"

Zephyr roared, then spiraled higher again. She followed along the back of the train, her wings casting a shadow over the cars. Brent fixated on the story of the barrier. Invisible but powerful, he sensed it expanding.

Upon arriving above the smokestack, Zephyr paused, then shot up into the sky. Higher…

Higher…

Higher…

A rippling of heat seared through Brent as they broke the first layer of clouds. He bit down on his lip, holding back a scream as it tugged on him.

Zephyr roared.

Then, with a beat, it subsided. The sun-shaped brand on his arm stopped throbbing.

The circus waited as only a speck of glistening lights below them.

Brent let go of the stories. As Nix curled up between his legs, Brent's own exhaustion took root. But he had to keep his eyes open, no matter the cost.

As they passed through the second layer of clouds, sunset welcomed them with open arms. But a deep pernicious yellow wreaking havoc along the edge of the sky stained the sunset sky. It danced along the cloud tops, scaring birds back to the earth and settling in Brent's heart.

I should've known it was nearby! the Diabolo remarked. *Getting soft being in your head.*

That's cause you're really me. I'm not you.

Nah.

Brent gripped tight to Zephyr's harness. Without a doubt, somewhere, a Diabolo waited, carving the skyscape out with its claws, setting a trap, and waiting for an enemy to show its face.

CHAPTER THIRTY-SIX

VESSEL

Yaz could hardly walk. Every day, Sir Jama had insisted she drink the strange silver liquid. And every night, nightmares riddled her head. She struggled to sleep, food tasted like lead, and whenever she tried to ask Sir Jama what was happening, he spoke about how proud he was of her endeavor. He promised her that once they reclaimed the Library, she would finally become a Mist Keeper.

But now, all she only wanted was to sleep.

Each day, she downed the liquid. In her dreams, she was a monster; each time, she was a different one. Some days, she walked along the edge of the giant cities in Yilk. Another time, she flew through the sky, destroying everything in her path. Her most recent dream took her down to the Glass City in Proveniro, where she waited over the water, watching as children played by the sea. She never remembered what happened in the dreams, only that she was there and that she was trying her best to get back to her master… her home.

She lost track of how many times she had those dreams, blending into her daily routine. In the morning, she would go explore the dragon fields with Caroline. The woman said little, often making small talk about Yaz's hobbies or about the weather. A few times, Yaz almost asked Caroline about her old apprentice, but she stopped herself. A sudden ache in her head pulled back on her questions and stored them in the far pockets of her mind. So instead, she just smiled and exchanged polite chit-chat with the woman before returning to the cavern on the hill again. There, Aelia, sometimes with Jiang's help, would make another pungent brew and tell Yaz to drink.

And, of course, Yaz obeyed.

She tried her best to listen in on Sir Jama's conversations with Aelia, Jiang, Alojzy, and Caroline. She caught glimpses of it: they wanted their library back, they searched for a few missing Mist Keepers, and they feared the ultimate backlash at hand. Alojzy spoke of events in Knoll, while Aelia discussed events in Mert, but Yaz struggled to keep up with the conversation. She wanted to understand; she tried to get Sir Jama to explain, pleading every day during their nightly discussion.

Sir Jama always said the same thing: "Trust us, Yasmin. You will do great things."

After days of this routine, Sir Jama woke Yaz up as a yellow sunrise flooded the Dragon Plains beneath their cavern.

"Yasmin, it is time…" His voice sliced through the air like a knife.

Yaz rolled over, yawning once. As she exhaled, yellow mist poured from her lips. "Sir Jama?"

"Come, Yasmin. It is time." Sir Jama recited again. He sat in Aelia's arms. His white eye focused with determination. As he spoke, chains of mist poured from his lips, helping Yaz to climb from the ground.

"What's happening?" Yaz asked. She blinked a few times, attempting to see past the onslaught of yellow filling her vision.

"It's time to reclaim the Library from the Evil," Sir Jama said. "We are ready."

Yaz blinked around the cavern. Only she, Sir Jama, Aelia, and Caroline stood in the room. "Where's everyone else?"

"Alojzy and Jiang have gone ahead to create a necessary distraction. They shall meet us at the Library."

"But don't we need an army?"

Ningursu smiled. "We have all the army we need."

"Huh?"

"You shall see Yasmin. For your power shall be magnificent."

Yaz stared hard at Sir Jama but didn't argue. Surely this ancient skull knew what was best.

"Come along. We must act in haste before our window of opportunity closes."

Yaz followed Sir Jama, Aelia, and Caroline back into the tunnels, glancing one last time over her shoulders at the yellowing plains just outside the cavern. Shadows of dragons soared through the sky. Yaz considered running in the opposite direction, hopping on the back of the creatures, and flying away. She missed her soft bed; she missed her dollies; in some ways, she even missed Ms. Kai and Mr. Nasr.

She shook away those desires in an instant, trudging along behind the Mist Keepers and into the heart of the tunnels.

The tunnels felt different this time. Each step bore a weight echoing along the cavernous walls. Thick mist gathered at their feet with stride. All else was silent and dark, but the crackling flames every few minutes, counting the moments from the wall.

They arrived at a tunnel junction to the sound of banging. Jiang stood there, throwing himself against a towering door, anger fueling every physical assault. He cursed in an unknown language before asking, "How have they locked the doors to keep us out?"

"You forget, Jiang, that they have magic." Sir Jama smiled.

Jiang spat.

"And you throwing yourself against the door has only alerted them to our presence. Your job was to merely scope the area."

"Nothing about this tunnel has changed!" Jiang barked.

"Pull back, Jiang." Mist chains exploded again from Sir Jama's mouth, and they tugged Jiang away from the door and to the far side of the junction.

Jiang groaned.

"Where did Alojzy go?" Sir Jama inquired once the mist faded.

"Went to open the other doorways like you asked, then headed back to Knoll."

"Very good. Then we are ready."

Jiang opened his mouth to say something, then shook back his long hair, glaring at the wall once again.

Aelia positioned Sir Jama in the center of the junction. She then guided Yaz over to Sir Jama and sat her down on the floor. The Mist Keepers exchanged a single nod.

Sir Jama began, "Yasmin, you have an immense power."

"Huh?" Yaz blinked.

"You have the amazing ability to empathize with the monsters known as the Diabolo. You've been controlling them in your sleep. Now, we shall use them to take back the Library."

"But those are dreams!" Yaz protested. "I don't know what I am doing!"

"That's okay, Yasmin. I have many years of experience. All I need for you to do is trust me, understood?"

Yaz glanced over her shoulder at the other Mist Keepers. They nodded in her direction.

She turned back to Sir Jama. "A'ight…"

"Good girl. Now hold out your hands."

Yaz gulped but did just as Sir Jama instructed. Tendrils of mist wrapped around her wrists.

"Now, Yasmin, I want you to close your eyes. Focus on what fills your vision…"

Yaz did as she was told. At first, darkness met the inside of her eyelids, but the longer she kept them close, the more she saw. First, a curtain of yellow flowed over her. Then, it was as if she watched out of hundreds of eyes: tall cities, empty deserts, gray forests, and lush swamps all greeted her in a picture show. She couldn't quite fixate on one. No. She saw it all.

"Good." Sir Jama spoke, distant. "Now inhale what you see, let it fill your senses, then exhale. I am here to help."

Yaz took a deep breath. Her stomach churned at the nauseating scent of rotten eggs and milk. It burned her eyes, dried her tongue, and buzzed in her ears. Her skin crawled. The monsters filled her; for a moment, she was no longer Yaz. She was the creatures all across the globe, hurling themselves on for an endless oblivion.

"And release!" Sir Jama ordered.

As she opened her mouth, a noise that reminded her of a steaming kettle exited her lips. It started as a low rumbled, then grew higher, and higher, and higher.

Until a yellow steam flooded out of her mouth.

It spiraled in the air, filling the junction with smoke.

As if on cue, the tunnels nearby rumbled, and just like the smoke from her mouth, monsters exited into the junction.

Yaz kept screaming, louder and louder. The monsters grew. The creatures roared.

Ningursu murmured something Yaz didn't understand, and the same words exited her own lips. Was it a command? An order?

Yaz didn't know. The world around her spun.

The monsters attacked the Library door, clawing it open with the power of an army and the anger of a mob.

But Yaz didn't know if they were successful. Her head grew heavy. Her eyes bled.

And she collapsed onto the ground with yellow mist gathering around her cheeks.

CHAPTER THIRTY-SEVEN

ARRIVAL IN YELLOW

Bria spent the next day venturing into the Necrowood with Lana in search of the tower after seeing Madame Owiti. They had visited Madame Owiti in the infirmary, asking the old seer for help to find the tower. She gave them guidance, describing the way the world churned around the tower with a layer of silver. But other than the dead trees, Madame Owiti had no specific landmarks to help them find it.

With only a confirmation that the tower still stood, Bria and Lana spent all day searching the Necrowood. While exploring the forest, though, Lana quizzed Bria on her magic. Reluctant at first, Bria gave in, and they spent hours exploring the way different nutrients and elements pulsated through the plants.

While Lana talked little about her life, she did talk about the book she gave Bria. She detailed the different elements she had read about over the years, often conversing with Hue about the intricacies of each element. Lana then urged Bria to trace along the veins of leaves for the electric pulses, the oxygen breaths, and the absorbed nutrients. With each touch, she sensed the different nutrients: iron caused her body to perk, zinc caused her little branch to bloom with leaves, and carbon transformed the yellow stains on her leaves to green. She couldn't name all of them, but from what Lana had researched over the years, there were over one hundred elements navigating the intricacies of the world. Bria didn't quite believe it, but with each day of practicing, she noticed her ability to manipulate her surroundings grew.

Beyond plants, her magic often caused everything else to turn to dust.

"Crud..." Bria grumbled as a stone crumbled in her hand. She stared at the powder, willing for it to come back to life. She'd been trying to manipulate it into an arrowhead, the same way she could command the branches into the shape of a sword or a ladder. But even as she could sense the way elements intermingled to form flint, she could not get it to obey. She let the dust fall to her fingers. "This isn't working."

"You definitely have the magic." Lana crossed her arms, staring at the pile of dust on the ground. "Unfortunately, I do not have the knowledge to instruct you on how to manipulate it. I base everything I know on conjecture."

"I wonder if Kek could help," Bria mused aloud.

"Who?"

"Someone I've met in my travels." Her mind thought back to Mert. *Could Edith help? She can manipulate metal. Is it the same idea?*

Lana stared into the forest. "I know you want to help us, and I want you to help us too...but perhaps it is time for you to move on. I'd hate to hold you back. You have healed well over the past few days."

Bria stared at her leaf-appendage and clenched her stick-like fingers. It was still odd, using the branch for a hand. While she could sense things in her clutches, she still couldn't *feel* with it, a constant reminder of what happened in the Tower. Lana was probably right. There was no reason to spend much longer in the Pit, not when she could take to the trees and produce life out of the dead. She could even use the time to destroy the Pools.

But where would she go?

She had to find Brent. That much she knew. They were a team, and without him by her side, she wasn't sure she'd be able to lead any charge against the Order, the Council, or even Kek.

"Even if I wanted to leave, I wouldn't even know where to begin," Bria whispered. "Before I even dive further into this…I need to find Brent. We're a team, and I can't do this without him. For now, I have to keep to my goals."

"Right. Brent. That boy you keep talking about." Lana shook her head. "You don't need him. You're clearly strong enough on your own."

"It's not like that! We're a team; we complement each other," Bria said. "He's my best friend…my confidante. I love him."

Lana rolled her eyes.

"Weren't you ever in love?" Bria asked.

"I was in something. Didn't last long after…well…what I did."

"Can I ask what you did?"

Lana scowled. "I murdered someone. Not much else to it, really."

Bria kept her composure. Nowadays, murder didn't cause her to bat an eye. She'd met people who had done far worse. She asked, "And why did you murder them?"

"Protection, I guess," Lana said as she peered at the sky. "The man I thought I loved…he wanted nothing to do with me after that. The moment you break the façade of being pure, they only see you as a demon. That's why love…it means nothing in the end. Everyone loves a myth."

"I've…killed someone too," Bria approached Lana.

"And your lover stood by you?"

"Brent understands things. He has this innate ability to see why something happened."

"You're idolizing him."

"No! It's the truth. I think you'd like him if you met him. He's…" Bria smiled to herself. "He's a mess, but he's sweet. And we work together. I can't take on the world without him by my side."

"Eh, whatever you say. But don't let his disappearance keep you from bettering yourself." Lana pointed her finger at her. "If you are given the chance to soar, take it."

"I will."

Lana turned her back. "Keep practicing in the meantime. I think we call it quits for tonight, though. It's getting dark, and we won't be able to find the tower by nightfall. We'll try again in the morning." She walked past Bria back towards the Pit. "I would be out of here in a heartbeat if I were in your place."

Bria watched in silence as Lana left. She knew Lana was right; the Pit wasn't safe. If they didn't find the Tower soon, then surely the Guard would find out she was here. The Guard had plastered her face all over Rosada. Even if the Guard didn't discover her, what would stop a vagrant from turning her in for a shot at freedom? She genuinely believed most people wouldn't, but she was sure, somewhere in the heart of the Pit, someone would want a chance at a new life.

She marched along the edge of the Necrowood, letting her mind wander. As she wandered, she found a few small silver puddles, easy to break with a mere wave of her hand. In their place, a single peony blossomed, a stain of color on the otherwise drab landscape. The plants moved easier to her now, humming and singing as she walked by them. Sometimes, she even swore that the stone spoke to her or the clouds in the sky.

Part of her wished they wouldn't. Part of her just wanted to curl up in her bed and revel in silence.

She hated to admit how much she missed Brent. Every time she thought of him and the way she could curl up beneath his arms, her heart ached. Bria yearned for those small moments: those times in bed early in the morning, where she could roll over and nuzzle into his side. She missed the way Nix slept on her feet and the way Brent smiled when a story blossomed on his tongue. His stories brought so much joy to others.

While she missed his stories, she longed for the connection and a chance to listen to him rationalize every thought. When she closed her eyes, she saw his handsome face, his silver eyes as bright as the moon, and his curls like the waves of the sea. She rarely gave him the satisfaction of knowing how he made her swoon, but he did.

At least when they were in Mert, she generally knew where he was, even if the monsters clawed into his psyche.

This was different. An air of uncertainty hung in the air. Did the Guard capture him? Was he thrown into some pit?

Was he in Knoll?

Or wandering the Rosadian landscape?

Or captured again by the Council or Kek?

She didn't know. And it was that uncertainty that made her stomach quiver.

With her head down, she limped out of the Necrowood and into the Pit. Well, the forest closest to the Pit wasn't quite dead anymore. She'd nurtured the canopy, helping the trees burst with green. With the color, the trees thanked her, and the Necrowood began its slow ascent back into the arms of life. Bria only helped a few trees at a time, her energy worn from practicing with Lana each day and her recovery still incomplete from the Tower as well as from her time in the Library. Even though weeks had passed since Ningursu clawed through her head, ignited her magic, and sent her heart pounding, she still sensed the results in her core. Using too much would leave her wilted. So, she couldn't use all her energy to save a forest.

Not now.

As she stepped out from under the trees, sunlight did not greet her as she expected. Instead, a deep smog rested over the sky, wreaking of sulfur and ash.

Her stomach churned.

The smell. The color. Even the taste. Everything flooded back to her.

This was no normal smog.

She raced into the center of the Pit. A few vagrants gathered, all eyeing the sky with confusion. Mothers held their children's hands while a few vagrants rushed into their tents, leaving others coughing by the firepit. Bria searched for Lana in the crowd. *Why is this happening now?*

The sky continued its descent into yellow. Yes, most definitely, Bria knew this without a doubt. A Diabolo was near Knoll. It pulsated with nightmares.

Marisol rushed over to her. "Rho! There you are! This is some weird-looking storm, isn't it?"

"This isn't any old storm!" Bria shouted over the wind.

"What do you mean? Isn't it just the smog making the sun look weird?"

"No. Haven't you heard about what happened in New-bird's Arm?"

"The Storm of Nightmares?"

"Yes. It's happening again. We need to get everyone inside as soon as possible."

Marisol eyed Bria carefully. "Are you sure?"

"I was there. I'm positive. Get everyone to safety." Bria glanced around the area. The air grew thicker with each parting moment. "Quickly."

"Listen, I trust you. I'd know if you were lying." Marisol winked. "Don't know if everyone else will trust you, though."

"I'll find Lana. She'll get them to listen."

Bria left Marisol to gather the different vagrants into their homes. She ignored the thunder rippling through the air, tasting as each branch of electricity in the distance called for her. With every step, she could feel the earth calling for her. Not just the trees now. The stones whispered; the water babbled; the sky screamed. Every step carried the weight of the world on her shoulders. She shook them off, though, focusing on finding Lana…or someone who might listen to the impending doom.

Yellow thickened with every step, collecting dust with burly breaths and mounting height. Nimbus clouds rose above the towers in the distance, higher than the Dead Forest, and masked every bit of color in the sky.

Except yellow.

"Everyone, get inside!" Bria shouted as she ran past a few vagrants. She slowed as she walked past Hue, hurrying down the path with Madame Owiti on her arm. For a quick moment, Bria exchanged a glance with the old woman. An understanding crossed her face.

They shared a mutual memory of these monsters in Mert.

A SHIELD OF COLOR

Lex kept her head low as the cadet with the burned face led her out of the infirmary. After what seemed like weeks of poking and prodding, they had decided to remove her from the infirmary. Professor Gratz never told her the results of the study. All Lex knew for sure was that she could see every color pulsating around the Guards, the doctors, and everyone; intentions glowed with the rainbow, and evil lurked in red and silver.

The cadet thrust her down the stairwell in chains. His aura bled bronze, flickering between silver and gold in different lighting. "C'mon. Get a move on. Sooner I get ya locked up, the sooner I can get food."

Lex gripped the handrails as she walked down the stairwell. Each step pulled at her. She wanted nothing more than to escape the pain; weakness grappled her body, sadness strangled her heart, and loneliness slipped through her veins. The Guard never brought her Garrett, they had taken Madame Owiti far away, and they had turned her husband into a traitor.

The cadet nudged Lex harder. She fell forward, toppling down the last couple steps and hitting the ground at the exit to the Tower. She held herself there, only moving when the cadet lifted her by both her arms and dragged her into the evening light.

Lex squinted. A yellow haze desiccated the land, like dust on the horizon or a handful of sunlight dripping through the clouds. As the cadet pulled her from the ground, the yellow grew brighter, as if staring directly into the sun itself.

But no sun hung in the sky.

Is it the sun god of Yilk wreaking havoc? Lex blinked a few times. It reminded her of the strange monsters that attacked Mert right before the Order arrived and forced her to flee. But then, the monsters produced only a soft yellow glow, weaving its way through the city, only a gentle aura filling the streets. This was stronger, blinding even.

"C'mon!" the cadet yelled. "Ain't no time to be looking at the sky!"

"It can't be wise to be out in the open..." Lex glanced at the young man.

"Then we better hurry and get inside, huh?"

Lex shook her head. "We should go back inside right now. We shouldn't be out here..."

The cadet yanked her forward. Lex stumbled along the path towards the truck. With every step, she swore the yellow brightened. Her worries escalated; she could almost picture Garrett, sobbing alone in his cell, begging for his mother or father. Did he have Preston? Was he close?

What about Madame Owiti? Was she alive?

She tripped again as she stepped forward. She turned to the sky. Shadows moved like monsters, and in her heart, she knew what was coming. Tears dripped from her eyes. "Please, we need to go inside. Can't you feel it? There's a monster!"

"I said shut up!" The cadet hit her. Hesitancy filled the assault, less commanding and done without true purpose. His aura flickered again.

"Look!" Lex begged.

"Stop trying to distract me, you fucking bitch! There ain't anything there. It's just a fucking storm—" The cadet's eyes trailed to the sky. His face paled. "No..."

"See!" Lex clutched the cadet's arm. "We need to get inside!"

The cadet didn't seem to hear her. "He's back."

Lex gawked.

"I need to tell Dad…" The cadet stared at her. "C'mon! Now!"

The cadet tugged on Lex's chains. She stumbled again as they approached the truck. Thunder rumbled in the sky. *No, this isn't the Sun God of Yilk. This is the anger of the Effluvium.* Lex gulped as she climbed into the back of the truck with a few more prisoners.

Even the sanctuary of the truck could not stop the fear building in Lex's body. The other prisoners sat beside her, hallowed faces and empty, twiddling their thumbs and shifting back and forth in their spot. Panic bubbled.

The cadet climbed into the driver's seat and began driving along the bumpy road. Rain picked up as they hurried along, causing the truck to swerve from one side to the next. Lex clutched the seat and tried to focus on anything but the thickening yellow. She observed the auras of the other prisoners, watched the way they shifted, and prayed to any god that dared to listen.

The storm rocked the truck. As they rushed along, the wheels shrieked, the road thudded, and the other prisoners mumbled prayers. Lex fell, deep down, into a sudden memory. Had this happened before to her? She remembered riding in a truck like this, with a horse at the helm;

she had chains on her wrists, and so many colors filled her vision.

She was a child.

She was alone.

This had all happened before, long ago.

Lex peered out the window, watching as the darkest tower emerged from the ashen sky. It stood without windows, a tall prison of hatred and despair. It might have been a nightmare, brought out by the monsters filling the sky.

But she remembered it.

The dark cells.

The endless cries.

The loneliness.

Again. She was returning.

The truck lurched forward, sending all the prisoners flying into the wall. Lex caught herself, then stole a glance out the front window.

The cadet sat frozen in the driver's seat.

A monster, with elongated fingers, a lopsided grin, and misaligned eyes, charred by fire and ash, rose above the treetops and skimmed the edge of the towers. Mist pulsed from its body. Even from inside the truck, its rotten and foul smells grappled at Lex's face.

Everyone's aura turned black.

"Fuck!" the cadet cursed as the truck rocked again. Lex gripped her seat. She had last felt this wave of nausea when the monster ripped through her shop in Mert. Seeing it now sent her back in time, filling her stomach with anger over Todd's ill decisions. It was like the storm was inside her, tainting her own aura and that of everyone around her. Each time the monster—or was it a storm?—screamed, her aura darkened.

No light.

No freedom.

Only fear.

Only darkness.

Lex shut her eyes tight as the truck skidded again. The cadet pressed on the brakes, and the truck teetered forward. Rain battered the windows, and the storm clawed outside the truck. Winds rocked the truck, pushing it one way, then the next, and—

With a flash of lightning and a roll of thunder, the truck spun out of control. The other prisoners in the truck screamed, and the cadet cursed at the top of his lungs. The radio he spoke into cut out.

Lex held her hands out in front of her face. She thought of Garrett, cold and alone, and of Madame Owiti, ill and worried. Her worries gathered in her chest, and she cradled them close. Worries. How she hated them. But at least they told her one thing: she still wore emotion deep in her soul.

She still bore humanity.

And she would keep fighting.

The truck toppled in slow motion as her worries gathered. From her fingertips, her aura extended. A protective shield of gold wrapped around her and the prisoners.

Crash.

Lex and the other prisoners tumbled forward as the truck landed on its side. Glass shattered. Bodies flew.

But her aura acted as a cushion.

And no blood poured from the rear of the van.

Garrett. Garrett. I'm coming for you, Garrett.

Panting, Lex clamored to her feet. Her head spun as she pushed past the debris towards the broken window. Outside, the storm continued to rage on, with no guards in sight against the skyline of Knoll.

She glanced back over her shoulder at the other prisoners. Everyone appeared okay. With the shattered windows, they had an escape.

Lex ignored her nerves and fears and pulled herself through the window. It was a tight squeeze, but after a couple weeks of little food, she'd dropped some weight around her waist and hips.

She clamored out of the truck and onto the road. Rain battered against her face as Lex breathed in the stormy air. Despite the nightmarish yellow riding through the sky, relief washed over her. Chains hung from her wrists, and the auras spun around her. But she was free. She could go find Garrett, she could go find Madame Owiti, and then they could run away to someplace safe. Back to Mert, perhaps.

Or maybe somewhere else far away.

She held her chained hands up above her head, using her aura as a shield against whatever monster rode in the sky. It wouldn't be able to see her if she held her gods close.

She had to believe that much.

Without looking back at the truck, Lex hurried along the road, carrying her son's name against her breast and aura close to her heart. *I'm coming, Garrett. I promise.*

CHAPTER THIRTY-NINE

ENLIGHTENMENT

Jemma stood in the back of the Aviary's Atrium, listening as Senator Cordova blessed the newly arriving prisoners. She kept her head low, mouthing along to prayer, begging that the Effluvium would help set the new prisoners free. Already, fourteen trucks had arrived with ten prisoners each, all bearing the black stamp, with demons climbing on their backs. Some stared with eyes of silver, or lips of storytellers, or the hands of Magii. Did all of them really hold demons in their heart?

Not every vagrant belonged to demons. Micca had told her that during their travels.

Even if Micca didn't deserve vagrancy, Jemma couldn't know the past of these others. Could she put her faith blindly into the hands of strangers?

Jemma awaited the final truck with anticipation: Christof's truck. At first, they said little else, but those quiet nights held a strange warmth in her heart. He'd become a companion in this strange landscape of Knoll's Gully, and she didn't want to lose him. Yet, the more often he visited her cloister, the more they opened up, speaking in hushed whispers as the candles waned. Together they prayed but also discussed their past; they danced around the topics of their nullified betrothals, instead discussing the joy the Effluvium brought to them and the future of Rosada. Christof asked her with a husky whisper why she became a Sister; she asked why he became a guard. The answers were similar, with one obvious goal: to change the world.

When Jemma first started this journey, she would have thought they had different means to the same end. But hadn't they both left in the dead of night without a word? Hadn't they both endured the storm?

After everything, Jemma wasn't even sure what she stood for anymore. Did she support the Magii? It was hard to say yes. Not after what she'd endured.

Thunder broke through her thoughts. With the sky's roar, Senator Cordova's prayers teetered. He strode with poise over to the small window that peered out of the atrium. His voice echoed with confidence. "A storm has arrived. Sister Jey Ma, please lock down the tower. I must go discuss this with Elder An Drew…and prepare."

"For a storm?" Jemma asked. She joined the senator by the window and gasped.

On the horizon, over the City of Knoll and out towards the Necrowood, a yellow storm tore open the sky. Wind bellowed, thunder crashed, and lightning shimmered. Like the Storm of Nightmares in Newbird's Arm, a monster rose from the ashes, locking her in permanent fear. She couldn't shake it, and every time she closed her eyes, a constant feeling of failure pooled in the center of her body.

"Oh…I see." Jemma remarked.

"Lock down the tower."

"Yes, of course…" Jemma glanced back at the guards, and her stomach tightened. *Still no Christof.* She turned back to Senator Cordova. "But sir! Not all the prisoners have arrived. You said there would be fifteen arrivals; we've only had fourteen!"

"If we lose the prisoners, so be it." The senator turned. "Lock down the tower."

Before Jemma could stop the senator, he disappeared down a hallway and into one of the heavy doors.

Jemma turned to the guards in the atrium, keeping her voice steady as she relayed the order. "You heard Senator Cordova. Lock down the Tower! The last thing we need are vagrants escaping during the storm. If we lose them, we fail the Effluvium!"

She feigned confidence, straightening her shoulders and watching in horror as the Guards moved like clockwork to secure the Aviary. Her mind kept fleeing to the last truck out in Knoll. Where was it? Would it make it in time? *Where's Christof?* She couldn't shake the dread over what might happen to him in the nightmarish storm. What if it ripped him to pieces? Last time, he and his father escaped its vengeful wrath. This time, might it finish the job?

Outside, the storm continued to wage a war. She and Christof both knew what happened during the Storm of Nightmares.

Except this was worse.

Through the small window, she watched as the storm ate away at the landscape. It ripped open buildings, tossed aside trucks, and sent debris flying. In the distance, the Necrowood almost seemed to dance with the storm. It might have been a trick of the light or the storm acting out, but Jemma swore she saw a dragon in the sky.

The questions rotated in her head as she gripped the windowsill. Were Brent and Bria near Knoll? Was this their fault? Or something worse, more powerful?

Jemma didn't know.

As she broke her paralysis to lock the window, the main door swung open. Christof ran in, dripping wet, blood pooling from his nose.

"Cadet Carver!" Jemma exclaimed as she ran to him.

The cadet met her gaze. "I need to speak with my father."

Then, his eyes rolled back into his head, and he collapsed on the floor.

Jemma waited in the hallway outside of the small room where Elder Un Dine let Christof rest, pretending to be enamored with the scripture written on the walls. It detailed the Effluvium's role in keeping the cities safe from the beasts of the forest, wrapping the trees in its embrace, and choking out the evil. Her attention fixated instead on the etching of the trees around the scripture while her ears listened to the discussion behind the door of Christof's room.

Captain Carver had arrived within the hour. He didn't even acknowledge Jemma, rushing into the room and yelling at his son without hesitation. His fury echoed through the walls, his questions repetitive and statements absurd.

"How could you let the prisoners escape!?!"

"I have never known a more useless guard!"

"One more fuck up like that, and I'm gonna throw your useless ass in the Pit."

"Fucking pathetic."

Jemma never heard Christof's responses. She stayed bowed in prayer outside, pretending to not be interested in the shouting as Captain Carver left the room. He stomped away, not noticing Jemma, his feet scuffing across the floor, his fingers laced around the whip on his hip.

Once he disappeared down the hallway, Jemma slipped into the room.

Her mouth grew dry upon seeing Christof.

He sat on the edge of the bed with his eyes shut, back hunched over in defeat. He wore no shirt. Sweat matted his torso. His muscles flexed as he gripped the uniform in his hands. Jemma froze as she stared at him; she'd seen men without clothes before, but there was something…stunning about Christof. His muscles, his body, the way he held himself…a vulnerability rested in his stature. Jemma yearned to cradle him and tell him it would all be okay.

She kept her poise, though. "Cadet. I've come to offer you a prayer of healing."

Christof grunted.

"And..." Jemma sat down beside him on the bed. "To make sure you are okay."

He glanced at her with jaded eyes. "Why do you care?"

"I worried you would get hurt out there in the storm." Jemma fiddled with the edge of her sleeve. "You have embraced the Effluvium in your life...and it would be a shame to lose someone like that."

"Hm." Christof glowered at the wall. "At least someone cares."

Jemma's heart ached at the sentiment. "Your father must—"

"Doubt it."

"He's your father, though."

"That don't matter to him! I'm just a no good fuck up in his eyes. I've been trying my whole damn life to impress my father. Joined the fucking Guard, tried to find myself a reputable wife, but no. He don't care about any of this damn cockamamie bullshite!"

She placed a hand on his arm. "You're not a failure."

Christof shoved her away. "Yeah. I am. I lost the girl I was gonna marry to some fucking demon-ridden slob. I got half my face burned off 'cause I was too much of an idiot. And now I can't even complete a damn prison transport!"

"Those failures do not define you in the eyes of the Effluvium."

"Effluvium this! Effluvium that! My father doesn't see it that way!"

"But I do!" Jemma protested.

Christof shot a glare back in her direction. As soon as their eyes met, his face softened, almost as though he would cry. He kept his emotions in check, though, straightening his shoulders, and keeping the staid presence of a guard. His voice echoed around the room. "What does it matter to you, Sister?"

Jemma's heart battered in her chest as she chose her next few words. "Because...I like you. I want to get to know more about you. I feel like even though we grew up together, I never really got a chance to know you. You're...you're enlightening."

Christof didn't blink. He stared at her with his jade eyes, hard as the stone, his lip pursed in a half scowl. Then he brought his burned hand to her face and tucked back a lock of hair. "Never really ever gave you much of a thought. You were just that pretty, pious girl back home. Ain't ever paid you a second glance. You're enlightening as well, Jemma Reds. It's a shame Harley never saw that."

"Brent had a mind of his own."

"He broke your heart."

"I don't think I ever gave him a heart that could be broken," Jemma laughed. "It would never work."

"So you don't have a twinge of hope that he is here, now, in Knoll?" Christof asked.

Jemma glanced to the window. Traces of yellow still hung in the evening sky while the wind died down into a steady whistle. She said, "It doesn't matter."

"But doesn't the storm seem familiar?"

Jemma fidgeted with the seam of her dress, then nodded. "Yes. It does."

"I bet Harley is here. That son of a bitch always brings trouble. My father thinks he's dead, but I don't think so. It's gonna follow him wherever he goes, I'm sure of it."

"But why would he be here?"

"To cause shite like he always has."

"But..." Jemma shook her head. Brent had always gotten into trouble, but had it been on purpose? Why did it follow him?

Perhaps he did have a demon on his back.

She glanced back at Christof. "If he is here...Bria might be as well."

Christof sighed and nodded. "Yeah...her too."

"Are you okay knowing that?"

"Yeah. It's just a fact of this shite. She's a bitch."

"I do not support that sort of language, Cadet!" Jemma scolded.

"Eh, well, I'm a guard, and I get to say what I want." Christof leaned his head back and stared at the ceiling.

Jemma held her hands over her lap, watching each of Christof's breaths as they rocked his body. There was something calming about watching him breathe. He took each one into his muscular chest and exhaled with a slight smile.

It made her stomach perform somersaults.

Christof continued, "I think...there are more enlightening people in this world than Bria Smidt. I'd been enamored by her for so long...but she is nothing more than a demon herself."

"I wouldn't say that."

"She came to Newbird's Arm with magic in her hands. She promised peace...but left with destruction in her wake. That's what the newspapers have said...and if that isn't a demon, I don't know what is."

Jemma didn't reply.

"I believe you are more *enlightening* than Bria Smidt." Christof eyed her.

"You really believe that?"

Christof bit his bottom lip, then nodded.

Jemma kept her eyes locked on him. Now she understood everything he had been through: burned by storms, tossed to the side, and overlooked by everyone. This guard just wanted someone to love him.

He needed more than the Effluvium in his life.

Jemma didn't break eye contact with him. Slowly, the guard pulled her close. His hot breath hit her cheek, his fingers digging deeper into her hair.

Their lips met.

This kiss carried more passion than Jemma had ever experienced. Her few kisses with Brent, all for show, held no passion or romance, just an obligation. But this kiss…she could have lost herself in it.

Christof held her with such desire that her entire body stiffened. His mouth consumed her lips, tongue tracing over her teeth, before pulling her closer. Jemma wrapped her arms around him, letting him pull her close, letting every single craving bubble out of hiding.

Christof pulled back and breathed into Jemma's neck. "I apologize, Sister. I know romance is held to a certain standard within the Temple."

"There is nothing in the scripture saying no." Jemma pressed her hand to his chest. Her body pounded, yearning for Christof's next touch.

"Are you sure?"

"I am sure." Jemma stepped back from Christof. She eyed him for a second. The scripture said nothing about love, intercourse, or marriage. While many Brothers and

Sisters of the Order devoted their lives entirely to scripture, many in the cloister explored different ways. This much she had learned during her short time in Knoll.

She hadn't quite explored it herself…until now.

With a storm raging and the land on fire, it was the perfect time to set off on this quest.

"I'm sure," Jemma whispered again.

Then, slowly, she unpinned the bun on her head, letting her red hair fall to her shoulders before strolling over to the door and locking it tight.

CHAPTER FORTY

SULFUR

B ria scaled the trees. With each passing moment, the fog grew thicker. Yellow. So much yellow ripped through the air. Coupled with the screams of the wind, she could only imagine the prowess of the monster producing its storm. The trees cried with every gust. As Bria balanced at the top of the canopy, weaving the dead branches together to form a platform, she nearly lost her footing, not once but twice.

She winced as streaks of rain bombarded her face. Bria struggled to see past her fingertips. *Focus. It's a part of nature.* She was no stranger to storms. Her heart racing, she opened her hands and let the water race over her. She focused on the elements within each drop of water—the good and the bad, feeding the earth below her. This time, instead of focusing her energy directly on the water, she focused outward, pushing the water away from her and the tree, allowing her to see her surroundings again.

The earth rumbled on the far edge of the forest, just at the edge where mountains met the Necrowood. A crack of lightning shot through the air.

What resembled a tornado spiraled out of the ground, filling the air with debris and fear. Bria held on to the tree, but her heart dropped. Despite knowing what was coming, it still ached to see: a monster, a Diabolo, rising from the ground, its distorted body more like a beast than a human. Its eyes glowed yellow, a constant reminder of its disfigured soul, tainted by misuse and mistreatment. Part of Bria ached for the Diabolo, a creature born of nothing but hate, destined to hunt something it could never obtain. Perhaps it hated magic because of its own creation, or perhaps, it hoped magic would cure it.

"Bria!" a voice called from the forest floor.

She looked down from her perch. Lana stood at the base of the tree, dripping wet.

"What's happening?" Lana called.

"I've seen this monster before!" Bria yelled back.

"Can you stop it!?"

"No, only Brent knows how." Bria frowned. "But I can distract it to make time for everyone to escape. Do you think you can help?"

"How?"

"Hold on!" Bria sent a branch-made ladder down to Lana. The woman climbed up, joining Bria on her platform. Once situated, Bria turned back to the monster, thinking aloud to herself. "Last time I distracted it, I lured it with a storm outside of Mert. It's attracted to magic, and even in a city of magic, it noticed me. This time I think its storm is too powerful...perhaps to counteract me. And if I used my magic, it would only come towards us instead. So..." Bria stared at the trees. "We confine it. At least for a little while. So people have a chance to escape and hide. Then we worry about how to defeat it."

"And why do you want my help? Seems like a waste of energy."

"Because your magic is like mine."

"I told you—"

"Yes, but you can still try!"

Lana sighed. "I can't do much."

"Any bit will help."

"And after we catch it?"

Bria pressed her fingers into the tree trunk, watching as the monster crawled across the landscape like a storm cloud. In its wake, branches flew, debris scattered, and thunder boomed. She turned back to Lana. "We try to destroy it. Or hope someone that knows how does."

"You mean your knight in shining armor?"

"Can you stop with that? Just because you had bad luck with love doesn't mean I will!"

"It wasn't bad luck. It was my fault."

"I doubt that."

"It is. You need to stop putting your trust in me, Bria. I'm not a good person."

"We don't have time—"

"You want to know why I'm in the Pit?"

"Do we have to do this now?" Bria shouted over the wind.

"I want you to know!" Lana snapped. "I like you, Bria. You're a good person. But you need to know this!"

"Lana—"

"I killed my daughter!"

Bria stopped, eyeing Lana as her heart skipped a beat. Lana told her she had killed, but to kill her own daughter? Bria never expected such a thing.

She didn't have time to process it.

"That was the past. This is now," Bria begged. "Please. You can be a hero now and stop this monster with me."

"I CAN'T HELP! My magic—"

"Is still there! Please...help me!"

Lana huffed, her face marred by tears and rain. Yet, she still gave an affirmative nod.

"Thank you," Bria whispered, then guided Lana's hand to the tree with her. How could Lana's small, thin hands kill? Lana would answer later. For now, they had a monster to fight.

Bria's thoughts returned to Brent. She wished in the deepest confines of her heart that Brent was there. Perhaps he was; perhaps that's why the Diabolo reared its ugly head. Did Brent finally lose it? Or did the Council uncover where they were?

She didn't have time to worry. Brent could take care of himself.

Usually.

Instead, she directed her energy inwards, tracing the pulse of the trees with her heartbeat and mind. Lana's pulse matched hers, and while the woman's magic was but a whisper compared to what Bria could sense, it helped. With a command in her heart, Bria ordered the trees nearby to grow, including hers. At least a hundred trees, or more, began their ascent into the sky. They wove together, taller than the towers, their spines bending and moving like sea anemones.

The monster turned its attention towards Bria. The strong magic attracted the monster, pulling it forward like a dog chasing food in the street. Its breath painted the world in rot; while the trees continued to grow, their leaves did not. Gray, black, white; the world turned monochrome with every breath and movement of the monster.

Lana pulled back once, her face pale and eyes wide. Bria nodded once at the woman. She'd given all she had to defend the Pit; now, Bria had to handle the rest.

She hoped that those with magic in the Pit stayed hidden. While some of them had talents that served well in a fight, they didn't understand this monster like her.

One wrong move, and they would become the Diabolo's lunch.

"A little closer…" Bria murmured as the monster flew over the tops of the trees.

It slowly became more and more visible: a torn open face with a flattened nose and white hair wrapping around its body. Just like its siblings, it bore no clear sex and no evident relation to humanity. It rode on the inhibition of terror and hate.

Nothing else.

Nothing more.

Once she saw the monster's teeth, she snapped the fingers on her good hand. Using her branch fingers, she commanded the trees to reach up, grab each of the monster's legs, and hold it in place. It riveted and shrieked, trying to escape the trees' clutches. Branches snapped as it tugged.

More trees grappled at the monsters' arms and torso, twisting and curving, taking a permanent form like a bonsai tree. Bria searched along the veins of the trees for different elements. She sensed the different nutrients, but the one she recognized was none other than that grotesque yellow rock.

Sulfur.

Not only did sulfur rip through the trees, but beneath the skin of the monster at large. Bria had sensed the strange substance on more than one occasion, gagging at the smell, trying her best to stay ahead of its evil grasp.

She let her senses wander past the trees and into the arms of the monster. It roared, tugging at her magic as it crawled over its body. Bria swore it would pull her into its arms at that exact moment.

But just like she'd been practicing with Lana, she put all her energy into that one element: sulfur. She let it fill her heart, her body, and warm her core.

Until it burst.

It wasn't dramatic like she'd seen with the other stones in the forest. Instead, the Diabolo merely roared in pain, then its body hunched over, graying. It continued to snarl, fighting against the dead trees. Bria kept them together, her heart pounding.

If she had been stronger, she might have been able to destroy it.

But the world of the Dead was beyond her reach.

At least it seems we're safe... Bria gulped. Dizziness threatened to toss her from the tree, but Lana's steady hand kept her in place.

The monster wheezed.

"I'm sorry," Bria mumbled. "I know it hurts. I'm sorry. I wish I could end it sooner..."

She meant it. She hated seeing this creature, born of pain, suffer. But even after removing a critical component of life, the monster continued to wither.

Because it wasn't alive.

And in that showed the true evil of Ningursu and his Mist Keepers. They created these monsters but gave them no way to die.

Except by their own hands.

And even they forgot it.

Bria slid to her knees. Lana pulled her into a hug as they watched the creature cry. Until its existence ended, it would stay there, haunting the landscape with its distant cries.

Another shriek joined its fear. It caught Bria's attention, and she directed her gaze to the sky.

Out of the clouds, a dragon emerged, pulsating with smoke and mist.

And it was flying straight for the Diabolo.

CHAPTER FORTY-ONE

DRAGON AGAINST DEMON

Brent spiraled through the sky, instructing Zephyr to dodge through the storm, his own head pounding by the onslaught of stories pouring out of the yellow mist. The residuals of the performance from mere minutes before pulled at his thoughts. He fought the urge to fall into the stories one at a time, focusing instead on the mountains ahead. Yellow spiraled out of the ground, winding through the air, masking the world in toxicity.

There, in the center of it all, emerged a Diabolo towering over the mountains and trees.

The landscape distorted as Brent directed Zephyr to fly towards the monster. Trees seemed to grow, reaching as high as the Diabolo if not higher. They grabbed onto its arms and legs, holding it in place. The creature roared.

Brent didn't want to get his hopes up, but the monster's prison could only belong to one person.

She has to still be in Knoll. He laughed and ushered Zephyr closer to the monster. The dragon shrieked as it neared, matching the Diabolo's blood-curdling cries.

Frankie the Diabolo's voice echoed in his head. *Something isn't right. That bitch of yours is doing something to it.*

Brent noticed it, too. The Diabolo had gone entirely gray, the mist around it coating the landscape in a way that reminded Brent of newspaper photographs. Tree branches tightened around the monster's skin every moment. Frankie was right; Bria, or whoever commanded the trees, was doing more than just holding the monster hostage.

Rain lambasted Brent as he directed Zephyr straight to the Diabolo. The monster continued to shriek and cry as if begging for a release. For a moment, Brent could taste every ounce of the monster's story: tales of killers carving open children, of spouses yearning for their significant other to return from war, and of doctors who thought they did no wrong. It was more than just evil; there was good hidden inside the Diabolo.

Where the voices of children sang.

Brent balanced himself on the saddle and held out his hand, letting the stories wash over him again. He ignored Frankie's cackles and Nix's whines, focusing on the stories in the monster's core. Around him, tales came to life: stories about warriors, about dragons, and about flying whales. He laughed at the audacity of each, but not for long.

Zephyr circled the Diabolo a few times, letting Brent knit the stories along his fingers. She blew away the smoke so he could see them all.

As well as see the demon holding them tight.

Brent locked eyes with the Diabolo. Sadness hung in the air as he reached out and captured the Diabolo's soul in his palm. Each of its stories traveled through him, and as he absorbed them into his soul, the monster began to fade.

"Goodbye. You're free now…" Brent whispered as Zephyr flew past the Diabolo one last time. In its place, specks of dust glistened like a rainbow in the sky.

And the moon hung bright.

My name is Brent Harley.

I free Diabolo from their chained lives.

I am free.

My name is Brent Harley.

I am me.

Frankie the Diabolo cackled. Brent shoved it down, closing his eyes tighter as Zephyr glided across the sky. Slowly, the beast lowered him into the Dead Forest, finding a small clearing between the towering trees. The trees remained in their permanent woven embrace, a visual reminder of how they captured the Diabolo and held it for ransom. No greenery bloomed beneath the moonlit sky.

All in the forest was quiet and dead.

Brent slid off Zephyr and hit the ground, grumbling to himself as he rolled over onto his back. He lay there for a minute, letting Nix lick his face. Finally, away from the commotion, his head caught fire. He saw all the stories at once and floundered in their embrace. Was he a mother yearning for a child? A father at war? A child screaming for chocolate? He didn't know.

He only had his name.

My name is Brent Harley.

My name is Brent Harley.

My name is—shite! He crawled along the floor of the forest to his bag. Each movement dragged him further into the Diabolo's tale; was his name Nedo? Did he love Mert? Or was he someone else?

The name *Brent Harley* sounded foreign on his tongue. His only hope lay in a vial. A single vial of silver.

He reached into his bag, found a syringe, and stuck it into the vial. The liquid filled the syringe, and with trembling fingers, he brought it to his arm.

The silver liquid relieved his thoughts, and the terror subsided.

Once again, he knew his name.

My name is Brent Harley. He glanced at Nix and patted the dog's head, then approached the dragon. She breathed out a puff of smoke, seeming to smile to herself, relief on her lips.

"You're free now, Zephyr. A'ight. I think…you can go wherever you want, y'know. If you wanna go back to Spinoza, it's in the east, I think. A long way away, but it's there. I think it's been a long time since you were there, though, I bet." Brent touched the dragon's snout. "Thank you for your help."

The dragon puffed out her chest, snorted, and bowed. Brent backed away, letting her beat her wings, and with a steady push of her hind legs, she took off into the sky, captured by the night air.

She disappeared into the clouds, a mere dot in the arms of the stars, once again free to roam the sky and count the stars.

CHAPTER FORTY-TWO

REUNITED BY TRUTH

Whales flew through the sky as the yellow storm dissipated.

And Bria laughed.

She dug her fingers into the tree, watching the story take hold. It had to be a story, without a doubt; the way the mist gathered around the whales, how they shifted in the sky, and the misty exterior on their fins all told the tale. This was none other than a creation by Brent Harley.

Well, except for the dragon Bria had seen passing in and out of the yellow clouds in the sky.

"Are those…flying whales?" Lana pulled Bria's attention away.

A smile laced over Bria's lips. "Yes. Brent's here."

"What does that have to do with flying whales?"

"Everything." Bria kept grinning. "I'll be back."

"Bria! Wait!"

Before Lana could stop her, Bria clamored into one of the bent trees. She found a steady perch at the top of the canopy. The Knoll skyline glowered in the distance while the remaining yellow clouds puffed with a gentle wind. A springtime humidity filled the air, caught on the back of the wind, rocking Bria's forehead with sweat.

Once again, in the distance, a dragon circled the trees, then descended into the forest.

With nothing else to go on, Bria headed in the direction of the dragon. The idea of Brent riding a dragon seemed preposterous, but it seemed like a strange coincidence for the dragon to appear at the same time as the story. She kept her hope tethered six feet away from her heart. The last thing she needed was another broken heart.

The clouds slowly moved out of the sky, while the dead trees of the Necrowood returned to their usual stance, gasping for breath as life left their bodies. They called for Bria to give them life. Bria shook away their demands.

Later.

She followed along the trees towards the clearing. A few birds cawed.

The beating of wings broke the silent night. As Bria neared, the dragon once more took to the air, breaking out of the treeline and into the sky.

"No!" she shouted.

The dragon didn't turn back, flying up...up...up...

And vanishing like mist into the sky.

"No...no...no!" She raced across the treetops. Where the trees finally parted, she jumped onto the ground, racing through the brambles.

A few bushes and sticks lay scattered on the ground where the dragon had landed. She grabbed a branch and broke it in frustration.

As the stick snapped, a dog barked.

Bria froze. *Don't hope. Don't cling to it. It can't be.* Her voice came as a whisper. "Nix?"

Another bark.

The trees parted.

Out of the bush, a dog lunged.

"NIX!" she cried out.

Nix jumped up and licked Bria's face. Laughing, Bria collapsed on the ground, hugging the dog tight, tears swelling in her eyes.

"I missed you," she choked on her words. If Nix was here, then that had to mean one thing—"Is Brent here?"

Nix barked once, then darted back into the brush. Bria chased after her, heart banging, a smile itching to pull at her lips.

Bria followed Nix through the trees to the clearing. There Brent sat against a tree, parsing through his bag, decked out in a purple suit. He removed his jar of medication with trembling fingers. As he put a pill in his mouth, his body relaxed.

A smile tugged at Bria's lips as she stepped towards him. Beneath her feet, a stick snapped.

Brent glanced up with his eyes wide. He blinked twice. "Bri?"

She waved.

He clamored to his feet, still staring, his crooked smile extending over his face. But then his brow furrowed. "You're not a story…right?"

"I don't think so."

He approached her. At arm's length, he reached out and touched her cheek.

When their skin touched, his smile returned. "Bria!"

"Hi," she laughed. Tears stung her eyes. It hadn't been long, only a few weeks, which was nothing compared to their time in Mert. But this felt different.

"It's you!" Brent laughed. Without his usual hesitation, he cupped her cheeks and kissed her, long and hard, beneath the arms of the Necrowood. Every few seconds, he pulled back, as if checking to make sure she was still there, before going back in for a kiss. Bria clung to Brent's purple shirt, never wanting to let him go ever again.

The kisses only stopped when Brent touched her branched arm. With gentle fingers, he traced the way the root moved down her neck from behind her ear, blending in seamlessly with her dark skin. The leaves and grooves gave away the arm's true nature.

"What happened?" he asked.

"It's a long story…" Bria pulled her hand back. "I'm okay, though. Really. Let's get out of here, then I'll tell you all about what happened."

"A'ight. Whenever you're ready." Brent stroked her cheek. She leaned into the warmth of his hand. Part of her worried if she closed her eyes, she might wake up to find him gone. All she wanted now was for him to hold her, to tell her it would be okay. She didn't care if it was a lie; it was what she yearned for more than anything.

"I missed you so much. I didn't know how I was going to find you…" Bria admitted, tracing her real fingers across his cheek.

"I knew you were heading for Knoll…just had to get there or something…I mean…yeah…" Brent replied. "Didn't intend to show up here on a dragon, but I ended up causing some shite with a circus and...well...I mean...yeah."

"You owe me that story."

"I'll tell you everything."

"You can tell me all about it on our way back to the Pit."

Brent froze. "The...Pit? Isn't that...what—the Pit?"

"Come on. You'll see."

The entire walk back to the Pit was filled with kisses and desire. Bria told Brent about her moments in the Tower while Brent detailed his wild adventure with the traveling circus. Between each story, they stopped, enthralled with each other again, before devolving into a fit of giggles.

Even though no one cared what they looked like, or what they did for that matter, embarrassment washed over Bria's face over the possibility of someone seeing them. Her giddy excitement brought her back to the schoolyard where she watched Brent tell his stories or to the senator's hedge mazes, where they explored different ways to touch and kiss.

Yet despite the excitement on their way to the tenement hall, by the time they arrived, exhaustion had longed washed over them. The moment Brent hit the bed, he passed out, shoes still laced, his long legs hanging off the end. Bria got him out of them before pulling the blanket over his body. She lay down beside him with Nix between them, listening to his breathing, but sleep did not find her. Instead, she watched as the night brushed the windowsill, counting the moment until dawn.

Sleep must have come at some point because the next thing she knew, morning trickles through the window. Brent still slept beside her, his arm now around her waist. She rolled over and took in his face. Stubble-covered, gaunt, and scarred. When he slept, he unveiled all his troubles. Awake, his bright eyes and smile hid it like a mask, a skill he'd gained over the past year.

After kissing his forehead, Bria slipped from his arm to use the restroom. Nix lifted her head slightly as Bria walked past, then fell back to sleep.

Memories of the previous night lingered as she stepped into the shower. As the cold water dripped down her body, she thought not just of Brent but of Lana. *I killed my daughter.* Her words echoed. Bria had processed little of it. Yet that statement alone caused her core to chill. What compelled her to kill? Bria trusted the woman…but that single question remained.

Bria struggled to braid her hair as she stepped out of the shower. Her branched fingers tangled with her hair, and she had to settle for a loose braid hanging against her shoulder after tugging a few strands from her head.

She cursed to herself as she left the bathroom, read-justing her arm as she hurried down the hall.

Lana waited at the end of the hallway by her room, pacing back and forth, head lowered. She raised her head as Bria approached. "Oh, good, you got home okay."

"Yeah, I got back last night," Bria said. "Are you okay?"

"I'm fine." Lana crossed her arms. "Just wanted to make sure you were okay."

"Yeah, yeah, I'm great. Really. Brent is—"

"Yes, he answered the door in a sparkling purple suit."

Bria grinned to herself. "He hasn't changed yet."

"I see. Well." Lana turned. "I only wanted to see if you got back safe."

"Lana! Wait!" Bria called out.

The woman paused.

"Last night, what you said about your daughter—"

"It's in the past."

"But why? She was your daughter..." Bria gulped. "Please...I want to understand. My mother...she tried to kill me. I never found out why..."

Lana replied with a whisper, "What I did won't fix your problems. Deal with your trauma in another way."

"I'm not—"

"I don't want to talk about it."

"But maybe I can help!"

"You can't help! How could you help? Nothing can replace what I did! I killed my daughter!"

"But why? That's all I want to know."

"Fine! You want to know what happened? I returned home from Knoll after the Smoke Riots with my head in a fog. The Order had corrupted me! Then, I gave birth to a beautiful baby girl only for her to have magic! So, the demons in my head told me to bury her alive...and that's what I did!" Lana snapped.

Bria reached behind her ear where her little branch originated. She kept her voice steady. "I was buried alive."

Lana stared at Bria, frozen in place, eyes wide. She opened her mouth to speak, but nothing came out. Only utter shock hung in the air. Bria gaped back at her. The truth tasted bitter; perhaps she had been ignoring it this whole time.

The story Brent used to tell came back to her like the wind: *The story goes, on a sad-sad note, that the Evil Witch Angelana killed her daughter.*

Lana broke the spell with a shake of her head and hissed, "Liar."

"I'm not—"

"I want you to leave."

"I—"

"It's for the best."

"Lana—"

"Goodbye, Bria." Lana disappeared down the hallway.

Bria couldn't bring herself to move. *How could I be so dense?*

The door next to her creaked open, and Brent stuck his head out. "Bria? You a'ight?"

Bria glanced at Brent. Tears filled her eyes, her mouth dry, and lips quivering.

"What…what's wrong? What is it—" Brent glanced down the hall after Lana. His eyes widened as he took in the stories. "Shite…Bria, that's—"

"Angelana Gonzo. My mother."

A Hero in Yellow

Yaz's head seared with yellow.

Her thoughts were yellow.

Everything was yellow.

Then came a blinding white light.

And she could see again.

She lay in a sterile white room, shivering. Candles hung from the walls, casting shadows over tables, while a plate of pastries waited on the table beside her.

What happened? The last thing she remembered, she'd stood in the junction.

Then came the screams.

The nightmares.

And yellow.

So much yellow.

Since the mist attacked her in the tunnels, she dreamt of riding among the clouds, looking down at the world. Monsters obeyed her every whim, bowing to her and crying her name. When she told them to attack a dragon, they attacked. When she told them to fight a thunderhead, they fought. And when she told them to tear open a door, they tore. And then, when she ordered them to grab an individual in a plague mask, they gripped.

Then the dream faded.

And she saw only yellow.

"Hello?" Yaz called out, lifting her head slightly. Straps kept her wrists locked to the bed. "Anyone?"

Moments later, a figure draped in blue strode into the room. After blinking for a few moments, she recognized Aelia standing over her, with a birdlike shadow against the wall and a twinkle in her dark eyes. "It's good to see you awake and, well, Yasmin. We've been concerned about your health since last night's endeavor."

"What happened? Where am I?" Yaz asked, straining against the straps on her wrists.

Aelia untied each of the straps around Yaz's wrists and helped her sit up in the bed. "You helped us win."

"What do you mean? Are we in the Library like Sir Jama wanted?"

"Yes, we have reclaimed the Library." Aelia placed a hand on Yaz's forehead and nodded. "Good. You seem better."

Yaz shifted in her place, her stomach grumbling.

"Eat. Ningursu shall be with you presently." Aelia handed Yaz the plate of pastries and smiled. The way the smile tugged at her lips looked forced; her eyes didn't glisten, as hollow as ever.

Yaz took the plate and began eating. Aelia left her once again, alone, in an unfamiliar room.

After picking away at the pastries, leaving behind the strawberries and icing, Yaz climbed out of bed and paced around the room. Every step caused her headache to worsen. But that didn't sadden her; after all, she had helped Sir Jama take his home. Certainly, he'd explain what happened, right?

She walked around the infirmary, peering into the different jars and vials on the tables. Many contained the same strange silver drink Aelia had given her. *Hopefully, I won't have to drink any more of that stuff now that we have the Library back.* Yaz stood on her tiptoes to peer out of the dusty window. Books lined the walls on the other side, glowing in the candlelight, while an ethereal mist coated the air.

Yaz pressed her face to the glass to get a better look. A staircase trailed down one side of the hall into an abyss of trees, shelves, and debris. This was not just a library; this was another world, beating beneath a glass walkway. She couldn't wait to explore it!

I can't wait to tell Mr. Nasr and Ms. Kai.

Her heart broke at the thought. Could she see them again? Or was this her home? What about her dollies and her skeletons? Had a stranger once again uprooted her?

No. Sir Jama wants what's best for me.

She stepped back as the door swung open again. Aelia carried Sir Jama in on a velvet pillow. The skull looked admittedly happier, more in his element than ever before, positioned with his chin high and a smirk on his lips. Yaz curtsied as he entered.

"Thank you, Aelia. You may leave." Sir Jama smiled at the Mist Keeper.

The woman placed Sir Jama on the table, then, without a word, strode out of the room.

"Sir Jama! What happened? I don't remember anything!" Yaz threw her hands back dramatically, staring around the room in utter amazement. "Aelia said we won!"

"We won, Yasmin, and it was all because of you! You summoned the monsters here, and you controlled them so we could use them to reclaim the Library."

"And the evil Magii are gone?"

"We have apprehended most of them. A few got away, but the most important one is now locked away in our crypts."

Yaz jumped in excitement. "I can't believe we did! I didn't even know what I was doing!"

"But you trusted me, and that is the most important part. Because of that, we won." Sir Jama spoke with such glee in his voice, Yaz couldn't believe it was the same skull. His white eye kept twinkling as if he had won a grand prize at a carnival.

"Will I be allowed to explore the Library? Or do I have to stay in here?" Yaz asked. She had so many questions bubbling on her tongue. Would Sir Jama answer them?

"Of course, Yasmin. You can delve into whatever you desire. You're a hero! In fact, I can even show you now." Sir Jama lifted his chin, beckoning Yasmin forward. She picked him off the table, carrying him gently upon his velvet throne.

The Library wrapped her in a cold embrace as she crossed onto the glass walkway. It wreaked of swamp, rotting paper, and rain, quite different compared to the small library in the Curio Shoppe Tower. But despite the terrible smell, it also glistened with aromatic mist, waltzing back and forth in the air. Yaz had never observed so many colors before, and she watched them with awe as she peered over the edge.

"Why is there a swamp down there?" Yaz asked. Mud coated the ground, trees and moss growing on shelves. Footprints lay scattered among the books. For a brief second, Yaz recalled the way the monsters had entered the Library, knocking everything down, tearing open doors. The destruction lay obvious before her. This was a war zone.

But she couldn't look away. There was something remarkable about the Library. It harbored magic that reminded Yaz of Sir Jama. This was his home, after all. No wonder he seemed so powerful!

"One of the evil Magii did this, Yasmin."

"Did you capture them?"

"No. She was not here when we attacked."

"It's terrible…" Yaz murmured. "Why would she do such a thing?"

"Because she has no heart. It is why we need to stop these Magii. Their magic makes them evil and vicious, so they destroy people like us…like Mist Keepers…because our magic is different." Sir Jama glanced at her with his empty eye. "And you'll be able to help stop them."

"Because I can control those monsters?"

"Precisely."

"But I don't know how I did it…" Yaz stared down at the swamp-riddled Library.

"I helped you this time. But we shall train you for the next time. All of us: Aelia, Alojzy, Jiang, Caroline, and me. We will make sure you understand what you can do with your magic." Sir Jama cocked his head at her. "Because you are so strong, Yasmin. Stronger than you know."

Yaz fiddled with her fingers. Strong? She didn't feel strong. Wasn't that why Mr. Nasr and Ms. Kai monitored her? She was only a child.

Strong.

She continued observing the swamp on the ground floor. Caroline walked along the edge, her face resembling a swamp beast, while a few misty individuals floated over the bookshelves, picking up books with downcast stares. Yaz could only imagine the nooks and crannies filling the Library, the places to explore, and all the goodies she would find hidden in the corners.

As if Sir Jama read her thoughts, he replied, "You'll get all the time in the world to explore our home, Yasmin. Don't worry. In fact, I implore you to explore."

"Really?"

"Yes. Really. Aelia needs to run a few tests on you, but afterwards, the Library is yours to conquer. I'll have Caroline join you and begin your teaching. Does that sound like a good idea?"

Yaz frowned and glanced back at Caroline. "Does she have to go with me?"

"I understand. You probably want to explore everything on your own. But we don't know everything the evil Magii did to our Library yet. Once we determine it is safe, then you will have freedom to roam. Is that fair?"

"I guess."

"Very good. Now let's head back to the infirmary. Aelia will finish checking on you while Jiang and I go to interrogate our prisoners."

"I thought you said they were gone?"

"I said we apprehended them. They are imprisoned in our crypts, yes. Don't worry. They won't be able to harm you." Sir Jama motioned to Yaz with his head. The mist tugged at her feet, leading her back towards the infirmary doors. "We are safe from their reign of terror, Yasmin. All thanks to you."

CHAPTER FORTY-FOUR

MOTHER

Bria lay on her bed, staring at the ceiling, her head still spinning. *Lana is my mother.* How had she not noticed before today? Brent's confirmation of her story only reaffirmed the truth. It was a story that Bria had heard too many times; the story of a child born with a camellia on her head, buried soon after her birth. But unlike the story Bria wore, Lana's story ended on a different note.

In her tale, the child died.

Bria tried her best to rationalize every part of the story. Perhaps there was another child out there, long ago, born with a flower growing from her head. And possibly, their mother had the name Angelana…Gonzo. It was preposterous. But she couldn't imagine that her mother, the woman who tried murdering her at birth, was the same woman that had helped her the last few days reignite her powers.

Angelana Gonzo hated magic. She didn't have it. Her grandmama would have told her.

Right?

Bria brought the blankets up to her chin, her head spinning as she analyzed every possibility. Beside her, Brent sat, silent. At first, Bria wanted to scream at him; it must be a trick, nothing more! But Bria couldn't blame him. His magic was out of his control in those aspects.

And after all, people can lie, but their stories will always speak the truth.

"Do you think she knows?" Bria finally asked as the afternoon sun danced over the windowsill. They spent all day huddled in silence. Brent brought her food, but she didn't eat. When they reunited, Bria expected a day of romance and smiles.

Not emptiness.

Brent glanced at her. "I dunno. She seemed kind of…I dunno…like she knew something? I…sorry. The story was too brief to figure out."

"It's fine."

"Are you a'ight though?"

"Yeah…I'm fine—" Bria stopped, catching Brent's disappointment. He read her lies like a book. She backtracked, "Or maybe not. I want to confront her on this, but she doesn't hear it..." Bria gulped. "My whole life, people told me that my mother, Angelana Gonzo, was a selfish, evil witch. I can't for the life of me rationalize that Lana is my mother. She's kind of hard-headed and droll, but she's been helping me. Look."

Bria reached for the book Lana gave her on the end table. She opened it to the first page that detailed elements interacting.

"An apothecary book?" Brent asked.

"Yes...but it details how different elements interact. She thinks that based on what happened in the Tower with the electricity, I might be able to control more than just plants. Which makes sense after everything that happened in the Library and with Kek." Bria stared at her branched hand. "She thinks I have control over elements. Like carbon...sulfur...all of those. I'm not sure how to feel about it."

"Well, I always thought you were powerful as hell." Brent closed the book. "And it sounds like Lana wants to help you."

"But I don't understand why! She tried to kill me because I have magic. Why would she want it to flourish now?"

"You'll have to ask her. I mean, I can always look at her story, but it's the more honest thing to do...to ask her, I mean. But...you don't have to either. She...she hurt you. I wouldn't want to force you to do any of that. It's your choice, Bri. Really."

Bria pulled her knees to her chest and sighed. "I guess."

They sat in silence for a few minutes while Bria pondered her options. It'd be so easy to ignore what Brent told her, go about her own battles destroying the Pools and hiding from the Council. But her past called to her. More than anything, she wanted to understand her powers. Kek had opened a window, Ningursu had opened her soul, and now Lana held the answer to the question Bria wondered for the longest time.

Why me?

She needed to find out.

Bria left Brent in the tenement hall. She had to do this alone. Despite how she yearned for Brent to be by her side, she only bore the memory of his touch as she trudged across the Pit towards the farmhouse. She paid quick glances towards Marisol, Chander, and a few others, waving slightly as she continued her journey.

This new quest wrapped her in its palms and cradled her close. It was a short voyage, without the twists and turns, but the revelation it held weighed on her heart like any other adventure.

Answers.

The mere idea kept her head together.

But as she reached the farm door and pushed it open, her throat tightened. What would she say?

She decided not to dwell on it and stepped inside the barn.

Lana sat on a hay bale, eyes heavy, a scowl on her lips. She straightened as Bria entered.

"What are you doing here!?"

Bria cut her off with a pointed statement: "Angelana Gonzo."

Lana stared at her, brow furrowed.

"That's your name, isn't it?" Tears stung Bria's eyes, but she held back the sobs building in her chest.

Lana clenched her jaw and looked away. "It doesn't matter."

"It matters to your daughter!"

"My daughter is dead!" Lana shouted. The barn rocked with her voice.

"No…" Bria clenched her hands, capturing the humidity in the air with her voice. "No. Your daughter was born with a flower on her head. You buried her alive…your daughter…your Rhodana…"

"You don't need to remind me! I wear that sin on my cheek every day." Lana pointed to the black stamp on her cheek. "What does it matter now?"

"I told you...I was buried alive! I'm your daughter!" Bria's voice cracked as she said the words.

"And I said you're lying." Lana glared. Yet, despite her anger, there remained an air of trepidation.

Bria licked her lips, keeping back the mixture of emotions brewing in her chest, restraining the desire to scream. "My name is Briannabella Sophia *Rhodana* Smidt...daughter of Noah Smidt, granddaughter of Beatriz Gonzo. And I was born with a camellia on my head only to be buried alive by my mother. You."

Angelana Gonzo stared at her, then shook her head. "Don't play with me. My daughter is dead."

"Why would I lie?"

The woman didn't respond. With a quick turn of her heels and a wave of red fabric, she rushed out of the barn, leaving Bria staring after her with a broken heart.

Bria darted after Lana. How could she not have noticed? Of course, *Lana* was Angelana Gonzo. She carried herself just like Bria's grandmama, her dark eyes as determined. She led the Pit through quiet rebellions, despite her lack of motivation and confidence. Even her magic bore the same base as Bria's magic. Madame Owiti had noticed it!

But Bria had turned a blind eye.

She raced from the building in Lana's direction. The woman shoved her way through the vagrants lining the paths. Comments passed by Bria's ears about the storm from the previous night. Some called out to her, asking for details. For now, Bria ignored them.

"Lana!" she shouted. "Can we please talk?"

The woman continued into the Necrowood. Bria hopped over a few newly blooming flowers, her heart pounding at every step. Tears continued down her cheeks, casting a blanket of gentle mist over the air. Of course, her own mother wouldn't confront her! Why would she think they could ever mend relations?

Why was she even chasing after her?

Bria slowed where the brambles and weeds thickened. Lana slipped into them, untouched by their thorns.

Bria followed suit, ignoring the way the thorns scraped at her skin. These weren't her plants; instead, they belonged to Lana. This was her secret hideaway, just like Bria's old home within the tunnels.

Bria pushed through the last wall of brambles. "Lana! Please talk to me! Please!"

She choked on her words. Lana sat in the middle of a bramble-made cage, head hanging in defeat. "Go away, Bria."

"Talk to me!" Bria gritted her teeth. "Please…"

"What is there to talk about?"

"Maybe the fact that you're my mother!" Bria clutched a nearby branch. "Did you know?"

Lana didn't move.

"DID YOU KNOW?" A branch flew past Bria and forced Lana to turn around to face her. The woman still would not meet Bria's gaze.

Lana mumbled, "I thought your magic was coincidental. And the flower. All of it. I didn't know you were alive. My mother never told me you survived…"

"Of course she didn't! You wanted to kill me!"

"Only to protect you!" Lana's voice broke. "You can't imagine what I went through! I left Knoll riddled with psychotics and shell-shock after months of being tortured! I didn't want a child, but I got pregnant with your father after he helped me escape… and then suddenly my daughter was born with my magic! Magic stronger than my own! The only thing I could even consider was getting rid of you!"

"You buried me alive!"

"I planted you so you'd survive!"

"Bullshit!"

Lana scoffed. "You survived, didn't you?"

"Like that helped me. I still ended up here." Bria shut her eyes. "The Order has still hunted me. They tortured me. So you buried me to save me, but I carried the burden that my mother didn't love me my whole life."

Lana looked away from her.

"And you won't even deny it." Bria's head fell.

"How could I love you if I didn't learn you survived? If I had known, I would have tried harder to get out…" Lana shook her head. "The guard completely deconstructed my file. Spun it on its head, called me a witch, and shipped me back to Knoll. I didn't even have time to say goodbye to my family. Like you, they probably don't even know I'm here."

Bria shook her head in disgust. It was true, though; no one spoke about what happened to Angelana Gonzo. Arrested by the guard and shipped away, no one had been certain where she resided.

"You don't understand, do you?" Lana snarled. "Your magic? If they had discovered you, they would have sent you Knoll the moment you were born. They would have tortured you as a babe. You'd be nothing but a shell if you even lived. I had seen it myself! I was scared!"

"Then why didn't you tell Grandmama? Or my dad? Or someone who would have listened!?!"

"Because I didn't know what my ma would do either! She didn't know about my magic! Only Pa knew 'cause he had some magic too!"

Bria asked, "Grandpapa had magic?"

"He didn't tell you?"

"No…"

Lana's face softened. "It wasn't as strong as yours or even mine. But it was there. That's why he was such a good gardener."

"I always thought it was a skill…"

"It was, yes, but he had that green thumb. He didn't tell me much, but he showed me a few tricks." Lana frowned. "He really never told you?"

"No one told me anything. For a long time…I just learned about it in the shadows. Grandmama, Grandpapa, Daddy, and Ric found out, but they never said anything. I was so young when Grandpapa passed away, so he might not have considered telling me." Bria wiped her eyes. "If you were there…you could have taught me."

Lana crossed her arms and glared towards the trees. "You did fine on your own."

"Yes, but—"

"You never needed me, Bria. I'm just a piece of shite mother who tried to kill her daughter, okay? Best forget about it."

"I don't want to forget!" Bria stepped forward. "My whole life, everyone told me you were some evil woman with some sort of wickedness embedded deep into her soul. I don't believe that! I've spent so much time with you here…and there is more to you than what the story said. Please, Lana. We don't need to behave like a mother and daughter, but you can't deny who we are. Please…"

Lana didn't respond, running her hands over the grass. Bria watched as a few clovers bloomed, then fell, gasping for air despite the touch of magic.

"It doesn't matter," Lana whispered. "None of it matters. What I did still occurred. I intended to kill you, even if I wasn't in the right state of mind."

"Not everything sent for slaughter dies." Bria sat across from Lana. She took her hand and held it over the grass. After a few moments, the clovers bloomed with white flowers, spreading out through the clearing. "Sometimes, the right people can bring it back to life."

Lana tugged her hand away.

The clovers wilted once again.

"When life gets a little petty, why not replace it with something pretty?" Bria recited.

"That's bullshite."

"Grandmama always—"

"I'm aware of my ma's motto. But sometimes, making the world pretty doesn't solve your problems. The world is an ugly place…you understand?"

"I'm not saying that—"

"So I think it best that you leave as soon as possible and go live your pretty little life. The Pit isn't a place for you. The longer you stay here, the sooner it'll be until you get caught."

"Lana—"

"It's for the best." Lana rose. She didn't look back as she marched through the brambles, leaving Bria alone amid the thorns.

CHAPTER FORTY-FIVE

MAGNETS

rent slowly dressed, staring out the door where Bria had vanished. His heart ached for her. He couldn't even fathom what went through her head. He had heard the stories for years now: the evil witch Angelana buried her daughter, Rhodana, alive. Even before Brent knew that Rhodana was Bria, he had told the story to children back home.

But it had always just been a story.

Bria confirmed it otherwise.

Now, with a single revelation, the story reinvented itself. Angelana Gonzo, the witch and bane of Bria's life, was none other but a woman with a muddy history. Brent caught a quick glimpse of it: a young woman traveling to see the world, only to be thrust into a life of servitude beneath the Order's reign; branded, cleansed, she continued her life, wounded and afraid. No wonder she'd gotten scared when her daughter was born with a flower growing from her head.

Brent took his time buttoning his shirt, missing the eyelets multiple times, before leaving the room with Nix on his heels. He stepped into the dusty road of the Pit, breathing the dead air for a moment. It tasted of stories from years past, and through the subtle headache in his head, the tales of the dead crusaded through his mind. How many people had died in this Pit? How many people still needed to be free from Hell?

He glanced towards the Necrowood. Bria's story trailed into the forest, disappearing among the trees. He let it go, instead turning down the path. Vague memories filled his head of the last time he was here after uncovering Bria's identity as Rho. The Pit had kept its dark essence. Tents bordered the distant wall towards the south, while decrepit buildings towered over the northern edge of the prison. Vagrants crouched on the side of the roads, huddled together in prayer and chatter. None of them looked at him. In the distance, towers moved along the landscape, forever shifting the skyline of Knoll like puzzle pieces.

A group of vagrants gathered around a firepit. One young woman glanced his way and called, "Hey! You're new! I mean, I'm new here too, but you're newer than me! I can tell. Haven't seen you before, and you don't have one of those ugly jumpsuits!"

"Oh, uh—"

She continued, full of pep and enthusiasm as she spoke, "What's your name?"

As if she pulled the truth out of him by a rope, he responded, "Brent."

"Brent! I recognize that name! Bria mentioned you. I thought I saw you with her last night!" The girl bounced on her heels. "I'm Marisol. I met Bria in the guard tower a couple weeks ago. She's amazing, isn't she?"

"Yeah, she is," Brent flushed slightly and picked at his wrist. "She's spectacular."

"Well, do you want something to eat? We were just waiting in line for our rations from Chef!"

"I got some food earlier—"

"Yeah, but that was then. This is now! C'mon!" Marisol took Brent by the arm and ushered him over to the line.

He didn't have a chance to say no, trying his best to ignore the story brewing on Marisol's fingertips. It was a soft story, a girl taken from her home, like all the tales lost in squalor. He sensed the sadness riding through her, masked by a cheery exterior and a set of bright eyes. Her magic wore her thin, giving her truths, however unnecessary.

Yet only Brent saw it.

Marisol introduced Brent to the group in line. He didn't catch all their names, but his attention stopped on a kid by the name of Chander. The kid hugged himself, avoiding contact with any one person, his stone eyes gazing past Brent towards the buildings. He didn't say a word, aged beyond his years with a single look.

"Chander! Meet Brent!" Marisol said.

The boy said nothing.

"Eh, don't mind him. His magic gets to his head sometimes." Marisol shrugged.

Brent watched the boy for a moment. The mist spun around him, almost interested in each of his movements. Chander hardly flinched, keeping his hands straight at his side and eyes empty.

"Are you a'ight?" Brent asked the kid.

The boy blinked, then shook his head.

"You wanna talk about it?"

"It doesn't stop," the child whispered.

"He means his magic," Marisol interjected. "He can see out of the eyes of the last person he touched."

Brent nodded. The mist gathered at the boy's head, masking his eyes. For a moment, Brent saw Chander's story frolicking just over his head. A young boy, carefree, until one day, he started to see things as they happened through the eyes of his mother, his father, and his sister and grandfather. It was too much for a child of twelve.

Only for him to see through the eyes of a guard one day. His family, gone. All slaughter, but for him and his sister, taken by a tower because of their magical inclinations.

Or at least his magic.

But why was the mist so attracted to him?

He knelt in front of the boy. "Listen, I know it's hard, right? So what I want you to do is this: whenever the sights get too bad, or your head hurts too much, repeat your name…then remember one thing you hold close. Your one constant. Tell me…what is one thing constantly there?"

Chander frowned. "My sister…"

"Then think of your sister…and think of the present. Whatever you have seen doesn't define you. Remember, you own your magic. You are in control."

"Are you in control of yours?"

"I try to be. It's difficult, and I'm still learning…but I try."

Chander gulped. His shoulders loosened, and when he reopened his eyes, a new glistening aura of childhood touched his irises. While they still bore exhaustion and fear, the boy at least took the words and stored them somewhere in his heart.

"Thank you," Chander whispered. "I'll try to remember that."

"We can work together, a'ight? I understand better than anyone how magic can make your head spin."

"What do you mean?"

"That's a long story." Brent climbed to his feet and smiled. "I'll tell it later tonight if you want. I got a lot of good stories if you wanna come listen."

"Can I bring my sister?"

"You can bring everyone."

Chander grinned. It was the type of smile that rarely appeared, from what Brent could gather, but it was there. He couldn't be sure if he'd be able to help the child, but he'd try.

Brent stepped forward in line to grab a bowl of bread and gruel. Marisol leaned to the side, arms crossed, watching with a wide smile on her face. "I've never seen anyone get Chander to smile!"

"I just...I dunno. I know what he's going through, sorta, I guess. With his magic, I mean." Brent picked at the bread. "I wanted to help."

"Golly, no wonder Bria likes you. You got a good heart!" Marisol giggled.

Brent felt his face turn red again.

He gathered himself at the side of the square to eat his food, sitting with a few other vagrants as they discussed the well-to-dos of Knoll's Gully. They spoke in hushed whispers, speaking of their desires to sneak into the towers or dismantle the government. It all sounded like a distant dream, tethered by reality. While they discussed possible ways of sneaking into the towers - through the sewers or via capture - none of it ever came to fruition. Brent saw it in the stories; every day, these groups gathered, whispering the same stories.

For how long?

He overheard them speak Bria's name; she'd become something of a legend, by the sounds of it. Her magic was legendary, exaggerated in parts, diminished in others. *They really see her as Rhodana the Forest Queen.* Brent placed his bowl down as he listened to a group.

"You think she will act, though?" One vagrant asked.

"She's gonna have to. She's the only one with the magic strong enough." Another added.

A third leaned forward as they spoke, "And the determination too."

Brent glanced over at Marisol, who was far too distracted by a conversation about the color of jumpsuits with another vagrant. *Does Bria know what they expect of her?*

"Ah! There she is!" The first vagrant shouted and rose to their feet.

Brent glanced over to the Necrowood. It wasn't Bria who emerged from the trees, but Angelana Gonzo, eyes bloodshot, face downcast. She bore an expression Brent had seen before but on Bria—one of utter fear and defeat. His own heart paused. Did something happen to Bria?

No.

It was Bria who had left Lana like this, that much Brent was certain.

"Lana!" the vagrant called. "We've been discussing—"

Lana spat in the vagrant's direction. "Not now! I'm done!"

The vagrant rose. "Lana, we were just planning—"

"You're planning nothing! There is no plan! No goal! Nothing! You understand? Nothing!" Lana clenched her fists. "Bria or Rho or whatever you want to call her will be leaving. Whatever ideas you have, throw them out! It was all a dream!"

Lana stormed into a nearby shack and slammed the door. The entire square stared.

"What was that about?" Marisol parroted everyone's thoughts.

The vagrant glanced at her. "After we saw what Ms. Bria could do, we started developing a plan to use her to infiltrate the towers. Lana was behind it, too, and we were gonna talk to Bria in the next couple of days. Guess that isn't happening…"

"Isn't it dangerous to break into the towers, though?"

"If we get rid of those damn towers here in Knoll, it means the Order's days are numbered, don'tcha know?" The vagrant shrugged. "It'll show everyone that the Order isn't in charge of everything. Bria already did that in Newbird's Arm, I'm sure you've heard, so we thought…with some help…she might be able to do it here."

"Oh! I see!" Marisol grinned at Brent. "You're a lucky man."

"Yeah…guess so. I'm…I'm gonna see if I can find her, I mean, to find out what happened with her and Lana."

"Smart idea."

Brent took his leave as the group continued to talk. It made him uncomfortable listening as they tried to plan out Bria's fate without her present. She always wanted to be in control of her own destiny.

He found Nix sniffing around the fire. The dog joined him, bouncing at his heels, as Brent followed Lana's story back into the forest from where she came.

In the forest, stories danced. Nonchalantly, Brent traced along them with the tips of his fingers, watching the mist gather at the edge of his nails. So many vagrants had tried to escape, only to die far away with no food or water. The Necrowood stretched on for days on foot, and even if they reached the mountains, they rarely had the stamina to survive. Their stories wove into the landscape, no more than a heartbeat crying out for help.

Brent reached forward, feeling along the mist for each path. He found a story of a man trying to climb the mountains, an old seer attempting to understand the world, and a child getting lost in the woods.

He gripped his hands, ignoring the sadness swelling in his throat. For their souls crying for him, reaching out from Hell, he had to be strong.

He had to be more than a Mist Keeper.

He had to be their companion. Their friend.

And like the time weeks before, he released the souls of multiple individuals hidden beneath the roots of the earth.

I won't forget my job, even if the Council has forgotten me.

Much to Brent's surprise, the Diabolo didn't come with a snarky remark. Instead, Brent felt nothing more than the distant drumming of the stories in his head.

And saw nothing more than the parting mist.

Once it had left his vision, he continued along the path of Lana's story, releasing souls as their stories popped up around him. He tugged and collected them naturally, bearing their stories close to his heart, until he arrived at a wall of brambles blocking his path. They wove together like a lattice, reminiscent of Bria's hideaway deep in the tunnels.

"Bri?" He tapped his fingers over the edge of the lattice, careful not to prick his fingers. "You there?"

A small hole opened, giving him enough room to crawl through to the other side.

Green welcomed him as he ducked through the thickets and vine. Bria sat there, in the center of the clearing, laced in the foliage, her eyes shut. Brent stood there in amazement. As the sunlight drizzled down over her, Bria looked like a goddess, a mother of the earth, and a queen. She was everything he dreamed about and more.

Brent started chuckling.

"What's so funny?" Bria asked without opening her eyes.

Brent crouched down, restraining another laugh. "Are you gonna stay like a tree forever or what?"

Bria scowled.

After wiping his eyes, Brent restrained himself, keeping his voice low. "Why are you a tree, Bri?"

"It makes me feel calm. Like I belong here." She still didn't glance at him.

"You gonna stay a tree?"

She shrugged.

"Bri..."

"Brent, really, I just want to be left alone."

"Oh, um, a'ight. I'll go then..." Brent stood and turned back to the thickets.

Bria stopped him. "Wait. No. Stay. I'm sorry. I didn't mean…" She finally opened her eyes. Bloodshot and tired, Brent swore she would break out in tears at any moment. She continued, "I'm…upset. It was like getting smacked in the face."

"I know. I'm sorry."

"It's not your fault."

"Yeah, but I confirmed it."

"I would have been upset if you didn't."

"Yeah, don't want to get on your bad side."

"You really don't. I'll turn you into a tree."

Brent chuckled and took Bria's good hand. He traced over the betrothal mark on her dark skin. Micca's voice came back to him: *Ask her to marry you.*

Brent shook his head. *Not yet.*

They sat there in silence, watching Nix roll around in the grass. Brent caught glimpses in the clearing of Bria and Lana's encounter, but he passed over them with a momentary wince, focusing instead on the dancing stories of the dead. He could easily weave his fingers through each tale and tug on them, releasing another soul. Every soul left a heavy mark on his heart, though, and spending too long in their stories fed the Diabolo, leaving his head spinning and reeling.

"I don't know what to do," Bria confessed.

"Hm?"

"I always had this image in my head of my mother. Then I find out it's Lana—someone who I have become acquainted with over the last couple of weeks—and she strikes down all my thoughts. I guess…I always believed my mother would be some witch like the story said." Bria ran her fingers over the grass as she spoke. "But she's not. She's complicated and hard-headed, but her heart is in the right place. I guess part of me hoped Lana would turn around and admit she regretted everything and loved me. Or that she watched me from the shadows. But she didn't…and she didn't live up to the idea I had in my head either of an evil woman either. If she was like the stories said…this might have been easier. But she's not, and I don't understand what it means for me."

Brent placed his arm over Bria's shoulder and pulled her close. He couldn't imagine what she felt. The betrayal, the heartache…all of it had to be ripping her apart.

And there was nothing he could do.

"She wants us gone…" Bria added. "She wants nothing to do with us anymore."

"I know. But she's probably scared, just like you." Brent stroked back a piece of Bria's hair. "Give her time."

"And if she still doesn't want to talk?"

"Then we leave. Go on our next adventure." Brent squeezed her fingers. "Just like we planned before this momentary…delay. A'ight?"

"But what if I lose you again?"

"I wish I could promise that I'll be right here. I mean…we're like magnets. That's what Micca called us. We're drawn together…but…sometimes we face the wrong way. I dunno. It's all this science stuff he says…but basically, I think he meant is…we'll always come back together, but if we, I guess, turn the wrong way or get torn in the wrong direction…it's not good."

"I guess that's part of being in a war," Bria said.

"But even before then. I mean, we've always had something thrown between us. Remember our first kiss? A week later, you and your father and Mr. West went on a trip to Hutch's Creek…"

"And you thought I left forever because it was a spur-of-the-moment trip." Bria half-smiled.

"Then you wrote to me…and I spent the next few days collecting wildflowers."

"I still remember when the train pulled up. You were standing there in an ill-fitted suit with a handful of flowers. You were so giddy and shy when I got off the train."

"I thought I ruined everything. We had become such good friends…" He bit down on his bottom lip to stop the tears. "I thought I lost you after the betrothal, too. We didn't talk much for a month…"

"I was heartbroken. But a few weeks later, I found you smoking by the cows, and you looked so pitiful."

"We should have run away then...don't know why we didn't." Brent sniffled. "I mean, I know why, but...we could have gotten some cabin somewhere, gotten married...it'd be a quiet life." He sucked in his lips. "Before the betrothal...I planned to ask you to marry me when you turned eighteen. It was just a couple months short..."

He paused, realizing what had exited his mouth. He'd never told Bria his intentions. Those dreams were torn from him, and he stuffed them deep in the crevasses of his heart.

"I would have said yes. Without a doubt," she whispered.

Brent glanced at her, a knot forming in his throat. "And now?"

"Are you asking?"

He nodded.

"My answer hasn't changed."

Brent closed his eyes, his bottom lip quivering as a single tear rolled down his cheek.

Bria caught it with her branched hand. "What's wrong?"

"I...I never thought I'd...that I'd end up with...I mean..." He cursed under his breath. "I never imagined that through everything, I would still end up with you. And you still said yes now, despite everything, and...with your mother and...I can't...I—"

"I didn't have to think about it. Because like you said, we're magnets. No matter how many times we're pulled apart, we'll come back together. Like the seasons touch hands throughout the year..."

"Like Life and Death brush lips..."

"Nothing can keep us apart for good." Bria laced her arms around Brent's neck. "So the answer will always be yes."

Brent stared at her for a moment. Something reignited inside of Bria in that moment; the happiness and determination of the Forest Queen continued its reign inside her heart. Brent could feel it bubbling to the surface, despite the fear and sadness that left permanent scars on Bria's face.

He always knew she would say yes. But it didn't stop him from riding the waves of excitement into her arms.

All to bless her with a kiss.

LIFEBLOOD

Bria and Brent stayed hidden in the brambles until sunset graced the horizon. With only dusk to guide them, Bria helped Brent through the branches and led him back through the Necrowood. She took the long way, letting the trees sing to her as she walked along the pathway. Brent caught stories on his fingers as they walked, focusing on the random tales throughout the forest. It almost felt normal, like the days they spent exploring the gardens in their early romance. If Bria closed her eyes, she almost felt it on her lips. The garden always left a sweet flavor on her tongue. But the Necrowood tasted of ash.

Walking beside Brent gave her a new sense of confidence. Something had changed about him over the past few weeks but in a good way. He didn't slump over as much, his smiles fuller and eyes sparkling. The stressors of Newbird's Arm and the Council no longer weighed on him, at least not in the same way.

Bria took his hands as they hopped across a couple of stones where the river flowed. She went to smile at him, then slowed, glimpsing the bubbling edges coated with silver.

*The Pool…*Bria sensed the peony heart rocking along the waves. Was she strong enough now to destroy it? She knelt beside it and placed her hand into the liquid. Cold. Lifeless.

Like the forest.

"It's everywhere," Bria said to Brent.

"What is?"

"The Pool. It's the lifeblood of this forest."

"More like death blood. Cause, y'know, the forest is dead or something…I mean."

"Semantics." Bria poked at the water. "We left the Library with the mission to destroy these Pools, and we haven't done any of that yet. I could destroy this one now."

"What would destroying this do to the forest, though?" Brent asked.

"Bring it back to life, maybe?"

"Do you know that for sure?"

"No, of course not. But the Order might be using it. And even if they're not, it's a pollutant. It's destroying the world. I can hear it. The trees are crying for me." Bria heaved. "They want me to give them life."

"We don't know for sure what this river...pool...thing leads to. It could...it might be nothing. By destroying it...we don't know. If it was in the Library, I mean, it might be different but...Kek and Ningursu, they've been influencing everything for a long time, haven't they?"

Bria stared at the river. "You mean the Pool might be more a part of the world than we realize?"

"And destroying it might have a detrimental outcome." Brent tugged on her hand. "Just...I think we should move slow on this or whatever. Start with our original goal of disconnecting the Order from the Council."

"Right." Bria scowled into the river.

Brent pulled her away from it. "We didn't expect to find a river of silver. This differs from the Pools. It's not as localized or anything, y'know?"

"Yes. I understand. Really." Bria sighed. "I just feel so small."

"You shouldn't, though. Look at everything you've done."

Bria shifted. "I caused a riot."

"Yeah, but you've fought Death Gods, escaped a prison tower—"

Bria jumped up. "The Tower! Of course!"

"What?"

"Before you returned, Lana and I were searching for the Tower. We thought we could use it to sneak into Knoll. Madame Owiti gave us a general idea where it is, but we hadn't found it yet...she only mentioned a silver river." Bria squeezed Brent's hands. "But until you mentioned it, I hadn't even thought about how you can help find it!"

"A story, you mean?"

"That's what you're good at, isn't it?"

"I mean, the forest is huge...and it's not like I have Zephyr or anything...but yeah...let's look..." His face relaxed, eyes scanning the surrounding forest. Mist gathered over the leaves and thickets. Brent smiled. "It's not far. This way."

They traveled along the river. Brent made comments about the stories in the air, his expression changing with different whiffs of the tale. He mumbled something about whales at one point, puffing out his cheeks as if he became the beast. It wasn't like they were searching for a tower—rather, they were just playing in the woods, like any other game.

It was in these moments that time flew. They didn't care about the weight of the world, the potential enemies, the possible beasts; instead, the moments existed as heartbeats.

And the final beat came with a shadow.

In the heart of the forest, far from the Pit, where the trees stood dead and barren, the Tower waited. It watched over them, glowering, its icy stare wrapped around Bria's heart.

Brent took her branched hand. "I see the story…with you and the tower…I can't…wow."

Bria eyed the tower. Scorch marks gathered along the wooden doors while charred branches lay on the ground. It seemed like a distant dream rather than a memory; the magic that coursed through her was like no other.

They ventured into the tower, ducking through the debris and hopping over stones. Bria ran her good hand along the wall, recalling the moments of terror as she and the other prisoners lay waste to the building. Inside, with no guards, it wasn't all that terrifying. The pipes creaked, the wood snapped, and the rooms echoed, but nothing moved.

The Tower wasn't all that large. Only six floors layered the facility, with the engine positioned in the center, beneath rows of scaffolding and paths. Bria didn't dare venture to the crypts in the basement where the guard kept her prisoner. Closing her eyes brought her back to those moments; the last thing she wanted was to be locked by her own memories.

They trailed along the scaffolding, gazing down into the engine. A layer of red petals coated the silver pool that once powered the Tower. But like the rest of the Necrowood, even those petals had begun to die. In its place, the silver pool continued to bubble; not as vibrant as before, it still hissed with magic, beckoning for Bria's attention.

"Well, we found it. But I'm not sure how they plan to move this thing…" Bria said. "It's just as dead as everything else."

"Maybe there are controls to start it up?" Brent asked.

"I think the Pool powered it. It's almost like they were using magic." Bria rubbed her wrists. "The restraints they used on me pulsed with electricity. It got worse whenever we used our magic. See the wires down there? They connect to the Pool." She pointed to the structure. "I don't know how it works…but they did it."

Brent's brow furrowed. His lip quivered. "Hypocrites."

They stared for a moment longer into the lackluster pool, then together continued venturing throughout the tower. Most of the other rooms were as expected: a mess hall and galley resided on the third floor, sleeping quarters on the fourth, and an armory on the fifth. Each one wrapped around the engine below, wires protruding from every direction.

In the captain's quarters, Brent paused in the doorway. He scanned the room, then left Bria's side to open the dresser. After rummaging for a few seconds, he removed a woolen cowl, one that Bria knew all too well.

"You found it," Bria said.

"It has a strong story." He draped it over her neck.

She squeezed his hand for a moment, then ushered him out of the room towards the next one.

The bridge looked out from the top floor, with levers and controls on the walls and floors. A single chair stared out the lookout window.

As they entered the bridge, the chair squeaked.

And spun.

Bria stepped back, holding tight to Brent's arm.

Sitting right in the chair, with a wide smile on her lips, was none other than Edith—the crazed metallurgist from Mert and one of Kek's confidantes.

Brent stiffened.

Edith's lips parted into a pernicious smile. "Ah. I was wondering when you two would show up."

"How d'you get here?" Bria gripped Brent's arm closer.

"The Pool."

"But…the one down there…I thought I destroyed it!"

"You destroyed it in the Necrowood, so the Necrowood brought it back. Made it easy to figure out your location.

Bria glanced over the edge of the scaffolding where the Pool bubbled. While the petals continued to wilt, its heart produced a quiet hum, whispering, *I'm alive.*

She turned back to Edith. "What are you doing here? I told Kek I want nothing to do with them."

"Ask your lover boy there. I'm sure he has already seen."

Bria turned back to Brent. His gaze traced over Edith, his face paling as each story entered his purview. His answer came as a whisper: "Ningursu reclaimed the Library."

"So much for Nedo killing his brother, huh?" Edith chuckled. "Weakling."

"Nedo never had the heart to kill." Brent shifted. Every time they mentioned the deceased ghost, Brent seemed to change the way he carried himself. What went on in his head? How many voices spoke to him? How long would they last?

"How did Ningursu find his way back?" Bria pulled the conversation in a different direction.

Edith shrugged. "The damn reapers got some new weapon or something. Able to do more with the Diabolo now or something. Doesn't matter. Didn't see it…as soon as they broke open the Library, Kek told me to flee. Took a bit, but your magic isn't hard to track with the right knowledge. So c'mon, we're gonna go reclaim the Library before the Council wreaks havoc."

"Why would we go with you?"

"Because I said so."

"That's not a reason."

"Listen girl, with the Council back in power, they will not sit in the shadows much longer. We're in a war—"

"We're not involved in *this* war."

"Oh?" Edith leaned forward. "You've destroyed Pools, ignited magic, fought Diabolo…this is *your* war."

"We're defending ourselves!"

"Must I remind you that your reaper is the only one who can destroy the Diabolo?"

Bria glanced at Brent. He'd been quiet, his gaze fixated at the wall, eyes dark. She tugged at his sleeve, but he didn't budge.

"Aw. The poor baby is traumatized. He's probably remembering all the fun we had." Edith smirked. She ran her hand over the metal of the chair. Out of it, she pulled a thin strip of metal, which she welded into a blade in the palm of her hands. She rotated it in her fingers. "Then he knows I'll drag you kicking and screaming if it means getting rid of these reapers."

"I have my own goals. Kek knew that too." Bria replied.

"And now Kek is locked in the crypts under Ningursu's watch. So, it will be best if you come along with me. I'd hate to hurt you—" With a lurch, Edith jumped from her seat and sent the newly made dagger spiraling through the air.

Yet, before she even left her spot, Brent tugged Bria away, and they stumbled back into the wall.

"I got you," Brent mumbled.

"How d'you know she was going to throw it?"

"I—"

Edith launched at them again, running her fingers along the stone and pulling out chains of metal. She laced them around her fingers, then sent them flying like whips.

As the chains lashed in their direction, Bria grabbed hold of them with her good hand. The metal burned into her skin, the elements reacting at her touch. If she just focused, she could hear them calling her name, enough so she might manipulate and guide them. *They belong to me. Like the forest. Like the tunnels. I can hear these elements talking.*

Bria laced her fingers around the chains and swung them. Rather than the chains landing on her and Brent, they launched back into the air and hit Edith in the face. The woman stumbled back.

Then shrieked.

This time, she lunged at Brent with no weapons. Bria raced after her, but Brent was faster. He stepped back.

The mist danced around him.

And in its place, three versions of Brent Harley stood. Edith toppled through one of them, hitting the side of the scaffolding overlooking the pool on the ground floor.

The mist-made versions of Brent remained for a moment before shifting back over the real Brent. Bria didn't have time to marvel at it. With adrenaline pumping in her chest, she pressed her hand against the wall. The tower rumbled around her. She searched it, listening to the elements.

Iron.

Iron was strong. Firm. It pulsed through her skin and across the world. She felt it in the tower and in the bars that prevented Edith from toppling into the Pool beneath them.

And with a mere blink, a mere beat, a mere prayer…Bria turned the bars of the scaffolding to dust.

Edith toppled down into the pool at the bottom of the tower.

And vanished with a splash.

But even with her gone, Bria's magic continued flourishing. Iron crumbled, but the peony heart of the Pool flourished. Bria listened to the walls speak, the electric pulse of the copper wires sang, and the Silver Pool below him. It was never dead, just dormant. She hadn't killed it those weeks ago, only pulling away its magic for a time. The Necrowood kept it alive. Edith reignited it.

Now the Tower could return to life.

"Bri!" Brent shouted.

She remained frozen. It was so easy now to immerse herself in the elements. One turn and she could create fire, another and she could create water. It was all at her fingertips.

Just how could she manipulate them?

It pulled at her heart, begging for her soul. What if she handed it over to the elements?

What if she gave life to the tower?

Brent's arms pulled her out of the reverie. He wrapped them around her waist and pulled her close, tugging her good hand away from the tower wall. Bria gasped out and collapsed against him, her heart racing, head searing.

"Bri? You a'ight?" Brent asked.

Bria nodded.

"I thought…you were…it was like you were becoming the tower."

Bria stared at her good hand. "I felt it. If I tried harder, the Tower would have come to life again."

"But at what cost?"

Bria met his gaze. His eyes pooled with fear.

Her answer was brief and pointed.

"I don't know."

CHAPTER FORTY-SEVEN

CONSTANT COLOR

The auras followed Lex. They painted the City of Knoll in colors she'd never seen: the brightest blues, the darkest yellows, the smoothest reds. She saw them in the buildings, in the faces of the strangers on the street, and in the clouds. Ever since she extended her own aura to protect those in the truck, the colors hadn't ceased.

With each step, though, her head seared as though on fire. Tears engulfed her vision. But she clung to her heart, to the one goal: Garrett. She would find her son and take him out of here. Part of her still clung to a dash of hope that Toddle might surprise her, that he might just save Garrett and meet her in an alleyway in town. But what about Garrett's dear brother, whether real or not? Would Preston be okay?

Lex always believed that Preston was there with Garrett. But what if he got separated? What if Garrett lay wallowing in a cell, separated for good from his twin?

She dug her nails into the wall and sobbed. The colors overwhelmed her as she walked. She couldn't tell if she had gotten closer to the towers or not. For the past few days, everything was a haze as she walked. At night, Lex found shelter in the alley, finding scraps of food thrown for the stray dogs to survive. Weakness became a companion, but she kept her head high.

Yet, the colors blinded her. She lost track of the other prisoners who escaped. Lex struggled to figure out how she got from one location to the next.

Survive.

She had to survive.

The colors dimmed at night when the mist came out to play. Like every night, Lex hid in an alley, staring towards the Tower of Aeterno. She had no clue how to reach it, the aura of the building wrapping around with hints of yellow, silver, and gold.

*Madame Owiti always understood what the auras told her. Why can't I? I just see the colors…*Lex rubbed her eyes. *Oh, dear Constable Gelida…can't you guide me?*

Despite her prayers, the auras didn't cease. Lex curled in the alleyway, hugging her knees to her chest and closing her eyes. She imagined what Garrett experienced in the tower, crying out for her, begging for his mama. If she listened hard enough, would he speak to her?

"I'm here, Garrett…" she said aloud.

Bwaaaamp. Bwaaaamp. Bwaaamp.

She jumped, the sound of the towers lurching her away from the prayer. Shadows moved above her of the towers in the distance, changing positions across the skyline of Knoll. Their glare remained over the city, peering out towards the Pit and across the tops of the Necrowood. Lex remembered watching them when she first found a home in the Pit many years ago. She would sit on the rooftop of one of the tenement halls with Toddle and watch them move. They had their first kiss watching them, almost like a sunset, imaging a time when they might steal a tower and race off into the sunset.

Lex had to admit she loved him. But he transformed when they lived in Mert…or maybe she changed. Was it her children that led her into the arms of magic? Madame Owiti?

*Madame Owiti…*Her heart ached. *They took her to the Pit, didn't they?*

Lex stumbled along the alleyway towards the street. How could she get to the Pit with no one seeing? It had been years since she'd lived there! But one thing remained in her mind: the Necrowood painted her memory with dark shadows and silver paths. She used to wander them in a haze, waiting for the day freedom might whisk her away.

She would dip her toes in the river and dream of auras.

Now, the dream had come true.

"The river…oh, thank you, dear Constable!" Lex raced out of the alley. If her memory served correctly, a river bordered the edge of Knoll, leading into the Necrowood. If she headed south, she might just end up in the Pit.

Or lost forever in the dead forest.

She gulped down her nerves and raced along the road towards the river. Whenever a shadow of a guard or a random passerby entered her field of vision, she ducked into the alleyways to prevent being caught. It was hard enough anyway; her pale skin shimmered in the moonlight, and her stature made it hard to squeeze into small hiding spots. *Hold the auras close. That's what Madame Owiti would say.* Lex didn't know what that meant, though. She just imagined a cloak of black over her and continued in the shadows, praying that no one would notice her.

The river bordering the city of Knoll reeked of sewage and death. A silver glow pulsed around the river, filling Lex's chest with warmth. There was something familiar about it; somehow, it reminded her of Madame Owiti's old orb. Silver. Humming. Perfect.

But Lex didn't dare touch it.

Last time she touched the silver orb, her body attacked itself with phantom rot.

Did Phantom Rot even exist, though? Now she saw auras. Her head pounded at each color, nausea a constant companion. But she didn't die despite the constant exposure to magic! Perhaps she was never allergic.

Creaking pulled her out of her memories. Lex glanced away from the water, eyes widening at the sight of a smaller tower moving along the river. Unlike the guard towers, this tower moved with a gimp. Different pieces of houses, of buildings, and of towers constructed it, like a hodgepodge of different facilities. Not a tower.

At least not like the ones in Knoll.

She squinted as the tower-like structure skidded to a stop before her. The door opened, and a woman with luscious black hair and heterochromatic eyes stuck her head out. A smile laced its way over her lips upon seeing Lex.

"Oh!" Lex stepped back into one of the dead trees along the water.

"Ah! Yes! There you are! We were looking for you!" the woman called.

"Me?"

"Come in, love. We'll explain everything!"

The woman led Lex into the tower. Lex followed with caution, but the moment she entered, all her fears faded. This was no tower. Inside, an array of goods reminiscent of her home in Mert greeted her. Different goodies, from potions to artifacts to magic trinkets abound, filled the bottom floor. She laughed, pressing her hands together as if in prayer. This was the closest she'd felt to home in weeks.

She followed the woman up the stairs as she marveled at the shop on the first floor. Despite her clear excitement, an aura of blues and grays filled the room: worry, dismay, and heartbreak. Something hung over the woman's head. Was it regret?

Lex couldn't be sure.

But despite the strangeness of the tower, the woman drew her forward, just like Madame Owiti drew Lex towards her in Mert.

As she reached the top of the stairs, the scent of chili powder and red pepper whisked across her face. Her stomach groaned at the smell of food.

"Come on. Yeshua should be finishing up," the woman waved her into the room.

A small kitchen greeted her, with spices and herbs dancing through the air. A stout, dark-skinned man with a scraggly beard ladled a few bowls of soup, his red eyes staring forward without blinking.

"Please have a seat, Elexis." The woman said.

"You know my name!" Lex exclaimed, her voice scratchy and out of practice. She hadn't spoken to anyone in days. It was like learning to speak again for the first time.

"Yes. Yeshua has been watching you."

Lex glanced at the man again. His red eyes glistened like Madame Owiti's eyes. She asked, "Is he a seer?"

"Ah, you already have a good intuition."

"Gisela, of course she does," the man spoke. His voice was higher pitched than Lex imagined. "She is a seer, after all."

"I'm a seer?" Lex stared in bewilderment. Yes, the auras graced her now. But during all her time in imprisonment, part of her thought it was just insanity. But then again, she had protected prisoners during that storm. Her mind raced with all the possibilities.

The woman, Gisela, led Lex to a seat. "Yes. Yeshua has been seeing you in his own visions."

"I never thought…it was always a dream…" Lex stared at the bowl of soup on the table. Her head pounded, but she brought the liquid to her lip and swallowed. After the first bite, she continued to inhale the food, basking in the meal.

"Haven't you ever wondered why you could see auras?" Gisela asked.

"I only started to see auras over the past few weeks. I thought I was going mad." Lex swallowed her spoonful of soup. "Some days, I yearned for magic, but when I was told I was allergic to it…I thought that dream had ended. I guess not, though. In fact, some memories have resurfaced…I think they tried to take my sight from me as a child."

"It is possible. There have been many experiments." Gisela glanced at Yeshua. "But I am glad to hear your powers have returned to you. Perhaps too much torture reignited them?"

"I don't know. Is that possible?"

"Well, whether it is or isn't, your powers are back, and that is very good because we need your help."

"My help?"

"Well, it won't just be you helping. If our *intel* is correct, there are quite a number of Magii who will help…although Yeshua hasn't provided me with all the details."

"No, I have yet to obtain all the details," Yeshua replied with a frown.

"Semantics," Gisela waved her hand.

Yeshua grunted and placed a spoonful of food in his mouth.

"We are gathering help from those with magic. Like you, Elexis." Gisela said.

"I really would like details, if possible," Lex pleaded. "You must understand, I have other priorities at the moment. The Order has taken my son from me. I need to rescue him and get out of here."

"And you shall, you shall," Gisela sighed. She paced towards the window, staring out at the Necrowood bobbing up and down around the tower. "But without your help…and the help of others whom Yeshua has seen in his visions—"

Once again, Yeshua grunted from his spot.

"Shush!" Gisela threw a glare at Yeshua, then continued, "As I was saying…without the help of Magii and seers like you, then there won't be a future for you and your son. Which is why we're heading to Knoll's Pit…there are some powerful Magii there if visions show correct. You are just one of many we need."

"So you see the future? Madame Owiti couldn't see the future. It was more like…current knowledge."

"Seers perceive many things. For Yeshua, that's the future," Gisela replied.

Lex almost smiled. *I love magic.* Her own exhaustion and fear prevented her from fully parting her lips, instead delving back into her bowl of soup. The colors mingled even in the food, bleeding with warmth, comfort, and trust. Life would be easier with the auras now. She'd know people's true feelings and not have to worry about lies or anger.

I wonder if Garrett's aura shines or if it has turned dull. She lowered her spoon. Still, Gisela's aura moaned with blue sadness and Yeshua's with empty sorrow. *What happened? Why the guilt?*

"If I may ask," Lex pressed, "why might there not be a future for me and Garrett? Surely the Constable Gelida or the Effluvium will protect us, yes?"

Gisela shook her head. "It's quite simple, really. Yeshua and I...we made a mistake."

"What kind of mistake?"

"We had a ward in our care that we promised to protect from evil. Well...we fear the evil will claim her. And with her in its grasp, the evil might just win."

CHAPTER FORTY-EIGHT

THE ORPHAN HERO

Yaz kept her head down as she followed Caroline through the tunnels. Exhaustion swept over her, and every time she closed her eyes, she dreamt of the monsters. Despite her excitement at exploring the Library, her ordeal left her bedridden for days, only able to walk a few steps before returning to her bed in the infirmary. While there, Aelia would occasionally give her a dose of the elixir, causing even greater nausea. Sir Jama promised she would improve and soon be able to explore; they just wanted her to do the best possible.

Soon, she could walk further, but the Library left her spinning. From the balcony, she watched as different Mist Keepers and ghosts disappeared into the shelves. To occupy her, Sir Jama invited ghost children to come play in the Library. Yaz never learned their names, and they all vanished within a day.

Despite being heralded as a hero by the Council, Yaz suffered alone, a mere orphan left in the mist.

Always the orphan, ripped from her home.

Almost as if the Council knew of her sadness, they sent Caroline to spend more time with her, much to Yaz's dismay. The woman made odd small talk, discussing Yaz's duty as a Mist Keeper. She never once looked straight at Yaz as she spoke, her melted face hanging onto the flesh, lacking the confidence bolstering in the tone of the other Mist Keepers. Why wasn't she happy? They were back home, weren't they? Sure, the Library looked like a swamp, but at least they were safe. Right?

"Where are we going?" Yaz finally mustered the courage to ask after they spent a bit of time walking through the tunnels.

Caroline glanced back at her and replied, "You must learn how to be a Mist Keeper if you are my apprentice. Ningursu asked me to take you on a release…to gauge where your abilities lie."

Yaz pouted. "Sir Jama couldn't help me?"

"Ningursu has not conducted a release in many thousands of years."

"Oh."

Yaz mulled over the term "release." Sir Jama had said she would become a Mist Keeper, a guardian of the dead souls in the world. He told her how she would release the souls of the dead. But that had been weeks ago. Did this mean the Council had won their war? Would she be able to go back to Mr. Nasr and Ms. Kai soon?

Caroline led her out of the tunnels and into a grassy plain, with rotund trees creating shadows in the distance. The arid air sliced at her cheeks, and with every step, dust kicked up around them. Yaz couldn't help but wonder where else the tunnels might take her if she raced away from Caroline.

I can't let down Sir Jama. She kept her head high as she continued following Caroline towards a small gravesite, where a strange trapezoid structure stared down at her. Mist spun in the air around the fixture, coating it in a golden aura.

"The people of Delilah bury their loved ones in tombs like this. This is one of the grander ones. Most are small, nestled away in cities," Caroline said as she ducked into a doorway on the outside of the structure. "There are a few fresh dead souls in here. Their Hells shall not be as pungent as those dead for a long while. We shall release them."

"A'ight..." Yaz squeaked, following behind Caroline. The inside of the pyramid glowed, with multicolored candles hanging on the wall, as if kept in place by magic. Caroline ran her finger over the flames, frowning to herself as one flame turned purple. For a brief second, Caroline's face turned from its usual droopy self to that of a middle-aged man with a receding hairline.

Yaz gaped but said nothing. What if Caroline didn't know her face changed?

"This way," Caroline motioned, her face once again its usual melted appearance.

She beckoned Yaz down one of the winding hallways. A few people knelt in front of a tomb as they walked, but neither of them turned as Yaz walked past with Caroline. They kept their heads bowed in a prayer that Yaz didn't understand. But their sorrow caused a small laugh to ripple through her body.

She covered her mouth. *That wasn't me.*

"Are you feeling okay, Yasmin?" Caroline asked.

"Yes. I'm a'ight," she lied.

"Nervous?"

"A little…" Yaz whispered. Every step closer to the dead brought a heavier wave of dread. Spots of yellow filled her vision, and aches arched through her body, threatening to eat her alive.

They entered a tomb decorated with opulent and gaudy decorations. A sarcophagus sat in the center, draped in gold, mist pulsating around it. Caroline neared it, running her hands over the metallic material.

"Now Yasmin, before I show you, I want to warn you it can be quite…difficult the first time. The stories dragged my first apprentice deep into their arms. So, if you get scared, let me know. I do not want to overwhelm you."

Yaz gulped. She didn't want Caroline to know how scared she was, but part of her wanted to run away from the scene as soon as possible. What if a dead body jumped from the tomb? What if it tried to eat her?

Caroline held out her hand. "Ready?"

Yaz took it. "Uh-huh."

A sanguine smile on her face, Caroline clutched Yaz's hand in hers and, with her free hand, stroked the top of the sarcophagus.

At first, nothing seemed to happen. Yaz blinked a few times. Was this a trick?

But then, yellow mist spiraled around the tomb.

And she was falling.

There was nothing.
Darkness.
Utter darkness.
Yaz walked forward, calling out Caroline's name.
She saw no one.

She heard not a sound.

Then, out of the dark, came light.

But the light was yellow. Smoggy.

Gas.

"Hello?" Yaz shouted. Her voice had no sound. It was an abyss. She was empty.

In the darkness, a figure approached. A monster. Moving.

It clawed its way to her.

Teeth parted. Nostrils flaring.

It wasn't one monster.

It was thousands.

They all surrounded her.

They bowed to her.

Then one came forward.

And attempted to eat her.

Yaz shrieked. Her eyes flew open, and her entire body thrashed. She still couldn't see. A blinding white light hung above, and while people spoke around her, she couldn't hear them. Just noise. Buzzing. Constant buzzing.

"Yasmin."

She recognized Sir Jama's voice as he spoke. His smooth tone dragged her out of the torture, wringing its hands in her head.

"Yasmin," he said again. "You're safe. It's okay."

She glanced around the room. Once again, she returned to the infirmary in the Library. Aelia watched from her workbench while Caroline stood against the wall, pale as a ghost. Sir Jama rested on his pillow on a nightstand, his voice still pleasant as a luxurious dessert.

"Welcome back, Yasmin." Sir Jama whispered.

"Where was I?" Yaz croaked, her throat stained with the fruits of her screams.

"You had an unfortunate reaction to the release."

"Unfortunate reaction?" Caroline spat. "Sir! She created a Diabolo by just EXISTING in the realm of Hell! We will not be able to train her, but you have forced her into the curse…you have set her up to fail!"

Aelia interjected, "Caroline, you should not talk. You set up your first apprentice for failure. Do not judge Master Ningursu's decisions for the girl. I am certain he has a plan."

"Plan? A plan? His plan is utter malarkey! He wants to destroy—"

"Silence, Caroline!" Sir Jama spat in her direction. A strip of mist flew from his mouth, silencing Caroline and the room at large.

Yaz furrowed her brow. What did Sir Jama want to destroy? Why did she matter? Yaz didn't want to do anything that might get her in trouble or harm. But maybe Sir Jama wanted to destroy evil. Yes, that had to be it.

Right?

Sir Jama turned back to Yaz, his voice once again calm. "Yasmin, your magic is far stronger than we thought. You have an innate connection with those monsters I showed you, the Diabolo. I think you will help them thrive. They are part of you now."

"Is that why I keep having nightmares?"

"Yes. But Aelia has been working on some cures for that. See that vial on the table?" Sir Jama motioned his chin at the glass beside Aelia. "That will help you relax. We want you to be at your calmest as more of these Diabolo connect with you. That way, they will listen to you."

"But what if I don't want them to listen to me? What if I want them to go away?"

"Yasmin, do you not understand the importance of guiding these lost creatures? They are uncertain and alone. But you, Yasmin, you will lead them to victory. Do you not want that sort of success in life? Do you not want to be a hero?"

Yaz drew her lips into a tight frown. She used to pretend she was a hero back in the towers.

Wasn't this what she had always wanted? Adventure?

"I want to be a hero."

Sir Jama nodded in Aelia's direction. She removed the glass from the workbench and brought it to Yaz. A strange murky liquid bubbled to the surface.

"This will help you sleep, Yasmin. Drink. You need the rest." Sir Jama reiterated.

Yaz sniffed the drink once, scowled at the rotten scent, but obliged. The drink smelled as bad as it tasted.

But as the last droplet hit her tongue, a feeling of utter bliss rocked her body.

And she drifted.

CHAPTER FORTY-NINE

THE EYES OF THE EFFLUVIUM

Jemma finished pulling her hair up into a bun on her head. Christof sat on the bed, his toned muscles oiled and defined in the dim candlelight. Slowly, he climbed up, walking over to Jemma and placing his hand on her lower waist. His lips traced her neck.

"Christof, I have to go meet with Senator Cordova. He called for my presence." Jemma shrugged his hands off her body.

"That's only upstairs. You have time, doll. Come back to bed..." He turned her around, pressing his finger into his chin, capturing every fraction of her gaze.

"I do not want the senator suspecting anything."

"I thought you said it was fine for relations to develop. Are you ashamed of me? Doll, you got nothing to be ashamed of..." His finger traced the side of her jaw.

"I just want to look professional...so they take me seriously. You understand that, right?"

Christof's finger trailed down her skin, resting on the crease of her breast. Whenever they weren't working, Jemma invited Christof into her chambers, where they shedded the skins of their past and enveloped the future in their mutual embrace.

Jemma had explained to Christof what she learned during her time in the Tower of Ab Aeterno's cloister. While the sisters, Rose and Ada, long ago had many lovers, neither of them could carry children. Out of respect for Rose and Ada, the Order kept one promise: Sisters of the Order could not bear children, although they could wed and exchange pleasantries. For Brothers of the Order, it had been far easier; if they impregnated someone else, no one batted an eye. But for the longest time, Sisters had to stay celibate to prevent the possibility of pregnancy. With modern elixirs, times had changed. Young Sisters could indeed engage in more romantic endeavors if they made sure their body and soul belonged to the Effluvium.

Jemma loved the way Christof touched her. He pulled her close with lust, he touched her wildest desires in bed, and he unlocked something deep down that she kept hidden. When she was traveling with Micca, she played the role of a pious young woman, blushing at the sight of male anatomy. Micca said there might be a wild woman in her yet.

He was right.

Christof pulled her close and kissed her hard again. She melted into his arms and almost let him woo her back into the bed, but she pushed him away. "Later. I must get ready for this meeting."

"Sister Jey Ma…" Christof bemoaned, his arms still wrapped tight on her waist. "Please…"

"Later, Cadet Carver." She shoved him away and finished pulling on her blue robe. "I have more important things to attend to."

Christof didn't protest. On the way out, he ran his fingers over her body one last time, causing a warmth to climb from her center and through her fingers. It was so strange, the feeling that lust had on the soul. Jemma wasn't sure if she would call it love; while she enjoyed Christof's company as they spent hours discussing scripture and destiny, it didn't have the compelling nature of true love.

Not in the way she had seen Brent stare after Bria or how Micca fell into Timothée's arms.

She refused to let it distract her. Wherever the Effluvium took her, she would oblige.

Jemma trudged down the road from the cloister towards the Aviary, keeping her head down as the wind bellowed and the mid-spring air sang. Guards marched past her, calling orders and loading into the watchtowers bordering the rivers. After the storm, everything changed; now, Knoll knew the fear left behind in Newbird's Arm.

Upon entering the Aviary, Jemma hurried downstairs, past the rows of cells where Magii moaned and cast curses her way. Sometimes, sparks of magic flew from the windows, but never enough to break free. Of the Magii she had met, most just sat in their cells, their eyes glassy and empty. They quivered in the face of the Effluvium but didn't submit to its demands. The demons rode too heavily on the Magii's back.

Jemma wasn't sure if she could save them.

She entered the meeting room in the basement where Senator Cordova, Elder An Drew, Captain Carver, and Professor Gratz sat around the table. Jemma bowed and whispered a greeting to the Effluvium, then sat herself down across from Professor Gratz.

"Hello, Sister Jey Ma." Senator Cordova beamed. "We are so happy you could make it. We hope you can provide some valuable insight into this conversation."

"Of course." Jemma bowed her head.

"As you are well aware, a few days ago, a Yellow Storm attacked Knoll, similar to what we experienced in Newbird's Arm many moons ago." Senator Cordova rose, pacing about the room. "Professor Gratz has analyzed the outcome of this storm and has some inspiring news for all of us. Professor?"

The Professor nodded. "Yes. It was quite interesting. As soon as the storm arrived, it caused our Magii's magic to act up much more than we remember…as if the storm were eating away at it. This allowed us to harness in triplicate the energy from the Magii for our own use." She frowned. "That being said, I worry it might have also awakened magic inside those who did not know they had it. We have already seen several prisoners experience greater bouts of magic. Others have gone missing, such as Ms. Dray…and we fear the yellow storm might have taken her and other prisoners."

"Why would that be?" Jemma asked. "Ms. Dray was sick…not magic."

"Before we put her in transport towards the Prison Tower, she was exhibiting…magic. We don't know how. Perhaps it was the oncoming storm's doing. She doesn't see us anymore. She only sees colors, and it seems she can tell every single person's motivation based on these colors. In fact, she has gone as far as to turn her husband away for being, and I quote, a 'self-righteous asshole.'" Professor Gratz scowled. "But it raises a concern…how many Magii did this storm awaken? Did it occur in Newbird's Arm? Where else is it occurring?"

Elder An Drew, usually a quiet man, molding the words with his bold accent. "We believe the storm, or monster if you will, feasts on magic. I have reached out to a few contacts and believe we can test this, but by feasting on magic, it also acts as bait. Magic reacts to stressors."

Jemma nodded in agreement.

"This is very dangerous for the Order of the Effluvium. Very dangerous indeed…" Senator Cordova paced around the room. "Unfortunately, few of us can see the true suffering of the Effluvium. But I see it. It is in pain. It needs our help."

"How do you see it, if I may ask?" Jemma inquired.

The senator grinned at her. "That is why I rounded you all up today. You are ones I can trust, yes?"

Everyone murmured in agreement.

"One of Elder An Drew's contacts has whipped up a…wine, so to speak, that will help us stare into the heart of the Effluvium. We will be able to see if it's struggling, see if it's thriving. Sister Jey Ma, do you remember what I showed you in Ab Aeterno?"

"Over the water…the Effluvium…" Jemma whispered.

"You shall see it everywhere. Over time, of course. Too much at once will overwhelm anyone." He turned to Elder An Drew. "Can you retrieve the wine from the cellar?"

"Of course." Elder An Drew nodded. He sulked off, his balding head glistening in the candlelight, reminiscent of an egg.

Senator Cordova turned back to them. "In the meantime, we must decide on a course of action. I worry the Pit might be a threat to us if magic is awake once again. We cannot have that."

"I can prepare my men to raid the Pit. Grab any likely subjects," Captain Carver said.

"Do so delicately. We do not need an uprising," Senator Cordova mused. "We shall need someone to venture to Newbird's Arm as well."

"Captain Palmer has almost recovered from her injuries. She is quite eager to begin her pursuits again after her encounter with the Terrorist."

Jemma hadn't met the captain attacked by Bria in the forest, but she'd heard rumors throughout the towers. The woman was ruthless; she would find the Magii now and bring peace to the Effluvium.

"Very well. If she is ready, then she may go. I have already sent a telegraph to Senator Heartz, warning her not to resist. Newbird's Arm does not have the manpower to fight off Knoll." Senator Cordova stretched his hands.

"I have also sent along my proposition to the Senate. If all goes according to plan, we will rid the province of magic once and for all."

"Ay." Captain Carver bowed his head.

Senator Cordova turned to Professor Gratz. "Etta, continue researching, as you have been. Once you can see the Effluvium, I am sure your answers shall come."

The Professor smiled slightly, though her eyes didn't sparkle with the grin.

Senator Cordova finally directed his attention to Jemma. "Sister Jey Ma, now I ask you, what else do you think needs to be done?"

Jemma stammered, "I-I'm sorry, sir, but why do you care about my opinion?"

"You wanted to be part of our decisions. So, tell me. What are your thoughts on all of this?"

Jemma stared at the table, running through everything she had just learned. It was a lot. Was magic really returning? She'd seen it in Ms. Dray and back in Newbird's Arm. She'd even seen it in the circus when she traveled with Micca. But she stayed in the towers otherwise. She had no real way of knowing what lay beyond it.

But there was one thing no one mentioned; even Captain Carver seemed to have missed it.

Didn't Christof tell him?

Or did they not listen?

"I think we should…" She licked her lip before continuing, "We must do our due diligence. If patterns hold, as I am sure Professor Gratz could say they do, then chances are there is someone, or something, linked to the Yellow Storm. We already know that Briannabella Smidt escaped Captain Palmer's custody. She was there during the Storm of Nightmares in Newbird's Arm. She caused an uprising. Isn't there reason to believe that she might still be here and that she is connected to the storm?"

Captain Carver butted in, "I also interrogated her during the early signs of magic in Newbird's Arm. She held to her conviction and never once agreed with the Order. If Senator Heartz hadn't stepped in, we woulda gotten her, I'm sure of it!"

"It is also possible, knowing their connection, that Brent Harley is here as well. I was betrothed to him for a few years, but it didn't work out. While he has not proven to be as dangerous, he has shown magic inclination. The Yellow Storm seems drawn to him." Jemma blinked a few times, utterly surprised at how easily the words came to her. She had seen the destruction laid out before her in the past few days. How could she look away now? How could she deny the stain Brent and Bria had left on the world?

She wanted to believe in good. She wanted to believe in them.

But it was too obvious now.

They had shattered the Effluvium.

"Did Christof not bring up something like this?" Senator Cordova asked Captain Carver.

"I brushed it off as hysterics. He always fixated on those two....to the point of obsession."

"But now Sister Jey Ma has proposed similar allegations. It would be unwise to not consider them."

"If Bria was in the Necrowood after destroying Captain Palmer's tower, maybe she ended up in the Pit?"

"I already asked about her in the Pit." Captain Carver muttered.

"They may have hidden her," Senator Cordova remarked.

"That contact is usually reliable. But I shall check again."

"Is there not a registry?" Jemma asked. "Wouldn't that help identify who belongs?"

"Pits ain't ever needed them," Captain Carver said.

"They didn't need them in Newbird's Arm, where the Guard knew all the prisoners. Here in Knoll, the Pit is tremendous. Why wouldn't you keep a registry?"

"Listen, Sister, I was given this charge a few months ago. I don't got answers for you."

Senator Cordova kept his composure. "Now, Captain. It is a valid question. I recall that years ago, we kept a registry, but after the Smoke Riots, many ended up imprisoned that we never did account for here in Knoll. With the increase in magic and demons, now might be the time to reinstate this process."

"Sir! Gathering all the vagrants would be an extreme undertaking."

"Then we do it slowly. We need to find any outliers." Captain Carver grumbled.

Senator Cordova returned to Jemma. "Thank you, Sister, for your insights. They are most enlightening."

"I am glad I could help."

"I knew I was right to ask you to join me."

The door swung open behind the senator. Elder An Drew strode in, carrying a bottle of sparkling red wine and a handful of narrow glasses. He placed each glass on the table in front of Jemma, Professor Gratz, and Captain Carver. As he poured the liquid from the bottle, it oozed like metallic blood into the cups. It reminded Jemma of the liquid in the Year Glass in Aeterno Tower.

But it couldn't be…right?

"I have been drinking this special mix for a few weeks now. It is…enlightening." Senator Cordova grinned. "It'll take time, but soon you shall see the truth. Drink."

Jemma raised the glass to her lips. The liquid was poignant, burning the insides of her throat as she swallowed. She forced it all down in a few large gulps.

Nothing changed.

But as she rose from the table, the world spun around her. Edges of objects seemed to beat with a strange miasma, causing her own throat to tighten. Tears dabbed the corners of her eyes.

I'm seeing it. Just barely. It's right here.

She would protect it for humanity and the Order, no matter the cost.

CHAPTER FIFTY

LINKED

Bria slept a great deal over the next couple of days. Despite Lana's request that she leave, the idea of abandoning the Pit seemed preposterous. Yet, equally, the thought of leaving her bed also filled her with dread. She didn't want to talk to anyone, keeping under the covers and hiding her head in the pillows. Brent didn't pester her; part of her soul had shattered, and she needed time to heal.

Worries filled her dreams, creating shadows of Lana, her grandmama, and her grandpapa. The dreams called her back to Newbird's Arm, begging for her attention and questions. Surely if Lana refused to speak, her grandmama might have some answers.

Right?

She sat up as Brent walked into their small room. Exhaustion nestled in his face. He'd been spending the days wandering the Necrowood, releasing souls and hunting stories. The events in the tower still hung over him. They'd discussed it in length, from Edith's arrival to Brent's strange new abilities. As he described it, the mist foreshadowed what Edith would do, then he used the mist to tell a story in the presence. His magic grew stronger by the day, and even though he didn't say, Bria could tell how it perplexed him.

Yet, despite everything, he still smiled as Bria sat up with that silly crooked grin and sparkling eyes.

"Morning, sleepy-head." Brent sat on the edge of the small cot and leaned over, kissing her on the forehead. Bria leaned into the kiss, holding his hands for a moment to her chest. His fingers trailed to a loose strand of hair on her shoulder and wrapped it around his fingers. "You feeling a'ight today?"

Bria shrugged.

He grimaced and brushed another strand of hair behind Bria's ear. "Still haven't seen much of Lana. Everyone says she's been hiding a bit and everything. Won't see anyone."

"Guess we have that in common…" Bria grumbled.

"You'll see me."

"That's because I don't have a choice."

Brent kissed her forehead again. Sometimes, when he kissed her like that, Bria could imagine a normal life. What would that have entailed? Perhaps she'd have been a gardener or something, and Brent...well, the only thing Bria could see him do was tell stories. Perhaps in a city like Mert, he might have been a bookstore clerk or worked with children.

That was a different life, though.

A life, Bria knew, she would never have.

Would they ever be able to have kids? Would they ever feel safe?

"Bri?" Brent nudged her. "You a'ight? You're...you're crying."

Bria touched the tears falling from her eyes and wiped them away. "Yeah, yeah, I'm fine."

"Bria..."

"It's been a lot, that's all. Maybe fresh air will help."

She didn't wait for Brent to object or pressure her further. Instead, Bria clamored out of bed and pulled on a jumpsuit and her cowl. She dug her nose into the wool. Despite everywhere the cowl had traveled, it still held a distant scent of her grandmama's home: lemon cakes and tea, with a soft fire burning.

I can't keep thanking you for finding it. She squeezed Brent's hand as they left the tenement hall. A few vagrants stole glances at her and Brent as they walked along the path. She kept her eyes down while Brent hunched over beside her. The wind caught his curls, sending them flying in the air, before landing as an uneven mess upon his head.

The nearby square bustled with the wind. Marisol ran over to Bria and threw an arm around her. "Rho! I was so worried! Are you okay?"

Marisol's magic coaxed Bria to tell the truth. "Oh…um…no, not really."

"What? Why? What's going on?"

"It's complicated." Bria moved away. "I'll tell you later."

"Oh. Okay. Fine." Marisol pouted.

Something about the square here reminded Bria of Newbird's Arm. The children followed in step with Brent, begging for a story, while vendors sold random goods. Only no gold or silver passed between vendors and patrons; all came from barter.

Bria could almost see her grandmama running through the square, taking stock and managing the vendors.

As the children gathered around Brent for a story and Nix lay down at his feet, Bria leaned against a nearby tree. Unlike in Newbird's Arm, Brent spoke his story freely. The children looked on with awe, marveling at his magic. In the front, Chander, the boy from the tower, gaped in awe. This was the freedom Brent always wanted.

But they were still in the Pit.

They were still prisoners.

Sure, they could leave via the Necrowood. But who would survive?

Perhaps Bria could lead them to freedom at last?

But then what? Rosada was still under the Order's hand.

She glanced towards the Towers, shifting along Knoll's skyline. The Order was always watching. They were always manipulating and melding those within their grasp.

And there were always captains asking people to count the lights.

We need to help these people…to help everyone across the province. She glanced back towards Brent. *But what? I can't take on the Order alone.*

Brent smiled at a few of the kids, patting Chander on the shoulder, before returning to Bria. "Feeling better?"

"I'm fine. Just…thinking."

"What about?" Brent sank next to her. In the past, he would have sat there smoking; it made Bria so happy that if anything came out of the mess with the Diabolo, at least he had stopped with the smokes.

"I want to go home...to Newbird's Arm. To talk with my grandmama. But I can't. At least not with all of this." She glanced around the Pit. "They might act like a town, but they're still a prison. The Guard still loads prisoners in daily. I greeted some of them..." Her eyes widened. "Shit."

"What?"

"Madame Owiti! She's here...in the Pit! Lana and I visited her a couple times, but I haven't had a chance to *talk* to her! Shit. I'm a terrible person!" Bria hopped up and started towards the infirmary.

"Wait? How is she here?" Brent chased after her. "Bri!"

"She said it was a long story. I kept promising to talk with her." Bria inhaled. "I feel terrible."

"I'm sure she'll understand. C'mon, I'll go with you."

Bria led the way to the infirmary, nodding towards a few of the vagrants. They always seemed to look at her.

She hated it.

But it was part of her life now.

They tiptoed together into the infirmary. Dr. Hue waved at Bria as they entered, then returned to her patient. Bria meandered to the far side of the room where Madame Owiti sat, her long gray hair woven into a disorderly braid. Her dark skin had paled, her jovial youthfulness diminished into crow's feet and smile lines. Her red eyes didn't shine the same way anymore.

"Madame Owiti!" Bria raced to her side. "I'm so sorry. I meant to visit you, but—"

"Deary, dear, stop worrying." Madame Owiti squeezed Bria's hands. "Madame Owiti knows what has happened."

"You knew Brent was here?"

"I know everything, yes, yes. Nothing is a secret from me."

Brent joined them. "What're you doing here, though? You were in Mert…"

"Oh, that's a story…" Madame Owiti grinned. "But I think you'll like it. Trust me, it's quite an entertaining one, yes, yes."

Madame Owiti detailed her voyage from Mert with the Dray family, only for them to be torn apart upon arriving in Rosada. They had no intentions of coming here, but after the Order redirected all flights for logistical purposes, they didn't really have a choice. They took away Lex for "testing," as Madame Owiti called it, while they parsed children out into separate facilities without their families nearby. The children didn't surprise Bria. She'd seen them herself, but it broke her heart.

"They are trying, yes they are, to eliminate magic to the best of their ability. Cleansings are rampant…and I worry, yes I do, that this is just the beginning. It has a funky color to it all. Yes, yes. But Madame Owiti is old and doesn't understand. They've run her dry…yes, they have." The old woman leaned her head back and sighed to herself.

Brent picked up on the one word. "*Harnessed?*"

"Yes. It goes buzz buzz, and suddenly magic isn't as…prevalent is the word. It's as if they are using the magic for something." Madame Owiti squinted at him. "It's not like magic can just disappear. It's energy."

"And energy can be converted…" Bria whispered.

"Yes, yes, that is right, yes."

Bria glanced between Brent and Madame Owiti, then whispered, "When I was in Captain Palmer's tower, there was a pool of silver there with wires connected to it. Like they were using the pool to power the tower. Marisol told me that once I destroyed the pool…the Tower stopped. I thought maybe the Pool was powering it, but…it was just a guess. This confirms it, though."

Madame Owiti sighed. "It would seem so, yes, yes."

"And they're taking more children? I mean, I already met Chander and the others, but…I was hoping…they were…I mean…" Brent's face twisted in frustration. "Are they branding them?"

Brent understood better than anyone the cost of a brand at a young age. He'd harbored one since he was a toddler, a permanent stain on his wrist, collecting with the newest marks up his arm.

"I wish I knew, yes, yes, I wish I did." Madame Owiti patted Brent's hand. "Yes, I apologize. I don't have any answers."

"Yeah, a'ight, whatever..." Brent stood up abruptly and marched out of the infirmary, his hands clenched at his side. Bria recognized the signs at once—the way Brent tightened his jaw and started squirming and how his gaze grew distant. She'd see him like this on multiple occasions. After his betrothal to Jemma, when his apprenticeship in the market fell through, and when he learned his curse as a Mist Keeper. Each one left him in an utter state of disarray, different from his time with the Diabolo.

"He'll be okay, deary dear." Madame Owiti smiled at her. "Give him time to breathe."

Bria replied. "It's a lot. All of this has been way too much..."

"Yes, yes, I am sure. Especially with everything you have learned, yes, yes?"

"You mean with Lana?"

"With your mother, yes, yes." Madame Owiti said. "Give it time. Your auras are strong."

"What does that matter?"

"Where I come from, far in the south where cities of glass roam, yes, yes, they say when the auras are so deeply connected, they shall never falter. You have that with Lana. I see it clear, yes, yes. Both green. Deep. Connected."

"But she didn't raise me. She's not my...*mother*."

"Yes, yes, that is true...but you are linked. As you are linked to the trees, the grass, and to your lover boy."

"Brent and my auras are linked?"

"Yes, yes. Very much so. You may call it destiny."

"I don't believe in destiny."

"Well, if not destiny, then it is the strength of your care for one another. But in my life, yes, yes, I think it is destiny. That is what we call it down in Proveniro; destiny, fate, by colors united."

"That doesn't mean Lana and I will see eye-to-eye. I wasn't raised to believe in such things."

"Those with your aura always do." Madame Owiti scoffed. "Raised differently, they are...the ones from there."

"Ones from where?"

"From where your family came, yes."

"I'm sorry, but I don't know a lot about my family history." Bria frowned. She never asked her grandmama or her father much about her history. After her mother buried her alive, a cloak fell over her family. It was better to live in the now, abandon history, and pave a new future.

"Then you must learn in order to thrive," Madame Owiti said. "But for now, it is best to return to your lover boy, yes, yes? I am tired, and you are too. We must save our strength."

"Oh...okay." Bria paused. "Can I ask one last question?"

"Quick, my dear."

"What led you out of Proveniro? Isn't it far south of here?"

"The Order took me from my brothers, sisters, mothers, and fathers, of course. I've been a prisoner of many pits here in Rosada over the past fifty years. Only until I arrived in Mert ten years ago did I finally get a taste of freedom. Only for a bit though...and oh, do I miss it...yes, yes."

"They went all the way to Proveniro to take you?"

Madame Owiti leaned back into her pillows. "Deary dear, Mert isn't the first place the Order has tried annexing. They've been dominating the continent for centuries, finding Magii and seers, stripping us of our humanity. Heims, Kainan, Volfium, Proveniro, Perennes, Janis...and more...the Order has been trying to rule since it first laid its foundation here. You fighting it will not just save Rosada but the world. Yes, yes…it is clear to me…yes."

Bria bowed her head. "I'm sorry…I didn't know."

"Because they do not want you to know such a history, no no. They want to paint their own story. But now"—Madame Owiti half-closed her eyes—"I must rest to save more history for another day, yes, yes."

"Okay. Thank you, Madame Owiti. I'll try to stop by again soon."

"Whatever you want, deary dear. Whatever you want."

Bria waved goodbye to Madame Owiti and tiptoed outside, the woman's words echoing over her. *Fighting the Order won't just save Rosada but the world.* She glanced over at a few of the patients. When she had stayed there, it hadn't occurred to her how young so many of them were. Children, adolescents, and teenagers withering away beneath the hand of the guard. Their black stamps glowered on their wrists, and their faces hung with the obvious hatred beaten into them over the months…or years. *Stopping the Order will end all of this. For here and everywhere.*

It also means ending the Council of Mist Keepers too.

She flexed her branched hand as she walked outside, harnessing the magic on her fingertips. Brent stood only a few paces away, leaning against a wooden pole. His fingernails dug into the fixture, and his free hand trembled.

Bria approached him, shaking away the new revelations, and placed a hand on his back. "Are you alright?"

"Now's a time where I really wish I still smoked..." Brent laughed nervously and scratched at his hand.

Bria stopped him. "What's bothering you the most? Talk to me."

"The kids..." He frowned. "And just...this. All of this. It's insane. And I keep seeing stories, and...this is all just a fucking mess."

"Don't blame yourself."

"But what if they have Alexandria?" Brent's voice cracked. He didn't talk about his younger sister often. "She has a brand. What if they took her?" He gulped. "She's branded because of me. I can't deny that."

"I'm sure she's safe. Your mother wouldn't have let them take her. Not after what happened to you."

Brent exhaled. "I just don't know."

"Your sister has shown no signs of magic..."

"She liked stories. And...I mean...I didn't have magic until I met Caroline."

"I think you always had a bit of magic. You're a storyteller."

"Hmph." Brent's shoulders sagged. "I still don't feel great about all this."

"Who would?"

"Apparently, the assholes in the Towers."

"Yeah, well, they're assholes. You're not." Bria wrapped her arm around Brent's waist and pulled him close. His body relaxed, though the anxiety on his face remained.

After a few minutes, he asked, "What was Madame Owiti telling you?"

"About her past…and the Order…and me…in her own round-about way. I think my grandparents knew more than they said. I need to go home. Perhaps my grandmama can help me." Bria glanced at the sky. Shadows shifted through the clouds. "She said something about my family's past. My whole life, that past, ended every conversation. We didn't talk about what happened with my mother, but we also didn't talk about *family* except in abstract. They were trying to protect me, but now I need to know the truth."

"I'll help you find it. We can find a way back to Newbird's Arm—"

"We have to help here first. Lana wants me gone, but…I'm not leaving. Even though I have no clue what I'm going to do now."

"We'll figure it out." Brent squeezed her hand.

She tightened her grip around his fingers, still watching the way the shadows moved in the sky. *Destiny.* She hated that word, just like she hated the ever-changing prophecy that chanted around her name.

Rhodana, the Forest Queen
She loves to laugh, she hates to scream,
She'll finally give in to her destiny
Rhodana

The song echoed in her head, a constant reminder of her journey. Could it ever leave her alone?

A shriek coming from the sky stopped the song, at least for a moment.

Bria redirected her attention once more to the clouds.

Out of them emerged the black shadow of a dragon, heading straight for the Pit.

CHAPTER FIFTY-ONE

THE DRAGON'S RETURN

The dragon landed in the Necrowood, its black wings whipping up the dirt, a steady mist drifting from its nostrils. Laughing, Brent raced through the forest with Bria as his guide. He thought Zephyr had left for good, but this dragon returned, no doubt. The beast's excited roar broke the sadness and revelations left behind in his soul by Madame Owiti's revelations.

"What're you doing here?" Brent asked when he reached the clearing where Zephyr landed.

The dragon huffed.

"Well, she decided to come back and give Santiago a piece of her mind," a voice shouted from the dragon's back.

None other than Micca Fein slid off the dragon, a massive grin on his face. Timothée slid off next, followed by Ms. Honey and Hortense. Once Hortense hit the ground, Ms. Honey helped their sister into a makeshift chair they had stored on the dragon's back. A couple other acrobats and performers slithered from the dragon's back as well, all grinning, their colorful outfits fit for a rainbow.

"What's going on?" Brent laughed. "How did this…where did you all come from?"

Micca patted Brent's shoulder. "Now it looks like I got a story to tell for once—oh shite, it's Beebelle!" Micca raced over to Bria and hugged her. Bria visibly recoiled for a second before accepting the hug and laughing. "I knew Brenty-Boy would find you! I told him, you're like magnets. And look at that fancy-schmancy hand!"

"It's nice to see you too, Micca." Bria smiled as she pulled her branched hand to her side.

Micca threw his arm around Brent again. "The old gang's back together. We can get into all sorts of trouble now!"

"Micca, hun," Timothée interjected as he removed a few bags from Zephyr's back. "Can we go two days with no trouble, please?"

"Aw, c'mon. Gotta have some adventure!"

"Why don't you fill your friends in on the story, hm?" Timothée kept his head low, not daring to look at Bria. His guilt bled through the stories, caressing Brent's skin like ants.

"I'm not good at that. Brent's good at that. Can't he just do that magic thing he told me about? With the story collecting?" Micca gave Brent a puppy-eyed stare.

"I could, but I kinda want to hear you tell a story now." Brent smirked and leaned against a tree.

"I'm gonna need alcohol to do that. Where can we get a good drink around here? Hm?" Micca glanced around. "I just see a bunch of fucking trees."

"I recommend you don't insult trees," Brent said.

Bria giggled beside him.

"You know what I mean! I need civilization. I ain't equipped for this forest life!" He took a stick and threw it, nearly missing Hortense as she pulled leaves out of her wheelchair. "C'mon! At least show me where the latrine is. I don't want to take a shite in front of you all, a'ight?"

Zephyr disappeared again into the sky, using the Effluvium as her mask. Yet even as she flew, a whisper rode on her wings; she had not left for good. Once she vanished, Brent and Bria helped the new arrivals carry their belongings into the Pit. Hortense set up in the first empty shack she saw after a frustrating voyage through the forest. Ms. Honey had to carry Hortense while Brent strung her chair on his back. The tattoo artist sighed with relief once they got to the Pit and disappeared at once into the shack. She lay out her tattooing equipment on the floor while Ms. Honey hung their colorful array of garments out to dry on the clothesline. A few of the vagrants spoke in excitement with the newly arriving acrobats, laughing at their performances and abilities. It pulled some of the focus off Brent and Bria to their relief. Yet, the remnants of Brent's own anxiety remained; watching the children in the Pit play with the acrobats hit him like a punch to the face. He'd been lucky; despite harboring the black stamp, the people of Newbird's Arm didn't toss him away.

Part of him expected to see Alexandria among the faces in the Pit.

Micca collapsed on a bench near the fire. It glowed orange, ash and ember lacing through the smoke into the sky. He found a jug of ale hiding behind a shack and poured everyone a mug. Brent sat on the bench opposite Micca, with Bria curled up against his side and Nix lying at his feet.

"A'ight, ya gonna tell me what the hell happened?" Brent pressured Micca.

"Yeah, yeah, hold on…" Micca downed his ale and leaned back.

Timothée nudged him. "Hun. Tell 'em."

"I needed some alcohol first. I told you, I'm not a good storyteller!"

"Micca, just tell him, or I will!" Timothée urged.

"Fine…FINE!" Micca sighed. "It was kinda awesome, really. After you did that crazy thing and escaped with Zephyr, Santiago went totally ballistic. Nearly killed a guy. The audience all thought it was part of the show and tipped a ton of coins, but it didn't matter. Santiago really wanted to find you, but then that weird ass storm happened. We took cover in the train and waited for his wrath in the morning."

"That was a weird night. Terrible nightmares," Timothée added.

"Yeah, you were crying like a baby!"

Timothée nudged Micca. "So were you!"

"Nu-uh!"

"Yes, you were!"

Micca crossed his arms. "Nope! I ain't ever a baby ever."

"Yeah, alright."

"Well, I wasn't as bad as Santiago, at least!" Micca glanced at Brent. "You shoulda seen him after that storm. He was about to blow a gasket. Got everyone lined up, trying to get us to rat you out. Was convinced I helped...which I did, but I didn't budge. He just didn't believe you did that all on your own. Granted, I didn't know you were that smart, either. But I guess you are. Or Beebelle done rubbed off on you."

"I mean, maybe a bit." Brent smiled at Bria.

"Just a little," Bria chided.

Brent elbowed her slightly, still grinning.

"Eh, well, that's good then. At least you got a bit of a brain or something." Micca took another swig of ale, his eyes glistening with every laugh. "But I guess Santiago didn't think you had much of a brain either 'cause he thought we knew. Was threatening beatings on everyone, even Lolli. Considered getting the guard involved.

"But then out of the sky came Zephyr. But not you. Just Zephyr. She came back just as Santiago was getting out his clubs and whips and all. She roared, and I guess that was enough to get us all to fight back against Santiago. Ms. Honey kinda took charge; it was like Zephyr and you being free broke some dumb spell or something. Santiago was keeping so many people prisoner. Not me...but Timothée was. And Ms. Honey and their sister...and all those other people."

Brent touched the sun tattoo on his forearm for a moment.

Micca continued, "So we kind of just banded together against Santiago, Lolli, and all of them. We sorta cornered them. But Santiago said we wouldn't be able to escape with the barrier in place. I thought that was a load of shite since you escaped. So a fight broke out. Like total mob warfare here or something! Just rioting in the carnival, magic going haywire. I ducked behind a barrel to hide 'cause I ain't able to fight no magic.

"Then Zephyr let out a loud ass shriek, and...well..." Micca started laughing. "She done eat Mr. Santiago...and Lolli too...right up like a tasty snack! She gobbled them up and everything! People vomited! It was terrifying! I thought it was hilarious. It was like one of your stories—the dragon just gobbled him up!"

Brent smiled towards the sky, where a trail of Zephyr's smoke still left a slight trace.

Micca continued his rambling tale, "So Timothée came back a few minutes later saying the barrier was down with Santiago's curse or whatever. We don't know if it was because of what you and Zephyr did or because Santiago done kicked the bucket. But it meant a bunch of his prisoners were free. So some of them took control of the train, while Timothée, Ms. Honey, Hortense, some acrobats, and me got out of there on Zephyr's back to start fresh. She took us straight to you too when we asked what happened....so she's a smart little lizard."

"More like big lizard. She is a dragon," Timothée interjected.

"Shush."

Brent sank back on the bench, staring out across the fire. He didn't think his small act of rebellion would lead to the end of a crazed circus performer's reign. It seemed so minuscule in hindsight. All he did was ride on the back of a dragon out of the circus...but he supposed sometimes smaller acts of rebellion could change history.

"So now we're here, and I dunno what we're doing next, but I'm so happy to see you found Beebelle! You were like some lovesick puppy when she wasn't with you, y'know." Micca kept rambling, even after Brent tossed a glare his way. "So, did you propose to her yet? After all this time, I hope you have because, well, it's ridiculous. I made you promise!"

Bria announced, "Yes, he proposed the other day."

"Bout fucking time!" Micca clapped Brent's shoulder. "So when's the wedding? Hm?"

"Oh, well, um...we...I mean...we can't really plan one. It's not like we have family around or anything..." He glanced at Bria. He didn't dare bring Lana into the conversation. "So...yeah."

"What're you talking about? Hortense can fix up your brand, so you got that official thing going for you! And you got your best friend right here. Sure, family ain't around…but you can do it again for them. Why not seal the deal, hm? That's what Timothée and I did! Look at what Hortense did to my brand!" Micca showed Brent the back of his hand. "See! Hortense made me this fancy-schmancy betrothal mark!"

It was certainly fancy. It looked like a train engine pulling train cars along the railway. Timothée lay his hand beside Micca's hand, where the caboose of the train connected to Micca's hand. Beneath the firelight, the train moved as if to a pulsing heartbeat.

"Hortense does a good job. Much nicer than those stupid Order brands. I'm sure Hortense could fix yours right up." Micca winked.

"She offered back on the train…" Brent mumbled.

"So you two gonna do it?"

"Micca…" Timothée groaned. "Let's give them some space to talk about it."

"This is six years in the making!"

"Micca!"

Grumbling, Micca rose, winking back once at Brent, before slumping off down one of the crooked streets. Brent remained in his seat, staring into the fire.

He had almost forgotten Bria heard everything, sitting right beside him, until she spoke. "We should do it."

"Huh?"

"Get our brands fixed and have a small ceremony or something like that."

"Really? You don't want to wait until we're back home…with family?"

"When will that be? Why not just…make it official while we can?" Bria took his hands. "I never had a dream of a grand wedding. It doesn't matter to me if we elope under a decrepit bridge. Brent, I love you. Besides…" She grinned. "Micca's right. This has been a six-year-long courtship."

"A'ight, yeah, let's do it. When do you want to, though?"

"Tomorrow? Before things…go wrong?"

Brent's face burned, but he kept smiling. "It's a date."

BALANCING ON THE EDGE

Bria kicked Brent out of their room early the next day. While she'd abandoned most of the traditional wedding elements for this affair—there would be no Temple, no plain matronly robe, and no prayers to the Effluvium—she absolved to keep the ones that made her smile. When she witnessed her father and Ric's union, she loved seeing their reactions after all day apart; there was something sweet and romantic about it all. The Order said it warded off demons and bad marriages.

Not that she believed in any of those ridiculous superstitions.

She spent the day blessing the floor with multicolored camellias from her little branch. She wove them together with a flick of her hand, and a luxurious dress made of the earth wrapped around her body. It fit her perfectly, laced into her branched arm and scars. As she peered in the mirror, she had to admit: she felt gorgeous.

As the sun kissed the trees with orange, someone knocked on the door.

"Brent, if it's you, you know you're not allowed in here!" She called.

The door opened. Lana stood in the entranceway.

Bria stared. "Oh. Hi."

"Hi," Lana mumbled. "I heard you and Brent are eloping."

"Yes, we are."

"That's very nice. I can only imagine my mother's reaction…" Lana picked at the peeling paint around the entrance.

"She was fond of Brent."

"And I am sure she only wants what was best for you."

"She does."

Lana rolled back her shoulders and sighed. "That's good. You deserve the best."

"Oh, um. Thank you, Lana."

She shrugged.

An uncomfortable silence rested in the air between them for a moment. Lana kept picking at the paint. Bria didn't say a thing, battling to braid her hair, keeping her eyes locked on Lana.

Finally, Lana glanced at Bria. "Do you need help?"

"Huh?" Bria stopped braiding her hair for a moment.

"Your hair. It seems like you're struggling with it. Because of your hand."

"Oh." Bria flexed her branched hand. "Yeah…that'd be helpful. Thank you."

Lana sat on the bed beside Bria and began weaving her hair. Bria fidgeted with her hands, picking at the bark on her skin.

"You're lucky you got your father's hair," Lana said. "My hair is so brittle, but yours is smooth."

Bria didn't reply.

Lana grew quiet. She finished Bria's hair, then stepped back to comment, "You…look nice."

Bria glanced at the multicolored camellia woven dress on her body, then touched her braid. "Oh…thanks."

"Even if it's not an actual wedding, I guess it's the symbolic gesture," Lana continued, struggling with her word choice. "What I'm saying is I'm happy for you. He seems like a good man."

"He's one of the best. But don't tell him I said that." Bria smiled. "He'd never let me live it down."

"Well, it's obvious he's smitten with you." Lana turned. "Congratulations."

"Thank you."

"Yeah…no problem." Lana left, glancing once over her shoulder before vanishing down the hall. Part of Bria wanted to call out to her, but she instead closed the door, returning to her own reflection in the mirror. *That was strange, but I guess it was something.*

Today, she would focus on herself, not Lana. So she pulled her thoughts back to the flowers she started weaving into her hair. It took all her energy to control her little branch as she placed a few flowers, with its fingers constantly trying to sprout new limbs.

Bria finished winding flowers into her braid, then, with bare feet, strode out of the tenement hall.

She had never really thought about her wedding day. It never really mattered. But dressed in camellias, walking through the Pit, where so many unfamiliar faces watched her in awe, it was not something she had ever imagined. They admired her, and she wanted to hide away, avoiding their wandering stares.

Micca waited for Bria in the center of the Pit, his hair combed back. After they told Micca of their plans to get their brands fixed and say a few traditional prayers with no fanfare, Micca objected on all counts. His words had been simple: "I ain't gonna see my two best friends have no wedding. Lemme handle it!"

Now he waited for her with a grin expanding from both corners of his cheeks. "Oh, Brent's gonna be so flustered when he sees you all dolled up like that."

Bria shrugged. "He gets flustered if I'm wearing a giant sweater too."

"He's a funny man." Micca chuckled and handed Bria a strip of cloth. "Y'know the custom, right? Can't see him until you say your vows."

"Right." Bria pulled the strip of cloth over her eyes.

Micca led Bria through the Pit. The ground beneath her shifted from stone to dirt. She recognized the way the forest sang for her, and she welcomed it with open arms.

"Ain't too far now. Just up ahead," Micca said. He guided her for another minute before helping her stand upon what felt like boxes.

Bria stood there in silence. Brent waited beside her, his presence beating with the wind and the mist. Micca guided their hands together. The blindfolds remained.

"A'ight, hold on. Let me get the paper. Tim helped me put it together 'cause I don't know shi—ah! Here it is."

Brent squeezed Bria's hand, rubbing his thumb against her skin.

"As per the Order...blah, blah...a'ight, we'll start here." Micca cleared his throat. "True love is blind, so they say; it has been blind for eternity. You'll wear your heart, you'll wear your emotions, and if your love is true, you do not need sight. Listen now, listen quick, to your love's heart and its beat. Do you love them? Speak the truth so all can hear."

Bria tightened her hand around Brent's hand, feeling the way life blinked through his skin, pulling for her. It soothed her, knowing that he had beaten back whatever curse threatened his life.

And she would never let him die until they'd both gone gray.

"Yes," Bria said first.

"Constantly," Brent added.

"Then tell each other, and only each other, as we all turn away." Micca shuffled. "Okay, I'm not looking."

Brent snorted.

Bria turned, running her fingers along his arm so she knew they faced each other. He had to be smiling.

That kind, bright smile.

She loved that smile.

"Briannabella Smidt—"

"Wait," Bria said. "Let me go first. You're going to up-stage me."

"A'ight, fine, a'ight."

Bria inhaled, choosing each word with care. "Brenton Rob Harley, I remember when we first met. It was not in school like we both believed, but in the garden. We were young. Kids. And there was a squirrel. You and Micca thought it was dead, and it upset you. You said that now the squirrel wouldn't be able to complete its quest, whatever that may be. I didn't realize until years later what that showed me. Your heart is big, and you're so kind, and you carved out a special spot in there just for me."

She lowered her voice, holding back a few tears. "When I found you in my tunnels, after everything we'd been through, I thought I would break. You're the only one who I ever wanted to share that part of my life with. I don't believe in fate, divine intervention, or even that the Effluvium has a guiding hand...but I think I got lucky finding a man like you. There aren't many others..." She bit down on her lip to stop herself from crying. "I promise to protect you, I promise to listen to you, and I promise to love you. No matter what happens."

Silence rested between them for a minute. Bria felt her face turn red, and her heart fluttered in her chest.

Brent's voice cracked as he formulated a reply. "Briannabella Sophia *Rhodana* Smidt...I think I am at a loss for words. I...I don't...Words can describe everything I feel about you. There's never been someone who has filled my heart so much. I remember when you first moved to Newbird's Arm and entered our classroom. You were shy, but I thought you looked nice. I didn't realize then how those feelings would bloom from us being strangers...to friends...to more.

"We've gone through so much together, so much more than most others. I...I mean, the moment I accepted the proposal from the Order to marry Jemma, I knew I made a mistake. My heart broke, and I thought I lost you. But you stayed by my side. You remained...my constant." Brent sniffled and shifted slightly. "Growing up, I don't think I ever admired someone like I admired you. You were the one thing, the one person in my life that ever truly stayed. Without you, I don't think I'd be the man I am today. You helped me so much, whether or not you realize it. I'm not saying you fixed me...quite the opposite. You helped me realize who I am and...and...I mean..." He gripped her hands tighter. "I can't imagine spending my life with anyone else. We're a team. I'll follow you to the end of the earth and back. And I promise to always stand by your side. Constantly."

Bria smiled. A few tears fell from her cheeks. "Constantly."

The wind rustled in the trees, wrapping around them with a blessing.

"Well, that was lovely," Micca stated with a twinge in his voice. "Now I must inquire...are there any objections? Or should I reject on principle?"

"I'll string you up in a tree," Bria hissed.

"So no objections? In that case, let's escape the darkness and into the light!" Micca took Bria's hands and guided them to Brent's face, letting her fingers rest on the blindfold. He did the same with Brent. "You may grant each other sight."

Brent removed Bria's first. She blinked a few times to reclaim her vision. She stood on a makeshift stage composed of balsa wood boxes. A discombobulated trellis waited above their heads, creating a crisscross pattern of shadows and moonlight. Brent stood before her with his blindfold on, garmented in a white button-down with suspenders, a dusty gray jacket over it. Even with the makeshift clothes he found, he did look rather dashing.

Standing on her tiptoes, Bria removed his blindfold. Brent met her gaze.

"Briannabella Smidt...wow...you look...wow...I mean..." He dabbed his eyes. "Wow."

"You look handsome too," Bria giggled.

Micca took the two blindfolds from them, then wrapped Bria's hands with Brent's hand, looping the fabric around where their betrothal marks stood. Soon, they would match.

Soon.

He stepped back and smiled at them. "We have bound another union! Let it be known to whoever is present." His voice added a jovial twinge again. "Which is me. I'm present. And that's all that matters. So...I guess that means you two should kiss already!"

Bria didn't wait. She pulled Brent down to her and kissed him.

Together, with their fingers entwined, Bria and Brent followed Micca out of the forest towards Hortense's makeshift tattoo shack along the edge of the Pit. Bria couldn't stop smiling. It was silly. The ceremony had been the three of them, with Micca's humorous interpretation of the sacred ceremony, but it meant the world. *Married...* she glanced at Brent. He was so handsome, so charming, and now, no matter what anyone said, they were together. A team. Forever.

Ms. Honey waited for them outside of Hortense's shack. They waved, grinning. "I knew that outfit would fit you!"

Brent adjusted his jacket. "Yeah, it did. Thanks."

"Come on in, lovelies. Hortense is waiting. Oh!" Ms. Honey turned to Bria. "You're absolutely gorgeous. I know we haven't really met you, but I heard so much— just not how *stunning* you are!"

Bria flushed as she followed Brent into the shack. Hortense had set up a table for them, easily maneuverable in her wheelchair, with sets of odd tools sprawled across the tablecloth. Bria's heart leapt, her skin crawling with uncertainty.

"You wanna do this still?" Brent asked.

"Yes. I don't want this…burn on my hand anymore. I want the world to know I'm married to you," she said.

"A'ight. If it hurts, let Hortense know, a'ight?"

"Please, I have a higher pain tolerance than you."

Brent rolled his eyes. "Sure."

She stepped on his foot, not hard or malicious, but enough to make him jump. "Oi!"

Hortense inserted herself into the conversation. "Could you two stop flirting already? It's repulsive." There was a smile in her voice, and her eyes glinted with amusement.

Bria kept grinning, and she placed her hand on the table with Brent's right hand beside her left hand, still wrapped in the cloth from the ceremony. Hortense unwrapped them to observe the mismatched triangles on their hands and nodded to herself. She traced the brands with her fingers. "Yes, I can work with this, yes. So I guess the question is how to tackle this horrid mark. Do you have any ideas?"

Brent shrugged. "I'm no artist."

"Neither am I…" Bria added.

"Well then…tell me things about the two of you. Where was your first date? Where did you fall in love? I gave Micca and Timothée the train because that's where they ended up. Before Santiago and Lolli met their timely ends, I marked them with a dragon. So tell me about you."

Bria stared at her hand for a moment before whispering, "The gardens. Our first kiss was on our way home from school…and we kissed in the gardens by the immortal camellias."

Brent's ears turned red. "I remember! You were picking a few of the flowers and putting them in my hair."

"They always wove nicely with your curls."

Hortense ran her fingers over their hands again. "Ah, yes, I see it now. Bear with me." She pulled Brent and Bria's hands closer to her. After warning them to signal her if it became too painful, Bria listened as the tattoo artist removed a few tools. Then she pricked Bria's skin.

Bria cursed.

"The first one always hurts. Sorry," Hortense mumbled. Another prick raced up her skin.

"Hey, hey, focus on me, a'ight?" Brent nudged her with his shoulder. Bria turned to him. In these moments, right at the edge of euphoria, his face was like a sunrise. His eyes dazzled. His lips peaked in a smile.

Bria yearned to take him into the forest, just to spend moments alone, kissing and weaving stories out of their own desires.

She kept staring at Brent for the duration of the tattoo session. Hortense hopped between working on Bria's hand, then back to Brent's hand without breaking stride. Brent winced a few times, stories surely drifting past his gaze and through his head, then threw a strained smile to keep Bria at ease. He joked about the state of his arm, coated with brands and scars, saying how someday they might cover his entire body. As much as Bria hated thinking about it, Brent had the unfortunate luck of, well, getting burnt and branded.

After a dragging hour, Hortense dosed both Bria and Brent's hands in a soothing ointment, then moved back from them.

Bria finally glanced at her hand.

Her mouth dropped open.

On her skin, woven through the old betrothal mark, was an artistic rendition of a camellia bush. The flowers seemed to blow across her skin, moving as she breathed in and out. The branches looped around her fingers, matching the root-like path on Brent's hands. While her hand beat with flowers, his beat with the desire of the earth. The roots fledged out, crossing his pale skin, reaching for life.

As she gasped, the roots on Brent's hand grew.

"Wow..." Brent gawked.

"The betrothal marks are connected to each other," Hortense said. "As long as your marks are pulsing, you'll know the other is okay. It sounds like you both end up in quite the pickle...so at least this will let you know the other is safe."

"It's perfect. Thank you." Bria whispered, flexing her fingers

"How much do we owe you?" Brent asked, reaching into his pocket for the nice coins he'd acquired.

"My treat," Hortense waved her hand. "You got us out of Santiago's grasp, so might as well return the favor."

Brent's smile returned. "Oh, thank you."

Hortense nodded, then pushed her wheelchair into the other room where Ms. Honey waited.

Bria laced her fingers with Brent's, unable to keep her eyes off the way their betrothal marks pulsated to one another. *Magic.* She would never get over it.

They walked out of the tent, where Nix waited for them, rolling around in the dirt. Micca waved from the distance while a handful of other vagrants seemed to watch as they exited. Bria pleaded with Micca not to throw a party after the fact, and whether it was her pleas or Timothée's ability to restrain Micca, it seemed to have worked. Only whispers spoke of the marriage, and while a few individuals threw congratulatory remarks in their direction, she and Brent disappeared into the arms of the forest without display.

As Bria walked into the forest, her camellia dress continued to flourish, sending petals raining in the cloudless sky. Her own happiness kept the wind calm, the trees humming; the world was bowing to her whim.

When they reached a quiet clearing away from the Pit, Bria waved her hands, ordering the branches and vines to form a wall around them, locking out any curious visitors.

Bria traced the lattice, recalling her hideaway beneath the earth. She could still see, as clear as day, when Brent sat in her hideaway chewing at a lemon. He seemed so foolish then, so young.

Had it only been a year and a half ago?

Brent placed a hand on Bria's shoulder and turned her around to meet him. They met each other's eyes for a moment, then Brent took Bria's face in his hands and brought it to his lips. He kissed her long and confident, falling to his knees so he was more at her level. Bria threw her head back as his lips moved to her neck, his hands to her waist, his breath to her skin.

"Brent..." she murmured and caught his eyes. For tonight only, they could finally hold each other without fear. Without desperation. Without tears. Bria wanted him without reservation. She yearned for his lips to touch every part of her body.

She dug her fingers into his curls. Bark crawled over her skin while the camellia dress floated away. Petals rained from the sky. As she gasped out in pleasure, she brought her branch hand to Brent's cheek, letting the stick-like fingers stroke the stubble on his cheeks.

As the last camellia fell from her body, she began un-buttoning Brent's shirt. His fingers drifted across her skin, capturing each beat with the tips of his fingers, and Bria let herself drift. She immersed herself in the pleasure as his fingers found the most sensitive sections of her skin. With her pleasure, she let her energy flood the clearing, calling for green to return, for the nutrients in the soil to magnify, and for life to come home.

It was more than love. For that moment, they were the heartbeat of the world, Life and Death balancing on the edge of peace and chaos.

What Must Come

Lex slept the best she had in weeks, the tower rumbling beneath her and lulling her into a sense of security. With Gisela and Yeshua, she felt almost secure; their auras bore trust, while their actions bore secrets. They didn't tell her much of what happened with their missing ward, but it was enough for Lex to realize the predicament of their situation. If Yeshua's sight was true, and Lex believed it was, then this missing child was in the hands of some strong forces.

And in these forces' grasps, she could bring about destruction worse than anyone imagined.

Yeshua's sight told them one thing, though: Knoll's Pit harbored an army of Magii, ready to fight. Together, they might stop all Hell from breaking loose.

As the tower screeched to a halt, Lex rolled out of her cot and pulled on the fresh clothes Gisela had laid out for her. They were a little tight, but she managed to squeeze into the lace front dress, then head down the stairs towards the shop on the first floor. Gisela stood at the counter, holding her hand in front of a candle.

"Ah, good morning, Lex. I was wondering when you would wake." Gisela said, her eyes not moving from the candle. She captured the flame in her hand, passed it between her fingertips, and extinguished it with a snap.

"Can you control fire? Like Eldsandi of the North?" Lex found her newest prayer of the day in the question; an obscure god from the natives of the Tom Lands in the northwestern region of the continent.

"No, I can control and see temperature. So I merely took away the heat of the flame…and extinguished it." Gisela glanced at Lex. "It proves little use in a war like this, though. But luckily, we shall have help."

"How much longer until we arrive in the Pit? Surely we can't delay much longer." Her thoughts traveled again to Garrett.

"We have already arrived. Look."

Lex neared the window. The dark trees of the Necrowood pooled out beyond her, with a soft musty glow peeking through the paths. In the distance, as always, the Towers of Knoll shifted along the landscape, creating the ever-changing skyline of Lex's nightmares.

"Yeshua has gone ahead to introduce himself and all…avoid scaring potential allies, as you imagine. I figured I'd let you sleep," Gisela said as she joined Lex. "But once you are ready, we can head over there. Unless you would rather stay in the tower…which, of course, I understand as well."

Lex glanced at the shop behind her. Yes, she would love to remain in the tower, but an inkling of hope sat in her chest: Madame Owiti waited for her in the Pit. Once she found her dear friend, then it was one step closer to Garrett.

"I'm ready," she replied to Gisela.

Gisela grinned, revealing her lipstick-stained teeth, and offered Lex a hand. Her hands warmed Lex's skin like a flame, and as they walked towards the door, the heat continued through Lex's body. She was safe, warm, and content with Yeshua and Gisela. Once she found Garrett, she wouldn't mind staying with them.

Even if it meant abandoning Toddle.

Her heart broke as she thought of her husband. She wanted him to join her, but could she trust him? He had made countless mistakes. What cajoled him into joining the guard? Was he really that clueless?

She didn't know.

But she refused to ponder the issue as well. She had to keep her head up and heart strong…for Garrett.

And for Preston.

Lex followed Gisela from the tower, stumbling through the thick silver water pooling around the foot of the tower before reaching the dry land of the Necrowood. Memories arrived on the branches of the trees. Upon closing her eyes, she once again was only a girl, wandering through the world, without color in her life.

No one helped her.

She was alone.

At least until Toddle came, broken and frayed. She put her energy into helping him.

Now, she would do it again, but this time…for her children.

The Pit was exactly as she remembered it, though. With webs of shacks, tents, and tenements filling the paths, it was like its own city. To Lex's surprise, a calm and happy aura spread throughout the Pit. Rather than distress, there was a wave of hope in the air.

And so much green.

She didn't know what it meant; perhaps Yeshua might tell her.

Or Madame Owiti.

The center of the Pit had always been a meeting space. It was where she sold her "readings" when first dropped off in the Pit; it was where Toddle punched a guard in the face; it was where she prayed to the moon, the sun, and the Effluvium. Nothing had changed about it.

Except for the tirade of circus performers acting out scenes around the fire.

Lex giggled at the sight but didn't dilly dally for long, waltzing behind Gisela as she approached Yeshua. He stood talking with a woman with a black stamp on her face, eyes dark. Her aura glowed deep green, in contrast to Yeshua's silver and Gisela's red.

"I still don't know if I can trust you. You just come wandering into my pit in some fancy tower and think we'll help you? With crazy cockamamie thing against the Order and such? Sounds like bullshit if you ask me." The woman said.

"As I mentioned before, with all the Magii in this Pit, we would be unstoppable," Yeshua replied. "I have seen—"

"We have many people who see. None of it is set in stone." The woman turned. "I'm no stranger to magic. The world might be burning, but I don't give a shit about saving it. I want to protect those under my watch."

"Then it is imperative you help us."

"Listen, I don't want to get involved. If you want a hero, go find my daughter. She's the one you want. We're only trying to survive."

The woman refused to humor the conversation any further. She merely turned with a sway of her hip, her head held high, while her aura bled with sadness. Yeshua glowered after her, his arms crossed, as he cursed under his breath.

"There are other fish in the sea that may help us, Yeshua, my love," Gisela said to him.

"Lana there. She's the de facto leader of the Pit. People follow her."

"But she is not the deciding voice." Gisela placed a hand on Yeshua's arm. Lex missed the tenderness of touch, the companionship; she hated to admit it, but part of her even longed for Toddle again. Or, at least, she wished for the life she had before they left Mert.

Before, when the world glowed bright.

Yeshua nodded to himself. "There is another seer here. I must confer with her about what she's seen."

Lex's heart lurched. *Really? Another seer?* She didn't want to get her hopes up, but could it be Madame Owiti?

Gisela and Yeshua exchanged a knowing nod, then led the way out of the main square. They said nothing to Lex, but she followed them, her heart thudding. Hope continued to bubble in her; was it her own ability as a seer, knowing that something good would happen? She always had an innate ability to detect good news, but she waved it off as luck and optimism.

Madame Owiti had to be here.

They reached the long-dilapidated hall used as an infirmary. Lex had spent many days here recovering from illnesses during her younger years. She used to know every doctor and nurse, every regular patient, and even the new ones. How much had changed?

Inside, everything appeared the same. Cots lined the walls, with a few nurses in torn uniforms assisting the sick. A doctor with straight black hair bounced between each of the patients. *Dr. Ortega must not be here anymore.* She frowned, remembering the balding doctor who tended her regularly. *I hope he has found peace.*

Her sorrow stopped as gold filled her vision. An aura, so bright and kind, beckoned to her from the far side of the infirmary. She blinked, letting the color situated.

Then, she cried out to the aura's owner, "Madame Owiti!"

The old woman glanced in Lex's direction. Her smile lit up the room, despite the exhaustion in her glassy red eyes. Her hair hung loose around her shoulders while skin drooped from her bones like a melted candle.

But there she waited, alive.

Lex pushed past Gisela and Yeshua, nearly trampling over the beds, before throwing herself into the old woman's arms.

"Oh, Lex, Lex, Lex." Madame Owiti cradled her close. "Oh yes, how I missed you, yes, yes."

"I didn't think I'd see you again," Lex sobbed. "They still have my sweet Garrett…and Toddle is an ass…and—"

"Toddle is doing what he thinks is right. Whether he is right is another issue, but he has done nothing out of malice."

"Then he's being plain dumb."

"I think it is best to say his mind works in peculiar ways, yes, yes?"

"I suppose, yes." Lex frowned. "I have so much to tell you."

"Yes, I am sure you do. I see your aura…it is no longer murky, yes, yes? Full of brightness, full of pride; oh yes, I see it. It's so beautiful."

"I see auras now! Yours is golden, Madame Owiti!"

"I knew you had it in you. Come, I desire fresh air. We must go for a walk before the day gets old. It is right…yes…today is the day I must go along the path of light."

"Pardon?"

"It is all well and good, Lex. Let us talk. We shall uncover where your Garrett is yet. Come. Let us walk."

"Walk where?"

"Where we must. Now help me rise."

Lex helped Madame Owiti out of bed. The old woman led her away from the infirmary hall, disregarding Yeshua and Gisela as they walked. The two followed Madame Owiti for a few minutes before stopping at the edge of the Pit as they headed into the Necrowood.

As they strolled, Lex told Madame Owiti how she had seen the auras of prisoners, guards, and objects. The old woman nodded to each word, stumbling over the brush, determination in her stride. Pride rested in her smile, and for a moment, Lex traveled back to her childhood when she told her faceless mother the same thing.

But her faceless mother in those memories sent her away.

Madame Owiti cradled each word and held Lex on a pedestal.

Even after Lex finished her story, they continued walking, deeper and deeper into the Necrowood, past patches of green and into a gray grip. The Pit had fallen out of view. Lex couldn't even see Yeshua and Gisela's tower. Would they find their way back to the Pit now? She trusted Madame Owiti, of course, but the Necrowood took its prisoners often and never set them free. It was the magic that kept Knoll's Pit submissive to the Guard and the Order.

Lex trusted Madame Owiti, though, and didn't bother asking where they were going. As they walked, the auras seemed to blend seamlessly into each other across the dying trees. Madame Owiti probably saw the true paths.

"I always knew you had the sight, Lex deary dear." Madame Owiti gripped her arm as they clamored over a log. "Now, you must learn to extend it."

"Is that what we are doing? Are you going to train me, like we used to say?"

"I am afraid I do not have that sort of time. But I must tell you, my deary dear, your sight will grow stronger if you hold tight to your emotions. Love your sons; wash away your hate; stay true to yourself. You have gone through Hell and back, but you will rise again."

"Like Eldsandi's phoenix," Lex recited, "who rose from flames and soared through the sky."

"Yes, yes." Madame Owiti slowed as they neared a clearing. Over a slight hill, the top of a dilapidated tower waited for them. She eyed it with care, then continued towards it, not hesitating at the tower's darkened eyes.

"Madame Owiti? Are you sure…it is quite angry with us!"

"It is a dead tower. We are safe. We are fine. Come, come." Madame Owiti waved for Lex to follow.

Lex glanced behind her once, into the dark arms of the Necrowood, then followed Madame Owiti inside the tower. A midnight aura fell over her as she walked, only to be suffocated by the bright white auras of vines, roots, and flowers crawling along the wall.

In the center of it all, silver glowed in a pool.

"It's like your orb!" Lex exclaimed.

Madame Owiti bowed her head as she reached the shore of the silver pool. "Yes, yes it is. Exactly like my orb."

"That's spectacular! So we can use it to see?"

"Perhaps you may someday. For now, this is the spot where we wait."

"For what?"

"What must come," Madame Owiti whispered.

"But what must come?"

"The end."

"The end?" Lex stared. "Madame Owiti…what do you mean? I apologize. My sight has yet to show me the truth. I only see auras."

"As is best." Madame Owiti took Lex's hand. "Just know, my dearest friend, that your role does not end with me or anyone else. I am just glad I can spend this time with you, the woman I consider my daughter. I apologize it must be so short."

Lex's stomach lurched. "What…what are you talking about, Madame Owiti?"

The old woman kept gazing into the silver lake. Bubbles foamed at the top of it.

"Madame Owiti?"

"Lex, you will be a key to bringing peace. Whatever role, no matter how big, it is paramount. Do not dwell on what will come. You will be strong." She cupped Lex's cheek. "And I bless you with that strength to complete the next chapter."

"What is going on, Madame Owiti? I don't like this."

"Your story is yours, dear Lex. Now I must go."

"Madame Owiti?!"

The old woman let go of Lex, kicked off her shoes, then waded into the lake. The bubbles continued to form in the lake.

Lex screamed her name again. Madame Owiti didn't turn.

Instead, she stopped right where the bubbles gathered.

Silence followed.

Then another pop.

Out of the water emerged a woman with frizzy red hair and a wild grin. She drew a dagger from her side. Her laughter sounded like a crow, shrieking about the tower, echoing through the sky.

Madame Owiti said something in a foreign tongue and lowered her head to the woman. A smile itched across her body. Without hesitation, she drove her dagger into Madame Owiti's chest.

"NO!" Lex cried out, rushing into the water and splashing it up around her ankles. It burned, tearing at her paper skin like the day her Phantom Rot came to life. But she didn't care. She had to save Madame Owiti.

She was too late. The old woman's body fell into the water. Red poured from her chest and into the silver liquid.

The redhead woman cackled again, then turned to Lex. Her smile grew wider. "Well, well, well. What do we do with you now, hm?"

WARFARE

Brent woke the next morning with Bria in his arms. He pulled her close the moment his eyes opened, nuzzling his nose into her hair. She sighed into his chest. Everything felt like a dream, but Brent didn't care. He just wanted to lie in Bria's arms forever, keeping her close, feeling the warmth gather on his skin.

Married. Brent smiled to himself, taking his fingers through Bria's hair. He stopped at her little branch by her ear. She'd always been his one constant, and now, with a tree pattern on the back of his hand, Brent knew he would never lose her.

They were together. That was all that mattered.

Bria's eyes fluttered open a few minutes later, the sun battering down on her face, casting rays over her freckles. She stretched, the muscles in her shoulders flexing, letting her branched arm rewind itself into its usual state. Unusual flowers, vines, and roots matted the clearing. Nix slept, a pathetic guard dog, at their feet.

"Morning," Brent whispered.

Bria wrinkled her nose. "Your breath stinks."

He blew a puff of air in her face.

"Ew! Stop! Brent!"

"We're married now. You get to share in my filth."

"Well, I want a divorce then." Bria shoved him playfully.

He pulled her on top of him. "I don't think so."

It surprised him when she responded by kissing him. She always had a way of making time stand still; he didn't care that they still lay on the forest floor in broad daylight; all that mattered to him was the smile on her face.

Hunger prevented them from spending too much time in the clearing. After a few playful kisses, they gathered themselves and walked arm-in-arm back to the Pit. Nix refused to wake, though, sleeping beneath a tree. When he tried to get her to come up, she merely rolled onto her back, belly in the air. She would follow later.

Together, Brent and Bria continued along, speaking in hushed whispers. Brent pointed out odd stories along the path while Bria ran her fingers over different objects, absorbing the elements just beneath her touch.

The Pit sat quietly as they returned, with a few vagrants eating around the fire. Brent grabbed a few pieces of bread and meat, leaving a coin on the bench beside the cook, before sitting with Bria by the fire. He began picking at the bread, watching for stories, absorbing the moment of peace resting in his life.

Who would have thought the Pit would be restful? It certainly wouldn't be permanent, but at least for the time being, he didn't have to worry about more than the Guard waiting over his shoulder.

His anxiety had him convinced something would go wrong on his wedding night. But everything ran without issue. It was all he could ask for nowadays.

"May I sit?"

Brent hadn't heard Lana approach. She stood across from them, holding a platter of food. Her eyes darted between Brent and Bria, unable to focus on either of them.

"Yes..." Bria replied.

Lana sat across from them. Silence stalled in the air for a moment, only broken by the chewing of food and the crackling of the flames.

"You two snuck off last night after everything," Lana stated.

"We...I mean...you know, we wanted to spend time together..." Brent flushed and kicked his feet.

"Ah yes, I am sure. But I did not have time to congratulate you both. It's rare to see two people so in love who have been through so much." Lana blinked a few times. "I am…happy for both of you."

"Oh, um, thanks."

Bria said nothing in response. It led to another long stretch of silence. Brent attempted to speak a few times, but words escaped him. This wasn't something he could mend; the story threads were too frayed.

"How much longer are you two staying here?" Lana asked. "Surely, with that dragon nearby, you two could fly off into the sunset and forget this Pit soon."

"We…we haven't discussed…" Brent glanced at Bria.

"It would be beneficial if you two could stay a bit longer."

Bria narrowed her eyes at Lana. "I thought *you* wanted us to leave as soon as possible."

Lana stirred the food on her plate and scowled. "There have been some changes since last night."

Brent exchanged a glance with Bria, then glanced around the Pit. All seemed calm in the stories at first glance.

Lana continued, "Two individuals came out of the forest saying they need the help of Magii. Apparently, it is pertinent regarding the survival of the world or something like that. I don't give a shit, though; it's not my problem. Don't know if I even trust them, to be honest."

Brent glanced over the Pit again. As he squinted harder this time, he saw a stout, balding man with red eyes meandering through the mist. Moments later, in the same story, a woman with long black hair and a woman who glowed like a moonbeam followed.

He recognized them all. "Lex is here…"

"Lex? Madame Owiti said she was locked away, though," Bria recalled.

Brent continued examining the story. "She came with the other two…Gisela and Yeshua are their names. I met them briefly at the circus after their ward went missing. I couldn't find her. My magic started acting all crazy when I looked and…yeah."

"Yeshua and Gisela…right, that was their names. They were trying to get me to rally troops like I believe in their cause. Bullshit." Lana rose from her spot and glared around the Pit. "We're trying to survive and escape here, not save the freaking world."

Bria asked, "Then why bother looking for the tower?"

Lana shrugged. "Protection. Nothing more. I never once said it was our job to save the world."

"But—"

"Whatever. You can go join those two loons if you wanna fight the Order or whatever you've got in your head. Think it's better to just get the hell out of here, though."

Without another word, Lana left, her head held high and shoulders strong. Brent had to admit that there was a similarity between the mother and daughter. The way Lana walked was how Bria used to carry herself in Newbird's Arm: a confident stride and a determined step.

Now, beside him, Bria stiffened.

"Go talk to her," Brent said. "I'll be right here when you get back."

"Is there anything to talk about? She means nothing to me."

"You know that's a lie."

Bria stared ahead, flaring her nostrils. At her feet, weeds sprouted.

"Go," Brent insisted.

Bria huffed. "Fine. Don't go getting into trouble, though."

"When do I get into trouble? Except for that one time."

Brent smirked.

Bria nudged him, then, after planting a kiss on his cheek, followed Lana. Brent leaned back, watching as she strode, the same resolve in her step as her mother. Around her, the stories continued to flourish. Part of him wanted to follow the tales, go find Gisela and Yeshua, and uncover more about what brought them to the Pit. But mostly, he wanted to sit on the bench and take in the pleasantries of the air. He still rode on the high of the night before, and when he closed his eyes, he composed stories of the forest coming to life.

He placed his empty plate on the ground as he continued watching the stories. Countless tales waltzed ahead of him and pried at his mind. As of late, his Diabolo had been quiet. He was sure it waited in the shadows to claw into his psyche. At least for a little while, everything seemed quiet.

Until Nix barked.

She bounded through the trees, hopping around Brent in an excited circle, her tail wagging.

"Nix? What's wrong?" Brent rose.

The dog jumped on his legs once, then raced back into the trees.

I swear, I can't catch a break, can I?

You're cursed. What'd you expect? the Diabolo hissed.

Ah, there you are, Frankie. Was wondering if I finally got rid of you.

I'm not going anywhere.

Brent ignored the Diabolo's continuous rambles as he followed Nix's story. By the time he reached the Necrowood's edge, Nix had long vanished into the trees. He never worried about the dog. She always found her way back. But the speed and agility that caused her to speed through the brush concerned him.

He clamored over a few more logs, following along the stream deeper into the forest. The Tower's shadow loomed over him. At first, all seemed normal.

But as he grew closer, the landscape changed. Floods of silver poured from the base of the Tower, dripping into the streams and rivers beneath the Tower's foundation. In the few days since he had last been there, the Pool had taken over, filling the forest and the path in which the Tower followed.

Nix barked again, racing back and forth in front of the entrance to the Tower.

"What is it?" Brent asked the dog.

She whined.

Then came a scream.

Brent sprinted into the Tower without noting the stories.

Lex stood at the edge of the Pool. She'd lost quite a bit of weight since Brent last saw her. Her finger quivered as she screamed, pointing into the center of the water where none other than Edith waded, knife extended directly into Madame Owiti's chest.

Edith unfurled the dagger and wiped it on her dress, smirking. Madame Owiti faltered, then, within a single beat, collapsed into the Pool.

"No! Why...what...fuck!" Brent pushed past Lex and waded into the water. Before Madame Owiti's body sank, he yanked her to shore. Her red eyes stared, hazed and blank. Panic rose in his throat like bile.

I have to save her! He placed his hand on her forehead.

But unlike other times he'd saved souls, her soul did not reach for him.

No story.

Nothing.

"No...what...what'd you do!?!" He snarled at Edith.

"What? You won't even say hello? How rude of you, Reaper." Edith placed the knife back in its halter. "I did what had to be done."

Brent held Madame Owiti's head, trying his best to latch onto a part of the story. It was empty. Vacant. Alone.

Like Merta... Nedo's voice echoed. Nedo had lost Merta when Kek killed her thousands of years ago for the sake of the Pools. No one could release her soul.

It was all the same.

"Oh, come now. Don't be so pathetic. She was gonna die soon, anyway." Edith kicked Madame Owiti's body away from Brent. It tumbled into the Pool. Red seeped into the silver liquid.

Lex whimpered beside them, her gaze not leaving Madame Owiti's body.

"I do what we need to survive." Edith approached him. She grabbed hold of the collar of his shirt and tugged him upward, placing the knife on the bottom of his chin. The rain picked up around them. "Now, we're gonna try all this fun and games again, understood? You're going to come with me. Got it?"

Brent clenched his fists. The mist swirled around them. "And why would I do that?"

"Because I've had some time to think, and I think if I trade you to the Council, they'll give me Kek. You're the Reapers' bane now, you know." She kept the blade against his skin. "My work here is done."

"You can't make me." Brent thrust Edith back, and the knife cut into his chin. He winced but kept focus on the mist swallowing his hands.

"Aw, what're you gonna do? Throw mist at me?"

"What's the worst that can happen?" Brent extended his hands. The mist pummeled from his fingertips, breathing with the smoke in the air, swallowing gulps of rain as it pattered from the sky. It wrapped around Edith in a powerful whirlwind. Brent rode on the stories of those lost in the forest, of those begging for help, and of those fighting their way through the traps. They surrounded them both.

Focus. Brent shut his eyes. He imagined a tale of guards battling with vagrants, forcing them into the deepest parts of the forest. He conducted the story like a choir, sending it off in each direction, locking both him and Edith on the stage. Edith lost her footing as one character ran past, and she fell into the mud at Brent's feet.

"You…you're a terrible woman…you…you…" Brent raised his foot in the air as if to kick her.

Do it. His Diabolo persisted.

"No, I…I can't…" He lowered his foot. It was too personal. Sending someone through a whirlwind of stories was one thing, but the act of hitting someone with his own body terrified him.

"Weak." Edith cackled, and in one swift movement, she grabbed his foot. Brent stumbled backwards, twisting out of Edith's grip, only to lose the surrounding stories. Edith jumped to her feet and ran her hands over a rock nearby. A new blade emerged from the stone. With a smirk on her face, she lunged once again at Brent. The blade met his stomach this time, skimming just over the top of his skin.

Brent groaned and took a knee. Blood soaked his shirt as he bit down on his lips, trying to refocus on the stories. Too many flittered about now, and he struggled to focus on just one.

"I'll go deeper next time…" Edith glowered, inching closer. "So, are you going to come with me or not? We can end this war."

"It's not my war," he groaned.

"Of course it's your war." Edith raised her dagger again and lunged forward.

Brent clamored back, her blade scraping his thigh. He fell back and gripped the ground.

Edith chuckled, standing above him with the dagger aimed at his chest. "You have one more chance...I don't think the Council will mind finding you maimed or—"

Boom.

Light filled Brent's vision. Like a moonbeam shining through the storm, it blinded everything. Edith screeched, dropping her knife to the side as she tried to cover her eyes. Buzzing roared, seared, and carved.

Then came the colors. Through it all, Brent swore he saw a figure walking towards Edith, skin glowing.

Lex. He tried to say her name, but his throat tightened.

The colors radiated and screamed. If colors told stories, these held anger and perdition. They sought no survivors but terror, destruction, and hate. White marched to purify; blue to bring justice and change; yellow to electrify and shock. Each story, each tale, the colors held.

But these were stories he couldn't control.

Brent covered his eyes. Even with his eyes shut, the light continued to blind him. The Diabolo screeched in his head, clawing down at his psyche.

Please, let it stop! Let it stop, dammit!

Did the voice belong to him or the Diabolo? Why did it feel like the colors suffocated him?

Please. Please…please stop.

Nix howled once.

"Please…"

Then all went quiet.

And dark.

Brent's eyes fluttered open as the final color drifted from his vision. Edith lay a few paces away from him, her chest rising and falling, skin pale, mouth ajar, and eyes shut. Lex stood over her. The delicate nature that she carried in her shop in Mert vanished right then; what she bore instead was the fury of a woman torn from happiness. She carried the weight of her missing sons, the burden of her lost friend, and the magnitude of a lonely existence. Brent saw her story in the fading colors and in her stance. He didn't need to ask. It was clear to him as the walls of the tower.

With the final color gone, Lex collapsed to the ground with a sob. Her voice rocked the air. "I'm sorry…"

"Since when do you have magic?" Brent asked her, leaning on his arm as he glanced around the Tower.

"The Effluvium only granted it to me recently…but I think…forever." Lex stared at her trembling hand. "When I saw this crazy woman attack you, I feared she might kill you, too. After what she did to Madame Owiti…I used the auras. I apologize if it hurt you, Brent."

"No, no…it's a'ight. I'm glad to be alive and shite…"

Lex wheezed, her attention turning back to Madame Owiti's bleeding body.

Brent joined Lex's side, glancing down at Edith on the ground. *She might wake soon. We gotta detain her.*

How are you going to do that? the Diabolo returned. *She'd escape you in a heartbeat. You're not exactly tough. And she controls metal! Can't put her in a cell!*

Brent glanced at his fingers. *I know you're trying to belittle me…but that gives me an idea.*

The Diabolo continued to make snide remarks, but Brent disregarded them. Instead, he held open the palm of his hand and wrapped the mist around his fingers. Like the chains Ningursu used to control the Mist Keepers, Brent composed his own restraints. Unlike Ningursu, though, these did not control Edith.

If I can create objects out of mist, even if temporary…will I be able to control people someday? Is this why Ningursu wants to stop me?

For now, that wasn't an issue to worry about now. Instead, his attention fell on the scene before him in the Tower.

The last thing he wanted the day after his wedding was a battle.

But then again, just like Edith said, this was his war.

CHAPTER FIFTY-FIVE

SACRIFICE

L ana! Wait!" Bria called, pushing past a few vagrants. Lana's red jumpsuit glistened in the path of beige, green, and white suits. "Lana!"

She didn't turn at Bria's calls.

"Lana, wait!"

At the edge of the path, she paused, glaring back over her shoulder at Bria. "What do you want?"

"To talk."

"What do we have to talk about?"

Bria sighed. "Listen, all of this has been awkward. But we need to talk about everything that is happening. We have too much in common to ignore and could fight together. After all, you're my...you gave...you're my grandmother's daughter."

"You mean I'm your mother?"

"Yes!"

Lana scoffed and began walking forward again.

Bria fell in step with her. "My life has been turned upside down because—"

"Your life isn't the only one that got turned upside down." Lana spat without looking at Bria.

"What?"

"I've been atoning for murder for years. I thought I killed you!" Her eyes flared. "If I had known, my life might be different. I've slept with scum, I've toiled in the sewage, I've lived life as a maggot…all because I *killed* you. My own mother wouldn't even tell me the truth!"

"It was to protect me…"

"What? From your evil mother?"

"From all of this!" Bria motioned to the Pit.

"Fat load of shite that did."

"It might not have worked in the end. But it didn't…just like you *killing* me didn't. But it protected me for a bit."

"All while she let me wither," Lana said. "I lost everything. Not just my home."

"But we can save—"

"We can't save anything. The world is dying. It isn't worth fighting for."

"But—"

"Magic is dying. It *has* died. And the world is ending with it. If I can feel it, then you can too." She glanced at Bria. "And what's the point of trying to save it?"

"Because *people* are dying."

"People die every day."

Bria half-laughed. "You don't believe that. You're helping people find their magic and—"

"I'm doing my best to help everyone survive. So, if you can excuse me..." Lana started towards the gate.

Bang!

A gunshot ripped through the conversation from up the path. Bria and Lana exchanged a glance, then, in unison, started running towards the front of the Pit.

Guards waited at the entrance, blocked by a few trucks, with their pistols aimed. In front of them all, with his wicked black eyes and sinister grin, stood none other than Captain Carver.

Bria ducked into the pushes with Lana, clenching her teeth as Captain Carver scanned the Pit. With the sunlight on him, Bria once again found herself face-to-face with him in the barracks in Newbird's Arm. He paced before her, asking her to count the light.

There are no lights here. Only the sun. She dug her fingers into the dirt.

Lana glanced at Bria. "Get into the trees. I'll take care of this."

"What? Are you sure?"

"I deal with them regularly."

"Oh, okay..."

"Plus, what good will it do if the Guard sees you?"

Bria already knew the answer.

She took the trees at once, enough where she saw the gate to the Pit and make out Captain Carver's glare and his snarling voice. Lana approached them. Her dark eyes focused on the captain, and her lips curved in a disappointed frown that Bria had seen far too many times on her own grandmother.

"Captain Carver! What is the meaning of this?" Lana called.

"Ah, Lana, good. I was hoping to get your attention." Captain Carver said.

"You could simply ask instead of shooting off your pistols."

Captain Carver scoffed. "We don't have time for games. We have reason to believe you're harboring two fugitives."

"I have no clue what you are talking about."

"I think you do. You knew about them before, and you know about them now. So tell me...where are Briannabella Smidt and Brenton Harley?"

"Those names do not ring a bell."

"Liar!"

"Do not accuse me of lying. I am aware of what happens in my home," Lana spat back.

"Home? You live in squalor!"

"It is all we have."

Captain Carver shook his head. "All we ask is you turn over these fugitives. Freedom may be in your cards if you do."

"I don't know what you're talking about."

"You're as stubborn as a mule."

"I'm only telling you the truth." Lana didn't falter.

"Very well." Captain Carver straightened his coat. "I suppose we have no choice but to interrogate and cleanse every member of the Pit. Someone is bound to break."

"Everyone in this pit has undergone a cleansing at least once!" Lana snapped. "How dare you issue that threat!"

"It is as Senator Cordova decrees."

"Well, it's bull!"

"Move aside, Lana." Captain Carver ordered.

"No. This is absolutely ridiculous. We are not harboring any fugitives!"

"I said move aside!" Captain Carver removed the whip from his belt.

Bria lurched forward, grabbing hold of the branch to prevent herself from falling. What could she do to stop this? Even if she never considered Lana her *mother*, this woman had offered a helping hand through some of her most confusing moments in the past few weeks.

Lana remained in place, eyeing Captain Carver as he removed his whip. *He always loved that whip.* Bria recalled how many times she would see half-naked vagrants in town, holding themselves in pain as lashes ripped open their back.

She remembered Brent's wounds.

"Move," Captain Carver ordered one last time.

Lana glowered. "Make me."

The captain raised his whip.

"No!" Bria screamed.

Captain Carver paused and glanced in Bria's direction. The branches blocked her from his sight, but his beady eyes continued to lace their way into her soul. "Who goes there?"

Bria didn't reply. Pulling back on her fears, she ordered the trees to grow, commandeer their branches, and help save the day. They expanded with every second, grabbing the different guards and stringing them up into the burning trees. Curses filled the air, followed by irregular gunshots. Bria did not let her gaze fall, giving the trees one goal: protection. Like the bark of a tree protecting the core, the trees could secure the Pit. They would thrive against a storm like Captain Carver or the Order.

Captain Carver smirked as the trees caved in towards him. "Ah, I knew the little terrorist was here." He raised his voice and called, "Come on out, Briannabella. Before anyone else gets hurt."

Bria held tight to her tree, hoping that the confusion would be enough for Lana to get away.

Except she didn't run.

I do what I need to survive. Lana's voice rang in her head.

Instead, Lana stepped forward as the vines and roots moved around them. "Leave, Captain Carver. Now. You haven't seen what I can do."

"Oh, so you are doing all this silly magic?" The captain snarled. "Liar."

"I am not lying." Lana unclenched her hand. For a single moment, a vine wrapped around her fingers.

Bria focused her energy, praying that it was enough to help with Lana's façade.

Captain Carver snarled. "I can't believe this. But then again, I shoulda known you had magic—especially considering you gave birth to a fucking terrorist!"

"My daughter is dead."

"No, she ain't."

"I killed her. Everyone knows that."

"No, she's alive."

"My daughter is dead!" Lana shot her hand out in front of her.

Bria used that as her cue: the fauna went flying around Lana, racing towards the captain.

Captain Carver acted with dexterity and shoved himself into Lana, causing her to hit the ground. The foliage scattered.

Bria didn't let the moment stop her. Instead, she focused on the guards in the trees. The vines and roots continued wrapping around the scene, closing in tighter on Captain Carver and Lana. It had to be methodical, to not give away her location, but she didn't know how much longer she could hide.

"Enough is enough. This ends now." The captain removed a pistol from his belt. In one swift movement, he aimed the pistol at the trees and shot four bullets in Bria's direction.

Bria jumped before the bullets hit her, landing on the ground hard.

Her connection with the trees floundered, and all the Guards fell from the tree after her.

The cracking of a whip and Lana's screams told Bria what happened next.

"No!" she cried out and raced towards the path, using the brush as her armor and shield. If she hadn't held back, if she had just let her magic take hold of her, this wouldn't be happening. But she put her trust in Lana, and now, blood spilled where Lana knelt before Captain Carver. She kept a determined glare in her eyes.

"It stopped when you hit me, Captain. As I told you, my daughter is dead." Lana said with such poise that Bria admired. "So beat me, cleanse me, do whatever you will. Even if my daughter were alive, she and I would share the same genes. She would know it's important to stay hidden. For the sake of everyone…including herself."

Lana's eyes met exactly where Bria stood in the brush. It was as if she spoke directly into Bria's soul, making her promise to stay put. Every piece of Bria's soul wanted to continue fighting.

You can't keep sacrificing yourself for everyone, she reminded herself.

"Very well. I'll make an example out of you yet." Captain Carver raised his whip and struck Lana across the face once more, and the woman withered to the ground.

The guards returned to Captain Carver's side, and after the whip cracked thrice more, they dragged Lana into a truck. A crowd gathered around the scene, paralyzed. With each glare from Captain Carver, they shrunk back into the shadows.

He handed them fear, and they took it, cradled it, and wore it against their chests.

No one moved or spoke as they dragged Lana away.

Captain Carver spat once on the ground, then trailed behind his guards, his head high, whip dragging at his side. Bria made a point of raising a root as he walked away. He slipped once, straightened his uniform, then vanished with the rest of the guard.

Even once they left, no one said a word.

Bria waited until the trucks left the gate to slip from the bushes. Guards remained around the border of the Pit, watching but without seeing. As if nothing happened, as if everything was the same, life in the Pit resumed with individuals suffering in squalor.

With heavy steps, Bria headed back into the heart of the Pit. Without Lana, the Pit almost felt...vacant. She had a commanding presence. *Why didn't I stop it?* She kept wondering. *I could stop all of this.* She inhaled. Bria wouldn't admit her defeat; she wouldn't cry now. No, she would find Lana. Even if Lana didn't think they could save the world, Bria wasn't quite ready to surrender.

They would fight. Or die trying.

FEEDING TIME

Yaz occupied herself by wandering around the second floor, exploring shelves, and pulling out any books her heart desired. She spent hours just observing; she watched the way the floor moved as she walked and the way the ghost-like people moved above, translucent and glowing. Yet, she avoided going downstairs into the forest-like abyss unless the Mist Keepers coerced her, and she never dated venture to the floor above either. The second floor became her endless home, just like how she hid away in the Tower.

Alone.

Always alone.

She hadn't left the Library since her incident with the release a few days earlier. At night, the monsters haunted her sleep, and sometimes an odd mist plumed from her fingertips. Aelia and Jiang kept giving her special elixirs to help, and sometimes Yaz swore she was on a cloud. At least the second floor seemed endless, and it gave her a chance to let her imagination run wild.

Over a few days, she took up playing a game of *Come-Find-Me* with a ghost on the second floor. The ghost never spoke, always cradling a charred doll to her chest. She flinched at the candles, and whenever Yaz called out to her, she ran away. She wasn't even sure if it was the same ghost or if the ghost could see her, but it let the otherwise repetitive days feel a bit more different.

After a couple of days, Yaz returned to the infirmary to find Caroline and the balding Mist Keeper, Alojzy, waiting for her. She shrunk at the man's stare. While Caroline looked monstrous, Alojzy's dark eyes almost never blinked, carrying the weight of anger and disappointment. His lips curved in a permanent frown on his snub-nosed face. "There you are."

"Sorry. I was playing with my ghost friend." Yaz mumbled.

"You should be studying and learning, not playing." Alojzy glowered at Caroline. "Did you not learn from your first apprentice?"

"She cannot complete releases. Has Ningursu not been providing you with a report?"

"He has, but you can still teach her. You are an embarrassment, Caroline. Really."

Caroline said nothing.

"Never the matter. We shall do some training today. Come, child. We have some new experiments to run." Alojzy motioned Yaz towards the door.

"Where are you taking her?" Caroline spat.

"Somewhere important." Alojzy stepped forward. "You are welcome to join me, Caroline. Perhaps you will learn a thing or two."

Yaz glanced back at Caroline and shrugged, then shuffled along behind Alojzy as he led them down the stairs. Jiang waited for them as well, a bottle of liquor on his hip.

"Have you sent the information along?" Alojzy asked Jiang.

"Yes. They've already set up what they need." Jiang replied.

"Good."

They said nothing else, leading Yaz into the tunnels. Her nerves prickled, and unconsciously she reached for Caroline's hand. She didn't flinch when Caroline squeezed it for comfort.

Alojzy was a quiet, stout man with determination in his eyes. As he walked, he unfurled a green robe from beneath his suit jacket and pulled it on, bringing light again around him. Matched with Jiang's constant glare and persistent frown, the two men looked like the stoic leaders Yaz had encountered while traveling across the continent. Some of them came to visit the Tower, but Mr. Nasr and Ms. Kai always sent Yaz to her room. Children did not belong in politics, so they said.

Now, strong leaders guided her, supported her.

She still feared them.

The tunnels darkened as they walked along, fewer fires flickering, the walls echoing each of their steps. They tapered off into a long winding staircase, twisting around in a spiral as if heading up the Towers. Yaz gripped the handrail. Despite the summer air dabbing her forehead with sweat, shivers of anticipation rocked her body.

Where were they going?

After walking in silence for a few moments longer, they arrived inside a tower marked by the presence of Guards. She shrunk in their presence, begging they didn't glance her way.

They only paid heed to Alojzy, calling him words like "brother" and "elder." The Guards said nothing to Caroline or Jiang, completely ignoring their existence. Yaz didn't know how they avoided staring! Jiang was a miniature giant, and even Caroline stood taller than most, with her misshapen face as a signature staple on her face.

Mist Keepers are strange... Yaz would have giggled if she wasn't so tired. The walk up towards the Tower caused her feet to ache. Her head pounded with each step. As they neared the top, yellow filled her vision, and the chants of the monsters filled her head.

Feed...

Eat...

Me...

Feed...

I want to...

Feed.

Yaz restrained the urge to vomit. With each step, the yellow grew more intense, as if reaching for something just beyond the wall.

"Yaz, are you feeling alright?" Caroline knelt at the girl's level.

She shook her head.

"What is the matter?"

"Hungry...the monster...it wants to eat."

"It shall eat soon." Alojzy tugged Yaz away from Caroline. "Come. Now."

"Alojzy!" Caroline called.

The man had already dragged Yaz to the top of the stairs. It reminded Yaz of the Curio Shoppe Tower, in a way. Electric wires pulsated along the wall, buzzing with ferocity, while a small window stared out at the worn-down city beneath the Tower. She stumbled along to keep up with Alojzy, but she swore as she walked. The hallway distorted around her. Everything spun.

Everything twirled.

Alojzy opened a doorway on the top floor. A woman with large glasses sat hunched beside a chair protruding with electric wires. Jiang followed in behind them and joined the woman, mumbling something to her. The woman nodded before calling into another room. Yaz struggled to hear anything. Only the monster continued reciting eager demands in her head.

Feed me.

Food is here.

I can taste it.

Feed me.

Yaz covered her ears, but the chants didn't cease.

The woman with wide glasses returned, followed by a captain in the guard. They led in a tired-looking woman with a black stamp on her face to the wire-ridden chair. Yaz stared at the woman, and as she sat there wide-eyed, the monsters buzzed with excitement in her ears.

Magic.

The woman tugged against the guard as they lowered her into the chair, shouting, "This is inhumane!"

"Shut it!" The guard strapped the woman into the chair. He then walked over, without breaking pace, to the lever on the far side of the wall. "This is for your own good."

He flicked the lever.

Electricity pulsed around the room.

Inside Yaz's heart, the monster pounded, racing to the surface, trying to escape Yaz's chest.

A scream escaped her lips.

What was happening? Yellow fizzled around the room.

Dancing. Twirling.

She couldn't see anyone.

She couldn't hear anyone.

I wanna go home. I don't wanna do this anymore.

Tears flooded her eyes.

It didn't matter.

Her mouth unhinged, and out poured an arm of mist, reaching out over the woman in the chair...almost as if trying to tear open her soul.

CHAPTER FIFTY-SEVEN

THE PUREST CLEANSE

Jemma stared through a one-way mirror at the cleansing chamber at the top of the Aviary with Senator Cordova. Elder An Drew had walked into the room on the other side with a little girl next to him. The little girl's silver eyes darted around the room behind her murky glasses, a yellow tinge on her skin that made her seem almost inhuman. Professor Gratz sat over the Buzzing Chair, working on adjusting the straps and wires.

"What is this about, Senator?" Jemma asked, arms crossed.

"Just watch, Jemma. Elder An Drew has been working with his contacts on this. We believe this will help purify the Effluvium, on all counts." Senator Cordova said.

"It's a child."

"A child, yes. But if this child works out, then we will finally understand how to cleanse the Effluvium at its roots. Is that not what you want?"

Jemma chewed on her bottom lip. The child didn't look well, her skin translucent and large glasses foggy. Perhaps it wasn't even a child, but a demon made to look like one.

The door to the Cleansing Chamber opened. Captain Carver dragged a woman with a stamp on her face into the chamber. The woman thrashed about, her gaze rabid and lips curse-ridden. The captain did not humor her, walking straight past the child to throw the woman into the chair. Professor Gratz worked in haste to strap the woman in, placing a cloth in her mouth before placing the metallic wires to her head. Once secure, Captain Carver tugged on the lever by the chair. Electricity flickered through the room, and the wires around the woman's body roared.

The woman screamed, flexing her body as the electricity tore through her. Jemma swore as the electricity bellowed that misty figures entered the room, one joining Professor Gratz's side while the other placed a hand on the child. Ever since Jemma started drinking that strange elixir Elder An Drew had provided, she'd gotten glimpses like this. Animated shadows followed her, and sometimes she swore she saw eyes staring at her through the Year Glass.

She didn't focus too long on the shadows, pulled away by the child's wails. With each detrimental sob, yellow mist ripped from her body, hovering over the woman buzzing away in the chair. Like the storm of nightmares, it clawed its way over the woman's body, hovering as if eating a meal.

The girl cried out and fell to her knees.

The woman in the chair hollered.

With every passing second, the scene darkened with mist. Jemma pressed her fingers to the glass, watching as the world shook just beyond the windowpanes. This was magic at its worst; destructive, hateful, and terrifying. Was that child always magic? Was she just a victim? And now the child exploded with yellow.

And the vagrant woman's screams shattered the air.

"What's happening?" She turned back to the senator.

"Just wait, Sister."

Jemma waited. The screams only continued. She wanted to call out, beg for it to stop.

But she had to trust Senator Cordova on this. Surely this was all done with proper calculations.

It felt like it would never end.

Until, as if in a blink of an eye, the yellow mist cleared. Elder An Drew had vanished with the girls, not leaving a single shadow in the room. Only Professor Gratz remained, checking the vitals of the vagrant in the chair, as well as Captain Carver, sitting against the wall with his arms crossed.

"What just happened?" Jemma asked again.

Senator Cordova motioned Jemma to follow him into the cleansing chamber. Professor Gratz had removed the wires from the woman's body, where her breaths pounded in shallow beats.

"Etta, what is the status?" Senator Cordova inquired.

Professor Gratz pricked the woman's finger and diluted it in a small dish of silver liquid. The blood filled the small pool, then vanished. "No active signs of magic now. We'll have to watch her for a few days to see if it resurfaces."

"Could someone please explain what this has been all about?" Jemma demanded, clenching her fists.

Senator Cordova beckoned Jemma towards the door. "Yes. Come along."

Jemma followed the senator out of the cleansing room. The adrenaline of the cleanse followed her, thudding down the stairwell and pounding in her ears. Even the Guards moved about the Tower in a haze as if the strange cleansing ritual had changed their world. They didn't even nod in Jemma's direction, their attention locked on whatever task was at hand.

"What you witnessed might be the purest way for us to cleanse magic once and for all." Senator Cordova finally said. "While the Five Levels of the Cleanse have been effective for many years, magic is coming out of the shadows, drawn out by those nightmarish storms. You know why?"

Jemma shook her head.

"Those storms are being led by monsters who wish to feast on magic. So, what if we found those monsters, harnessed them, and let them feast, hm? Wouldn't that end these storms? Wouldn't that let us obliterate magic?"

Jemma squinted at the senator. "Are you telling me the little girl is one of those monsters?"

"She is a vessel who Elder An Drew and his accomplices have been training for many weeks. If she is successful, we can create an army of magic eaters...vessels for these monsters that are otherwise too insane to function. It can be organized, less chaotic, and focused on one goal."

"Destroying magic, you mean?"

"Precisely."

Senator Cordova ran his hand over the wall as he spoke, his eyes hard focused. "A monster that eats magic...yes, it seems contradictory. But the monster is born of the Effluvium's anger. And thus, with it, we shall be able to prosper at last."

"We're sacrificing a child, though."

"A sacrifice for the greater good."

"But…does she know what she is doing? She's only a child," Jemma asked.

"Elder An Drew has promised that they are educating her on her role."

"But why her?"

"Why anyone?" Senator Cordova shrugged. "Her eyes are blessed by demons, and she has a sensitivity to the mist. It fits the bill, just like that old betrothed of yours, Brenton Harley."

"Are you saying that he was supposed to harbor the monster?"

"It is possible. Elder An Drew has worked on this for a while. But unfortunately, Mr. Harley proved to be un-compliant with their cause."

Jemma stared, thinking of the child and the way this duty yanked childhood from her. Was this really best for the Effluvium if it harmed a child? Children deserved their innocence and freedom. Not to carry the weight on their shoulders. Even after everything that had happened with Brent, it still bothered Jemma how he received a black stamp at a young age. No child deserved treatment like a demon.

Even one that might serve as a vessel.

Her voice quavered on her next words. "What if I do it instead?"

"Pardon?"

"What if I learn to control the monster? I'm already drinking that elixir for sight. What if I also take over the power? I have the purity of the Effluvium deep in my soul." Jemma bowed her head. "I cannot let a child sacrifice herself. It seems wrong."

"I am not sure if it is possible. Elder An Drew has been studying for ages, but..." Senator Cordova nodded. "It could bring this to the next level. You are older and aware of the cause. This may be what we need. I shall discuss with Elder An Drew and ask for his opinion. In the meantime, Jemma, keep your heart pure and devoted. Keep your heart filled with the Effluvium's embrace."

Senator Cordova departed at the bottom of the stairwell. In a daze, Jemma headed out of the Aviary towards the Cloister. Her head spun, yet she still gathered a prayer on her lips. She prayed for protection, for safety, and for peace and tranquility. If it meant harnessing monsters to obliterate magic...then so be it.

She'd seen what magic could do, after all.

Christof waited for her in the bedroom. He lay on the bed, shirt off, his muscles glistening with a twinge of sweat.

She climbed onto the bed beside him, resting her head on his chest. Christof didn't speak, focusing on unpinning her hair and letting it fall to her shoulders. His hands began their slow descent down her back, undoing each of her dress's buttons. It was an unconscious ritual, one that Jemma fell into without a thought.

Christof angled her chin up to face him, then kissed her hard on the lips. She couldn't return the affection, her own mind wandering farther away with each moment.

"Okay, I'll bite, doll. What's wrong?" Christof asked.

"Things are a lot darker in the Effluvium than we imagined. But I'm going to fix it."

CHAPTER FIFTY-EIGHT

DESPONDENCE

Anguish hung over the Pit, coupled with silence and uncertainty. Brent immersed himself in the stories while helping prepare Madame Owiti's body for burial after Dr. Hue patched up the scars and wounds left behind by Edith. They locked the metallurgist in a sturdy wooden cage with no metals in the back of the barn, leaving her cursing and roaring in anger. Marisol offered to integrate Edith about her arrival, but Brent told her to reserve it for later. A deeper sadness shook the Pit. Madame Owiti's stories hung in the air, about a nomadic woman bouncing from place to place, uprooted by the Order, trying her best to survive. The best years of her life she spent in Mert; she thought she would die there. But ultimately, with her soul back with the earth, her story was nothing more than momentary jumps back and forth through her life.

He didn't have the energy to focus on them.

Instead, he helped bury her body, returning it to the earth. Lex watched it all, not speaking, her own eyes glassy and empty. Beside her, the two travelers Brent met at the circus, Gisela and Yeshua, stood, their gazes determined. Micca, Timothée, and the rest from the circus joined, as well as a few of the prisoners who came with Bria from the tower. Marisol remained as bubbly as ever, attempting to keep smiles on everyone's faces. Even the boy who came with her, Chander, kept his head high. Ever since Brent spoke to him, the boy had been doing better. He kept his gaze focused, his eyes forward, and even smiled at his little sister.

No one spoke during the burial proceedings.

Even Lex, the one who heralded Madame Owiti, had no words to say. The brutal murder, the blood in the silver pool, they said everything.

Brent waited in the back, stealing glances towards the Necrowood, where Bria watched from the trees with Nix. Ever since the Guard took Lana, she'd been more distant than ever. She spent hours each day in the Necrowood, returning to the Pit only once the sun set. She didn't sleep and rarely ate, speaking in only single-word sentences. Brent didn't try to get her to talk. He knew better than that. Yet it pained him to see her in this reclusive state. He wanted more than anything to help her sort through her emotions, but she kept him at arms-length.

She would come to him once ready. He had to be patient.

The burial ceremony ended with a moment of solace. Each person brought a handful of dirt to the grave. Lex carried the most, and with the top layer solidified, she threw herself down and sobbed. Around her, flowers bloomed.

Brent glanced back at Bria. She held out her branched hand, nodded once, then disappeared into the Necrowood with Nix.

"Is Beebelle a'ight?" Micca joined Brent's side.

"She's…trying to figure out her next steps, I think. I'm not gonna rush her," Brent said.

"Well, if you need my help…y'know where to find me." Micca took a few steps forward, then glanced back. "Timothée talked to me."

Brent froze. "Oh?"

"About how…he told the Guard about Bria."

"Oh. Yeah…he told me."

"Yeah, he said that." Micca smiled. "I'm pissed at him, but…I understand, y'know? He was scared and thought he could get out of Santiago's grip."

"So you didn't break up with him?"

"Nah. I like that man all too much. Just gonna give him a hard time."

Brent relaxed his shoulders. "Oh. Okay."

"Don't get why you and Beebelle aren't angrier, though."

Brent kicked the ground. "I was angry…furious. And I don't think I'd trust Timothée with anything big, but…like you said…I understand. Freedom's a tempting offer. Makes me wonder why no one has ratted Bria or me out to the Guard. They're looking for us, after all."

"Eh, I think it's cause you and Beebelle represent something to everyone here. Or people ain't paying attention."

"What d'you mean?"

"You two represent hope and change to those watching. Many people are out on the roof. I've been in the Pit long enough to see all that. Booze becomes more important than two wannabe heroes."

"Guess so."

"Even if they turned you in, it'd be the same as what happened with Tim. Fate always sends those of us with the Black Stamp back to the Pit." Micca glanced at Brent's wrist.

Brent traced the outline of his black stamp. *No matter what, I'll always be marked.*

"Nevertheless..." Micca grinned. "I'm gonna go bother Timothée. He ain't gotten rid of me yet." He removed a smoke from his pocket, then started back towards Timothée, Hortense, and Ms. Honey. Watching the group of performers warmed Brent's heart; in some ways, he would always be a part of the carnival.

Brent didn't join them. Instead, he approached Lex as she knelt beside Madame Owiti's grave. The woman didn't look at him, her own red eyes stained and glassy.

"She was like a mother to me," Lex mumbled.

Brent glanced over the story in the air. "She loved you like a daughter."

"And now I see all these...things. I pray to whatever god is listening that I can save my son. But I am so tired...it is as if the Effluvium has sucked my life from me. My head hurts. My eyes sting. I never should have left Mert." Lex wiped her eyes. "I wonder what the city is like right now."

"Not sure." Brent placed his hand on the dirt, once again trying to find Madame Owiti's story. "I didn't...I didn't learn about my magic until a year ago. It's scary. My world got turned upside down...but...I mean...you adapt. I don't know what it's like seeing the colors or anything, but someone once told me I should...I mean...there's a mantra I should recite. My name, my home, etcetera. But...the one thing I hold tight is my constant in life. For me, that's…it's Bria. I…she's always there for me. So find the thing that's constant for you, and you might be able to use it to home in on this magic now." Brent stole a glance behind him. He noticed that the boy, Chander, listened as well, eyes wide. "You too. Find the thing that always makes you smile."

The boy said nothing.

Lex stared at the grave again. Tears built up in her eyes. "Thank you."

"Yeah, of course."

As he turned to leave, Lex threw her arms around Brent and squeezed him tight. Brent returned the embrace, letting her story wash over him for a second. Months ago, her sad tale—about a girl taken from her home, tortured by the guard, and sent to the Pit—might have overwhelmed him. Now, with his medication, his meditation, and his mediation of the Diabolo, the story only stung for a moment. It would never go away, but at least he owned the stories.

Mostly.

As he released Lex, the two newcomers, Gisela and Yeshua, approached them.

"Ah yes, you're the story boy from the circus," Yeshua commented.

"Yeah, sorry about the…fit I had last time. It was…there were a lot of children or something and...yeah..." Brent eyed them again. "What are you do-ing here?"

"We're looking for recruits," Gisela commented.

"I'm not interested."

"We know you're a Mist Keeper."

"What?" Brent stood in disbelief. He had been careful not to flaunt his Mist Keeper status. No one had known in the circus; he was just an illusionist, a storyteller...who could control mist. As far as he knew, the Mist Keepers weren't even a common legend.

Unless...

He eyed them carefully, then motioned them to the side, away from Lex and the others.

"You're some of Kek's immortals, aren't you?"

"In a way, yes," Gisela said.

"We've been carrying some knowledge for centuries that is finally coming to fruition. If we don't act soon, the world might end as we know it," Yeshua added. "Though it may already be too late."

"You're a seer then?"

"Yes."

"Yeah...so...if you're here...what have you seen? I'm aware that the Mist Keepers reclaimed the Council. That's why Edith is here."

"Ah yes. We'll deal with Edith," Gisela said. "That is why we fear everything is in motion. We have tried for years to stop it. But it may be too late. Yeshua saw a potential future many years ago. He held it tight, only telling me. I'll spare you the details of it, but it basically predicts a time when once more, two apprentices of Death will both be trained on separate plains. One, a rebel. The other, naïve. Under this circumstance, though we are unsure how or in what way, a new reality might reign."

"And it has already begun," Yeshua said.

Brent furrowed his brow. "So, you mean, the Council has a new apprentice?"

"That is what we believe. And it is why the Council could reclaim the Library. It is why Kek is in prison. The balance between life and death is at stake," Gisela replied. "That's why we're gathering allies. But finding you…and realizing who you are…might give us an advantage."

Brent scratched at the black stamp on his wrist, eyeing their stories. Years of travels shrouded in mist flooded his vision, true intention lost by age. But he knew one thing for sure. Once again, he was another pawn in a game.

"Does this have to do with your missing ward? The one you asked me to find at the circus?"

Gisela and Yeshua nodded.

His stomach fell. "They're using a child as their next apprentice?"

Another nod.

Brent cursed and tugged at his hair. "Why would they think...why would they use a child!?"

"That we don't know. But it could change everything," Yeshua murmured.

"Don't be dramatic, dear," Gisela added.

"It's true."

Brent cursed again. Could he get one day without everything falling apart? Just once?

After taking a long swig of whiskey from Micca's liquor stash, Brent fumbled after Bria's story into the Necrowood. Something about the alcohol made the stories sharper. He saw a forest once born of green. Then came the silver rivers, the mist, and death. How it came together, Brent couldn't see. But the forest wilted, and he was once again in the bones of the trees.

He found Bria sitting in the doorway to the tower, her eyes shut, her little branch looping its way through the stones. More nature than human, she might as well have been a forest nymph or dryad from one of Brent's stories.

A twig snapped beneath his feet as he approached. Nix woke up beside Bria, woofed, then darted in Brent's direction.

Bria opened her eyes only once, blinked, then closed them again.

Brent said not a word as he sat down across from Bria.

For a while, they sat there, not speaking. The wind sang a harmony as it danced through the trees. But nothing more. Brent didn't even know how to breach the subject with Bria. There were too many stones, and pulling out the wrong one might leave a path of destruction in its wake.

"I should have stopped them," Bria finally whispered.

Brent didn't need to ask her to clarify. "You had no control over it."

"I did, though. Lana told me not to do anything, but I shouldn't have listened. She's struggled enough because of me—"

"Bri...don't you dare say that. You would yell at me for saying something like that."

Bria gulped. "You're right. I'm sorry. I need to fix it, though."

"Hiding in the forest won't do anything, though."

"No. You're right. It won't." She gripped the forest floor. "That's why...I think I've come up with a plan."

Brent couldn't help but smile. Relief washed over him to hear that Bria hadn't just been sitting around in her own sadness; that was something he did, but he always saw Bria as someone who did more than that. She was the forest queen, Rhodana, and her song played wherever

668

they walked. He heard it in the trees, in the air, and in the stones. Of course, Bria was concocting a plan.

Why did he ever doubt her?

"Before the Diabolo came, Lana and a few of the others here in the Pit were discussing finding this tower and re-activating it…so they could escape. The Guard uses the towers to navigate the Necrowood…so in theory, the vagrants could too. I think if we get this thing fixed and cleaned…I might be able to…reactivate it. With my magic. Then we can get into Knoll undetected, get Lana and the others out, destroy their personal Pool…end all of this madness." Bria stroked the stone.

"I thought we talked about this. We can't be sure what activating this tower will do to you!"

"But we have to try! I will not sit around and do nothing!" Bria glanced towards the sky. "I can do it. I just need to rest for a couple more days. It's the best option. Yes, I considered going on my own, but…I need help. *I* can't fight alone…I've learned that much."

"And I'll be right here with you." Brent shifted next to her, taking her hand in his and bringing it to his lips. She leaned into his arm, and for a few moments, they let the comfortable silence take them again. Brent didn't want to interrupt any plans going through her head. Would she be able to reactive the tower? He hoped so. But would she be okay after giving it the power?

"I'd be lying if I didn't say I was scared. This won't kill me…but…controlling a tower?" Bria half laughed. "It's crazy."

"You're gonna be a'ight." He brought the betrothal mark to his lips and kissed it. "And we're gonna be okay. Despite all this shite."

"Do you truly believe that?"

"Yeah…I do…but…" His heart fell. "There is one thing…"

"Hm?"

"I spoke with Gisela and Yeshua…the two who arrived with Lex…"

"Oh?"

"Well…they brought some news…" Brent's stomach tightened as he said the next words: "The Council found a new apprentice."

CHAPTER FIFTY-NINE

CLAIRVOYANCY

Each day bled with a different color. Lex sometimes saw only yellow. Other times, she saw greens. Today, it was blue. She recited Garrett and Preston's names, praying to every god imaginable that her boys would be okay. But otherwise, she was no more than a ghost wandering the Pit, begging for her life to end.

Her head burned, eyes watered, and lips quivered. Food didn't sit right in her stomach, and she spent half her time in the latrine. Every step hurt. It was as if Madame Owiti's death tore any bit of hope she still held in her chest from her.

Only the thought of finding Garrett kept her alive.

She didn't quite pay attention to the conversations happening around her. During the day, Lex stayed close to either Brent, Bria, or the boy named Chander. They produced auras that comforted her, so it didn't feel like her chest would break. Chander was a quiet child who said little; she didn't ask much either, but there was a warmth from his aura. Then, of course, Brent and Bria were kind, offering reassurance and promises that everything would be okay.

Any time she neared Gisela or Yeshua, a wave of fear washed over her, so she stayed away from them. As kind as they had been in her rescue, their secrets wore the auras thin. The surrounding colors constantly shifted, and part of her didn't trust them. What motivated them? What future did they see? She kept her head down and didn't dare say a word. *I am probably paranoid after everything.*

Her interest spiked when Bria returned. Lex sat on a bench, picking at a piece of stale bread, when Bria emerged from the Necrowood. Bria had embraced her natural tendency to lead in the past few days, a complete transformation from the quiet girl Lex first met in her shop. There was still that hesitancy, that fear, but she wore it closer. Lex witnessed it in her aura, too; she remembered Madame Owiti once commenting on how gorgeous Bria's aura was, but also how it seemed to fade. Now it glowed with determination and passion.

Lex wondered if her own aura had faded in its place.

Bria sat down beside Brent and turned to Dr. Hue and the rest. Her voice strained as she spoke. "I can ignite parts of the tower. But I haven't tried to ignite it all at once. I think it operates on the silver pool. With enough magic, it thrives."

Dr. Hue nodded. "I spoke with some engineers here, including that mechanic friend of yours…Mike? Micca? Whatever. We think we can get it working, just enough to drag us to Knoll."

"I think getting it operational won't be the difficult part. It's making sure we have a plan once we get there."

"And not getting caught," one vagrant added.

A few more vagrants started talking over each other, voicing their concerns about the potential difficulties in the plan. They all wanted to save their comrades and force the Order to its knees, but each question and statement drowned out the next one. Their auras each glowed as they shouted, their anger and distaste pulling at the different colors on their skin. Lex brought her knees to her stomach and held her hand over her ears.

Focus. Your one constant. You do everything for Garrett and Preston. Think of Garrett and Preston. Imagine their auras, their voices, their smiles…imagine Garrett and Preston.

She closed her eyes, pushing aside the commotion and picturing her sons. She imagined not just Garrett with his crayon drawings but Preston too. They sat together on the floor of her little shop, giggling as they colored. Their words sounded like nothing more than gibberish, but their connection remained strong. Their auras complemented each other, black and white, intermingling as one.

They glowed so bright.

She could almost touch them.

"Garrett…" She sobbed. "Preston…"

She blinked, but she no longer sat in the Pit. Instead, she was in a cell, crying on the floor. Beside her lay Garrett, his hands interlocked with Preston. They looked identical: skinny, tear-struck, and empty. A few broken crayons lay beside them, with sketches painting the walls of Lex, of Todd, of Madame Owiti, and of freedom.

"Garr-bear? Pressy?" Lex cooed.

The boys glanced in her direction, wide-eyed. They said her name, but their lips produced no sound.

"I'm right here. I'm coming for you," Lex bemoaned.

Garrett and Preston both reached for her, but their fingers slid through her skin like a ghost. Tears welled in her eyes.

"I'm coming. I promise."

The boys both turned away from her, focusing their attention on the bars of their cell. Lex moved with them to glance down the hallway. While she couldn't hear anything, the shadows of footsteps bobbed up and down in the lantern light.

Three auras entered Lex's vision: murky brown, red-like blood, and a dull gray. She blinked a few times, then the owners of the aura came into view.

Captain Carver.

Senator Cordova.

And her husband, Toddle Dray.

They spoke but with no sound.

Why don't you punch them in the face, Toddle? Why don't you rescue our sons? You could take these men.

Then again, she no longer knew her husband.

The men continued to speak. As hard as Lex tried, she couldn't read their lips. Todd's face was as unreadable as his aura: empty and broken.

"Boys, I need you to stay strong." Lex turned back to Garrett and Preston. They quivered in the corner, away from their father and the pernicious men beside him. If they heard her, they showed no reaction. "You must stay strong and keep your gods close. Whoever or whatever you believe in, please keep strong. I'll be there soon."

The twins showed no response.

"I promise...Mommy loves you..." She reached for them. "I love...I love—"

Lex...

She shook her head. The colors faded.

Lex...

She pleaded the voices would stop. They had to leave her alone.

Wake up, Lex...

"Please. Let me stay with them. Please!"

"Lex!"

She squeezed her eyes shut. After a few moments, light flooded her eyes again.

And she lay in the dirt, the sunlight hanging over her head, tears staining her cheeks. Bria, Brent, Chander, Dr. Hue, and all the others stood over her.

"Lex? Are you a'ight?" Brent knelt beside her.

He's such a good kid. Lex swallowed, letting tears fall down her cheeks as she pressed her head into the dirt. Every color, every noise seared in her head. All she wanted was to sleep. To forget. To dream.

"Do you need to go to the infirmary?" Dr. Hue asked. "We can treat you there."

Lex didn't respond.

"Can you at least tell us what's wrong?"

She found her voice. "I saw Garrett...and Preston."

"Your sons?" Brent asked.

Lex nodded.

"As in…you saw them…right now? In the Towers?"

She nodded again.

Brent glanced back at Bria and exchanged a look only close friends and lovers share. Lex didn't interpret it, instead pressing her head further back into the dirt. Perhaps if she tried hard enough, she would see Garrett and Preston again. Perhaps she could save them.

"Let's get you to the infirmary. Get you a nice cot and a warm meal, alright, Lex?" Dr. Hue cooed. "It'll be alright."

Lex shook her head. How could she ever be alright again when auras burned through her soul?

Lex dreamt of the towers. In her dreams, she walked along the paths, invisible to the guards as she entered the tower. It was a tall, windowless tower with individuals carrying gray auras. The paths widened and narrow, the stairs creaked, and the lights flickered as she walked.

She was a ghost, moving along, casting no shadow and shining no light. The paths bowed to her whims, and the colors showed her the way.

Down into the Aviary's crypts.

Down where the prisoners wept.

And down where her sons waited.

This time, she watched from outside the cell.

"I found you," she called.

But they didn't hear her.

Nothing more than a shadow.

Fading…

Fading…

Fading…

Until she woke again, this time lying on the cot, covered in sweat.

The colors of the infirmary were less prominent than her dreams. A few nurses, as well as Dr. Hue, moved like streaks of white, yellow, and blue, tending to the wounded, the elderly, and the sick. They used nothing more than the outdated supplies, deposited in piles from the Guard, left to rot in the Pit. It was enough to at least keep people alive.

I was in the tower. I was walking in the tower! Lex pulled herself off the bed and glanced around the room. She hadn't just seen color; she'd seen more; she placed a looking glass on the towers in the distance and thrived.

She'd followed the paths to her sons.

She knew exactly where in the Aviary they waited for her.

Despite the weakness in her legs, Lex pulled herself out of bed and hobbled towards the exit. Dr. Hue attempted to stop her, but Lex ignored her. She disregarded the way the colors blinded her as she moved, focusing on the vibrant green aura pooling from the edge of the Necrowood. When she had first arrived in the Pit, entering the Necrowood was taboo. But with this aura calling for her, it was easy to navigate.

She found herself drawn to the tower where Madame Owiti died. Her heart ached as she followed the riverbank, the glare of the tower tugging into her soul. Multiple vagrants worked intently, with engineers, mechanics, and others from the Pit helping to reignite the tower.

A mechanic working on one of the tower's stilts noticed her first. "Oi Brent! Bri! We got a visitor!"

Brent and Bria came over to the mechanic's side. Upon seeing it was Lex, they clamored down the ladder towards her.

"Lex! What are you doing here? Hue said you'd be resting." Bria asked.

"I need to talk to you both…I can help. With all of this."

"Are you sure? I mean…you haven't been…you've been sick." Brent asked. "I know you wanna save your sons, but we can—"

Lex interjected, "I can see the towers and the path to get to them. I don't know how…but the auras and the colors…they've come together to tell me. Please, I can help. Let me help."

Once again, the two exchanged that sacred glance.

Bria interpreted it for Lex. "Are you sure you're up for it?"

"I need to find my sons. This might be the only way I can help." Lex begged. "Please. Let me help. In the goddess's name, let me help! They're all I have."

Brent and Bria nodded at each other.

"Yeah, a'ight, yeah." Brent motioned for Lex to follow them. "Why don't you have a seat, and we can figure all this shite out, a'ight?"

"Thank you." Lex almost sobbed.

This was it then; she would find her sons. She'd go out screaming if she had to, but she would bring her sons to safety.

Even if it ended her life.

Captain of the Ship

It took a couple of days to get the tower ready. Every moment crawled, and with each passing second, Bria worried they might be too late in their rescue attempt. What Gisela and Yeshua told Brent also hung in the air; they didn't know how long they had until whatever terror struck. Were the gears already in motion?

They couldn't wait to act much longer. Even if they wanted to go down into the Library to stop the Mist Keepers, Brent confirmed the Council locked the tunnels. They could only act in the so-called Living World.

Rumors spread throughout the Pit as the day of their attack neared. People spoke of children captured throughout the province. Meanwhile, the Guard checked regularly on the well-being of the Pit. Dr. Hue deterred the Guard away from any individuals of interest, while Bria, Brent, and the others worked in the heart of the Necrowood.

They had come up with a plan, although not all pieces had come together. While Micca remained with the tower, serving as the "Executive Engineer," as he called it, Timothée would take the children and ill up the mountain beyond the Necrowood on the dragon, Zephyr. The dragon had returned the day before as if she knew about her job in this war. Sentient, Brent called her; the circus treated her like a monster for too long. Now, she would stand with those who cared for her. Meanwhile, Gisela and Yeshua agreed to join in the fight, but from afar. They'd travel in their own tower and serve as residual forces. Their fight, per their words, was not with the Order.

A question lingered about disguises. They had a few uniforms from the tower, but how else could they get past the checkpoints? The tower would be easily identifiable as Captain Palmer's steed. Heralded by vagrants? They'd be a target.

Brent came up with the solution. He described his ability to create disguises from illusions, like Caroline. While he'd only ever done it to himself back in Aeterno Village, he said with enough focus, he'd be able to maintain the story…at least temporarily.

With that, things fell into place.

Bria buried herself in the preparation, even ignoring the pangs in her side from her monthly bleed. It snuck up on her, irregular as usual, and despite the nausea that seeped through her, she kept working. She rarely went back to the tenement hall, often falling asleep in the forest with Nix by her side. Brent would find her in the morning with a bowl of porridge, where they'd sit in comfortable silence. They didn't need to talk.

A few times, she considered going to see Edith. But when she passed the barn, her courage faded. What could that woman say? She killed Madame Owiti, and she tortured Brent. Why would Bria ever give her the benefit of the doubt?

Finally, there was Lex. The woman had stayed close to the tower ever since her episode the other day. Her gaze always looked blank, her mind far away from preparing the tower. Bria didn't interrupt her, instead letting her make mention of the different towers as she felt fit. She described the glistening Tower of Ab Aeterno where a tremendous Year Glass of silver waited, the Aviary where prisoners screamed and suffered, and the one she dubbed the Windowless Tower, where the prisoners waited for their fate. Other towers waited as well: the Temple of Knoll, the Guard Towers, the infirmary, and the Senator's Home. But these had little points of interest.

Bria didn't sleep the night before they planned to depart. She lay awake in the tenement hall, finally returning to a bed for the first time in days. Brent slept beside her, his chest rising and falling with his breaths. They made a home in the bed early in the evening, filled with uncertain kisses and final touches. She sank into Brent's touch, letting his fingers navigate over her body and send her into a moment of pure euphoria and bliss. For that moment, she forgot her worries.

But despite the moment of bliss, she still did not find sleep. Uncertainty over whether the plan would succeed, if her leadership skills would be acceptable, or if they would all survive hung in her heart.

Bria climbed out of bed and tiptoed across the room. Nix raised her head, then rolled on her side, leaning against Brent's body.

Brent woke with a groan. "Bri…"

"Go back to sleep," she whispered.

He opened one eye. "What're you doing?"

"I need to clear my head…I'm going for a walk is all."

He sat up and rubbed his eyes, squinting into the darkness. "Talk to me."

"Brent…I'm fine—"

"Bria."

Sighing, she sank onto the floor and buried her face in her hands. "Why me?"

"Why you?"

"Why am I in charge of this? Brent…we're barely adults. I turn twenty-one in another moon! I—I don't know what I'm doing."

Brent sat beside her and took her hand. "I don't think anyone knows what they're doing. I've seen…I mean, the stories I've seen…no one seems to know much of anything. But at least you're trying to do something."

"What if I fail?"

"You won't."

"But—"

"I've never known Bria Smidt to fail."

"I—"

"You won't fail. That's my job, a'ight. I make dumb mistakes. You're not allowed to take my job."

"Brent—"

"Nope. They belong to me." He nudged her.

Bria gripped both his hands, staring at his new betrothal mark. The root-shaped mark tugged at his wrist, holding the promise that they were still together…no matter what happened in the morning.

She turned to face Brent, lacing her legs across his lap. He stiffened.

Bria pressed her hands against his chest, then kissed him. Deep. She let her lips wrap around his lips, her body sinking into his embrace. They'd already given into each other once that night, but she needed him again. Now, more than ever, she needed to feel something. Passion. Romance.

Love.

Brent caught her hands as she began to remove her nightshirt. "Something else is bothering you."

"I need to take my mind off all of this," Bria whispered. "please..."

"Bria."

She gulped, feeling the way Brent's eyes stared into her, watching her every move. Her throat tightened as the final bit of worry escaped from her lips, "What if something goes wrong and...and...I lose you? For real this time?"

"You won't," Brent promised. "We'll always find a way back to each other. We're like...damn, this is gonna be a lame comparison, but...we're Life and Death, you know? You bring life to the world, ignite it, and carry the change. I'm the one who records the past, carries the souls to the next realm...well...when I'm allowed to cause of all those fucking pricks. We can function without each other, do our duty and everything, but we are...we can't exist without each other. No matter what, we'll reunite."

Bria snorted. "What kind of poetic statement is that? I thought we were magnets."

"Eh, this sounds better."

She lined her hand up with Brent's palm, watching how their betrothal marks interacted. Hortense did a phenomenal job lacing them together with a promise of forever, of companionship, and of love.

Bria's voice caught in her throat as she spoke the next words. "I love you so much, Brent. I don't want to lose you."

"You won't. I promise."

Sleep eventually came, only for Bria to wake up to the Brent shaking her shoulder. She slept later than she intended, the mid-morning sunlight peeking through the broken window and reflecting off the mirror. Her head ached as she got out of bed, slowly getting dressed as Brent took his medication and struggled with the buttons of his shirt. Bria helped him with the last one, planting another kiss on his cheek. Oh, how she wanted to stay with him, curled up in his embrace.

But it was now or never. They had to act.

Already, the vagrants lined the edge of the Necrowood. While Dr. Hue would stay behind to tend to any wounded, many others chose opted to fight. Bria kept her hand laced around Brent's wrist, and after telling Nix to stay with Dr. Hue, she began her trek into the Necrowood. No one spoke. Together, they would march to their victory.

Or their death.

No. We're going to do this. In and out. Once the towers are destroyed, no one can stop us. We're Magii. We're storytellers. We're fighters.

Bria straightened her back and climbed onto the stairs leading into the tower. The vagrants watched her, with Micca standing by one of the gear-ridden legs. It took her back to the day in Newbird's Arm when the vagrants and townsfolk gathered in protest against the new rule of the Order. Newbird's Arm thrived, but she never returned. This time, she would stay and fight until the end.

"We're doing this for a few things today..." She glanced at Brent, who nodded once in her direction. "There are forces at work beyond our control, but if we can fight them, even for a little while, we might just be able to save some people. The Order has suppressed the true nature of humanity for too long. They fear magic, and maybe rightfully so. Because we can, without a doubt, win in a fight like this. But it's not just magic, but stories, but rebels—they give us no chance to live. Now, they're taking those of us who have already atoned. Lana is one. But also, those who have done no wrong...like the children. No one is brave enough to stand up. So, what do we have to lose?"

Bria glanced at her hands. "I was not thrown into the Pit, I escaped here, but I can tell you this: Knoll's Pit is more alive than most cities in Rosada. In so many places—Newbird's Arm, Hutch's Creek, Aeterno Village, and others—-people don't laugh. But here, you dance. You sing. And you are alive. So let's change the world, together, one tower at a time."

The vagrants cheered. Bria shrank and stared at her shaking hands.

Brent joined her side and squeezed her shoulders, a smile prominent on his face. "See? They look to you."

"Why, though?"

"Isn't it obvious? It's cause you are…you're Rhodana, the Forest Queen. Listen…"

She glanced back over at the gathering. A gentle hum caught their lips.

Rhodana, the forest queen
She loves to laugh; she hates to scream
She promised the world a reverie.
Rhodana.
She'll lead us back, no matter circumstance
Fight the bad with a mere glance
She'll take the world for a wild spin.

As always, the song changed each time. Kek once told Bria it was a prophecy, though she didn't quite believe that. It was merely a story, passed down from generation to generation, changing on each person's lips. Stories are never the same.

But what if the song predicted her ending?

If this version was indeed the prophecy, then at least it sounded like she would win.

"Beebelle!" Micca called from his spot by the geared leg. "We're ready whenever you are, a'ight? Everything is working all hunky-dory!"

"Did Timothée already take everyone to the mountain who wanted to go?" Brent asked.

"Ay. He said he'll join us down below. Zephyr wants blood." Micca winked. "Your friend Lex is already in the tower, and those two buffoons…what're their names? Right, Gisela and Yeshua? They're taking the long way around the city. Said they know what they're doing. We're all ready to go otherwise, though."

"Thank you, Micca. You've been a gem," Bria whispered. Sweat gathered on her brow as she turned towards the tower.

It was time.

She released Brent's hand, squeezing it once more for good measure, then marched into the center of the tower. The group joined her, everyone detouring to different positions: artillery, maintenance, navigation, or medical. They took their roles with ease.

I'm captain of this ship. I can do this.

She never thought she would be a captain…but today, that changed. Now, she had not just a vessel but a crew, and they were ready to follow her lead. Was it because she was Lana's daughter? Or did they know what happened to her? Did they know about the rebellion she began?

It didn't matter.

Bria stole one last glance at Brent. He stood by the door, watching each person enter carefully. As they passed him, a story surrounded them, his magic disguising each newcomer as a member of the guard. He already wore a story on him of a uniform. Bria squirmed at the sight: Brent Harley and a guard uniform just didn't mix. It reminded her too much of Cadet Lawry, or Christof, or Captain Carver.

She glanced down at her own body. A misty exterior hid her as well, disguising her in a captain's uniform. Bria gagged but then looked away.

Right now, she had a different job to do.

She marched down the stairs into the engine room at the bottom of the tower. Heat trickled around her, the gears screaming and demanding fuel. But despite the wires and dull electric currents, the silver pool provided no life. Dead peonies floated on the surface.

If I can use its magic, I can give it back. Just a jolt is all it needs.

She dragged her finger over the surface of the water. What if Ningursu watched her from his all-seeing pool in the Library? If he was truly back, surely he was looking for her and Brent.

With so many pools in the world, how would he know when or where to look?

Bria refused to let the fear get to her. Instead, she pressed her fingers into the silver liquid. It melded around both her real and branched fingers, begging for life. The dead peonies gathered at her wrist.

And like with the trees in the forest, she did just that. Before, she pulled at the peony heart, bringing the flowers to the surface. Now, she replanted its heart with the left-over seed, giving to it her life, her power, and her sanity.

The electricity buzzed around her. With all her might, she directed it along the currents of her body and into the Pool.

Nothing happened.

Then, the Pool bubbled.

With it, the tower creaked. The engine roared.

And with one uneven step at a time, the tower began to move.

CHAPTER SIXTY-ONE

HOW TO MASK AN ATTACK

Brent leaned over the railing, staring down into the heart of the tower, his arms wrapped around Bria. She leaned into him, half-asleep, still recovering from reigniting the tower. He urged her to sleep after, and for a couple hours, she hid in the Captain's Chambers. Meanwhile, Brent kept his attention on the story at hand: he told the tale of guards operating an unworn tower as it creaked along the river.

It didn't move fast, moaning and droning for hours as they neared the city. No one stopped them as the tower, disguised with the story as any other guard tower, passed out of the Necrowood. A few guards even saluted them along the riverbank. One vagrant manned the radio on the ground floor, using standard codes to communicate with the Aviary, the prime tower of Knoll.

If Brent didn't know any better, he would have thought they *were* in a guard tower.

The towers of Knoll peered through the windows at them, growing closer each minute as they traced along the edge of the city. From their perch, Brent made out how empty and broken the city appeared. While Knoll heralded itself as the military capital of the nation, the infrastructure sat in squalor. It might as well have been an extension of the Pit; the people he made out in the city below lived in rags, kept their heads down, and their tired eyes fixated on nothing at all.

They weren't just liberating the Pit. It was for Rosada.

Everyone would breathe again with the Order's reign gone. The towers served as a symbol; destroy the towers, and the Order lost its power.

That was the plan, wasn't it?

The tower screeched, finding a place along the river with the other towers in the fleet. Bria shifted in Brent's arm, immediately straightening her back, assuming her stance as captain.

"We're here," she whispered.

"Let's go find Lex."

Brent and Bria strolled into the navigation room where Lex had been saying. Unlike the rest of the crew, Brent didn't bother coating her with a story. Despite her reignited magic, the Phantom Rot left a mark on her. Exhaustion, weakness, and tremors rocked her body. Brent couldn't tell if it was the exposure to magic in the tower, her own newfound abilities as a seer, or something else.

Yet he refused to be responsible for Lex's further struggles.

"The tower is laying its anchors," Bria said to Lex. "Are you ready?"

Lex glanced at them, her red eyes heavy but determined. She nodded. "My son is in the Aviary, deep beneath it all. I will find him there. But…" Lex's eyes widened. "There are some, not many, but some, stuck in Aeterno Village. The woman…the one with the green aura. She's there."

"Lana?"

"Yes. She and others, they're at the hands of the brown and gray and black auras…and yellow." Lex's face paled. "There's yellow."

Bria and Brent exchanged a knowing glance.

My friends will never leave. Brent's Diabolo cackled. As of late, Frankie had been quiet.

Yeah, well, maybe you should tell them to have fun elsewhere.

Can't. You won't let me talk to them.

Brent sighed.

But Bria had already calculated her next move. "I'll go to Aeterno then. Take care of the Pool in the process…"

"You can't do it alone," Brent retorted.

"No. I can. I have to." She turned back to Brent and took his hands. "Ab Aeterno will be the most heavily guarded tower. Besides, you need to be with the others when you head to the Aviary so you can maintain the story."

"Right…the story…" Brent squinted around the tower. His head continued to hurt from the constant tale. In the back of his mind, the story operated like the constant nagging of anxiety. He didn't need to focus to keep it going, the natural tale of the tower almost begging to be heard. What would happen once they exited, though? He had already discussed the tale with everyone marching to the Aviary, but the worry of letting the story get out of hand remained.

What if a whale intervened in his story?

Or ostriches?

Or worse…a talking pineapple?

Brent kept to the back of the crowd with Lex and Micca as the doors to the tower opened. Bria stood at the front, the story of a confident captain laced over her body.

An actual guard greeted them upon the door's opening. Brent didn't hear what Bria said, but she kept her head high. A few of the disguised vagrants beside her assisted in the lingo and discussions, but otherwise, she handled the conversation with ease.

"You ready?" Micca asked Brent.

He nodded. Since they couldn't disguise Lex with magic, he and Micca took up a different charade: she was a prisoner they found running through the Necrowood. Disheveled, exhausted, it was easy to pretend she'd been on the run for days. Still, while it was all an act, Brent took Lex's arm with care, hoisting her along as the line moved.

His stomach churned, keeping his gaze straight and firm. The stories pounded around him, and every few steps, the mist caught a ridiculous tale of two mice racing through the tower or guards betting on a game of cards. With each new tale, Brent bit his tongue, recalling the basic story of the guard.

March. Defend. Order.

Persevere.

The late spring air hung with humidity as Brent exited the tower. Bria waited outside, watching each person leave, a captain at her post. When he exited, they couldn't touch, but they exchanged a knowing nod. It said everything, but most importantly, *I'll see you soon.*

They held each other gaze for a few moments longer, then Bria disappeared into the shadows of the trees. The story fell from her skin as she headed towards Ab Aeterno in the distance. *Good luck, Bria. Stay strong.*

Micca tugged at his sleeve. "Stay focused, mate. We got a job to do. You can give her googly eyes later, a'ight?"

"Yeah, okay." Brent adjusted his grip around Lex's arm. She didn't say a word, her own attention locked on the Aviary gazing over the yard. The Aviary was almost as tall as Ab Aeterno but without the glamor and pride. With no windows, it stood as one stone block. Waiting. Watching.

Harboring stories of death.

Brent felt the tug on him as he marched with the other false guards towards the Aviary. They moved in small groups, using the night and the stories as shields. He had to ignore the tugging, his own fear mounting in his chest as he walked. How long could he keep this cloak over the others? He was disguising at least twenty other people. There was no way it would last.

Not when the external stories bore death.

Each step pulled him further into the stories. His hands grew clammy, and his mouth grew numb. *Focus. You are a guard. We are all guards. Focus.*

He embraced the story on his skin as he walked. Now, he imagined himself as Cadet Chet Lawry, marching with his chest puffed out, his hands clenched around a prisoner's arm. In control. In command.

Leading.

Marching.

I am Chet Lawry, Senior Cadet of the—

Stop. No. Not that story.

He hadn't delved that deep into the Diabolo in months. The terrible stories remained in the creases of his mind. He couldn't escape, no matter how hard he tried.

You will always belong to me.

"Fuck…" Brent grunted. When Micca glanced at him, he merely shook his head. The stories grew stronger as they strode forward, the Aviary mere minutes away. They blended together, just like the stories of the children at the circus and like the stories of the prisoners beneath the Library. The worst scenarios always left the deepest scars, and those stories stayed for centuries.

Why couldn't the tales of kindness and bliss stay strong? Why did harm have to stay with humanity?

The closer they got to the Aviary, the more their group fanned out along different paths. The stories flickered more, but everyone knew the plan: enter the tower and free the prisoners. Brent and Micca continued straight for the entrance, keeping a grip on Lex. Her skin grew clammy as they walked, her body shook, and her veins bulged. Fragility became her new being; she might have been a piece of paper.

"Oi! Whatcha got there, mates?" The guard at the entrance of the tower barked.

Micca responded, leaving Brent to maintain their story-filled disguise. "Found this fucker running about here. Thought we'd bring her back."

The real guard glared at Lex. "Very good then, cadets. Ya can go hand her to me and get back to your posts."

"Nah, mate. This one is our delivery," Micca growled. "We want credit for finding her. Our captain said we could have it. Found her fucking in the forest."

"The Aviary is under lockdown. We don't want none of you cadets in there. Lieutenants only, ya hear?"

"Nah, I don't hear. In fact—" Micca removed one of his small windup toys from his pocket. "My little buddy ain't gonna like that."

"Wha—"

Micca tossed his windup toy on the ground. It moved its arms up and down as it approached the guards.

Then exploded.

Smoke rose around them, and Micca dragged Brent and Lex through the cloud and straight into the tower. The stories slipped from their skin, and by the time they passed through the doors, they stood again as Brent, Micca, and Lex.

As soon as Brent saw them disappear, he found another story. He pulled back on the tales of the guard, disguising him and Micca in different uniforms. With it, stories of knights riding ostriches, jugglers performing feats with fruit, and a gaggle of geese waddling along the path joined. He didn't bother shaking them, keeping his focus on the uniforms as more of their comrades slipped into the tower.

"Spread out," someone shouted. "Quick!"

Brent glanced next to him as they hurried. Lex walked along with her eyes wide. She held her hand out, and auras flickered before her: blacks, greens, whites, and reds. Every color imaginable flooded their vision. She sang, "Follow the colors of the rainbow. Black, gray, brown...that is all bad. Follow the rainbow. It is the true Effluvium." She blinked once. "They keep the children below."

"We'll help you find them," Brent replied.

"No. I must find Garrett all by myself. It is my destiny; I must go."

"Lex—"

Bwaaamp. Bwaaamp. Bwaaamp.

The alarm blared. Brent stumbled back, holding his hands over his ears, trying his best to maintain the story. It flickered in and out, clinging to more confusing stories dancing across the tower. None of it made sense anymore, but that didn't matter. It was enough to confuse the Guard.

Bwaaamp. Bwaaamp. Bwaaamp.

Another round of alarms exploded. On the last shriek of the alarm, an explosion followed. Smoke coated the room with black.

Hold the stories. Hold them, dammit!

Brent coughed out and waved his hands in front of his face. Gunshots rang. Shouts echoed. Cries shook.

When it cleared, the stories remained bantering in the tower. Warriors from ages old and new fought along the tower with the Guards and the vagrants. Ostriches, donkeys, and other animals screeched. Stories of prisoners, and perhaps real ones, dealt hands of magic.

Chaos assumed its permanent place in the tower.

It was all Brent knew.

All he understood.

No coherency.

Nothing.

He started laughing at it. The noise slipped out of him like a pathetic elephant. Brent pressed his hand to his lips to hide it, but he couldn't stop.

"Oi!" Micca tugged his arm.

"I…can't…" He guffawed, holding his stomach as the laughter continued.

"Brent! Mate!"

"I'm trying—"

"No—"

"Give me a—"

"Lex is missing!"

That stopped Brent's laughing.

As Micca said, Lex had vanished into the smoke and stories.

CHAPTER SIXTY-TWO

STRONGHOLD

Bria moved like a shadow in the trees, glancing back a few more times towards the Tower and Brent before they disappeared from her view. The story dripped from her skin as she hurried along, and by the time she reached the river, she once again stood only as Bria Smidt.

Or perhaps she was Rhodana.

She stared at the murky water before her. Streaks of silver pooled from the forest. The pool really had become the lifeblood of the Necrowood and Knoll…and soon, it might take over the entire world.

Had it always been like this? Or did recent events exasperate it?

She didn't have time to destroy it. That wasn't the target right now.

No, she focused only on Ab Aeterno as it gazed into eternity with arms spread out over Effluvium.

Or did the Effluvium control the tower?

Did the Order control the Council, or did the Council control the Order?

Were they one and the same?

Bria shook her head and climbed into a nearby tree, using the branches to cross over the river and land on the other side of the bank. Ab Aeterno continued to watch her, glistening with its Year Glasses. Unlike the other group, who could walk straight into the Aviary, she relied on stealth.

I am Rhodana the Forest Queen. I will keep my promise.

Reverie or not.

She used the trees to circle the tower, hiding in the branches and minimal leaves. Even in the late spring, the trees did not bloom. Everything, like the Necrowood, remained dead. It demanded life from her, but she didn't have the energy to spare. The phantom echoes from the tower sank into her stomach; she still recalled how the stones groaned, how the electricity sang, and how the pipes creaked. It pulled towards her in more ways than one, and if she had a chance to breathe, she might have explored the extent of her abilities.

For now, she stayed with the trees, using her little branch to stabilize each position. Higher and higher, she climbed until she reached the dead pine trees bordering Ab Aeterno.

Still too far to jump. She glared at the gap between the last pine tree and the tower. Each stone moved a different way, but none of them would be of help. She hadn't the skill to grow stone.

But she could give life to the dead vines knitting their way across the tower.

Bria summoned vigor back into them with a mere movement of her hand. Green blossomed along their narrow bodies. Once rejuvenated, Bria ordered them to carry her across the threshold and onto the uneven stones of the tower.

The vines hugged her to the wall for support while her little branch dug in between the stones. *Focus.* Bria squeezed the rocks. Did she have enough innate talent to manipulate these stones now? She had to get to the roof of the tower. But the stones didn't have the grips she needed to climb.

But I can make grips. She reached for the stones. At her touch, she ordered it to move. While it didn't move with the ease of the plants, the stones moved out enough to create a small ledge. She gripped each one and ascended the tower.

Bwaaamp. Bwaaamp.

Bria froze in her ascent. The siren blared in the distance from the Aviary. *They've been discovered.* She clung to a stone. If she went back now, she'd be able to help them.

But she might be too late.

No. She had to keep going. That much was certain.

Bria continued her climb. Fatigue clawed at her body, already worn from sending magic through the tower earlier.

Her back muscles roared as she reached the top. She clamored over onto the roof and collapsed, inhaling sharply. As much as she wanted to lie there for ages, she knew she didn't have that option. Instead, she rolled over and hurried along, in stealth, along the crystalized atrium. In the center, peering down at Knoll, stood the silver-bleeding Year Glass. She hid from its view between the pillars. *This is how they're communicating.*

Bria stepped towards the Year Glass, keeping to the shadows to prevent anyone from seeing her. It extended out the top of the atrium, serving more as a lookout than an object marking time. Beyond the silver liquid dripping down the sides, shadows moved inside the Year Glass.

She tore her attention away, focusing instead on the task at hand. Her heart thudded, reaching for the Pool. It would be so easy to end this all now.

Bria ducked down beneath the watch of the Year Glass and crawled along the rooftop, keeping out of view. Her goal initially was to find an entrance into the tower, but now—

I have to do this.

She placed her hand on the base of the Year Glass.

At her touch, the liquid changed.

"Ah, Briannabella."

Her stomach dropped.

In the reflection of the Year Glass, she saw none other than the Head of the Council himself, Ningursu.

"How did you know I was here?" Bria asked.

"I always know."

"That's a lie. If you knew, you would have found us by now."

"I have eyes and ears everywhere."

Another lie.

"I think it is time you and Brenton return to the Library, don't you think? We can end this." Ningursu said.

"You're the one who started it," Bria snapped. "And you're the one continuing it."

"You destroyed my Library."

"Only after you took control of my magic. For someone who hates magic, you seem to enjoy using it."

"It is not magic I hate, Briannabella. It is that which is unnatural. Kek disrupted the balance with immortality;

Brenton has disrupted the order of the world with his poor decisions; you…well, you are destroying everything we have spent millennia building. I want to keep the balance. You are a rational young woman. You must understand." Ningursu's shadow flickered in the Year Glass. "Come back to the Library."

Bria laughed to herself, running her finger over the glass. Ningursu's powers clawed at her skin. He still had a hold on her, a remnant from when they held her prisoner in the Library. She would never let him control her again.

"Come back." Ningursu pried again.

Bria raised her head and smiled. "No."

Ningursu's white eye flared. "No?"

"No!" Bria threw her hand against the wall of the Year Glass. The peony heart buzzed beneath her fingers and tugged at her heart. The moment she touched the wall, the flowers bloomed, taking away the protective coat of silver and pushing against the glass.

Ningursu's screams pounded in her ears. She half expected to see yellow trickle through the sky and take Knoll by storm. But this time, no Diabolo emerged.

But it didn't stop the storm from coming.

Bwaaamp. Bwaaamp. Bwaamp.

Bria froze. In the distance, a siren blared.

And right before her, as the final peony bloomed, the Year Glass shattered, leaving the atrium open and fully exposed to the shadows within the glass.

Yet these shadows did not belong to the Council. Beyond the broken Year Glass, a room waited. In the center of the room, around a table, stood none other than Senator Cordova and the Mist Keeper, the known architect, Alojzy. Senator Cordova gawked with wide blue eyes, his silver hair like the last remaining glimmer of the Pool. Beside him, Alojzy wore a vermillion robe, the symbol of the Order closest to his chest identifying himself as an Elder.

His dark eyes widened, and with a mere glance, Bria's entire world twisted.

Twists and turns, right and left, up and down, all became one. A maze.

Commotion tore.

The trees bent in weird shapes, the sky spun, and the ground tilted back and forth.

Below, screams bellowed from the pews. Commotion reigned.

They didn't need a Diabolo to enter Hell.

I had to do this. This is what I was working towards, and I couldn't keep procrastinating any longer.

Yet terror marked her return.

Was it worth it?

She took a step back, away from Senator Cordova and Alojzy. If they spoke to her, she didn't hear over her pounding heart and twisting head. *I have two options: jump or surrender.* Bria flexed her little branch, watching the way its fingers moved. On her good hand, her flower brand continued to bloom. As far as she could tell, Brent was okay.

Or keep fighting.

Bria outstretched her branched hand. The vines laced their way into the stones, and as she touched them, she felt the way each metal and element interacted. Over time, nature always took back the world; why not accelerate it?

If this was the true Tower of Ab Aeterno, she might have hesitated. But the elements told a different story; this tower was young, not much older than her. Whatever it once stood for fell the moment it traveled to Knoll. She was sure Brent could interpret the actual tale, but for now, she had the age in her pocket. This was no relic, no sacred object.

History might not repeat her tale the same way.

In fact, letting this tower fall might just secure the label.

She was Queen Rhodana of the Forest, destined to take back the world.

But I don't want to be known for destruction. She flexed her hands, letting the magic slow. Vines twisted around her, but the world continued to spin. The tower swayed as she took a single step back towards the edge.

"I don't want to hurt anyone." Her voice sounded distant as she spoke. "Call off the alarms, tell the Guard to retreat, and leave Knoll…and your tower will stand."

Senator Cordova chuckled. "You expect me to turn Knoll, the stronghold of Rosada, over to a crazed Magii?"

"It's already with a crazed senator." Bria blinked a few times. Alojzy's distortion mist continued wrapping around her. She couldn't even see the Mist Keeper standing by the table anymore.

"I don't have time for this. Captain Carver!" Senator Cordova called.

Bria's stomach dropped as the captain entered the room, his eyes flaring, lips curled in a smirk. He didn't bother to hand out any pleasantries. Instead, he raised his pistol in the air.

Bria held up her good hand. "If you shoot me, the tower falls! I'm keeping it together."

"She's lying." The captain snarled.

Alojzy spoke at last, his voice slithering through the conversation. "No. She isn't."

"Elder An Drew is right, Captain. Lower the pistol," the senator ordered. "I think we can negotiate with this girl. She's a rational one."

Bria clenched her teeth, another bout of nausea rocking her with vertigo. She kept herself grounded, focusing on her senses: the way the stone sighed under magic, the way the smoke stifled her nose, the way Senator Cordova's face scrunched in frustration, the way the sirens blared from the Aviary, and the way her mouth tasted of sweat. Each scent told her of the present. She wouldn't slip.

She couldn't.

But before anyone said another word, a gunshot ripped through the commotion from the pews beneath her.

Below them stood a cadet holding a pistol aimed directly at Bria. Smoke blew from the barrel, covering his face.

Then came the pain slicing through Bria's body.

She looked down at her stomach. Blood gathered.

Her senses wavered.

And with the tower, she collapsed.

CHAPTER SIXTY-THREE

MONOCHROME

tories surrounded Lex. That was the only way to describe what she saw. As the commotion grew, tales of warriors riding ostriches, whales floating in the air, and other such anomalies filled her vision. She used the chaos to slip away from Micca and Brent and follow the trickling auras towards the stairwell.

She moved like a ghost through the ground floor towards the narrow stairwells hidden against the wall. If anyone noticed her, they did not act, letting her follow her intuition down into the belly of the beast.

"Lex! Wait!" Brent called out.

Lex turned as she reached the stairwell.

Brent and Micca rushed over to her. "We're coming with you."

"I thought you would tell me to wait…" Lex said.

"Girl, this is your mission and your son. We ain't gonna stop you. Just let us help." Micca grinned.

Lex bowed her head, then turned to the stairwell and began her descent into the story-filled prison beneath them. Behind her, Brent fidgeted, his own attention wavering with each passing story. Lex never understood his magic, but as the notorious Story Collector, she knew this was his doing.

She didn't marvel at the stories. Her own body pounded with pain as they dove deeper and deeper into the Aviary. The auras flickered. Every step weighed heavier, and she gasped for air after every few seconds. In her chest, her heart thudded in uneven palpitations.

She refused to falter until she found Garrett.

The voyage down into the crypts carried on for ages. Each step, with Micca and Brent by her side, took forever. As they grew closer, new auras mingled with Garrett's gold one. It caused her head to spin, and she felt weak with each stride forward. Was this her phantom rot, eating away at her insides, telling her magic was too much?

Now, surrounded by untamed magic, her body screamed in sorrow and hate. She wanted nothing more than to curl up on the stone ground and let sleep wash over her. It had gotten worse with the passing days. But she would keep fighting.

She had to get to Garrett, no matter what.

Lex clung to the handrail, taking each step with a disheartened breath. When she finally reached the bottom of the basement, her breaths rallied in her throat in utter dismay. Brent used his stories to distract the guard waiting at the bottom, forming a story of a miniature dragon. When the dragon opened its jaw to eat the guards, they sank back in fear, and the group passed without circumstance. With the guards out of the picture, Lex's knees finally buckled. She coughed up phlegm and blood as the room spun. The lights blended. Colors turned gray.

I have to find them.

Brent helped her sit up, and after a few deep breaths, Lex found the colors and her footing, then continued along the hallway. The basement was dark, like a crypt almost, and it wreaked of putrid-smelling gas. Pipes and wires, like the ones in the Buzzing room, lined the hall, sparking with hints of electricity and locking doors shut.

Lex peered into the first room. Twelve children lay on cots no older than ten years of age. Her heart ached at the sight.

"We can't leave them here." She glanced at Micca and Brent.

Brent moved his fingers through the mist again. This time, a guard appeared, with a mist-like exterior. The fake guard approached the door and unlocked it, then disappeared into nothing.

"C'mon, kids. Get a move on and get outta here. People are upstairs willing to help," Micca called.

Lex didn't have time to watch every child. She waddled along to the next cell, a prayer on her lips, begging every god, goddess, and deity that her sons were okay.

Each cell had more children. How many had the Order taken from across the province already? How many were still coming? Who were these children? Not all of them carried an aura of magic. But what they did all have was a hurt spirit. Their auras no longer glowed, their faces no longer bright. No child deserved to go through such a fate.

Ever.

Did Todd know this was happening? Certainly not. Lex refused to believe that her husband of ten years would know about children being kept prisoner.

Surely, he would have freed Garrett if he did!

Lex peered into another room. This one was less secure, with only a small lock on the door. Small cots lined the room, with toddlers and babes sleeping peacefully. Pressing her face into the glass, Lex scanned the room. The mere sight caught her in another round of nausea.

These poor children appeared fragile and broken, like a collection of glass dolls.

"Garrett…are you in there, baby? Mommy's here—I'm coming!" She scanned the beds, banging her fist against the window as tears rolled down her cheeks. A few of the toddlers awoke, but they did not cry, instead staring at the door in shock and horror. They might have been skeletons, completely unaffected by the noise or the commotion.

Completely and utterly transformed into empty souls.

Their auras did not prosper. In fact, they all but sat still and vacant.

Nothing.

Even once Brent came over with a story to unlock the door with mist, the children still did not flinch.

Lex pushed past Brent and into the room, tracing the area with her eyes, searching for an aura that she didn't know. How could she pick out Garrett's aura from the lot? She hadn't seen it before when she dreamt of the towers. Would it be like Todd's, too weak to fight? Or like hers?

She didn't even know the color of her own aura.

She glanced at her fingertips. But trying to push her boundaries and see her own colors sent a headache pouring over her. She stumbled slightly. Why did she feel so ill? Why did all the colors wrap around her and send her spiraling?

As she wandered among the rows of emancipated children, blood gathered in her mouth. The magic here was so strong.

It suffocated her.

And it was threatening to send her falling against the floor.

But she kept walking. An aura caught her eye in the corner, glowing silver and red. Despite everything else, this one had more strength, reaching out for her like a lost child. She followed the colors until they led her to the back corner.

"Garrett!" she gasped.

Her son, her sweet little boy, lay in a cot, his face gaunt and filled with terror. The joy that once thrived in his red eyes seemed empty as if severed from his body. Now, he was nothing more than a mere ghost.

No.

He was a ghost.

"Preston?" She neared the boy.

A whimper caught in his throat.

"Preston…it's me. It's Mommy."

The boy brought his hands to his ears, closing his eyes tight, his lips quivering. He wouldn't meet her gaze.

His aura is like burning smoke. She gathered him close in her arms. He squirmed, not daring to meet her gaze.

"It's Mommy. It's Mommy, Preston. It's okay. Mommy is here."

He didn't speak. Did he know how? He died before he could form full sentences. But he'd been Garrett's playmate since then.

But this was different. This was fear, trauma, and suffering filling his body like a plague. It suffocated him.

Lex clung tight to her son, rocking him back and forth. Brent and Micca neared her.

"Lex, there ain't nobody here," Micca whispered.

Brent eyed Preston. "Yes, there is someone. You just can't see him…"

"Preston is here," Lex whispered into her son's hair.

"Y'know, I ain't even gonna try to understand this magic shite," Micca said.

Lex ignored the two men bantering. "We're going to get safe and sound, okey-dokey? You're with Mommy now."

"Garr…" Preston moaned.

"We'll find him."

"No…no…no!" the toddler protested.

She continued hugging him, but he didn't embrace her back. Preston writhed and cried, trying to escape her arms. He wouldn't acknowledge her. He wouldn't even look in her eyes.

Beside her, Brent half chuckled as stories of dancing aardvarks filled the room. It didn't get a reaction from Preston. The boy was a ghost in both self and body.

"You best get outta here. Both of you," Micca said. "You're losing it, Brent. I'll get the rest of kids outta here, a'ight? Take Lex up."

Brent nodded with another guffaw. His eyes flickered between different colors.

Lex ignored him. Instead, with Preston squirming in her arms, she hurried back to the stairwell. As she arrived at the top of the stairwell, the tower shook. Lex used one hand to steady herself against the wall as the lights flickered. The entire building seemed to shift as if twisting in and out of reality.

The colors twisted.

Her head roared.

Her heart galloped.

With every step, her body grew numb. She tried shifting Preston in her arms as she exited the Aviary, but her feet only wanted to rock to one side.

She couldn't differentiate purple from yellow, red from blue, or green from pink. Everything had turned monochrome. Why? What was happening?

"We're almost there, Preston..." Lex's words came out jumbled and distorted.

Each step moved slower. She lost sight of Brent in the commotion, completely enamored again by the colors, the mist, and the stories. She stumbled and coughed. Blood pooled on her lips.

"I got you," a husky voice said.

She didn't reject the arm that guided her. Through her own pain and headache, she couldn't see until the late spring air ambushed her, attacking her cheeks like daggers, shoving her to the side. Every single step hurt more. Every single movement caused her body to quiver. When would she be able to rest?

Outside, it was war, but she only saw blurs. Colors washed over her. Knives cut into her head. Why? Why was everything so bright? Why couldn't she just see again?

"I got you," the voice said again.

She turned towards the voice. "Toddle?"

He stared at her, his eyes tired, his uniform stained with sweat. His usual short stubble had formed a beard, and his face wore a burden of little smiling. But for the first time since she'd received her magic, his aura shone gold.

"I'm here. You're okay."

"Toddle...we need to find Garrett." Lex held Preston tighter. "I know you can't see him...I know you don't believe in this…but I have Preston. But Garrett is missing, and we have to find him. Please…”

“First, we need to get you to safety. I’m not leaving you again, a’ight?”

“Garrett is our priority.” Lex sobbed, another wave of sickness clinging to her throat. “Please. You need to find him.”

“We will.”

“No. You will.” Lex gazed up at Todd, hoping he might understand. “And when you do, you will reconnect him with Preston.”

“And where will Preston be?”

“With friends,” Lex sobbed out. “Brent, Bria, and the lot…he’ll be with them. We can trust them.”

“And you?”

“You already know.”

Todd cursed under his breath but didn’t argue. That time had passed. Instead, he embraced her tight. Lex leaned him to him, thankful that for one last time, she was with her husband. It didn’t matter how gunpowder and mist roared across the landscape. They’d found each other again.

Tears filled her eyes as she turned her attention to the stars. Lex swore she saw the shadow of a dragon moving in and out of the clouds.

With her last bit of energy, she held out her hand, casting a white aura in the beast's direction. Its shape swooped through the sky, circling the towers once, before hitting the ground just a few paces away. Lex stared on, unable to move.

No color remained.

All black and white.

"Holy shite!" Todd cursed. "What the—it's a dragon?"

"Toddle…you need to go find Garrett. Before it's too late."

"I'm staying with you."

"Toddle! Go!" Lex shoved his arm off her and stepped towards the dragon.

A man with a curly mustache jumped off the back of the beast. She recognized him from the Pit but didn't remember his name.

He approached Lex, glancing between her, Todd, and Preston. "You a'ight there, Lex?"

"My son…he needs…please take my son…" Lex gasped. Her throat continued tightening. She couldn't breathe. "My son…"

The man gathered the child in his arms and stared down at her. Preston still did not react, eyes fixated straight ahead at the tower.

"Save him…" Lex begged again, then squeezed Preston's little hand. "We'll find Garrett. Mommy loves you."

"We ain't leaving ya," the man said. "C'mon. Ya can make it to Zephyr, can't ya?"

Lex shook her head.

"Timothée! Lex!"

Micca joined her side, an entourage of children behind him and sweat matting his head.

Lex couldn't bear to look at him, instead turning back one last time to face Toddle.

"Find our son."

"Lex—"

"Nothing matters unless you find him."

"Elexis!"

"Find him…please…" Lex pressed her head to the dirt. She couldn't see anymore. She couldn't do anything.

Her eyelids drooped.

Was someone saying her name?

Was she floating?

It didn't matter.

Her last breath came but never finished.

CHAPTER SIXTY-FOUR

KNOLL'S FALL

Jemma pulled herself from the rubble, her entire body aching as she scanned her surroundings. Everything had happened so fast. First, the sirens bellowing in the distance woke her and Christof. He left her, racing from the cloister up to the Tower of Ab Aeterno, while she dressed. She had to shake off the Effluvium as it oscillated in her vision, but once she arrived in the pews, the Effluvium would not rest. Instead, commotion reigned.

The Year Glass shattered just as she entered.

And hundreds of red petals fell to the floor.

Jemma couldn't quite focus on the whole situation, her heart breaking with the holiest of the Year Glasses.

But she knew what she saw next.

Bria stood in the atrium above with Senator Cordova, Elder An Drew, and Captain Carver. With every statement, every movement, the walls of Ab Aeterno creaked.

Then, she caught a glimpse of Christof in the center of the pews. He raised his pistol, eyes focused, lips curved in a frown.

Jemma screamed for him to stop.

But he didn't listen.

He shot his pistol thrice.

Silence followed.

Bria stumbled.

Then the tower crumbled.

Now, hoisting herself out of the rubble, Jemma thanked the Effluvium for safety. She ached, but overall, she was okay.

Christof had already climbed from the debris, stomping along through the benches and pillars, his face as red as a tomato.

Jemma raced to his side. "Christof!"

"Get outta here, Jem."

"Christof—"

"I said get out before that bitch goes ma—Dad?" He stopped a few paces ahead of her. "Dad?!"

Jemma joined his side.

Captain Carver lay before them, his body twisted and mangled, blood staining his uniform.

He didn't breathe.

"DAD!" Christof shook his father's body. Nothing happened.

"Christof…I'm so sorry." Jemma touched his arm.

He clenched his fists. It almost looked like he might cry.

Then he stopped, gulped, and stood.

Jemma reached for him. "Christof—wait, what're you doing!?"

He raced off into the pews, swearing. Jemma chased after him, jumping over the rubble and wrapping around the benches. It wasn't hard to lose track of the cadet as he led her to where vines and petals gathered like a garden in the rubble.

Bria lay amidst them, gripping the floor, her body shaking. Blood dribbled from her lips, nose, and stomach.

"You!" Christof shouted and pulled Bria from the ground. He held her up by the collar of her shirt as he spat into her face. "You fucking broad! I should've killed you and your fucking bastard Harley all those months ago. You fucker—"

Jemma had never seen Christof snap. While his rage left gossip in Newbird's Arm, he always carried himself in a certain light that made her think it was all hearsay. Now, he bore hatred, betrayal, and distaste all in one look. She understood; Christof had expressed his utter dismay over the failed betrothal, over Bria's demonic nature, and over the life he once dreamt of having.

And, even as Christof raised his hand to hit Bria, Jemma had no desire to stop him.

This was the girl that caused the world to spin on its head. If she hadn't torn down the Pit, if she hadn't attracted yellow-stained monsters, Jemma would still be home. Brother Roy Al would still be alive. Peace would still have its arms wrapped around the province.

So Jemma stood there, unaffected as Christof beat Bria. He used his fists as weapons, slamming each punch harder and harder into Bria's small body. She tried to fight, sending branches and flowers at Christof, but her fall from the Year Glass left her weak. Each branch flew past with no true goal. Christof caught them with ease, snapping them, before returning to his beating.

Jemma could not look away.

Will death cure her magic? Or will it just go to the next person? Jemma had never considered this. But why not just destroy all the Magii? Wouldn't that be better?

But then again, their magic brought light to the cities. It supplied more power than she ever imagined.

If only they could harness it to bring excellence to the world.

The barrel of a gun on her neck pulled Jemma from the scene. She glanced over her shoulder at a woman with a black stamp on her cheek.

The same woman she'd seen in the Cleansing Room in the Aviary.

"Christof," Jemma squeaked.

He glanced over at her.

The woman spoke from behind Jemma. "Drop the girl, and the Sister won't get hurt."

"Who are you?" Christof asked.

"Does it matter? I have a gun. One bullet is all it takes."

The pistol clicked behind her. Jemma's whole body stiffened.

"Christof, please," Jemma sobbed.

Christof eyed Jemma, then dropped Bria's broken body to the floor like a rag doll.

The woman released Jemma and approached Bria, leaving Jemma to race over to Christof. He embraced her.

The woman lifted Bria off the ground and walked away from them towards the shattered entranceway. She kept her eyes on them, ready to pounce if anyone dared ask. Vines gathered at her feet, and the wind blew. As the woman reached the doorway, the darkness engulfed her, and she and Bria vanished.

"Thank you for choosing me," Jemma whispered.

"Yeah...woulda been dumb not to. Got my point across anyhow." Christof kept his arm around her. His face told a different story. Bright pink with narrow eyes, his bloodlust had only begun.

"We should find Senator Cordova," Jemma whispered.

"He's probably dead. Just like my father..." Christof's entire body shook with anger. "She killed him."

"And you killed her."

"We don't know that," Christof snarled. "She and that fucking...Harley...they have this fucking way of beating death."

"I like to think the Effluvium will do the right thing."

"And it shall," a voice said from behind them.

Jemma turned. Senator Cordova approached them, covered in soot and bruises but walking with the same determination as ever. Jemma almost fell to her knees. *He survived!*

She released Christof's arm and bowed her head. "Senator, I am relieved to see you are okay."

"Yes, Elder An Drew and I survived. But we must get to safety before these vagrants take control of the city," the senator said.

"You can't seriously be thinking of abandoning Knoll?" Christof snapped.

"We knew this was a possibility. If the vagrants started an uprising, we did not have the resources to defend against them here…especially if it comes to Magii. We must reconvene and plan accordingly, secure Rosada before it is too late."

"Senator—"

"I have already sent my best captains to secure other cities before the uprising spreads. We shall prevail. This is merely a…hiccough, if you will."

"But Senator!" Christof objected.

"Cadet Carver, you are not in a place to argue with me. Now, go sound the alarm. It is best we leave Knoll as soon as possible." Senator Cordova turned to Jemma. "Sister…you're with me."

Jemma followed Senator Cordova through a narrow network of tunnels beneath the Tower of Ab Aeterno. They left behind the dead and the living, venturing away from the commotion to where safety would reign. Jemma balanced on a beam of conflict. On one hand, she knew Knoll held no future for her; on the other, she wanted to help search for survivors and bless those who had long passed. Saying no to Senator Cordova wasn't an option, so she followed him deep beneath the tower in silence.

"Elder An Drew will join us shortly. Dr. Gratz should be waiting for us, though," Senator Cordova said as they neared the end of the tunnel.

"And Christof? What about him?"

"He'll join one of the towers heading north. You will see your beau soon enough, Jemma. But I want you safe. It is paramount now that you are our vessel."

Jemma had almost forgotten. It felt like a lifetime ago when she'd seen the child trying to "eat" magic. While they had offered nothing else to her yet, Jemma had held onto hope that she could save that child.

Senator Cordova continued, "Once we find safety, we will work on that. Now you see, yes? You understand the detriment of magic."

"Yes."

"Very good. Very good indeed." Senator Cordova nodded to himself as they ascended the stairwell.

At the top of the stairs, the night sky greeted them. The dead trees of the Necrowood waited, with a silver river lacing its way through the forest. Waiting on the riverbank stood a misshapen tower composed of different structures and vehicles. A woman stood on the platform, and upon seeing Senator Cordova and Jemma, she waved her arms in their direction.

The woman greeted them at the edge of the platform. Her voice sounded like honey as she spoke, her dual-toned eyes darting between the two of them. "Ah, Donovan. I apologize about what ensued. We thought they were only heading to the Aviary. Yeshua failed to predict such horrors."

"I do not blame you, Gisela. Thank you." Senator Cordova took the woman's hands and kissed them. "Sister, this is Gisela Kai. She and her husband, Yeshua Nasr, have traveled far and wide for many years. We hired them to help protect us from the oncoming magic."

"We have seen the potential futures…and it is for the best."

Gisela led them into the tower. A small shop, filled with odd artifacts and items, occupied the bottom floor. A stout man with red eyes and a balding head sat behind the counter, fixated on a basin of silver. Beside him, Professor Etta Gratz stood, holding a small child with equally red eyes on her hip. The child squirmed, face gaunt and emotionless.

"Ah, Etta! Good. You brought the child."

"Ay, yes, I did." Professor Gratz said. "Why did you ask for him, though?"

"All in due time. Once Elder An Drew joins us, I'll be able to explain everything."

"And where is the Elder?"

"He is finalizing a few things. I trust his expertise. He will be by our side soon."

Jemma eyed her new companions. Exhaustion seeped into her body, but she didn't wish to sleep. The Effluvium needed protecting. Around her, it no longer bore the simple soft glow, but it glowed with discontent. Dust-ridden and marred by smoke, the Effluvium needed help. Magic had tainted it.

"I shall go start the tower then," the man, Yeshua, said, then ventured upstairs.

Jemma took a seat on a stool by the counter. Senator Cordova sat beside her, an uncomfortable smile lurching across his mouth.

"Why are you smiling, Senator?" Jemma asked. "We have experienced great tragedy."

"Out of tragedy comes change," the senator said. "Today is the beginning of change, Sister Jey Ma."

"We have lost Captain Carver…Knoll has fallen…what can we do now?"

"Oh, Sister Jey Ma," Senator Cordova turned her towards the window. In the distance, the smoking remains of the towers of Knoll stood. "Now, we have reason. We can show those Senators in the Capitol the pure destruction of magic, of stories, and of vagrancy. Alas, Knoll will no longer be the 'evil child' of Rosada. Now, they shall see why we must act. We shall be in control."

"I'm sorry, sir…we?"

"As our new weapon and vessel, you will be the one to lead this charge." Senator Cordova took her hands. "You will abolish all magic."

Jemma sucked on her lips. She'd already seen the Effluvium. Now she would be more. She always wanted more.

This was it.

The chance to rid the world of demons.

The chance to bring peace to all.

She had to let go of everything holding her back from success. No more hesitations. No more mercy.

She would be one with the Effluvium.

"What do I need to do?" Sister Jey Ma asked.

"For now, rest up. This will be a long, harrowing process. But you shall be fantastic, dear Sister. You are what the world needs."

Sister Jey Ma bowed her head. Excitement and fear swirled around her stomach.

"Now"—Senator Cordova walked back to his spot by the counter—"it is time to leave Knoll behind. We have much bigger places to go, much better places to dictate. Knoll, for all intents and purposes, has fallen. It is nothing more than ash and smoke."

The tower rumbled around them as Senator Cordova finished.

All the while, in the distance, a final siren blared.

Bwaaamp. Bwaaamp. Bwaaamp.

Yes, Knoll had fallen.

But it would maintain Order across Rosada.

For peace, prosperity, and the Effluvium.

Intertwined

Brent stumbled out of the Aviary, laughing to himself. The stories had twisted together, producing tales of guards, of flying pigs, and of heroic mushrooms. He lost sight of Lex in all of it as she wandered out into the commotion. At first, he followed the colors glowing from her skin, but even that became too much, and he slid against a wall and continued to guffaw.

I'm losing damn my mind. Brent hugged himself.

Always knew this would happen. Just a matter of time, the Diabolo hissed.

Go away. Brent inhaled and ran his fingers over the root-shape betrothal mark on his hand. *Focus. Stay grounded. Just focus.*

He breathed in and out a few more times, focusing his attention on a single story of a butterfly in the breeze. It flittered about before flying off into the distance. It was such a small story; usually, that would never catch his attention. With his powers overwhelming him, everything remained.

He had to cling to the present.

Brent turned his attention to Ab Aeterno. The tower swayed in the distance like a leaf in the breeze. For a moment, all was quiet. The world stood still.

Then, in a single heartbeat, dust and smoke engulfed the tower.

"BRIA!" All the stories slipped away from him, and Brent stood alone in the commotion beneath the Aviary. Everything stopped around him. Even the guards and vagrants stopped their fighting, standing in horror as the dust settled.

Brent took a step forward as the smoke cleared. Ab Aeterno still stood but as no more than a shell. Half the tower stood in shambles, while the other half wore a cape of smoke.

A beat passed.

Another.

Then the screams.

And the fighting around him resumed.

This time, he needed no story for the commotion to hide him. Vagrants, guards, and civilians lashed at each other's throats. In the sky, Zephyr lunged forward, making her descent with a puff of mist and a roar. Guards fled in fear while the Magii unfurled their power. Fire, water, earth, air; each element found its own way into the battle. Confusion reigned. Even some prisoners took up arms, while others vanished into the commotion with the children on their hips, too weary to fight and too weak to stand. Gunshots roared through not just the tower yard but out into the city.

Explosions echoed.

Smoke reigned.

Screams encompassed.

And death won.

Brent stepped forward as a new onslaught of stories followed. He could create more distractions and use his stories to fight, but he failed to summon his ability. The world was on fire. People were dying.

And I'm a Mist Keeper. I have a job to do.

He walked into the center of the yard, using a mist as a cloak to protect him from the commotion. Was this truly how the Mist Keepers hid? They redirected attention from them, using the Effluvium as their mask? It gave him a sense of duty, and with his arm outstretched, he reached for the stories of the dead.

The stories intertwined, all in one.

A single bullet to the head.
A dagger to throat
and the culprit met by flames.
The flames ate away,
Another dead.
An individual who murdered the helpless,
dead.
Each story came and danced with the other,
sending ripples through the city.
Dead.
Another.
Also dead.
A woman holding her babe tight,
Aura bright,
Her heart breaking,
Her skin rupturing,
A last breath taken in arms
Of love and hate.
Dead.
Gone.
But stories remain.

Brent traced each tale through the mist. Hundred of stories wrapped around him—not just of those dead in battle but of years of torture and neglect. How many people had died at the hands of the Order?

How many at the hands of the Council?

The stories enamored him. Brent sank into their embrace. Was he a mother rescuing her child? A guard sacrificing his life for duty and loyalty? A seer who saw too much? Or one that saw too little? A sister of the Order who wanted to save the world? Or a child who only wished to play?

Who was he?

Did he know?

My name is…

Give up.

My name is…

Give in.

My name is…

Come now, open up to me. It's fine.

Someone smacking him in the face brought Brent back.

He placed his hand on his cheek. "What the fuck!?!"

"Well, you were busy having a fit, so I thought I would help you out." His assailant replied.

Brent raised his head. Caroline stood over him, a smirk on her melting face. It had gotten worse since he last saw her. The skin dripped from her bones while dark circles formed pits around her blue eyes. Blotches covered her hands. Her hair, once a deep luscious black, now hung thin and gray. Despite it all, she still painted her lips red and held her head high.

"Caroline…what are you doing here?" Brent asked.

"Well, I came to do my job, but I see you have already taken care of it."

"So you're actually working for once?"

"I have been slacking…" Her smirk fell. "It is good to see you, Brent. I am glad you are successful in your endeavors."

"If you're so glad, then why did you take up a new apprentice?" Brent rubbed the back of his neck as he rose to his feet. The stories continued their distant thud, but he ignored them.

"How do you know about that?"

"A seer told me. So answer me!"

"We thought you were catatonic," Caroline stated.

"Catatonic?"

"You are seeing stories everywhere."

"I was fine when you last saw me!"

"It was not my choice. It was Ningursu's choice to choose a new apprentice."

"He chose a child!" Brent shouted.

"We do not have time, Brent. You must get out of here—"

"No! Don't hide this bullshite from me again! What's going on?"

Caroline shook her head. "It is long and complicated."

"Then you better make it short and simple. I'm not dealing with this fucking bullshite anymore. Why a child?" Brent let the mist wrap around his hands.

Caroline stepped back. "Brent—"

"Tell me. This has as much to do with me as it does to do with you."

She held her hands up. "I do not have all the information, but from what I gather, Ningursu believes a child would be the ideal weapon."

"What!?!"

"Ningursu is trying to turn her into a weapon. A vessel, if you will, so she could carry a Diabolo across the world without it wreaking havoc. She is not strong enough for it, though." Caroline trembled. "She's dying."

Brent gawked. Around him, the world shook. He gripped the strands of mist tighter. "Why?"

"Brent, do you really have time for—"

"WHY!?" The mist raced past him, knocking Caroline off her feet. She stumbled back.

Upon finding her footing, Caroline straightened her dress and stared in Brent's direction. "It has always been about control. Really…you should know this by now."

"Just answer the question!"

"Brent, you have seen Ningursu. He uses the Mist Keepers as his eyes. He claimed control of Kek's pool. It is why he can control me. And it is why he dares to dive into the minds of the influential religious order on the planet. Because then, if they fear him, if they obey him…then he will be in charge." Caroline did not miss a beat as she spoke.

"But that's not the role of Death. We're guides. We're…we're the ones guiding people out of Hell. We're…"

"The judge, the jury, and the warden," Caroline stated. "But Ningursu wants to be more. He sees it as his right after millennia. He has the power, he can see all, and he wants no one to stand in his way. Magic does that. Bria does that. *You* do that."

"So, he used a child as a weapon?"

"He has used many as weapons. I can feel him now, tearing into my skull. That is why I beg of you—" Caroline paused as an explosion went off in the distance. "No, I implore you. Find Bria and leave. Before he knows where you are. Before he comes for you. Please."

"And the child?"

"It is too late for her."

"It can't be too late for her!"

"It is. I have seen her collapsing. She is confused most of the time. I will try my best to save her, but please, go."

"But—"

"GO!" Caroline swung her arms out. The mist flew around her, and in an instant, she vanished.

"Shite!" Brent tried to chase after her. Even if he couldn't track Caroline, he knew one thing: he had to find Bria. His feet pounded against the pavement as he wove through the continuing fight, using the mist to dodge any potential weapons and shield himself from harm. He traced the surrounding for any story, or clue, to find Bria.

He slowed himself at the edge of Ab Aeterno and traced the area. The world around the tower twisted like a maze, mist trickling through the ruins. It reminded him of the Library, the way it would change shape and bend at the whims of Alojzy. Even the stories didn't stick, twisting with the mist. He caught a glimpse of Bria's story as she broke the Year Glass above and the way she fell as the tower crumbled. The stories of the Guard, the Brothers and Sisters, and the civilians fleeing marked the commotion. Death, to his surprise, did not taint the tales but for one terrible story of a man motivated by hate. He did not touch that tale; he would not give that man a chance at the afterlife.

"BRENT! Is that you?" a figure near the silver river called.

He squinted. "Lana?!"

Lana walked towards him along the edge of the silver river, carrying someone in her arms. She looked defeated, her black hair cropped short, her body bruised and exhausted.

Brent's stomach dropped.

In her arms, she held Bria's limp body. Blood stained Bria's clothes and skin, and her breaths caught the air in uneven gasps. As soon as Brent arrived, Lana placed Bria into his arms, then cupped her hands into the river.

"Hold her head up," Lana said as she brought the liquid to Bria's lips.

Brent obliged, biting back the tears. "What happened?"

"She destroyed the tower. I was in one of the cells when it collapsed and escaped. *Lucky me.* But she fell. Looks like someone shot her, but the wound isn't too deep. She took a beating from some butt-faced guard, though. If we get her to Dr. Hue in time, I think she'll make it." She wrung out her hands, then stood. "C'mon. No time to waste. Let's get into the Necrowood."

"Oh…okay."

Brent followed Lana into the Necrowood, beckoning the mist to cloak them as they left the terror of the tower yard. Gunshots still fired. Hearts still beat. He focused only on Bria as they walked, listening as she took each breath, holding her tight as she shuddered. They said little as they walked deeper into the forest. The wood twisted around them, but they pushed forward.

As the battle disappeared into the distance, silence became a newfound friend. The Necrowood spoke like death, without a single breath of wind or a chirp of the bird. Brent welcomed it, letting Bria's breaths be the melody.

And when she turned her head and mumbled, that was the song.

"Wait, Lana, she's stirring…" Brent placed Bria against a nearby tree. "Bri?"

Lana joined his side.

"Bri?" he tried again. "You a'ight? You there?"

"Brent…" she mumbled.

"I'm right here." He brushed her bangs out of her eyes. "A'ight? We're gonna get you fixed up."

"I didn't mean to…"

Lana spoke, "Wasn't your fault, girl. They caused it to happen."

"I was…I didn't mean to…" she repeated. "I…I didn't…I killed…but I didn't mean to."

Brent cupped her cheeks. "Look at me."

She shook her head.

"Look at me, please."

She opened her less bruised eye.

"You did amazing. None of this was your fault. I know it's not…I see your story." He brushed back her tears as he glanced around her. "I know you don't like that, but I do right now. You had no intentions of doing wrong. You were shot. That was why it fell. You did everything right."

Bria shook her head. "I'm…I don't…I want…."

"Shh. It's gonna be a'ight. Knoll has fallen. It's gonna be a'ight."

Bria met Brent's gaze, then turned towards Lana, then back to Brent. Her eyes scanned the area, still tearful, but despite her pain and her injuries, she was alive.

"There's a girl behind you…" she croaked.

"What?"

"Behind you…"

Brent turned. A young girl with round glasses stood between the trees.

Yellow smoke pulsated from her skin.

CHAPTER SIXTY-SIX

NOT SO EVIL

Yaz wanted to go home. She wanted to be back in Ms. Kai and Mr. Nasr's tower. She wanted to be exploring forests, collecting skeletons, and playing games with her toys.

Instead, she lay in a cell, deep beneath the Library. Sir Jama told her it was for her own good. The cell would protect her from the monsters and give her a chance to recover. They gave her a comfortable bed and a few books. But the dark hallways scared her. Prisoners cried out, moaning and cursing in unfamiliar languages. Only Jiang came to visit, often disappearing into the depths of the crypt with a few large bottles on his hip. He would drop off food but otherwise say nothing, his focus entirely on the strange brews along his side.

Yaz didn't ask him anything. She merely ate her food in silence, watching through the bars of the cage at the prisoners across the hall. They bore ghostly eyes, their words meaningless, while mist pulsated from their bodies. Part of Yaz's soul reached for them, wishing to help them out of whatever Hell locked them tight.

At night, Yaz dreamt of monsters. Some nights, she only saw yellow. Other nights, silver. One time, she even saw the body of a blonde-haired woman, wandering across a desert, guided along by a man with scars on his face. That nightmare faded again into yellow, leaving Yaz to cry alone again in darkness.

She didn't keep track of time. She only waited, dreamt, and ate. Sir Jama would come.

He had to come.

And eventually, despite everything, he did.

Alojzy carried him down into the crypts, placing him on a pillow across from Yaz. He smiled at her, his one white eye seeming to glow.

"How are you feeling, Yasmin?" Sir Jama asked.

"Am I allowed out? It's dark down here, and I wanna go outside," Yaz mumbled.

"Well, let's see Yasmin. How is your head? Are you still having nightmares?"

Yaz nodded.

"What a pity. I believe we pushed you too far and too fast. You are not strong enough yet to control the monsters."

"I'm trying!" Yaz hit her hands on the floor. "I'm really trying!"

"It is all okay, Yasmin. We have a new person in mind to help with the monsters. That way, you no longer have to bear the burden alone. A young woman in Knoll has volunteered her body and mind for the monster's endeavor. This will give you a chance to go out and be a Mist Keeper and not worry about the monsters. Isn't that better, Yasmin? Don't you want to help save souls?"

Yaz hugged herself and shook her head. "I wanna go home."

"This is your home now."

"But it's scary and lonely, and you won't let me do anything I want! I wanna go home!"

"You will come to appreciate it here."

"Ms. Kai is probably looking for me, though!"

"She is not, Yasmin. No one has cared about you. You are alone."

Yaz whimpered.

Alone. She hated that word more than anything.

It was how she felt in their tower.

And now she was alone here. She didn't belong, even with a talking skull!

"You are one of us," Sir Jama reiterated.

But it sounded like a lie.

Alojzy finally spoke. His little hair stuck out at all ends, his face covered in soot. His red robe, usually pristine and in order, carried tears and dirt. But his voice remained as stern as ever. "Ningursu, sir, perhaps we should let her out. She may need some fresh air…"

"Yes, that may be wise." Ningursu opened his mouth. A tendril of mist flew from his lips, unlocking the cage doors. Yaz shuddered, climbed to her feet, then tiptoed forward. Tears fell from her cheeks.

"It will be okay, dear child. This burden will no longer be yours to bear." Alojzy smiled, his lips twitching.

"Once the new vessel has been adapted, yes. Until then, you have a role to play, Yasmin." Sir Jama said.

"I don't wanna…" Yaz sniffled.

"We need you, Yasmin. One of the evildoers has been located, and you can defeat her once and for all. Do you understand, Yasmin?"

"No. I don't wanna."

"Once it is over with, you can be free, Yasmin," Alojzy said. "You'll be free at last."

"And I can go home?"

"If that is what you wish."

Yaz stared past Alojzy and Ningursu, then nodded once. "Okay. I understand."

But Yaz didn't know if she understood. She didn't know if she wanted to destroy this so-called evildoer.

She didn't even know if Sir Jama was right.

Alojzy led Yaz through the tunnels to a dead forest. Night reigned. The trees looked like skeletons dancing against twilight. Mist gathered at their feet, flickering between white and yellow.

"Alojzy." Someone said.

Yaz turned. Caroline emerged between the trees, her cloak blending in with the night air.

"Caroline, what are you doing here? Don't you have work to do?" Alojzy asked.

"I have finished for today. What are you doing with my apprentice?" Caroline kept her gaze fixated on Alojzy.

"She is not your apprentice. She belongs to the Council."

"No, she is my apprentice. I'm the eighth member, and she shall be the ninth. I think any decisions need to be made with me present."

"Ningursu doesn't think so."

"Do you think I care?" Caroline took a step forward. Mist trembled at her fingertips. She paid a quick glance in Yaz's direction and mouthed a single word.

"Run."

Mist exploded around them.

Yaz broke out into a run.

She pushed through the brush. The forest twisted like a maze. Where would she go? Home?

Where was that? She didn't know.

The trees continued to distort. Was she trapped in a nightmare? The ground crunched as she ran; the wind bellowed. Yellow flooded in and out of her eyes, leaving her trapped in an embrace of uncertainty. *Don't look back.*

She stumbled out through the trees onto a riverbank. Just up the path from her, a couple of individuals huddled by the water. Yaz sucked down her fear and tiptoed towards them: a tall man who spun with mist, a young woman, passed out on the ground covered in roots, and another woman who Yaz recognized from her first attempt to "eat magic" in the towers.

Her stomach grumbled. Inside her body, the monsters bellowed with delight. She could taste magic on her tongue, like rain, cleansing her body after a long day in the mud. Her body vibrated with excitement, the monsters clawing to the front of her psyche. They wanted to feast.

These individuals held magic close.

So much that the monsters could taste it from afar.

Yaz tried to shake them off, taking another step towards the group. As she stepped forward, the man turned and peered in Yaz's direction. He mouthed something, but Yaz couldn't hear him.

The monsters bubbled in her chest.

"I don't wanna," she moaned. Yellow mist pooled from her mouth, tendrils reaching for the small group. "I'm sorry...I don't wanna..."

Despite the monsters reaching through her skin, the man did not seem frightened. He approached her, still speaking, his voice blending with the buzzing in her head.

The forest twisted around her. Yellow exploded from her fingertips, down her body, and across her skin. It latched onto the trees, tugging at the different branches, eating away at the magic and life. Her monsters feasted.

But she fell.

She couldn't contain it. Everything hurt. The creatures tore from her body and ripped open her soul.

Yaz cried and pounded her fists against the ground.

She couldn't control these strange monsters.

She couldn't do anything.

"I don't wanna! I don't wanna!"

She gasped for air, and as if coming up from the bottom of the ocean, she could breathe once again. The yellow dissipated, its elongated fingers stopping just above the young woman writhing on the ground. Yaz clenched her hands over her head, hiding her face in the ground. None of her thoughts made sense anymore. She wanted to eat the magic, but she wanted to play. She yearned to slice open the people standing before her, but she also wanted to sleep. The conflicting emotions battled in her head.

What belonged to her? What belonged to the monsters?

Would the monsters ever leave her alone?

"I wanna go home..." she sobbed.

"I know," a voice cooed. The man had knelt beside her, his hand on her back, the yellow mist clinging to his skin. Around him, illusions of the past captured them; stories of monsters, but also of children playing. As more stories appeared, Yaz's body lightened, as if something lifted the weight from her heart. The monsters stopped screaming. She no longer desired magic.

"What's your name?" the man asked, his voice gentle.

"My name?" Yaz repeated.

"Yes. Your name." He smiled, combing his fingers through the illusions. They danced on his fingers. "If it helps, I'll go first. My name is Brent."

"Brent," the girl whispered. "I'm Yaz."

"Nice to meet you, Yaz. Don't worry...you're safe now. I took the monster from you."

"You took the monster..." She stared at him. Something seemed familiar about him. Then it clicked: she saw him at the circus another lifetime ago. "Are you the one Sir Jama hates?"

"Sir Jama?"

"Sorry...Ningursu. He said you were evil..." Yaz blinked. "But you're not so evil. You...you took away the nightmares."

Brent smiled. "I try." He glanced back over at the two women. The younger woman had sunken into the ground, her body sewn with vines and roots. Magic rippled around her. The grass greened, and the silver river rippled.

He turned back to Yaz. "Come with us. We'll protect you."

"But Sir Jama..."

"It's a'ight."

"No! He always knows. He sees...and he's coming...he wants me back. He's coming," she cried. "He's coming, and he won't let me go."

Brent helped Yaz off the ground. "Then we gotta fight. I'm not gonna let him take you, a'ight?"

Yaz continued to bawl. She couldn't escape. Already, something tugged at her body, begging for attention. With the passing wind, the heavy air, the forest twisted and turned once again.

And then snapped.

Mist exploded from the trees, encompassing Yaz and Brent. She couldn't see the other two women anymore. Instead, Caroline and Alojzy strode out of the mist like demons hunting for prey. But Caroline did not bear her face but that of Ningursu, peering with two pernicious eyes.

Yaz reached for Brent's hand and squeezed it.

"It's a'ight. I got you," Brent promised.

Yaz nodded, holding her breath as the Ningursu-version of Caroline approached them. His voice boomed. "Ah, Brenton. It has been quite a while."

"Fuck off." Brent clenched his free fist. Mist-made daggers formed in his hand.

"Now, now. You will not harm your dear teacher, will you?"

Brent's hand loosened, and the daggers disappeared. Yaz tightened her grip around his arm.

"That's a good lad." Ningursu smirked. "It has been some time now since we met at the circus, yes? That meeting didn't go well, did it?"

"You were with Yaz then, weren't you? You were hiding her?" Brent asked.

"Yasmin has been a good little girl. Very strong. Very powerful. Very obedient. But you stole that power from her now, didn't you? Now she'll just wither away beneath our curse. Die, as the curse entails."

Yaz squirmed. She didn't know what Ningursu meant. For the first time since she met the Council, she felt alive again. Her mind was clear, her heart light. Why would she die?

"The curse can be broken. I'm proof of that," Brent stated.

"Oh, Brenton, don't be so foolish. Why do you think Hell follows you wherever you go? The curse is trying to slaughter you dead, but you refuse." Ningursu sighed. "But no matter. We have a new Mist Keeper now. Good little Yasmin will be much better than you."

"She's a child!"

"Children are obedient."

"She's terrified!"

"She will learn."

"That's a load of bullshite!"

"You always had a tongue, Brenton."

Yaz finally stood up. "I don't wanna be a Mist Keeper anymore! I wanna go home!"

"Stay out of this, Yasmin. You don't know what you want." Ningursu barked.

"But I do! I don't wanna be a monster; I wanna go home and play with my dollies."

"You have no home. We're your home now."

Yaz shook her head, tears working their way through her body. For a moment, her body quivered as if the monsters would return. But her body and head belonged to her alone. She was safe.

"Stop!" Brent shouted. He glanced over his shoulder at the wall of mist, then back at Ningursu. "I'll come back to the Library. You can do whatever you want with me, but just…let Yaz go. She's…she's a child. It's…it's not right. Please. I don't care what happens…but you can't…she's a child." He swallowed and whispered again, "She's a child."

Ningursu simpered, "You always were a good man, Brenton."

Brent's shoulders slumped. "Promise me she'll be free to go. And…" Brent raised his head. "I want answers. I don't want to die not knowing *why*."

"Why what? Use your words, Brenton."

"Why everything!" Brent shouted. "Why do you hate Magii? Why did you use a little girl as a vessel? Why do you hate ME? I've been running across the world. If my life were a story, it would scrawl across many pages of an epic novel. Just tell me…WHY?"

Ningursu bowed his head. "Very well, Brenton. If you want answers, I shall tell you."

The wind picked up around them. Yaz fell back as a gust blew over her. The mist spiraled and swayed, hiding everything. She suffocated, gasping as the air escaped her lungs. Her lips became chapped, her eyes grew dry, and her skin went clammy. A tornado of illusions filled her vision; in one, she saw a little girl running away from home.

The next, a girl playing with dolls alone.

Another, a girl in a shop, diligently working.

Always alone.

It was her story, her tale.

Perhaps Ningursu was right. She had no home.

It would have been so much easier if she had never found Ningursu's skull. She'd still be with Ms. Kai and Mr. Nasr, exploring the world, collecting unique items, and dreaming of a better life.

Yaz covered her ears with her hands and cried. With her tears, the mist ceased, and she once again stood in the dead forest.

Brent and the other Mist Keepers had vanished.

But this time, Yaz wasn't alone.

The older woman still knelt beside the younger woman by the river.

"You're safe, girl," the woman called out.

"I—"

With a loud gasp, the body of the young woman lying on the ground seized. Her chest rose, then fell with a thud. The older woman jumped, panicked.

Everything stood still.

But why did it seem like the trees were getting thicker? Did the ground around the young woman suddenly become greener?

"Bria? BRIA!?" the older woman shouted.

Roots and vines sprouted around the young woman's body, lacing their way through the ground. She then exhaled. White flowers blossomed in her hair, spreading across the ground and mingling with the silver water.

Then, with a single beat, the forest exploded with life.

More green, more flowers, more everything. It wasn't just a simple spell. Life radiated from the woman before Yaz.

Yaz stumbled back, avoiding the vines as they reached out over the ground.

"What's happening now?" Yaz asked the older woman. This wasn't the Mist Keepers. That much she knew.

The woman didn't look at Yaz as she answered, "She's healing."

CHAPTER SIXTY-SEVEN

MASTER OF THE MIST

When the mist finally settled, Brent found himself in the Library. His heart raced. Everything happened so fast; he hadn't the chance to say goodbye to Bria. Was she going to be okay? Would she forgive him?

I'm sorry, Bri. I couldn't let a child suffer. In truth, he knew she wouldn't either.

She'd already proved that.

But as he stood in the Library, Bria was all he could think about. Her mark remained from the battle months earlier. It was worse than he remembered: a swamp spread out through the shelves, still draining after the battle all those moons ago. Yet, it wasn't just the destruction that made his heart empty. The Library no longer held the allure that once greeted him. Instead, its stories pulsed with death, with hatred, and with envy.

He'd uncovered its secrets.

Alojzy and Caroline gripped his arms tight as they led him up the stairs. Jiang joined them, keeping a stern eye on Brent like any common guard. Brent did not fight it. He walked with his head held high, his lips drawn in a straight line.

He would not let them see the worry creeping through his thoughts.

He would not show them his fright.

He was here on his own accord. If that meant death, so be it.

You're not allowed to die. Bria's voice rang in his ears. She told him that back when he first became an apprentice to the Mist Keepers.

It was a promise.

He would try to keep it.

As he walked, ghosts watched. Murmurs followed his movements. They would whisper his stories for days to come.

Even if his life ended today, at least he knew he left a mark.

The victors would decide what that mark meant.

But you're not allowed to die.

Aelia stood by the infirmary on the second floor, eyes narrow. When he glanced at her, she looked away, hiding in the mist of her story. He saw a woman focused on her work, determined to make the world better, only to poison it instead. The story didn't stay long, and Brent found himself once again drawn to Caroline's story as they reached the second set of stairs.

Sorrow clouded Caroline's eyes as they walked.

"I'm sorry," Brent whispered to her.

"You did what was right. I should be sorry," Caroline replied.

"At least you'll stop melting."

Caroline touched the dripping skin on her face and shook her head. "I do not think this has anything to do with you, Brent. It was inevitable my magic would one day fail. I can't keep up this illusion forever. It can get exhausting after centuries."

Brent sucked on his lips. He hadn't stopped to consider how much Caroline had gone through in the past hundreds of years. These past couple of years had been enough to drain him. What would a hundred years of being a Mist Keeper do?

Would he ever be able to find out?

"Enough conversation. Get in!" Jiang ripped the door to Ningursu's office open at the top of the stairs.

A mist-made chain laced around Brent's wrists as the door opened and dragged him into the room.

He squinted into the haze. Ningursu sat on a stack of books, but with mist twirling in the room and the gentle glow of the candles, it almost made him look like he was floating. Alojzy and Jiang took their places against the wall while Caroline joined Brent's side. Aelia entered last, guarding the door like a hawk.

The room itself no longer bore its old wave of glamor. In fact, it was nothing more than a wall of silver mirrors, reflecting different scenes across the world, around a desk. Books sat stacked around it, but none lay open. Every bit of knowledge, every bit of pride that once defined the office vanished.

Brent straightened his back and spoke first. "Hello, Ningursu."

"Brenton…" Ningursu's single white eye flickered. "It has been quite a long time since we've been face-to-face, hasn't it?"

"I've found it to be too short."

"Ah well, time is a mystery, is it not?" Ningursu sighed. "Very well. You will wish it was longer, though, for your minutes are limited. The curse is at its end."

Brent scoffed. "There's no curse."

"Oh, don't be so daft, Brenton. You knew long ago that you were cursed to die. It was only a matter of time before death came knocking."

"Death isn't knocking on my doorstep. There is no curse."

"Do not be ridiculous, Brenton."

"I'm not being ridiculous…you are! You're a fucking manipulative liar who is using us as tools!"

"Pardon?"

"Did I stutter?" Brent glowered. "You've created this lie around some curse for centuries! There's no curse! If there was, you would have told me to bring Yaz back as well. Mist Keepers are not cursed to die! You just create us to control us! Why, though? I don't understand! Why have you been acting with the Order? Why did you use Yaz? Why are you obsessed with trying to control Bria? If you're gonna kill me, at least tell me that much!"

Ningursu chuckled to himself. "Oh, Brenton, you don't understand."

"Try me."

"Magic is a disease. It disrupts the true nature of the world. The Mist Keepers are meant to maintain a balance between Life and Death, but when you have Magii and seers and Immortals infecting it, things go wrong." Ningursu closed his eye. "We created the Diabolo to stop that. We wanted Yaz to be our vessel, our test, to see if we could harness the Diabolo's ability and stop magic once and for all."

"All of that is bullshite, and you know it. You just don't want someone to be stronger than you. You want to control when people live and die. That's why you scare us with a curse. That's why you are fearful of the Palaver or of seers. That's why you hate Bria!" Brent stared at his hand for a moment. His tattoo wove from his fingers to his forearms, like a forest giving bloom. "I promised her I wouldn't die. And I still won't."

Ningursu did not flinch. "You do not have a choice, Brenton. You have done wrong to the Council and the world. You killed my brother, and for that, you must pay."

"Your brother wanted to go." Brent twisted his neck, feeling Nedo's story come to the forefront of his lips. He exhaled once, and on his tongue, as vivid as he was at the silver lake, came Nedo's own voice: *"I wanted to end an eternity of slavery, brother. That was not a life but a death lived over and over again. Brenton provided peace. So I took it."*

Ningursu snarled. "You cannot fool me."

Brent's voice returned, riding on Nedo's confidence. "It is the truth."

"Even if it is, there are more charges." Ningursu bit down, tugging at the mist-made chain, pulling Brent towards him. "You started the madness with the Diabolo, Brenton."

"I destroyed that Diabolo."

I'm still here, the monster whispered.

Brent ignored it, keeping his attention on Ningursu. "You're the one who brought them back."

"Oh, but that was only after you violated more rules, Brenton. You let a Magii into our Library on multiple occasions—"

"She did nothing wrong."

"You colluded with the Palaver."

"They saved me!"

"You vandalized the library, you've performed unauthorized releases—"

"To save souls…you know, our job?"

"You never learned."

"Because no one taught me!" Brent stared hard at Ningursu. "You left me floundering in my own confusion! You never taught me shite!"

Ningursu continued without reacting, "You are a disgrace to this Council, Brenton. You will never be a Mist Keeper."

"I already am a Mist Keeper."

Silence.

Ningursu tugged on the chains with his mouth, and Brent stumbled forward to the head's desk. "Enough. It's time."

"Time for what?" Caroline barked. "What is happening?"

"By my power, by my word, Brenton Rob Harley, you are hereby eradicated."

Brent did not flinch. His heart did not sink.

No. I'm not. I never will be.

You think that will protect you? his Diabolo cackled.

I promised Bria I wouldn't die. So I won't.

"Eradicated? What does that mean?" Caroline demanded.

No one spoke.

"Can someone answer me?"

"Say goodbye to your first apprentice, Caroline," Ningursu responded.

"What?"

"It's a'ight. I got a feeling this is just the beginning," Brent said to her.

"You're behaving like a fool for someone about to die," Jiang remarked from his spot against the wall. Alojzy nodded in agreement.

Ningursu tossed a glare at Jiang, then returned to Brent. "Any last words, Brenton?"

Brent met Ningursu's gaze. Confidence marred him. "I've seen your story. You're just as human as I am."

"Not begging for your life?"

"No…I'm not." Brent didn't know why. Somehow, despite everything, he didn't fear the fate Ningursu offered. He'd seen the world burn.

And he made a promise.

I'm not allowed to die.

He held that prayer close to his heart. If anything, he'd live on as a story.

"Very well, Brenton," Ningursu said. "I bid you farewell. It is a shame this didn't work out."

"I'll see you soon."

Ningursu closed his eyes and opened his mouth.

Black mist pummeled from his mouth.

Everything started buzzing. The smoke gathered around Brent, pulling at his skin, at his mouth, at his eyes. He lost his footing and collapsed to the ground. Were the walls shaking? Was he? Cold, warm, frigid, humid; the temperatures kept changing. Time merely wandered. His head erupted with fire.

Why couldn't he breathe?

Why did everything keep screaming?

Did paintings talk?

Did the ceiling dive?

Where was he now?

Were his surroundings moving in slow motion?

Or was he just moving fast?

Was that Bria crying?

No. He had to escape.

He had to run.

Into the mist…

Mist.

Mist…

Everywhere.

It decorated his skin. It pulled at his nails.

Was it in his head?

Did someone scream nearby?

Keep yourself together.

You are the Story Collector.

And you made a promise.

You promised.

You will not die.

For Bria.

For everyone.

He brought his fingers up to his face. They had begun to fade, blending seamlessly into the surrounding. Once, he opened and closed them, watching as they faded with his palms…his wrist…

I won't become just a story. My name is Brent Harley.

I am the Story Collector.

He clenched his palms and outstretched his arms. When he opened them again, his fingers had laced with the mist. Around him, the stories churned. Tales of centuries past flew, stories about those who long lived in the Library: of Caroline, of Alojzy, of Malaika, of Jiang, of Julietta, of Tomás, of Aelia, and of Ningursu. They intermingled with tales of ghosts, tales of failed apprentices, and tales of Diabolo. They danced, they sang, they spun; all the stories continued.

And they kept him alive.

"Sir! What is happening?" Jiang called.

"He's dead!" Caroline cried. "What else?!?"

"No, he's not dead," Aelia hissed, her voice like ice. "He's more than that."

"He's pure," Ningursu added, his voice but a whisper.

A laugh rumbled in Brent's stomach. For months now, the mist had wrapped around him, and he learned its stories and its embrace. He was one with the mist, just as it was one with him.

Brent guffawed. "I'm more than a pawn in your game, Ningursu. I'm the Effluvium. I'm the stories! I'm a part of this!"

"Grab him!" Ningursu roared.

Brent used the mist as a shield and vanished into its embrace.

"Lock the Library and the Tunnels!" Ningursu screamed. "We cannot let him escape!"

Brent continued to bellow, and he spun out of Ningursu's office, unable to control his movements as he rode in the mist's embrace.

Whether they liked it or not, he was still standing.

Whether they liked it or not, he was still alive.

And whether they liked it or not, he was a Mist Keeper.

WANT TO FIND OUT WHAT HAPPENS NEXT?

Find out in...

THE STORY COLLECTOR'S ALMANAC

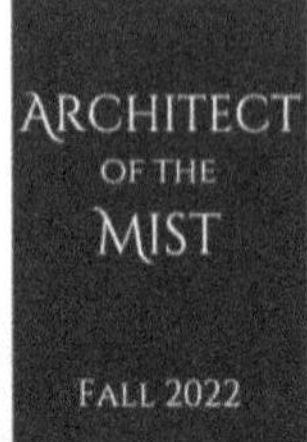

Also by E.S. Barrison...

Tales from the Effluvium
Speak Easy

The Unsought Fairytale Collection
Tuppence
Focaccia

Author's Note

Thank you so much for taking the time to read *The Towers of Knoll*.

If you enjoyed this book, I would appreciate it if you could:

Review this book. Reviews are a great help to an author. If you enjoyed this book, please consider leaving a review.

Tell Others. When you share this book with others on social media, you're allowing others to discover this story. Word-of-mouth is one of the best sources of marketing for an author.

Connect with me. If you want to find out about my upcoming releases, stop by my website at www.esbarrison-author.com or connect with me on social media.

Thank you!

E.S. Barrison

ACKNOWLEDGMENTS

To all the following, my thanks, for your support, friendship, and kindness throughout this process:

To all my beta readers—Matthew, Betta, and Amber—thank you for your insights to make this book shine.

To my parents, for accepting that their daughter has hundreds of characters in her head.

To Moira, my cover artist, for putting so much effort in this cover.

To Charlie, my editor, for helping me decide the best directions for my characters and to round out their perfections and flaws.

To Matthew, for actually reading my writing and giving your thoughts, however ridiculous they may be. I still won't be putting *that scene* in there. Sorry.

And finally, to my readers, Thank you for sticking by my side through this story. So much more will be coming soon.

Without all of your support, this story would not have been possible.

ABOUT THE AUTHOR

E.S. Barrison has been writing and creating stories for as long as she can remember. After graduating from the University of Florida, she has spent the past few years wrangling her experiences to compose unique worlds with diverse characters. Currently, E.S. lives in Orlando, Florida with her family.

http://www.esbarrison-author.com